COME YESTERDAY

Bridget Faure

a Stone Sky novel

ISBN-13:
978-0615917313 (Stone Sky Publishing)

ISBN-10:
0615917313

DEDICATION:

Thanks to my fantastic husband, Ben, for realizing how important developing this dream has been to me, for putting hardwood floors, A/C and insulation in the garden shed so that I'd have a great little place to write. Thanks to my patient children, Corey and Janey, for putting up with the days when I was trying to bring Adena and Preston to life on paper and for just being awesome kids. I am so very proud of you both. Thanks to my family and friends so far away for believing that I would one day finish this endeavor, even while others thought I was nuts for trying. To my sisters, Tammy and Alicia for their encouragement even though we very seldom get to see each other. Thanks to God for the dream that sparked the idea for Come Yesterday and above all I thank Him for all the special people I've been blessed to know in my life —Especially, my two wonderful mothers, Evie Jean and Jane and my Daddy, Ron. You are my rock! To my partner over at Stone Sky, Ms. LeAnne for her help and inspiration and her unconditional friendship, and last but not least, thanks to you (wonderful reader) for spending your hard earned money and time to read the following pages.

I love every single one of you.

Prologue

THE UNIVERSE IS A MAGNIFICENT TIMEPIECE. All that we know, what we think we know and that which we've yet to discover, spins and turns in a perfect dance. A movement with purpose and meaning that none of us can see or grasp as to why or how. But it is not for us to know why or how. Only that it is an intricate balance between free will and destiny. Past and present culminating into one dimension that we do not understand. The future. We think we know what we want, but what we think we desire is meager to what the universe has in store.

The timepiece. Every thing, every creature, every person, every speck of dust has its own cog, or pin or gear or spring. God is the master watchmaker. He keeps everything in perpetual motion. But time passes quickly and time passes slowly. Perhaps God in his infinite wisdom presses his finger with gentle resistance to slow the works for His purpose, or He may replace a set of gears; swapping one for another, a better fit than the ones before and all for the sake of perfect timing.

I imagine God closing a crystal over the face of His timepiece and smiling down upon us all then gently placing it in his shirt pocket near his heart for safekeeping, and taking a stroll through Heaven in contemplation of all that He created.

This is how I've come to rationalize the universe; our existence as a whole. I've been permitted the briefest glimpse of an infinitesimal piece of the puzzle —of the enigma known as Time —and still, my simple human mind could not possibly comprehend more information than I am now privy to. For what is Time? Really. With no beginning and no end. Why, -it is nothing less than the heartbeat of God.

My name is Adena Whitmore, born March 17th, 1970 in a small house on the banks of Lake St. John in Ferriday, Louisiana. I believe my second life began the day I met Preston Grace, May 2009. Yes, I said my *second* life. But I cannot begin my story in Louisiana. Let's go back a century.

Let us begin in London.

Havering-Atte- Bower, London — March 17th, 1908.

AT NINE-YEARS-OLD, DILLY watched Nathaniel Preston Grace and Ania Katherine Grace turn to face their families, all smiles and happy tears. Dilly blinked one bitter-sweet tear to her cheek; a hello for the couple who'd so graciously opened their home to her —and one more mournful good-bye to her dear mother. As she pondered thoughts far beyond her tender age, she looked down to find her five-year-old brother, Adam, dancing a silly jig that told her he really needed to wee.

After Mass, Dilly ushered Adam through the nave of St. John's and as the children passed Miss Constance Edwards, they heard the first of many insults to come from their new aunt.

"Irish Rats," Constance hissed; the venom in her voice a perfect accessory to her harsh beauty.

Dilly urged Adam onward until they stepped through the massive entrance onto the village green in front of the church, although, not so green just yet; the cold of winter still had a firm grip on the stony ground. She shivered within herself, breathing deeply the cold March air, thankful to be freed of the overwhelming odor of lavender oil engulfing that horrid woman she scarcely knew.

Adam tugged at Dilly's pale mint velvet sleeve, snaring one of her platinum curls. "Dilly? Are there *really* rats in the church? I'd like a look."

Dilly winced as she freed her hair from Adam's fingers, pretending she hadn't heard the raven haired spinster at all. "Adam, I thought you had to wee." His tiny face scowled a bit as Dilly led him on to his needed destination.

Necessities taken care of, Adam ran just beyond the stone wall that surrounds the headstones in front of the church, heading fast as his little legs would carry him to the old stocks and the whipping post still standing next to a colossal twisted tree.

He mightn't do such if he knew what those were for. She thought as she watched her brother play obliviously astride the double stocks as if he were riding a horse.

The rustle of several layers of silk swished too near to her feet to not demand a look. Dilly turned her head only to find Constance, leering long and hard with a nasty grin on her face.

"At least the *little* rat knows his place."

She blinked twice, her face never betraying her. Unruffled on the surface, she refocused on her brother, bottling the rage inside and waiting quietly as Constance sauntered away alone.

Her head held high, Dilly pulled a steeled curtain of dignity around her narrow alabaster shoulders, knowing one thing to be absolute. No matter who raised her, she'd never forget her proud Irish roots.

Long after the festivities of the day and after everyone in the Grace home had turned in, Dilly left her brother sleeping in their small shared bed then cautiously made her way through the blackness on the second floor of the three-story farmhouse.

With no moon to spill its merciful faint light into the windows and no candle to light her path, she inched along the tongue-and-grove wall, blindly feeling her way forward. At last, her fingers slid over the third cold glass doorknob to her right and she knew the stairs were close. The groan of a floor plank halted her progress but for only a moment as she quickly surmised it was but her own slight steps making the old house creak. A few steps farther and she could feel the wool rug at the first step of the stairs with her outstretched toe. Another tell-tale creak stopped her decent.

Dilly's innocent mind began to conjure the worst sorts of horrible creatures as she turned her head to peer over her shoulder; alas she couldn't see a thing. "Anyone there?" She asked, her little heart tripping with fear. Danger seemed to emanate from someplace too close, prickling her skin. A sinister presence lingered. Something? Someone?

Dilly shivered in the cold hallway as the coal in the stoves had long since turned to ash. She stood perfectly still in the looming silence, listening and waiting -holding her breath to better hear what she couldn't see. The faint sound of air moving back and forth registered in her ears. Was that someone else breathing?

Something stirred the air and a waft of lavender assailed Dilly's nose. No other warning, save for that sweet stench, could prepare the child for the two cold bony hands in the shadows thrusting her slight body down, down and down.

Dilly grasped blindly at nothing but empty space as she tried in vain to stop her fall. Her tiny hands could find no purchase, her body no release from the momentum of the push that had sent her into such a treacherous tumble. And she knew, even with her young mind, that the precise second her body made its final impact against the hard slate landing below, her delicate arm had snapped in two. She lay awkwardly, cradling her pain and she cried for her own mother. A mother who could not come.

The echo of a heavy iron latch clattered open on the first floor hastily followed by heavy footsteps ascending the first flight.

Constance hurried to Dilly's side before Preston could reach her. She yanked the child upright then with a cooing whisper in her ear, "Utter one word and next time it'll be your brother. The both of you should have died with your filthy mum!"

Dilly's mind reeled and her anger exploded; flailing at Constance's much taller body. "*Filthy*? My mother was —a virtuous woman. —And you're a *witch*! You *pushed* me on purp- OW!" Her howls of defiance punctuated with kicks and jabs until Constance wrenched her broken arm. The searing pain silenced her.

"I could quite easily snap your neck before he gets here. A tragic accident. Happens all the time. –Now, do try to remember. Not. One. Word." A sinister chuckle and Constance retreated.

As Mr. Nathaniel Preston Grace, known by those closest to him as simply Preston, approached, the yellow circle of light from his lantern fell upon the child standing there, leaning against the wall, cowering, weeping and afraid, her fair hair a tangled mess, her nose bloodied - casting a scarlet smear across her porcelain cheek. Immediately, he noted the dreadful distortion of her right arm.

"Gracious child. We must get you to Dr. Bainbridge at once." He stooped to carefully lift her tiny feather-light frame then stood and did his best to console her.

He felt a bit out of his depth at first, having no children of his own as of yet. And the child, not quite comfortable in his presence for even though they shared a home, the fact remained that he was still a stranger to her. Yet there they were, the babe and the giant it seemed, as Dilly was indeed a slight little girl and Preston himself had passed six and a half feet before his sixteenth birthday.

Dilly had been careful around Mr. Grace thus far, not sure of his disposition. He was still a young man of twenty-six years however Ms. Katherine was only seventeen and an angel and a Godsend and was sweet as fresh cream to be sure. But Dilly, even amidst her pain and her fear, noted how gentle the colossal man had been while lifting her, so careful not to frighten, so careful not to hurt her arm further. He was indeed a gentle man. She could tell this now. Although the tears still tumbled down her cheeks in the yellow light of his lamp, Dilly half smiled as bravely as she could and with that, Mr. Grace started down the stairs.

But Dilly's mind began to race. Terrified to leave Adam alone with that ghastly woman lurking about the house, Dilly begged Mr. Grace to please bring him along, insisting he'd awake frightened if he discovered he was alone. He assured her that he'd happily oblige and asked if she was able to walk.

Wiping her tears with her good hand, she nodded valiantly and stuck closely to his side while she silently weighed whether or not she should tell Mr. Grace that her broken arm was no accident. She quickly decided it would be a detrimental decision to do so and thus she kept her lips shut tight. Just as Constance had ordered, although, poor sweet Dilly, just a babe herself, could not begin to fathom why the strange woman hated her so.

With the warm lump of a boy sleeping soundly on Preston's strong thick shoulder, he tucked both of the children into the carriage seat of his 1902 Albion then returned to the house to get a wool blanket to keep them warm on their short journey.

He opened the front door to his home only to find Constance waiting in the foyer, an oil lamp flickering from a small table behind her; casting a silhouette of her slender legs beneath her gossamer gowns.

She toyed with her long black braid draped willfully near her breast. "A good man shouldn't be troubled with extra burdens, Preston. Why, oh *why* did you let Katherine bring them here?"

Preston looked positively puzzled. It had only taken a moment and a kind ear to understand *why*. Katherine had spotted the pair through a window of the shop where her wedding gown was to be made and yet the place was boarded shut. The proprietor, the children's mother, had passed on of consumption and for fear of being sent to an orphanage, the siblings had hidden, left unnoticed and utterly alone for three long, hungry weeks.

His beloved Katherine had been positively adamant on helping the children and there had been no tolerance from her parents for such things, especially now that they were set to travel to India together.

Katherine had packed her clothes and brought the children to the Grace Estate despite what society might have to say. That was why he'd loved her so. Her selflessness, her fortitude. Her loving heart and the face and fair hair of an angel. His angel. His Katherine.

He cleared his throat, gathered his wits and stared down at Constance with a look of indignation heavy on his brow. "I do not dictate the size or capabilities of my bride's heart. I'll thank you to respect her wishes. And mine." He attempted to brush past her.

Constance scoffed almost silently but the sound did not escape Preston's ear. He turned on his boots to thunder down from his towering height. Just so, he remembered the sleeping boy and the courageous little girl waiting just a few steps from the front door. "Least you not forget *Miss* Edwards; *you* are the only burden I bear. However, I made a promise to my wife that so long as you are without a husband and your parents remain abroad that you shall have a roof over your head."

Audaciously, she stepped too close as though she had in mind to thank him in some appalling manner.

Conscious of her ill behavior, Preston chose to retreat an arm's length. He stared down at the woman in such a way as to leave no doubt of his current and future intentions. "Do not mistake me for one of those bastard-breeding Neanderthals led about by the front of his breeches. The roof over your head need not be *this* roof." Exasperated and weary of speaking to his sister-in-law, he stalked away to retrieve the blanket; ever so thankful to find Constance absent when he returned to the foyer.

Little Dilly snuffled and sniffed in the bouncing automobile as they rode north. *Poor child*, Preston thought. She had been at his home for weeks and he knew she still felt out of place seeing as how she'd scarcely said two words the past couple of days. Especially since learning Constance would be moving in to stay. He didn't think the child cared much for the woman, not that he could blame her for her good sense. He didn't care for Constance either.

His mind wandered as they traveled headlong into the cold windy night, perhaps with purpose whether he was yet aware or not. But to think those poor children were completely alone. No relations at all. Heaven knows their fate had Katherine not found them. His mind sparked at once with a light in his heart.

Being ever mindful of her tender emotions, Preston asked, "Dilly, what did you call your father? God rest his soul."

"Da." Her small voice replied just loud enough to carry over the racket of the engine.

Da. Of course. He loved the Irish lilt to Dilly's soft voice. "Well then, what do you say to addressing me as Pop? Or Pa, if you prefer. *Sir* and *Mr. Grace* … bah! It all sounds a bit stuffy. Wouldn't you agree?"

Despite the hit and miss clamor of the Albion as they continued into the night, he caught one short burst of the melodious laughter that could only belong to a little girl. He breathed a sigh at the first true sign of her ease. She'd been terribly distressed and understandably so. She'd lost a great deal in her young life. Far too much, too soon and so much, so quickly had changed.

"You see, Dilly," Preston continued and his chest swelled a bit more with each passing second, "Katherine and I —well, we very much would like for you and Adam to be a permanent part of our family. –What do you say?"

She stayed quiet for a moment before looking up to find his face in the darkness. "You mean to say —you're *not* going to send us away?"

Preston's heart broke in two as he looked down and although he could not see her small face clearly, he imagined that ever present burden of consternation upon her brow. "Certainly not, Dilly. We would never. We've only been searching for your relatives because we thought it best. Not because we didn't want you."

Dilly bowed her head and Preston wasn't sure if she were contemplating his words or perhaps her arm was hurting. Until she raised her head, eyes closed, and as she made the sign of the cross, he saw her lips silently say, *Amen*. "Mam and Da, God rest their souls. —I'll call Ms. Katherine Mum if she likes."

He offered her a smile of sympathy. "I think Katherine will be very pleased." He made a right onto Wiggin's lane then glanced down at her again. "What were you praying for, Dilly? If I may ask?"

She tilted her head and looked directly at him. "I thanked the Lord for his gracious abundance. I thanked him for you."

Preston could not believe this child was merely nine years of age. He looked down at the crowns of the two small heads bobbing and bouncing with the bumps in the lane. One startlingly blonde, the other a warm cinnamon, both positively blessed with shiny curls. They smelled of soap and the unique sweetness that seemed to cling to children's dewy skin. They smelled of innocence and youth. And he vowed to protect them.

Silently seething, Constance stood alone in the shadows with the acid taste of rejection in her mouth. No man had ever refused her. Discounting Preston's rebuff, a new hatred boiled within the empty chambers of her heart as she considered the reason *why* Katherine should be so fatigued as to not be awakened by that wretched brat wailing on the stairs or the coughing of that ridiculous automobile puttering across the courtyard. No doubt, she was *tired* -the man-stealing wench! She was recovering from her first marital romp in Preston's bed!

Nothing could rival Katherine's unyielding beauty. Her silken light brown tresses, golden brown eyes, skin of fresh cream. Her simpering kindness made Constance want to wretch. How'd she love to bury her sewing scissors into her sister's heart that very night! But Constance knew she had to hold her patience. She had to be strong. Without wavering, she knew she would follow through with her plan.

After all, *she* had seen Preston first. She had made it her daily ritual to run into him in town, at church, at market and all had gone well in her favor, or so she'd thought, until the day she'd discovered the trail that crossed Preston's uncles farm and she'd donned her favorite walking dress and set out to 'bump' into Preston again, only to find him at the site of the old church ruins with her younger sister. Before Constance's very eyes, with his sweet name stuck in her throat, she'd watched Preston toss the leather reins over the neck of his finest mare then turn to take Katherine in his arms and he'd kissed her. He'd reached for her without hesitation like a thirsty man for water; like a starving man for bread.

How many times had they met here? How many times had he kissed her this way?

Too stunned to speak, Constance watched and she burned. And she saw Katherine's face – the very look in her eyes and Preston's as well when that kiss had at last ended. And Constance knew at once she'd inadvertently witnessed the precise moment that Preston and Katherine had fallen in love.

Preston fell to one knee, breathless and smiling and Katherine began to cry as he pulled from his shirt pocket a green velvet bag cinched at the neck with a tiny satin cord. But Constance could not watch what she feared was coming next.

Constance ran that day, faster than her legs had ever carried her before. She ran and she fell and she cried and she flung herself down the long trail toward home not caring that the intruding twigs and limbs and the underbrush tore at her dress and scratched her cheeks. She ran until her lungs were ready to burst with the burning fires within. Had she had a way to do so when she saw the lovers' lips meet; she would have set the forest ablaze to be rid of them both.

Her temper flared, her hatred grew and her life had suddenly changed. For Constance knew things. She knew things she shouldn't and up until that point in her nineteen years of life, she'd never dreamed she would actually seek to hurt someone, least of all her sister with the dark knowledge she possessed. But she was clever. No one knew she held this secret. No one knew how much she loved Preston. And no one would ever know how much she now hated her sister.

The passing of a year had done nothing to remedy Constance's blistering heart.

With the stabbing memories fresh in her mind, Constance hurried up the stairs in a billowing cloud of pale pink chiffon; her oil lamp leaving a lingering trail of soot that matched the blackness of her heart. She tugged a worn leather satchel from beneath her bed containing her most cherished book. A book filled with Hell-born mayhem that in the past had seen scores burned alive. Tonight she would set the stars for her future. And that future did not include those vermin Irish rats nor her sister for that matter.

Constance toed silently over the maze of fine Asian rugs throughout the first floor, making her way to the hidden servant's door in the hallway to stash a stack of parchment. Glancing over her shoulder, she checked for any sign of Katherine waking then gripped the edge of the heavy wall to slide the secret panel aside then disappeared into the very heart of Preston and Katherine's home.

Her covetous heart kept time with the rhythm of the ancient spell she whispered in a tongue long thought to be dead. No one would miss her this night as she hid amongst the cobwebs in the narrow abandoned stairwell to refine the binding details to the poem. The curse. They were ingeniously one in the same.

She worked diligently and without mercy throughout the night in the tiny servants' access to the attic that hadn't been used in over twenty years.

A dark new moon had been spent in the name of greed and lust and jealousy and the sun began to rise on her blackest of deeds. Leaving the marred moments to history, Constance glided soundlessly to her room on the third floor to watch the sun finish rising and paint with its golden rays the splendid colors of her future paradise.

Satisfaction had at last filled the empty chambers of her heart.

All that remained was to wait for Preston and Katherine's first born. Swift death to the innocent and all her dreams would come true. She would get what she wanted most.

Preston!

In this life…or the next.

1

Adena Whittington- High Springs, Florida -May 31, 2009

STANDING PRECARIOUSLY ON THE EDGE of the cliff, I wait. Hesitation holds me atop the outcropping of rock, but I want to leap more than I want to draw even one last breath. Something waits, although I can't see the source of the nebulous pull I feel tugging at my will. Far below, a lush green valley, the rocky gray foothills shrouded in fog. Cool brackish mist clings to my face and hair. The smooth rocks beneath my feet, cold and wet. The smell of new rain, grass, and earth permeates my senses as the most haunting whisper travels on the back of the winds, teasing my ears with its alluring invitation. 'It won't hurt when you fall. I'll catch you. I promise.' Eyes closed, I lean fearlessly into the wind. My heart lurches up and I begin to fall.

My eyes flew open to the skull-cracking buzz of my alarm clock, yanking me from the same bizarre dream I'd had the previous three nights. And I couldn't understand it. I grew up in Louisiana and raised my kids here in High Springs, Florida -flat lands through and through- I'd never even been that close to a cliff and suicide just isn't my style.

I bound my long thick snarl of dark brown waves in a crazed pile on top of my head, meticulously made my bed just as I do every morning then dragged myself downstairs for some coffee.

The resounding stillness of my house made me anxious as hell and I couldn't help but wonder if the dream of the strange cliff and that beckoning whisper had anything to do with my soon-to-be empty nest.

Who was I kidding; my children were practically already gone. Both of them would officially move to Gainesville this summer. A stone's throw away, yes – but still. I felt like an era of my life had ended. Gavin just finished his first year of college and Beth would be starting this fall.

Tossing the dream aside, I cracked the kitchen window over the sink, hoping the typical humidity of north central Florida on this last gorgeous Sunday in May, wasn't too heavy to let some fresh air in.

Fat Chance.

Sipping my coffee, I lingered over Gavin and Beth's photos chronologically down the foyer walls. The pudgy baby years. Missing teeth. Awkward tweens. Their senior portraits. How painfully fast they grow. Angry at myself, I wiped yet another bout of tears away as I'd done this very thing more than I care to admit lately.

I stopped short when I came to GG Delia's picture. (GG for great-grandma) She seemed to smile from the frayed black and white photo, taken just after the turn of the century in Dublin. How beautiful she'd been as a young girl, her platinum hair in ringlets. And again, as she always seemed to manage, even in death, the look in her piercing Irish eyes scolded me. For moping. She'd been my best friend in the whole world. God, how I still miss her.

I was nearly a mirror image of her. I had her elaborate curls, green eyes, clear skin and straight teeth. She was extraordinarily fair, like a porcelain doll, whereas I, on the other hand, had inherited the rich russet Cherokee colors from my father's side of the family along with a dash of Creole to boot.

How sad and how cruel old age can be. She'd suffered a stroke that left her nearly unable to speak. It had been on a Thursday morning, fourteen years ago that I held her hand at her bedside. Grappling to tell me something, the muscles on one side of her mouth refused to fully comply; her mind too damaged to produce a coherent thought. But I'll die with her words fresh in my mind.

"Adena, —Come find GG." She said and gripped my hand. Only GG *ever* called me Adena. To everyone else I'm just Dena.

"I'm right here, GG." I assured her and rubbed her cold bent fingers then brushed her silken silver curls away from her face.

"Memwees," she'd swallowed then closed her eyes so tight in frustration. She couldn't get the word out right and she knew it. "Memwees." She'd tried again. I wasn't sure what she meant. "Mem-a-wees." She said it very slowly with pleading in her still deep green eyes.

I took a guess. "Memories, GG? Is that what you're trying to say?"

She smiled but only one side of her mouth obeyed her will. "Yes. You – have my- memwees."

I only smiled. And then I *thought* I'd understood. I hugged her. "Of course I'll never forget you, GG." This made me cry. She wanted me to remember her. How could I ever forget?

She'd closed her eyes, and sighed so hard, seemingly defeated. And I could clearly see that this was not what she meant. She was trying to tell me something and I had no idea what. The urgency in her eyes when she'd opened them punched a hole in my heart. "Come and *find* me. Take memwees and find me. At home. Find me at *home*."

We *were* at home. We were in her house on the banks of Lake St. John in Ferriday, Louisiana where she had lived and reigned over my family since her and my great-grandfather, Joseph Albright, moved there sometime in the 1920s. My mind opened suddenly.

"You want me to go to Ireland, GG. To Dublin?" She was born there. Of course.

She smiled then. Feebly. She was so tired. "My memwees not live there. Not here. *Home*. Adena, listen to the *music* of your heart and follow me *home*."

The last of her words were crystal clear and her eyes were sharp with intelligence. Those were the last words she ever said. Her eyes held such severity; I knew it meant something far beyond my understanding- to her.

The following year, my husband, Trent, and I moved with our small children to Florida.

The cry of shorebirds echoed in the finest tin-can quality from my lap top speakers announcing the opening of a chat; mercifully breaking my pain-riddled reverie. I walked to my desk in the corner of the dining room and as soon as I saw the message, I sat down to reply.

Owen Stanley, my best friend and fellow writer, could be as long winded as a Baptist preacher at high noon on Sunday. In summation, he began by insulting my husband, which equals saying hello for him. He also needed my help editing his latest project and wanted to meet at Shep's Restaurant, a popular spot located in the historic Chesapeake Hotel in Gainesville.

I spent the afternoon at the elementary school to finish packing away my classroom to move into the new third grade annex this fall. Teaching paid the bills long before the publishing gods entered my life and I never saw fit to quit.

I adore children and love teaching. But no one at Magnolia Elementary knows I'm a writer which is to my preference. I don't care much for the lime-light not to mention my stories lean toward all things dark and daunting. The principal doesn't approve of such. He wouldn't even purchase those world-popular wizard stories for the school. He's a closed-minded idiot with no imagination and too old to change nor will he listen to reason. Too busy preaching fire and brimstone to let the kids exercise the muscles of their imagination. Hence, if he ever caught wind of the darker subjects of *my* writing, or rather, God forbid a parent did, he'd have my head on a chopping block and I guarantee, *yesterday* wouldn't be fast enough to expedite the deed.

Why stay then? I've been there for twelve years. Old habits die hard I suppose. And writing doesn't come with a retirement plan.

At 5:15 I dropped the last box of art supplies into the multipurpose room for summer storage. I managed to dodge most of the chit-chat with the other teachers not relishing the thought of being pigeon-holed by conversations of boyfriends, husbands or family vacations as none-of-the-above was on my immediate agenda.

I didn't mean to be bitter but for the past year or two …or three, my relationship with Trent had simmered down to a series of notes left on the counter all signed with an obligatory 'I love you'. The notes are simply courtesies to let me know where he's working for the next few days or sometimes weeks. The truth is, we've come to avoid phone conversations, too obvious that we rarely have much to say. He's a general contractor and he's gone a lot. Emotionally, he's been gone for years. And to be fair, maybe I have, too.

I slid into my old Mustang and quickly assessed my appearance. Favorite jeans, fudge colored v-neck and a beaded necklace to match although I smelled like crayons, and the ever present salty scent of play-dough. Long past caring, I headed south for some well earned down time with Owen.

In the ten-minute trek to Gainesville, the sky had fast become bruised with dark purple clouds converging from every direction. The humidity so warm and heavy, it felt like ten St. Bernards panting in my car and the A/C never had worked all that great.

Parking in the college town, usually a nightmare, I drove a three block grid around the old hotel. Two blocks away, I waited five minutes for some disgusting guy that was three knuckles deep into his nose to back out of his spot already.

I was finally able to dump a handful of quarters into the meter but as I closed the heavy door of my car, I warily gauged the undulating darkness overhead. The sky looked like it was preparing to wage war with the earth. And there I was standing right smack in the middle of the battlefield.

Gambler that I am, I set off down the sidewalk, one eye to the ever darkening sky then kicked it into second gear, hurrying past a long string of storefronts, all sporting orange and blue signs idolizing the UF Gators. Lightening forked straight over my head, shortly followed by a brutal rumble. One particularly menacing thunderhead approached from the west, building and boiling with astonishing speed. Another flash, another crack and then, *of course*, the clouds released their fury all at once. Too late to think of an umbrella, too far to turn around, I ran like hell through the stinging rain to make it across the intersection ahead, the relentless wind lashing my hair into my eyes like tiny bullwhips the entire way.

I'd never seen such an abrupt change in the weather. The sky actually appeared angry; violent even. Gale force winds drove the rain horizontally in wide white sheets. I stumbled a few times, still hurrying and trying to keep my bearings but the raindrops actually hurt as they struck against my skin. Each one felt like a bee sting.

I could hardly see through the deluge but I could hear the cars passing slowly, splashing water onto the sidewalk so I stayed close to the buildings. But there was nothing to stand *under*.

Finally, and thankfully I could see the white brick hotel standing out like a shining beacon. Anxious to make it to the huge green and white awning, I ran faster only to nearly hear the laughter of God himself as I could now see the rain gushing over the awning in a ten foot wide waterfall. The only way past it, was through it. I held my breath and in I went.

Instantly, everything seemed so much quieter inside with the storm at last muted; shut away by the doors behind me. I tried to dry my dripping hands on my jeans. Pointless as there was not one article of clothing on my body that was not literally soaked to my skin.

The Chesapeake had no fish nets or lobster traps as one might expect given the name of the place. On the contrary, it resembled an old English Manor oddly adorned with Wild West memorabilia. It looked like Wyatt Earp married Jane Eyre and they had a fight to see who'd do the decorating. So far as I could tell, nobody won.

One more adornment had been added since the last time I was there. As I approached the entrance to Shep's Restaurant on the right side of the well appointed lobby, I saw a shiny brass sign on the door that said, *CLOSED FOR RENOVATIONS.*

Fan-friggin-tastic!

Seeing no sign of Owen, I went to the bar on the south end of the lobby to wait. The sound of laughter and delighted conversation bubbled all around me, the tinkling of dishes and mugs being served. Bitching and moaning from at least a dozen others who'd gotten soaked like me. A rodeo on a wide screen was in progress, indiscernible music drifted in the background. Young men in spotless baseball uniforms milled about just waiting for the rain to stop.

Mmm. Right. Good luck with that. I thought as I looked out the doors again.

Wet, irritated and getting crankier by the second, I picked up a narrow red menu to peruse the limited choices.

A British voice pricked my ears from somewhere behind. I glanced up at a wall length mirror behind the bar. It had those little gold streaks running through it like the veins in marble and in it, I saw the reflection of a remarkably handsome, tall young man in a dapper black suit addressing a room attendant pushing a cart of crisp folded linens and towels.

He'd so politely asked her, "Pardon me, Miss. Could I trouble you for one of those?" He gestured to something on her cart. I then saw him via the mirror turn and walk directly beside me.

Oh, God! Seriously?

"Hello Miss, get a little wet?" He said while offering me a small hand towel.

"The world loves a funny guy. But thanks." I accepted the kindness of the stranger, patted my face dry and squeezed some of the water from the ends of my hair.

Every bit of 6' 3", the young man -not *illegal* young, but young all the same- took his suit jacket off to hang it neatly on the stool next to me. I caught a glimpse of the color of his eyes. The blue-green hue of the Gulf of Mexico. If you've ever seen its shallow waters on a calm sunny morning, it's a color difficult to forget.

He ran one hand back and forth through his hair then sighed like a man trying to release the tensions of a day gone bad. He pulled the stool next to me out with one hand and tugged at his tie to loosen the noose-like hold with the other. "I think it's been a bugger of a day all round."

I concurred with a fervent nod.

At the same time, we asked, "Where are you from?" We both laughed as he sat down.

"You first." I conceded and tried to tuck my wayward wet curls behind my ear.

"No, Miss. Ladies first. Always." He smiled the most dazzling smile I'd ever seen.

"A real gentleman? I thought you guys were extinct. Or at the very least on the endangered species list." I said in a conspiratorial whisper so as not to give his location away to the local hunters. I cast a meaningful glance at a table filled with college aged girls all giggling and staring at his back. Or his backside I gathered.

His shoulders shook a little with quiet laughter. "They are elusive creatures but I'm not one of them." In direct contrast with his denial, he quickly swished his jacket from his chair then draped it across my shoulders. I opened my mouth to decline his genial offer but he held up one finger. "If you're going to accuse me of being a gent, then you could, at the very least, allow me to behave as one." Again, with that crooked but lovely smile. He then proceeded to finger through a small hanging menu of spirits.

I promptly received five dagger-laced leers from the aforementioned girls.

"Thanks." I had to admit it felt better. His jacket still carried his warmth and it smelled like...I convinced myself not to go there. Smelling strange men is bound to be wrong.

He cut his eyes toward me then made a gesture with his hand as he said, "I'm still waiting."

"For *what*? Oh," My mind drew a blank as I filtered through it trying to remember where I was from. "Louisiana, originally. But I live just north of here." I managed to spit out before enough time lapsed to look like a dumbass. Maybe. I glanced at my watch and vowed that Owen had exactly ten minutes to get his ass in this room or I'd leave for a glass of wine and a hot bath.

I heard a voice from somewhere, distant but clear. *Don't be frightened, dear. I'll do my best to protect you.*

The voice seized my heart for one mind-ripping second. I whipped my head around to find the source but there was no one near enough other than the man next to me. The really wacky thing ... it sounded like GG, my long departed great-grandmother.

Thirty-seven is not old enough to have a mid-life crisis! Is it? What the hell would I be frightened of anyway? And protect me from what, exactly?

"Pleasure to make your acquaintance. Preston Grace." He waited with curious eyes and an encouraging grin until I realized he was waiting for my response.

Something along the lines of my name. I swear I was running like a V-8 with five bad sparkplugs. Damn rain!

"Adena Whittington. —But everybody calls me Dena. Nice to meet you, too."

"*Adena,*" He said my name as if trying it out like a new flavor of ice-cream. He looked at me in a way that felt like a touch. I shivered but at least I could blame it on being wet.

My cell buzzed from my purse. I dug it out and read the text.   -*Raining. Think I saw Noah's Ark pass me on the way home. Where r u?*-

"No shit, it's raining. *Genius!*" I mumbled then dug my thumbs into the keys as though Owen could feel every ounce of my aggravation. -*I'm at The Chesapeake ya jackass!*- (send) Without waiting for his reply, I stabbed the phone back into the side pocket then looked up to find the *gent* next to me laughing to himself. At *me* no doubt.

The bartender seemed anxious for my order so I glanced at the menu again then ordered the first thing I saw. A blackened Mahi sandwich and a glass of Merlot. I knew I'd live to regret that. Blackened does not simply mean *burn it till you can't tell the fish wasn't fresh*. Alas, that is usually what I get. Preston played it safe and ordered a cheeseburger and a Dewar's.

His smooth deep voice, like a perfect musical note, seemed to reach deeper into my ear. I'd always been a sucker for a British accent anyway. He could have looked like a toad and I'd have listened to him all night, which as it happens there was nothing remotely toad-like about him. He had the kind of face that just made me want to sigh and stare stupidly. But I resisted.

However, I did decide to give in to the previous denied pleasure. I took note of his scent with every single breath. I couldn't have ignored it if I tried. I was wrapped in a heavenly mix of musk, vanilla, citrus and cedar via his warm jacket and there was just something undeniably manly about it. I inhaled quietly; no one would notice. Discretion was easy when you have to breathe anyway. Not that a soul in this lounge or even this entire hotel is even looking my way or even knows me for that matter. I could sniff the guy like a bloodhound and no one would care. Well, *he* might.

One side of my brain began to argue with the other. *Stop that Dena. He's practically a kid.* The other side said, *Screw you! He's not* my *kid.* I bit the inside of my lip to stop the gibberish in my head. *He's too young. And I'm too married.*

He pulled a pretzel from a small basket on the bar and popped it into his mouth. "Louisiana. I've heard it's quite the place to see." He turned his head and smiled.

I smiled back, a little more contented to have someone to talk to. My mind wondered briefly back to the gravel roads of my youth. "It is. It's a wonderful place to call home. The people are a little crazy but in the best way."

I wrapped his jacket tighter around myself and stared at the amber wood of the bar remembering how much I missed my perfect childhood. Until tragedy I try not to speak of, tainted those silver memories. The reasons I don't visit home very much.

He startled me a bit when he flinched at an image on the wide screen just to our left showing a bull rider getting trampled by a bull named Iron Guts. Seconds later, the cowboy jumped to his feet, dusted his hat off and waved it to the crowd much to Preston's amazement.

I laughed at his wide-eyed gaze. "You've never been to a rodeo have you?" As if that were completely out of the question.

He arched one brow with mock arrogance. "I've been to Texas *and* I've seen *Urban Cowboys*. Does that count?"

I rolled my eyes and grinned.

"Ever been to England?" He asked then popped another pretzel into his mouth.

"No. I'd love to someday." I smiled at him and added, "But I've seen *Harrie Potter*, does *that* count?"

He nearly choked on his pretzel. "Touché, Love! You nailed me." He leaned back, inhaled deeply. "Smells like leather and old wood in here. I *love* the smell of leather." He nodded a quick thanks to the bartender and reached to take our drinks, then passed my wine glass to me.

I smiled inside at this small thing we had in common then took the first sip of merlot. "I used to spend *hours* in the barn behind our house because of the way the tack smelled." I wrinkled my nose a little. "Sounds weird I bet."

He shook his head a bit, took a drink of his scotch then crunched on a cube of ice. "I *still* do that. Do you ride?"

"I had a quarter horse when I was a girl. Used to barrel race a little as a teenager." This answer danced far too close to the memories I generally keep locked away. But Preston's good mood was catchy and although I usually resist digging up the bones of my past, he'd asked me to describe my favorite bits about growing up in Louisiana.

I told him I grew up on Lake St. John just a few miles west of the Mississippi River near Natchez, and for the sake of simplicity we both pretended he knew where that was. I circled the memories that hurt the most and described instead how I missed watching the sun paint the lake in the evening. How it looked like glowing copper shining through the black silhouettes of the cypress trees. How those haunting trees looked like ancient wizards to me when I was a little girl; how the trunks looked like robes flowing right into the water and the Spanish moss draped over every branch made me think of an old man's beard and his long gray hair. And that if I stood still long enough, I believed those old wizards would tell me their ancient secrets.

I told him of the hours I'd spent sitting in the barn surrounded by the smell of sweet feed, oats and the saddles on the walls, writing tales of alligators and herons and make-believe creatures from the swamps.

I loved to pick the okra in GGs garden, watch the Saints play on TV and go fishing with Daddy and his older brother, Uncle Ray, in his little green john boat. Riding my Honda 110 on the levy, playing in the dense black dirt with my cousin Carolyn, Uncle Ray's daughter, who lived next door. The coolness beneath the shade of a wild pecan tree, swinging fearlessly from an old frayed rope into the lake; always seeking refuge from the summer heat. The delectable smell of Mama's kitchen every night. The march to Grandpa Joe's little white church just down the road every single Sunday.

I stopped as I could feel the distant memories beginning to choke me. I was probably boring the poor man to tears anyway.

Preston crossed his arms causing his white dress shirt to strain across his shoulders. "You get more fascinating by the second, Adena. That was positively lovely."

I shrugged off the compliment. Maybe normally he was a shut in and hadn't talked to anyone in a while.

"You should write a book about the place. You know the type —for tourism. You paint quite a picture."

I smiled but didn't say anything because I hadn't had the good fortune to eke out a descent sentence in over two months. My muse was either dead or pissed off at me. In all likelihood it was the latter since I had basically ignored her throughout the school year. It used to be easy to juggle both, but lately it's been…difficult. Besides, tourism was more Owen's forte` than mine.

Thankfully, with only a little prodding, he returned the favor and took me on a trip across the Atlantic to a small village called Havering-atte-Bower, located on the northeast outskirts of London in the borough of Havering; the county of Essex. He grinned hugely having included all of this on purpose solely to confuse me. It worked to be certain but eventually, I caught on.

He spoke of a pub called The Hawbush in nearby Romford that he and his cousin Robert used to frequent before it closed —then of a family tradition where he, and his younger sister Teena, his parents, Doreen and Nate, and a little girl named Kelley, although I didn't catch the relation, would head to the banks of the Thames every June to watch the rowing teams compete in the Henley Royal Regatta. He described the St. John's church where his family had attended for generations. The beautiful land they lived on, the stables and long lush pastures and a pear orchard so big that you couldn't see where it ended.

I could picture it all perfectly as if I'd seen it all first-hand in some other life. Greener than green, rainy and cool. And I could see in the way he spoke, the endearing expression in his eyes, that he loved that little piece of London as much as I loved the muddy banks of my lake.

Taking my eyes off him was like trying to peel a price tag off a china plate. Difficult at best. His dark brown hair with hints of auburn was short and neat, a little longer on top. Two day's stubble on his jaw. Judging by the way his shirt clung to him in certain places, he was muscular; tall and lean but broad shouldered. A one inch scar disturbed his right eyebrow, thwarting his otherwise perfection. And he was young, mid twenties. Maybe. His eyes looked older in a way. Mysterious eyes that held something back. Smiling eyes that seemed to hide a great deal of pain. Or maybe it simply took looking through that same filter to recognize the mask.

The rodeo on the big screen was showing ladies barrel racing now. Preston commented, "I have one that looks just like that."

"You have a teenage girl bedazzled in rhinestones and satin fringe? Lucky you."

He turned his head slowly toward me, a smirk playing havoc with his tantalizing smile. "The *horse*. I have a quarter horse. Her name is Dolly." And we laughed together. He looked at the screen again and nodded in appreciation. "So this is barrel racing?" He gestured with another nod toward the television.

I answered with yet another nod.

"And you said before that you used to do this?"

"Yep. Many moons ago and of course, not as fast as those girls. But yes, for fun I did."

He looked impressed and I wanted to laugh. I admitted openly that the only thing I'd ever done in an actual rodeo was chase a petrified little pig with a red ribbon tied to its tail along with about fifty other little kids scrambling after it in a neighboring town at the Jonesville rodeo in hopes of winning twenty dollars.

I never got close; although one year I did manage to stay on a grown sheep long enough to win fifty dollars and a fake gold belt buckle slightly bigger than my own head. I was ten years old. This sounds simple enough, but believe me, sheep do not move like horses and they will bounce your brains out.

We laughed together, breathlessly, tearfully, and without abandon until our ribs ached.

No two people more different, we chatted over everything and nothing at all until the bartender brought our food and fresh drinks in Styrofoam to-go dishes and for the first time I realized, the lobby and the bar was nearly empty. Half the lights had even been turned off. It wasn't that late, they just tended to wrap things up early on Sunday evenings.

Preston smiled wickedly. "Care to accompany me upstairs?"

I'd just taken another drink and damn near spewed wine out of my nose.

"My apologies. I was only joking. I didn't mean my suite. There's a covered balcony on the fifth floor. We can continue our conversation and I can smoke. Unless you prefer eating alone —in the dark." He gestured to the obvious desolation around us.

I glanced over my shoulder toward the glass front doors to see the rain still coming down in a torrent. I couldn't even see the sidewalk despite the floodlights under the awning and darkness had fallen to boot. Maybe it was later than I thought.

"I guess so." I said feeling a smidge like an idiot for assuming he meant anything else by the invitation.

He tossed a tip next to his plate and told the bartender to put everything on his bill.

The bodiless voice echoed directly in my ear. *Follow the music of your heart, Adena. Follow me home. Come and find me.*

There was no mistaking it. It was GG! She's the only person who ever called me Adena. And those were the exact words she'd so desperately said to me the day she passed on. I whipped my head around again, searching in vain. I knew she wasn't there. Preston and I were the only people left. I chalked up the experience to all that talk of back home. That's all it was. Just memories. And I missed her. That's all.

Upstairs on the balcony, the heavy rain blurred the city lights. I sat down in a huge Adirondack chair fighting the urge to shake in my wet clothes; the winds suddenly unseasonably cool so late in May.

"Thanks for dinner. That was really sweet." I told him.

He lounged in another oversized chair, facing me; his ankles crossed conveying the perfect picture of leisure. "It's only a sandwich. Perhaps I could treat you to a proper dinner some time."

"Maybe," I replied without thinking. Then the self-righteous bitch in my head, my conscience, began to yell at me for flirting.

Oh shut up! I thought. No harm, no foul. As soon as the rain let up, I'd get in my car and *go home*. To a big fat empty house.

On the other hand, Preston was the most exciting diversion I'd had in a while. Just sitting there chatting away eating a not-so-good fish sandwich was the most fun I'd had in too long. Okay, as sad as that simple truth was, on the inside, I felt like a happy Labrador, wagging his tail too fast to walk straight, so I'd enjoy it while it lasted. My inner voice could just suck it. I had come out to enjoy an evening with a friend who happened to be a male and I was doing nothing else to the contrary. So, what's the difference?

Okay! I very well know the answer to that! I never wanted to sniff Owen per say. And he didn't look anything like Preston but who on earth did?

Preston finished his burger, rattled the ice in his glass then leaned his head back to watch the black sky. "I love a thunder storm." His eyes darted to mine and he smiled. "The lightening amazes me. Especially here. Even last night, when it wasn't raining, the flashes seemed to jump from cloud to cloud, but I never saw it meet the earth."

Heat lightening. Not uncommon in Florida.

He sat up straighter, unintentionally closer to me, his eyes still on the sky as another bolt sizzled through the atmosphere. I blinked twice and hoped he didn't notice the way I'd stared at the excitement in his amazing eyes. Repetitions of brilliant blue streaks turned night to day for about three seconds. Thunder the likes of a crack of a .308 rifle made the building shimmy.

Preston raised his voice over the increasing din of the storm; blocking his face from the attacking mist that had now found its way into the somewhat dry patio. "Perhaps we should have a look at the news! Looks like things are getting a bit nasty out."

I didn't hesitate to get out of the gloom. Weather like that made me nervous as a little cat in a big dog kennel. We walked just around the corner to his suite. Once inside, I reveled in the stillness of the room. No more wind. Warmer, dryer, quiet. The lingering aroma of Hazelnut coffee hung in the air of the small space offering at least a charade of the comforts of home.

He flipped the TV to the local news; squares of red were splayed all over a regional weather map and a flashing newsfeed streamed across the bottom of the screen. All of Alachua County was under a tornado watch.

Tornado. There went my two seconds of comfort. My throat constricted and I felt like an elephant was dancing the Hokey Pokey on my chest, and just about the time the big gray peanut-eating beast was *shaking it all about*, he'd effectively squashed all the air from my lungs.

"Looks like you're trapped here for a bit longer than you were expecting." Preston said as he sat on the couch and turned the volume up.

My nervous system started to short circuit. Cold sweat. Can't breathe. Knees locked.

"Don't worry. I'm not a psychopath." He defended himself as he misunderstood my reaction.

My hands clinging frantically to the black granite wet bar in a white-knuckle panic, I tried not to look at the Doppler images but I couldn't help it. Green meant rain. No sweat. Red was heavy rain. Alright. But purple! That's usually what turns my brain to cold grits. Hard, lumpy and good for nothing.

Preston walked over with a marked measure of concern on his brow and as he put his arm around my trembling shoulders, he looked carefully into my eyes. My silly heart did a double back flip, missed two beats then stuttered back to almost normal.

Wow! What was that?

"Adena, are you —frightened by the weather?"

I shook my head tight and quick. "Mm-mm, those...*things*." I jabbed a finger towards the television but refused to look at it again. Stupid phobia!

I knew the funnel symbol was floating in the corner of the screen as the reporter blathered away about the possibilities to come. Where to go in case *The Thing* formed from some demon cloud. That was by far the dumbest shit I'd ever heard. Like hiding *anywhere* could offer any protection from something so immense, so powerful, so...*deathly*. *The Things* were blind with no conscience, obliterating whatever they touched.

"Ah, I see." Preston leaned over and spoke low in my ear. "So you'll fly atop the withers of a horse at break-neck speed, but it takes the likes of a tornado to make you nervous. Interesting." He stood to his full height then reached for my hands and let my fists just rest in his palms, his eyes darting back and forth, from one to the other. "Try to relax, Adena. You're frightened. I see that. But you're only holding on to your own fear. And your very pretty nails are literally biting into your skin. Now just try to concentrate on my voice and do as I say."

I managed something like *okay* between teeth clenched so tight, it made my jaw hurt.

"Breathe in," he spoke softly and I listened with my eyes closed to his slow intake of air and tried to match my breathing with his. "Good. Now breathe out."

His voice, a soothing baritone giving me simple commands effortless to follow. And slowly, little by little, my hands uncurled in his and I felt the blood trickle to the deprived tips of my fingers. I inhaled through my nose, blew out a final purifying breath and opened my eyes. I looked up into his. His eyes were so soft, the color so tranquil. The Gulf of Mexico. Preston's eyes. One could easily drown in either.

He'd hypnotized me into a peaceful state it seemed. But the wind howled and another rip of thunder shattered my beautiful glass bubble he'd created for me and my body went rigid again. He reached across the short counter to retrieve a simple glass bottle with a whole pear miraculously trapped inside then poured it in two glasses.

He offered one to me. "When all else fails, a little brandy makes it better. Or so my father says. Don't drink it too quickly."

I marveled at the delicious taste and aroma of pears. Thankfully, with each drink, my senses began to dull. Abandoning his own glass, he slipped his hands beneath my hair, just along my scalp and began moving his fingertips in gentle circles near my temples.

That did it. Every muscle in my body betrayed me and my knees caved. It'd been too long since I'd been touched by a man. And I'm only human. My body responded on its own. He caught me and I gazed up at his face, feeling like I was in a dream, more dazed than I should be.

"Adena, are you all right? I told you not to drink it too quickly. I don't want you to think I'm *trying* to get you smashed."

"I don't think that was from the drinks." I said trying to come to my senses, feeling just a bit like a moron.

"Oh. Sorry." He raised his eyebrows once and shoved his hands in his pockets as if to keep them to himself.

I took another sip to let go of the awkwardness. "This tastes like a Jolly Rancher. Just with a wicked kick."

He smiled and wrinkled his nose. "Yes, but go easy. A bit of hard candy won't leave you with a hangover. I'm not sure it will mix well with your merlot."

Ew. Good point.

I picked up the bottle from the counter to study the pear inside. It was then that I saw the ornate black and gold label. *Katherine's Private Stock – Grace Orchards since 1842*

"Grace? As in *your* family's orchards?" I asked. He nodded with a modest smile. I held the bottle high to see the pear again.

He chuckled as he answered the obvious question on my mind. "The bottle is placed over the pear when it's still very small. It grows inside."

I nodded once, duly impressed. By far, the coolest thing I'd ever seen.

I almost took a seat on the couch, but remembering my wet jeans and the very expensive looking leather sofa, I opted for a stool at the short counter instead.

He looked at me funny and smiled, tapping his finger on his chin. "Now, let's see if we can get you out of those wretched wet clothes." He waited for my aghast expression, which he readily received then tossed his head back and laughed. "I was only going to offer you something to wear. You don't look very comfortable." He grinned again and appeared to be stifling the urge to laugh. "You're welcome to anything I have. And by all means, lock the bedroom door if it makes you feel safer."

My fingers had already turned all pruny so the thought of being warm and dry was just too good to pass on. Upon entering the smallish bathroom, I stopped dead short at my reflection in an unexpected wall-sized mirror. No wonder Preston was trying not to laugh. I looked like I'd been dragged through the swamps, beaten half to death, then left to die. I actually had two leaves stuck in my hair. *Nice.* I'd been too busy looking at him in the mirror at the bar to notice that I looked like an actual wild woman.

I scrubbed my face clean, dried my hair, then pulled it up in a clip just to get it off my neck. I drained the rest of the pear brandy from my glass, added a dab of perfume to my wrists and I almost felt like myself again.

I found a crisp blue dress shirt and a pair of those long board shorts that looked like they might fit. I'm five foot eight and wear a size ten. (On a good day). Bubble butt be damned, I eat what I want. I looked in the mirror again and laughed at myself in his clothes. Very hobo-ish.

A rather beat up guitar case propped against the dresser caught my eye as I passed through the bedroom to rejoin Preston in the living room of the suite. I spared the instrument a passing glance, idly wondering if he was any good at it or, if like so many that are doomed to travel regularly, simply pick and play out of sheer boredom. The thought evaporated as soon as I realized that Preston was gone. I looked to the left into the small kitchenette and to the right into the sitting area as well, yet he was nowhere to be seen.

I must admit, disappointment flooded my very existence in a strange and dangerous way. I was attracted to him to say the least. I'd be a liar and a fool to pretend otherwise.

Comforted in his generous offer of dry clothes, I strolled past the sofa to the far left of the living room to a large-paned corner window then pulled back the white gossamer sheers to see if the weather might be letting up.

I found him instead, leaning casually against the opposing brick wall of the balcony smoking and talking on his cell where the mist couldn't reach quite enough to saturate. His tie hung loose and he'd unfastened the top button on his perfectly starched white shirt. One foot perched on the wall behind him, he flicked the rose end of his cigarette and the wind carried the tiniest embers only a fraction into the mist to die. This image of Preston, this beautiful young man, sent gooseflesh dancing along my arms until an involuntary shiver literally shook me enough to snap me out of my stare.

Sheesh! Why did I have to run into a man who looked like a friggin' Tim McGraw video? The one where he sings, *She's My Kind of Rain*.

I lingered at the window, trying to decipher if the hard tapping I was hearing was really hail. But the thought of that scared me silly again. Thankfully, the merlot plus the yummy pear brandy was definitely keeping the storm from plucking my nerves too badly.

I settled onto the couch and pulled the long shirt down past my knees; my head getting fuzzier by the minute with the few drinks I'd had. Somewhere very far away I could hear the battle between my conscience and someone I wasn't familiar with, going on and on as I stared mindlessly at a rerun of *M*A*S*H*. Preston came through the door and laughed at something the character, Hawk Eye, had said as he sat next to me but I couldn't concentrate on the episode.

My conscience was quickly becoming a nag.

You shouldn't be here. You should go. You're gambling everything if you stay here much longer. You're way too old for him anyway!

HEY NOW! I shouted within my own barrage of why this entire situation could be bad. Mostly, because that last bit pissed me off — even if it *was* self-inflicted by my very own thoughts. But the simple truth remained that I hadn't *done* anything wrong. I was stuck there. But there was another voice; a sweeter echo in my head, and she was taking my side. I liked her. She understood. I told her so, only in my mind, and we thoroughly told my nagging conscience to shut her fat yap. I laughed at the silly image of a little cartoon angel and devil perched on my shoulders.

Preston chuckled softly, put his arm around me and gave me a quick squeeze. "Glad you're happy. That's loads better than flipping out." He laughed again. "You must be a good girl. Three little drinks and you're completely off your face."

Off my face? Must be a British thing. But yes. Two is generally my absolute limit. I'm not an established drinker and I never could hold my own.

The man smelled incredible. It couldn't just be his cologne. I knew my judgment was questionable but I could swear that his scent was literally making me high. I caught myself breathing deeper to take in this sweet bit of heaven as I slipped off to that place somewhere between awake and dreaming until I felt him lead my head and shoulders to rest in his lap. I opened my eyes to see him smiling down at me.

"Didn't mean to wake you. Thought you'd be more comfortable this way." He took the clip out of my hair and fanned it over his thigh.

My eyes closed again. "This way or that; doesn't matter. It all feels wonderful."

Was that a thought or an audible statement? Judging by the chuckle that came from his chest, I guessed it must have been the latter. *Dangit!*

"Adena, are you alright being here? With me, I mean. I'll call for a taxi if you like." Instantly, a blinding flash shot across the windows, the room went black and another whip-crack of thunder ripped the air.

A sliver of fear trickled down my spine; piercing my protective mask of alcohol. I'd almost forgotten the damn storm. I turned over and snuggled face-first into his tummy which ultimately I found to be hard as a rock. "I don't wanna go out there. Besides, I like my new friend and you smell really good."

He laughed harder than before and my head jiggled with the motion, shaking me out of my buzzed oblivion. A shallow wave of sobriety made me realize the way I was laying across him was completely inappropriate. Especially considering my ear was resting against his crotch!

I tried to sit up but my head spun. Then the room. That numbness that wells just under my chin before heaving made me swallow hard. "Ugh, no car rides. But I should get my own room. If I throw up on you, I'm 100% positive I will die."

He patted my shoulder, reassuring me without words that everything would be fine. He got up but I didn't dare raise my head to see where he went not that I could see anyway; the lights were still out. I heard the fridge open and the rattling of ice as he said, "The hotel is booked. There's a tournament of sorts nearby. Baseball, apparently. The lobby was positively swarming with teen-aged boys this afternoon." A few seconds passed; I heard a drawer slide open and shut. "Not to mention the wine and spirits conference I'd mentioned earlier has the immediate area fairly full up."

I turned my face to feel the cool leather of the couch to sooth as I remembered that part of our conversation downstairs. He was here for the conference in place of his father. Three of their brandies had been recently recognized for an award I couldn't remember the name of. I suppose it must have been quite an honor for him to fly across the Atlantic to represent his family.

At any rate, his British accent and light prattle was soothing to hear. Familiar. Almost expected for some reason. I couldn't put my finger on it. His voice seemed *more* in some weird and wonderful way. Like it was an echo lost forever in my own mind searching and swimming to break through the barrier of my own consciousness. It was a composition; my favorite melody and I knew the lyrics to the piece by heart.

But strangely woven throughout this beautiful composition were voices. Crying and pleading. Searching in desperation. So many voices creating a painful confusion. The cries were not distinct enough to hear clearly the words so desperately calling but they seemed to be searching. Searching in vain. There was also a taste of malice as well. Regret and something else. Foreboding and fearful.

What happened to my beautiful melody? What happened to Preston's voice? I couldn't find him. Where am I? Why is it so dark?

My head spun violently and I was on the couch very much in the present. My music had ceased; the lights had come back on and my skull felt as though it may possibly have a hairline fracture in it.

What the hell is in that brandy? LSD?

My thoughts faltered as he lifted my shoulders, arranged my head in his lap again then pressed an ice-cold compress to my throat. Ah…so perfect. After a minute or so, the sickly spinning began to slow.

"Thank you." I whispered and tried to hold the compress myself but my hand bumped into his. He gently pushed my hand away with his little finger.

"Just relax and feel better, Love. Sleep if you can. You're perfectly safe here."

I smiled a little, liking the way he said that. Probably just a matter of the way he spoke. He probably called all women *Love*, the way men in the south call them Sweetie or Sugar. And I did feel safe. He pulled one long ringlet of my hair at a time over his leg. It relaxed me and soothed the ache in my head. I wanted so much to look up at him. And I did momentarily but the whisper touches of his fingers against my cheek lulled me further into sleep. At first, I fought to remain aware but eventually I succumbed to the beautiful cloud pulling me under. My beautiful melody returned and it was just us, no scary sounds, no pleading voices and no fear.

At some point in the night, my head sank into a cloud of pillows. A soft down comforter covered me. I knew he'd leaned very close. I could smell his skin again. I also knew I had a new favorite smell now.

I felt his fingers slide slowly over the ring on my left hand as he whispered, "Why do you look so familiar to me?"

What?

There was no more. I was dreaming. Maybe it was all a dream. It had to be.

Vivid images of a vacation I'd taken with my father long ago trickled into my subconscious. I was fifteen at a hotel swimming pool in Texas entertaining a little boy around seven or eight years old. The memory, probably triggered by Preston's accent, as that family had been from England as well. His name was Scooter Banks and he'd proposed to me that summer with a gaudy purple ring from a gumball machine. He'd had the same haunting yet beautiful blue-green eyes.

The images morphed and I was on the edge of that mysterious cliff again, searching for the voice that beckoned for me to jump. *It won't hurt when you fall. I'll catch you. I promise.* —The same image that had now inexplicably haunted me for the fourth night in a row.

My eyes fluttered sleepily in the dark at a sound somewhat akin to a train barreling through a building made of lead crystal. A startling jerk of my body hauled me sideways across the mattress, covers and all. Arms with such strength that I could not escape and I'd not had adequate time to remember where I was but instinct necessitated my shriek and the struggle that followed. Fight or Flight —one or the other is human instinct. I was attempting to do both.

Despite it all, the strong arms held me fixed against his chest as he kicked the bathroom door open and practically dumped me into the tub. He'd wedged himself in as well then covered us with the thick comforter and two big blocks of something. One touch and I realized the blocks were the thick leather cushions from the sofa. Both of us in an awkward fetal position, we simply waited.

I realized at last what was happening. It was my own personal version of Hell. The cold porcelain against my legs matched the icy feeling paralyzing my body. My heart thudded hard as if trying to pump mud through my veins. A deafening, high pitched shrill from all around made me cover my ears. I cringed and hid my face against his chest bracing myself for what was coming and I prayed until the pleas ripped from my throat but my voice was lost in the violence —if I'd made a sound at all.

A sickening bang and the building shook to its core. Cracking sounds all around like everything was coming to pieces. An earsplitting crash, the sound of glass imploding, followed by random objects battering the walls. We held each other tighter with each blast; Preston's arms curled around my head, his broad hand protecting the side of my face.

The hotel groaned in absolute protest against the eternal ripping, snashing, and growling from the wind tunnel titan tearing its way in.

I won't let her take you, Adena! I won't let her have you as well! I heard the strange female voice again, that came from nowhere and everywhere at once. GG's voice. But it couldn't be. All the same, the voice came again and again with the same vow. My sanity had officially slipped off the fence.

Preston shifted his entire body over me -a protective shield from head to toe- just as the bathroom door blasted open sending a shower of debris on top of us. The new weight pressed down substantially; there seemed to be no more air, my ears popped viciously and it was difficult to breathe. Preston's lips crushed against my forehead and again against my temple. My head spun frantically. It felt like a kiss. A kiss goodbye. We were going to die!

And then... everything stopped. A dead silence cloaked us.

We lay there without a word, our hearts pounding like sledgehammers, each of us trying to hear if it were all really over. I threw my arms around his neck and started sobbing, trying to find some center of gravity. Terror still gripping my heart and relief spilling out that the monster had spared us and gone away. My mind struggled desperately to process the nightmare.

"It's alright, Love. I've got you." He let me cling to him, gently rocking me like a child until I calmed down.

I finally loosened my death grip and wiped at my eyes, trying to see anything in the blackness beneath the blankets. "I'm sorry." My voice, a raspy half-whisper from screaming.

"Don't be silly. That was absolutely horrifying." He whispered so close, I felt his breath tickle my cheek.

I could hear and feel the wild beat of our hearts, could feel each warm rush of his breath on my face. And although I couldn't see him, I felt every single heated part of him so very close, still holding me. The stubble on his chin brushed my cheek and I felt a tingling sensation in the depths of my belly. He pressed his lips cautiously to mine and all traces of panic melted away as if I'd never had a single fear in my life. He held my face; caressing my cheeks with his thumbs as his tongue touched my mouth urging me to let him inside. And I didn't stop him. I felt as though my heart and my mind had broken through to another dimension, one that I was all too happy to be in.

I felt his hand against the small of my back pressing me closer, as he traced the line of my jaw with his lips. His tongue eased out to taste my neck. His teeth raked across my skin and I shuddered. He breathed my name into my ear, the most beautiful sound I'd ever heard.

My fingers tunneled through his thick hair and I kissed him back. In one fluid movement, he pulled us up to our knees, tossing the stifling comforter away. His hand wound loosely in the back of my hair, molding me to the arch of his body -his lips trailing down my throat until he'd buried his face as far as the buttons on the blue shirt would allow. He kissed me just above my cleavage and I felt as though I'd just fallen from a plane, the rush of adrenaline more than I'd ever felt and I gasped at the sensuous feel of his perfect lips against my skin. But we had to stop.

"Preston," I breathed his name and tried to make sense of what just happened.

"I'm sorry." He whispered shakily and rested his forehead on my chest, his breath flowing in hot waves down my shirt. "We should go. It's probably… not safe in here any longer."

I couldn't help but detect the double meaning.

Emerging from the bathroom, we were welcomed by the hypnotic strobe of the emergency lights fixed high in one corner of the bedroom; the atmosphere humid but chilled as though we were standing outside. The bedroom door hung crooked, nearly freed of its hinges.

Preston looked down at my bare feet. "Don't move," A protective demand, "There's glass everywhere. I'll go check for a safe way out."

He disappeared and with every flash of light, I could see that the entire room glistened with shards of glass. Four improbably perfect holes now adorned the wall by the door. I saw a sliver of 2x4 skewering the mattress precisely where I'd been sleeping. My mouth went bone-dry.

The closet door was still intact so without moving my feet, I twisted to open it and right away spotted a far-too-big pair of tennis shoes. I scrunched my toes to the ends then shuffled my way to the door just as Preston popped around the corner. We scared each other half to death.

Immediately he picked me straight up. "Exactly which of your toes are you *not* fond of?"

When he lifted me, his shoes flopped clumsily down to the soggy and once beautiful coffee-colored carpet. He chuckled and sat me back down allowing me to place each foot back into his shoes again before letting me go.

I walked into the living room and couldn't move. The destruction that took all of two heartbeats was an imposing wake up to how lucky we were to be alive. Where once draped a white gossamer sheer now hung a sadly shredded web over what used to be a grand window, the entertainment center smashed into the floor and a wet layer of dirt and grime covered what little remained.

"Now that's what I call art." Preston said in amazement. I followed his awestruck gaze and just above the couch was one of the teakwood patio chairs from the balcony stabbed directly into the wall as though it were nothing more than a push pin in a corkboard. I then came to understand what the four holes in the bedroom were. The legs had punched all the way through.

The gaping hole that used to be the left corner of the living room revealed that the awning on the balcony was gone, the aluminum banister ripped off and a large crescent of concrete of the balcony floor was chewed away, leaving rods of bent rebar sticking out like broken bones. A traffic light teetered precariously on the edge. Preston scared the hell out of me when he hopped over a substantial crack in the cement to tug it completely onto the concrete to prevent it from killing anyone below.

I could have been in shock. Having never been in shock I couldn't possibly explain what I was feeling. I wandered alone back through to the bedroom. The only thing I could think of was to gather my belongings if I could find them. I dug beneath the bits of rubble, the couch cushions, and the heavy comforter until I found my purse and my wet clothes from last night. I redressed in them even though they still felt horribly wet and cold. I couldn't find my sandals anywhere.

When Preston returned and saw me, he smiled in a way that made my body temperature do strange things —like double, then plummet leaving me ever so slightly dizzy. He touched the button placket of his blue shirt I'd put back on over my own. He smiled, subtly reminding me that it was actually his. His touch seemed to ground me; wake me up in a way.

"It *used* to be yours, OK? I survived a tornado in it. This is now *my* lucky shirt." I said matter-of-factly and I think I may have even sounded normal.

He placed his finger beneath my chin and pulled my face toward his. "In that case, I think it's only fair to say that you're my lucky girl." He held my hand in his; his thumb slid over the diamond ring on my left hand. His smile faded as he hesitated, the dilemma in his eyes apparent.

I nodded once to confirm the truth but said nothing.

He turned away, his arms tense, hands balled. "Dammit! Why does *everything* in my life have to be so bloody complicated?" Two long strides away then in a blink he had me in his arms, muttering something I didn't catch.

His kiss was hard and I could feel the reverberations of his anger surging through me. I consumed it, made it mine as well. In some twisted way, it made *him* mine for whatever brief moment I could keep him. He pressed me close against him making me yield to his hands as if he could force reality away so that it never touched us again. But the distant sirens too quickly pierced the silence of the predawn hour, sounding the end of our time together. The building would certainly be evacuated any second.

He'd left me breathless again, not really knowing what else to say, what to do, what to think. However, the smile on my face was like a high-tension spring. The more I tried to suppress it, the more it wanted to bounce back in place. But why? I'd just kissed another man. Repeatedly! What the hell was I thinking?

But I knew what I was thinking. I liked kissing him.

Preston squatted down to check the condition of the old guitar inside the busted black case. I heard him whisper, 'Sorry mate,' almost to himself then closed it the best that he could. I had a feeling he went nowhere without that guitar and I was sad for him although I didn't know the story behind it.

I knew I should leave, that was obvious, but I didn't want to leave *him*. Excuses rallied in my mind as I remembered him mentioning some psycho driver who he'd sworn had almost killed him before delivering him to the hotel, so I knew he didn't have a rental.

"Preston, um…if you need a lift somewhere, I could take you."

He chuckled only slightly then grimaced as he grabbed a worn leather duffel from the bottom of the closet and gathered what had luckily been spared. "You're assuming you still *have* a car?"

Son of a bitch! That thought hadn't even crossed my mind. How many emotional highs and lows could a person handle in twelve hours? After all of this, if there was so much as a scratch on my Mustang, I'd flip smooth out of my mind.

I headed cautiously down the stairs illuminated by the eerie red emergency lighting. Preston stopped to tell a policeman which room had been his. We assured him we were in good health and he told us we could leave. The silent walk down the shiny wet, debris strewn streets was nerve racking. Two agonizing blocks down, I stopped in my tracks and sighed in relief that my car remained unscathed. I know it's ridiculous to worry about material things, especially after what we'd just lived through, but that car was special.

Preston stopped next to me under a dead streetlamp, his eyes following the shadowed lines of my navy blue sixty-five Shelby.

"You're kidding." He said as he looked over the roof at me.

I unlocked my door and reached to open his. He put his guitar and the leather bag in the back seat, thoroughly examining the original interior then ran his hand over the dash as he sat.

"Would you consider selling it?" He actually looked hopeful.

I stuck the key in the ignition. "You're delirious. Did I choke you in the tub? Take deep breaths, you'll feel better. I've had this car since I was sixteen. It's *not* for sale." I cranked it reveling in the beefy sound. "So, where can I take you?"

"Any hotel will do." His mood seemed to plummet along with mine. I'd hoped we could hold on to the lighthearted moment when he admired my car.

I pulled away from the curb, carefully dodging a few mangled panels that once belonged to some unfortunate building. Fire engines swarmed the scene eager to get the chaos under control.

We rode in silence although a couple times, I thought he might say something but he stopped each time and stared at the sky; a sunrise masterpiece with wisps of lavender, orange and pink seemed to demand his attention. Or perhaps it gave him an excuse to keep his words to himself.

Two exits up I-75, I pulled off to a Hampton Inn then eased to the front doors so he wouldn't have to carry his luggage across the parking lot. What little he had. The storm had indeed managed to suck out most of his traveling wardrobe.

"Thanks." He hesitated, again as if he wanted to say something. Instead, he just shook his head, turned to me and smiled a little. "It was lovely meeting you, Adena."

"You too, Preston." Good-bye just seemed too detrimental to say. Not that it made any difference. I'd never see him again.

The closing of the heavy steel door hurt my ears, not that he slammed it. It just meant *good-bye* whether we said it or not. He leaned over to peek through the window, gave me a little wave then walked away. I watched him open the double doors then disappear inside.

I'd never felt so absolutely alone in my life.

You'd think I'd forgotten how to drive. I had to make myself put the car in gear and pull away. Mile after mile, each one behind hurt worse than the one before. I honestly *tried* to be rational, ticking off the reasons, one by one, why it was all wrong. He's too young. I'm married. And for Christ's sake he didn't even live in the same country! So, why was it such a battle to just go home? To hold on to my sensibilities and not turn around and floor it as fast as I could just to be near him? Half way to High Springs, I realized I was crying.

Oh, the hell with it! Logic and common sense can be so overrated. I'd lived my entire life being the good girl; doing what I'm supposed to do. Tires squealing, I looped around to go south and stayed heavy on the gas all the way back. I pulled into the parking lot so fast that my car bottomed out with a loud metallic grunt and I had to stand on the brake to prevent hitting the yellow concrete parking bumper. Before I could change my mind, although that didn't seem to be a likely possibility, I got out and yanked off Preston's cumbersome shoes, knowing I couldn't run in them. Not without planting my front teeth in the asphalt anyway.

In no time at all I found myself panting in front of the long reception desk inside attended by a tall blonde woman wearing a very tired smile.

"Excuse me, Ma'am. I'm looking for Preston Grace. He just checked in."

She shook her head and covered a yawn as she stapled two receipts together. "No one has checked in since last night. I'm the only one who's been here. Sorry."

My heart sank. He'd gone somewhere else already, called a cab or something. I turned to go, resolved to get over what I hoped was just a transitory state of lunacy.

"Oh, Miss?" She called just as I had my hand on the door. "There *was* one gentleman who came in a few minutes ago, but he didn't check in. Is the man you're looking for really tall? Dark-ish hair?"

I swallowed hard and nodded. "Excruciatingly handsome?"

"I wouldn't know. I don't normally work night shifts and I'm so tired I can't see. She pointed down an empty hallway. "Go to the end and take a left. He was looking for a drink."

I nodded my thanks and set off at a brisk pace, hearing only my bare feet against the short pile carpet. The hallway got longer it seemed the quicker I moved. Finally, I turned to the left and stopped so fast I nearly fell. There he sat staring at the diamond pattern on the carpet surrounded by vending machines. He glanced up and did a double take. He didn't say a word.

I braced myself against the frame of the open door, my chest heaving, and I wanted to say something. Anything! But I'd lost my nerve. How could I be so delusional as to think he'd even be happy to see me? A big dose of rejection is just what I needed to top off my day. On the flip side of normal, I slid down the doorframe until I was squatting, running my hands through my hair not caring what he thought anymore. No doubt, he'd already gathered I was not a normal human being.

He walked closer, kneeled down beside me and touched my shoulder. "Adena, *why* did you come back?"

I shook my head and tried to make my mouth work. "I can't... I tried...I'm crazy, I mean, *this* is crazy. No, I was right before. *I'm* crazy." My babble made no sense to anyone but me. With a thought clearing breath, I leaned my cheek against his hand still on my shoulder and closed my eyes to whisper, "Preston, if you're not that interested just tell me and I'll go."

He took my hands and gently pulled me to my feet. I'd forgotten my inexplicable crying in the car until he brushed the wetness from my cheek. "Don't ever waste your precious tears on me. I will never make you cry on purpose."

The rattling hum of a compressor kicked on in one of the drink machines but everything else was quiet. He smiled. He looked happy, hopeful even and I imagine my face looked the same. But then his hopefulness faded. He took my hand and rubbed his thumb slowly over the back of it.

"Adena, —Wednesday morning I leave for London. I've been here for three days handling business for my father because he isn't well. I'd have told you that part earlier... but a few hours ago; well, I simply had no idea I would need to." A worried crease disfigured the space between his brows.

Trent and Beth were visiting his mother up in Georgia. Gavin and his friend Brian went to the old lakeside in Louisiana, for a few days of debauchery no doubt. They called it fishing but I knew better. I fidgeted, nervous about what I was considering but I knew my house would be empty until my family came back.

"Will you come with me?"

He touched my cheek and smiled. "Adena, I'd follow you anywhere."

"To my place?"

His hand dropped to his side and his face grew serious while at the same time his doubtful smirk and pinched brow seemed to question my intelligence. "I can't imagine that's your best idea." He straightened his back and crossed his arms. "Adena, before we take the first step onto this road-of-no-return, please explain why you're willing to *risk* everything."

I reached up to touch the scar just over his right eyebrow. "Because, just the thought of you being hurt in anyway, it's like a burning torture that I can't explain." Trancelike, I touched his lips and felt them slightly part beneath my fingertips. "Because, when you kiss me, the whole world melts away. —Because you *are* a gentleman, no matter how reluctant you are to admit it. And because your voice is like an echo I've heard my entire life." Overwhelmed at the truth of my own words, I swallowed then smiled and caught his bewildered stare. "And at the risk of sounding like a spoiled two-year-old —just because I want to."

His quick crooked smile and the look in his blue-green eyes stole my breath as he cradled my face in his hands and kissed me until I thought the vending machines might catch fire from the heat in my skin. His right hand moved down to grip my bottom, pulling my body flat against his to prove I'd been wrong about him being a gentleman. Nice try. I didn't care.

As we were leaving, the blonde woman at the counter looked up and cooed, "Awe, ya'll found each other."

Preston smiled down at me. "It appears we have."

Fate has found you both. The voice of GG echoed in my ear. This time I stopped and looked around, puzzling over the thought of true insanity.

It took me a minute to realize Preston was warily watching me with a smug smile on his face. "Exactly how long are you going to pretend you don't hear her?"

I froze and stared up at him.

2

STUNNED AND REFUSING TO ADMIT I'd heard what I thought I'd heard, from him or from…GG, I stared up at him, my face feeling purely stupid. "*What?*"

He shook his head, turned to face me directly and stared with astonishing purpose into my eyes. "Please don't deny it, Adena. Else, I'll walk away this instant and leave myself at the mercy of the closest nut farm."

"You can… *hear* her?"

He nodded quickly. "At first I thought it was a voice drifting from one of the other televisions in the lobby. Until I noticed your reaction to her." He saw my car in the parking lot, touched his hand to my back, very subtly prompting my frozen body to move. "You looked as though you were looking for someone in particular. You *recognized* the voice. Am I correct?"

My mouth opened and closed repeatedly like a fish gaping out of water. He held his hand out and wiggled his fingers. He didn't verbally ask for my keys but I handed them over nonetheless. I managed to choke out the directions to High Springs. It was easy enough; just go north on I-75 to exit 399. (Although his instinctual tendency to drive on the left side of the road even after we'd left the interstate was enough to make a person a little jittery.)

After taking the second right since the exit, we made our way through the large upscale development of *Waterscapes* with all its wondering streams, well placed yet totally fake waterfalls and man-made ponds and acres and acres of tidy grass covered parks and strict 'no dog' zones. The place screamed 'look but don't touch' and I'd grown to hate it. It was like living in a painted picture and nothing resembled nature despite the lush greenness. The sprinklers came on every morning at 6:00. The gardeners came through every Tuesday and Saturday to maintain the community grounds.

When Trent and I first moved here, this polished control of the environment seemed to sooth my OCD tendencies. Over the years this faded and I'd done my level best to ignore my growing dislike for it. Today it got on my last nerve.

We pulled into the drive in the center of the nearly deserted cul-de-sac —ours was the only house at the end of the street —I walked up the crushed marble path that curved through my purposely random rose garden toward the front door then glanced over my shoulder to find Preston running his fingertips over a cluster of new red-orange rose buds sparkling with the fallen rain. Their fragrance filled the air.

He smiled and looked over his shoulder then back at me. "You don't quite belong here do you?"

I shrugged a bit. "I belong any place I choose to I guess. I just like things a bit on the wild side. I find it to be closer to its proper order that way. At least outside."

His eyes lingered briefly over the myriad of roses, taking in every color and sort, the short bushes, the tall, climbing vines on trellises. "You did all of this yourself then?"

I put the key in the door and twisted. "Yep. Wait till you see the back yard. It's my sanctuary."

As we walked into the foyer, I noticed him looking at the pictures on the walls on his way slowly through and to the left into the living room.

"Why is it you are only in the *one* family photo?" He actually looked annoyed. "Your doting husband never saw fit to photograph you to decorate his castle?" He asked only half-joking.

"That probably has more to do with the fact that I detest having my picture taken. He's not the doting type anyway."

He glanced around at the bungalow, a virtual beach retreat although High Springs is not a coastal town. Pictures of lighthouses, watercolor paintings of sea turtles and ships at sea adorn the walls. "I take it you like the shore."

I laughed. "Is it that obvious?"

"It's actually quite relaxing. I expect a salty ocean breeze any minute."

"Mission accomplished."

He laughed a bit and I didn't know why. I looked at him inquiring with my eyes as to what was so funny. He shrugged. "I was only thinking of my place. It's nautical. Sort of. Very different than the bright airy colors you have here. But, in a way, we have a similar love for the ocean."

This made me smile. I went to the kitchen and got two cold bottles of water from the fridge then I found Preston in the foyer looking at more photos on the wall. He took the bottle I was holding out to him. "Thanks." His eyes lingered over the faces of my children then back to me. "You seem to have found your tongue again. Now, if I may... who it is that keeps speaking to you? And perhaps you could explain why *I*

41

should be able to hear her as well?"

I frowned and I could feel my eyebrows do something I didn't think they'd ever done before. "What do I look like? The friggin' Wizard of Oz? I don't know why you can hear her."

"Fair enough." He conceded. "And?" He prompted.

I sighed and turned my attention to the wall then touched an antique oval frame. "Her. Delia Mac Dermot Albright. My Irish great-grandmother." I was surprised at the matter-of-fact tone of my voice. How calmly I could discuss living in the land of crazy. Of course, he'd heard her too, so I guessed we were both bona fide citizens of Crazyville. He didn't seem overly bothered and he didn't ask me anything else about it. And that was good, because I had no other answers to give.

I was dead on my feet and I realized Preston was, too. His eyes looked like they were about to close. "You wanna go lie down?" I pointed upstairs as he took a drink.

He stared at me as he swallowed his water. "Adena, it would take the shifting of the earth beneath me to get me to take a nap in your husband's bed."

I shrugged and mumbled half to myself. "Well, that makes two men who won't sleep in it." I walked to the living room and gestured to the beige throw on the back of the couch. "If you're comfortable here, you can use that, just get some rest."

"Yes, Ma'am." He said like an obedient child. He sat down, stretched like a cat until he was completely horizontal then grabbed my hand and pulled me down on top of him and we both laughed despite the rather treacherous morning we'd shared. We settled quite naturally against each other; one of his hands on my back, the other in my hair. A whole flock of butterflies fluttered away inside me. He felt so good. Like GG's old quilt on a cold night, only *way* better.

"Adena," he spoke so low, it was barely more than a deep vibration against my cheek, "I need to know —if you still love him."

I stayed quiet as I considered the weight of his question, running my fingers under the starched lapel of his shirt. I wanted to be honest with him as well as myself. "We've been married for nineteen years, best friends since we were kids, and I'll always care for him. I'll always love him in a way. But we're not *in* love anymore. —We haven't been for a while."

He didn't say anything else. I snuggled against him and the rise and fall of his chest seemed to rock me to sleep. I could hear the beat of his heart and it was a tempo I could live by.

Blinding slices of sun forced an unwanted consciousness upon me. I noted the clock's hands on the opposite wall sitting at 6:05 p.m. I got up carefully and tip-toed to the windows looking over the patio and the back yard then shifted the Bahamian shutters so that the shafts of light fell on the floor. I took one long glance at Preston to affirm he was still asleep then hurried upstairs to the master bath.

The hot water seemed to dissolve some internal mechanism that kept me from going to pieces and thus the tears and the sobs came quickly and thoroughly. The tornado lasted a minute, maybe more, but it seemed like an eternity at the time.

Maybe it wasn't the tornado at all. I could never have predicted that infidelity would be a character trait I would adopt. I'd always been faithful to Trent. But somehow, not knowing Preston at all suddenly seemed to deny faithfulness to myself. Some crazy other part of me had been awakened upon his smile. His touch. Perhaps when he kissed me. – Yes. Yes, that was the moment my life had been altered.

My tears faltered and stopped. I finally gathered myself, knowing the tornado could have resulted in something so much worse. I met a man. I didn't die.

Just as I was about to pick up my shampoo, the light went out. I cursed under my breath.

An airy chuckle startled me. "It's only me, Love." His voice rolled over me like suede and the door closed, leaving us in steam-filled shadows. He stepped into the glass enclosure, his tall silhouette so close. The incredible scent of him enveloped me and suddenly I didn't mind at all that he was there. Truth be known, I didn't mind *that* much to begin with.

"I thought you weren't gonna come up here?" I teased him.

"I said I wouldn't take a nap in your husband's bed. Never said anything about his shower. Besides, I'm not after what you think. Turn around." He picked up the shampoo and poured it in his hands.

It felt glorious, the strength in his fingers gently kneading away every thought in my head. He tilted my head to let the suds run off then draped my hair over the front of my left shoulder. His lips skimmed my ear, sending both a chill and a flame dancing along my skin. His lips, teeth and tongue kissed the nape of my neck just as he would my mouth causing my heart, not to mention my long neglected hormones, to go into overdrive. His fingers dug into my bare hips as he pulled himself against me.

"I swear this isn't why I came up here." He whispered heavily then turned me to face him, capturing my face in his hands and kissing me until I thought my heart would explode.

My hands explored the long sinuous muscles of his back while the water cascaded down us in little waterfalls. The showerhead sent forth an unexpected splutter of ice-cold torture. I squealed and escaped the wrath of the failing water heater.

I laughed at the sound of his chattering teeth as he wrung out his boxers and tossed them over to the floor. I laughed again at his idea of hardcore prevention. Still wrapped in my towel, I sat on the corner of my bed and watched. He was stunning, even through the distorted bubbles in the glass.

With his towel fixed low across his hips, his skin covered with gooseflesh, he stepped into my bedroom and I could now see every defined muscle as the amber evening sunlight filled my room.

Note to self: send thank you note to God. Wow.

His eyes grew wide as he stared down at me. "*Why* are you still not dressed?"

I leaned back on my elbows. "Because I was enjoying the show."

"Oh, no you don't. I told you I'm not getting in that bed." He jammed his fists defiantly on his hips as if to make his point more clear.

I smiled innocently and crossed my legs. "Didn't ask you to."

"Oh, yes you did. And you're still doing it. Come on, get up and let's talk."

I scooted off the bed and crossed myself. "Need I remind you that *you* are the one who got in the shower with a naked lady?"

He raised both brows and turned an adorable shade of pink. "Guilty as charged." His eyes roamed appreciably over the sage walls, gold silk duvet, burgundy velvet drapes, a framed print of Rembrandt's *A Bathing Woman* and a replicated byzantine mosaic on the wall. "Every other room in ocean blue or sunset yellows. This one looks like a Venetian palace. Why is that?"

I shrugged and took in the wasted atmosphere. "I think it's romantic. Not that it ever induced a romantic moment since I finished it. Trent hates it."

He put his arms around my waist. "Pardon my saying so, but Trent's an idiot. It induces quite a few romantic notions as far as I'm concerned." He smiled one sided then leaned over to touch his lips to mine but froze in mid pucker. He shook his head and backed away running his hands through his hair. "Your *towel* is astonishingly distracting. Come to think of it, the room has very little to do with anything. You could be standing in a bloody card board hut and I'd still—" He cut himself off, closed his eyes and drew a deep breath through his nose as he cracked his neck before he continued. "Just hear me out." He took another deep breath and put a little space between us, his hands perched on his hips again. His expression was that of a detective trying to piece together vital clues. "We accidentally met. We had a bit to drink. We had a near brush with *Death*. We've had some ... passionate moments." His roguish smile told me he'd enjoyed that part. "Don't you think we should take a small step back and try to see what is really going on here? Especially since *you* are the one who has so much to lose."

His sincerity only made me admire him more. And I was grateful he'd decided to let the whole 'hearing GG thing' drop.

I strolled slowly to my dresser until I saw an old picture of Trent and me. It was like looking at two old friends that neither of us had seen nor spoken too in far too long. That happy couple only existed in those old pictures now.

I turned to face Preston, still thinking. I appreciated his concern. However, the many thoughts churning in my mind left it feeling as if I could pour it in a glass. At the same time, I thought with new clarity — or so I tried to convince myself. I sat back down on the corner of the bed. Holding my hands in my lap, I stared at my wedding ring and I could think of nothing to say. There were too many words jumbled in my head on the subject and yet I, the writer, the teacher, could not get them to come together.

He sat next to me and held my hand between both of his. "Adena, please don't make a colossal mistake on my account. Make certain this is what you really want."

I looked up from our hands and met his unbelievable eyes. I only nodded. He was right.

He smiled down at me with more dimples than any one man should be allowed to have. "You know what I've just remembered?"

"What's that handsome?"

"My clothes are still in your car."

I went to get his clothes then quickly made my way to the kitchen.

After sleeping half the day away with no breakfast, I was ravenous. Having found some gumbo in the fridge, I popped two bowls full into the microwave. After watching the first few rotations, I heard Preston coming down the stairs. I looked up to find him in faded jeans and a white button down oxford with the cuffs rolled up.

Oh sweet Jesus, he looks even younger. I physically cringed at the thought. I'd have to ask him eventually. My brain refused to think he was younger than twenty-four.

His nose seemed to lead him into the kitchen. "What *is* that divine smell?"

"Gumbo."

He looked at me dubiously to say the least. Apparently the word *gumbo* did not sound appealing. But he didn't comment as he sat in one of the bar stools at the cobalt-blue tiled counter. He looked so at home. So at ease sitting there in my kitchen.

I filled two glasses with ice then grabbed the tea pitcher from the fridge. Preston was seriously eyeballing me. Then I realized why. "I have Lipton, not Earl Gray. Try some?"

He took a cautionary sip of the cold sweet tea, wrinkled his nose and stuck his tongue out like a kid who'd just tried boiled spinach for the first time. I think he actually gagged but I couldn't tell as I was doubled over laughing. He got up and helped himself to a Coke in the fridge. The microwave beeped and I turned around to pull the bowls out then pushed one over with a spoon to see if he wanted to try it.

He stirred the gumbo around a bit then put the spoon back down. "This looks an awful lot like muddy water with mystery bits fallen in it." His eyes darted to mine. "No offense."

I fell into a fit of hysterics again. Upon recovery, I conjured a jar of file` gumbo from the spice rack and sprinkled a little of the gray-black powder on top of each.

His eyes and the turn of his mouth looked doubtful. "*Mmm*, I'm sure it will taste loads better, now that it has fresh *dirt* on it." He peered up at me from under his eyelashes.

My ribs were killing me but I composed myself and started eating. He stared at me like I was eating live crickets.

"It can't possibly be as ghastly as the tea." He gathered at last. Preparing for the worst, I supposed, he sat up straighter, wrinkled his nose, and tried the concoction. He sat there a second with his eyes closed then they popped open. "You might have mentioned it was spicy."

"You really *don't* know anything about Louisiana do you?"

"I know New Orleans is there. Mmm... that's about it. This is actually delicious." He appeared to be carefully looking for something in his bowl. "Does this have seafood in it?"

"Usually, yes. Today, no. Just chicken and sausage. Why?"

He deflated with a sigh of relief. "I'm allergic to shellfish." He smiled and took another bite. "You suppose anyone would notice if I were to purchase the empty lot next door?"

It reminded me that he'd be gone too soon; too far away. I didn't know how people did this sort of thing anyway. Until now. But how were we going to get around the fact that we'd hardly ever see each other. And you can't get to know someone in *two* days. I didn't want to think about it anymore. It already hurt that we had so little time and that was dangerous. For me.

The phone rang. It was Trent but surprisingly I held my panic. Turns out all I had to do was listen.

"...and Mama's roof is officially shot, so we'll be here till that shit's done. Hell, Beth don't care she thinks the neighbor kid is *hot*. Little weirdo. His hair is purple..."

Preston began backing out of the kitchen like he wanted to let us talk. "Come back here," I said before I'd thought better of it.

Crap!

Preston clamped his eyes shut, looking an awful lot like a man just kicked in the groin.

Trent asked, "Who are you talking to?"

Think fast, Stupid! "I found the cutest little stray last night and he is *so* cute." I pulled Preston back to me, stood on my tiptoes and planted noisy kisses all over his face.

His mouth dropped open in astonishment. "What the bloody buggering hell are you doing?" Instantly, his lips disappeared in a strange way. He'd sort of sucked them into his mouth then clapped his hand over them with a loud slap.

I bit my lip to keep from laughing. I couldn't tell if he were refraining from bad language or really letting it fly and I had no time to freak over Trent hearing Preston's voice because he started laughing and asked if I was watching one of those funny shows on BBC. I could do nothing *but* laugh as if in agreement. I was losing my mind.

Trent chuckled again and asked, "You don't really have a dirty stray in the house, do you?"

"Oh, I just gave him a bath." And at that point I had to cover the phone because the whole scene was just ridiculous. A mini argument then ensued over a fictitious stray dog which I won by saying he was never home to be bothered by a dog anyway. Trent admitted as much and even decided it might be good to keep the dog so he could keep me company. I put the phone in its cradle wondering what in the hell had gotten into me.

Preston had retired to the couch, utter disbelief coloring his face while he flipped mindlessly through an old CD holder filled with disks and the inevitable empty cases holding nothing more than the album cover art and lyrics.

"Let me guess?" He began as he plucked one notorious black and red label free and waved it at me. "Your favorite tune is *Highway to Hell*. Because *you* are a wicked and evil woman. *And* you're going straight to Hell when you die. You know that right?"

"Nope. Trent's the AC/DC fan. Not me. Mine is *London Bound*." I walked over and sat in his lap.

He blinked twice, his smile faded and he looked at me in a curious way. I laughed at the obvious connection but Preston did not. On the contrary, he looked wounded, frozen almost but he seemed to shake it off. He sighed then slapped my hip. "I desperately need a smoke. Show me to your sanctuary."

Odd, I thought briefly but refrained from any comment.

Upon his request, we stepped through the French doors and took the couple of steps across the small open air patio to find yellow Lantana blooming along either side of the flagstone path that led to the gazebo. Baskets of bright red geraniums hung in the arches and a Morning Glory vine loaded with purple trumpets threatened to take over the cypress lattice between.

I sat down on the glider and watched as Preston pulled a blue box of Dunhills from his shirt pocket, lit one and took a long drag as he distantly admired the yard filled with colorful perennials and the worn paths that cut through them. His eyes followed the gnarled twisting trunk of a Wisteria vine climbing the wooden privacy fence. But the colors did not pop under the now overcast sky nor in the presence of Preston's sudden gray mood.

He took a seat next to me on the glider. I stole his cigarette, drew on it once and gave it back.

Some of his jovial mood returned and he pretended to swat at my hands and scold me. "You *don't* smoke. I've spent exactly," He looked at his watch and chuckled as he finished, "twenty-four and a half hours with you and you've not smoked once."

"I quit seven years ago." Something had drastically changed despite his attempt at hiding it. "Preston, what's wrong?"

He took a last drag then dropped the butt into an empty flower pot. "*London Bound*. My best mate wrote a song by the same name. It just unearthed some really dark days for a bit." He forced a smile. "I'm sorry. I *know* it's not the same. He was never signed." His words drowned in sadness. That was plain to any ear. Less obvious was the sound of regret. I couldn't figure why but I wouldn't ask. I could tell this was simply a 'don't pry' situation.

But my brow furrowed on its own as I remembered where I'd found the song so long ago and I remember well that, it too, had been by an unsigned artist. I knew this because I had searched and searched for any other songs by the guy.

Preston reached down to turn on a small radio, likely to change his mood and the subject, but my thoughts and his actions had happened simultaneously and before I could stop him, the CD inside whirred to life and the funky rhythm of a blues riff was displaced in the air. A soft silent rain began to fall and Preston's adam's apple bobbed as he swallowed. He blinked rapidly then changed the function switch from CD to Radio.

"*Where* did you find it?" He whispered hoarsely, his eyes fixed trance-like to the radio.

"A blog." I began carefully and a bit unsure. "It was posted by some guy named Spencer." Preston flinched as if I'd hit him. "Your *friend* wrote that?" I asked, astonished at the odds. He nodded and the intense sorrow in his eyes told me the rest. "Is he ..."

He nodded too quickly cutting off my next possible word. Dead. Gone. Etc. "He passed on," He finished for me as he leaned over to rest the radio next to his feet. "That song is twelve years old. I never would have imagined it was floating about on the web."

A strum on a guitar drifted lazily from the speakers, *Raining on Sunday* by Keith Urban. Unexpectedly, Preston stood up, offered me his hand then pulled me close. We'd only just started to sway but he slowed his lead and looked down into my eyes as if he were trying to read something there. A slight shake of his head and he sighed deeply.

"Adena, there are —certain things I've neglected to tell you. But if I could beg your patience, they can wait. I'm only asking you to trust me. Can you?"

Without hesitation I answered, "Of course I can. Whenever you're ready."

He offered a smile of gratitude then bent to kiss me, resuming his role of effectively sweeping me off my feet. He was such a good dancer. Was there anything he wasn't good at when it came to winning me over? Somehow, I couldn't imagine.

We danced the breadth of the gazebo until finally he laughed and it was a musical sound to hear such absolute relief from whatever thoughts had stopped him before. I won't lie. Curiosity was setting my mind ablaze. What could he possibly *need* to tell me and yet it could wait? Although it was likely one of those things that would someday haunt me, tonight I was curious about other things. And not one single one of those things had a damn thing to do with whatever he had to tell me later.

Amusement danced in the depths of his blue-green eyes and just as abruptly as the shift in his mood, he scooped me up and stepped into the rain. "Now you'll never forget it was raining on Sunday the day we met." He spun me around till I was dizzy then set me on my toes, then after the following moments of hysterical laughter he resumed, once again, rocking us in a perfect rhythm to the last few notes of the seductive country ballad.

He hooked his finger beneath my chin and kissed me so tenderly, second by second, edging his way further into my heart. The surrender in that moment was tangible. The risks we were taking evaporated, along with everything else, until there was nothing left but us.

His hair was sodden and hanging slightly in his eyes, raindrops dripping from his lashes. Water trickled down his skin in ribbons, following the sharp angles of his jaw until they dripped from his chin. His jeans, heavy with rain, hung low on his hips. I stared into his eyes in the fading light, praying he could read my thoughts —hoping he could see what I wanted more than anything. After a few endless seconds surrounded by the gentle sounds of the summer rain, he smiled. I took that as an indication that our minds were on the same lovely path. My fingers had never been so sure, as I slowly unbuttoned his shirt. Shrugging the clinging shirt off his shoulders, he let it fall to the ground then held my hands against the firmness of his stomach more to bind them gently than anything. His beseeching eyes searched mine, asking me again to be sure. I'd never been more certain of anything in my life. Sane? Well, now that was an entirely different question. One he didn't ask.

With agonizing anticipation, I kissed his chest letting the rain warmed by his skin into my mouth, the sensation unparalleled as if I could drink the very essence of him. A slow fire began to burn in that deepest unidentified part behind my stomach, and by the way he groaned, he felt it too.

His voice was deep and full of need, "Here?"

"Well, you seem to have an aversion for my bed. And besides, I've never made love in the rain." I slipped my fingertips into the waist of his jeans and pried the button open.

"Neither have I." He undressed me at his leisure. The wet clothes slid away, the cool rain and his persuasive warm hands on my bare skin were almost more than I could stand.

To stand absolutely nude, exposed to the elements, exposed openly to a new lover is the most vulnerable feeling one can ever possibly experience. As well as all that, it was indeed the most erotic and sensual sensation I'd ever had.

Circling my waist with one arm, Preston eased us onto the soft sod below.

Hovering over me, he whispered, "Do me a favor, Adena." His eyes held something between anger and absolute veracity. And it was the most severe, demanding and honest look I'd ever seen in anyone. I nodded in response, too stunned by his pleading stare to speak. "Don't close your eyes. Don't forget it's *me*."

He caught my bottom lip in his teeth then slowly pulled his lips down my throat. Stopping to kiss. Slowing to taste. He continued this flaming trail down the center of my belly, he kissed every one of my ribs, and the embers inside me burned white hot until I thought surely I would be incinerated. He licked the rain from my breasts until my body trembled to have him. His kiss, almost fierce as he centered himself at last —lacing his fingers into mine, sliding them up over my head and letting his weight come down on me gently. So slowly he pushed himself inside, the immense pleasure so instant, my body arched against him, my hands gripping his, inviting him to go deeper. And he did. Again and again with the exquisite euphoria of both pleasure and pain. The raw power of his kiss only accelerated our ascent to a higher elevation, from one plane of heaven to the next.

Seeing Preston's silhouette over me with the darkening sky behind him, feeling the ever tap-tap-tapping of the rain, then the parting of the clouds to see the first stars was so overwhelming that I felt we were making love on the Milky Way.

Flying. Falling. Floating. Until we both reached the very highest point of the universe. Then exploding into mind shattering bliss. He held me close as we watched the stars come out in all their sparkling splendor, stroking my shoulder with the tips of his fingers. I didn't think the night could get any better. Didn't think I could get any higher.

Until quietly he whispered, "I can't let you go now."

GG's voice drifted in the breeze. She's tried to kill you both. More than once. She'll try again. Be very careful my dears.

Preston cleared his throat. "Did you hear something?"

I lied. "No."

"Then neither did I. –Humph. I wonder who's trying to kill us."

3

I LAY THERE STARING AT the texture of my bedroom ceiling, not entirely convinced that the previous day had actually happened. I sat up, rubbed my eyes to push away the fog of sleep, and scanned the room until my eyes fell upon a crimson rose on my nightstand, lying on top of a note.

Good Morning Angel,

I'll be back in a bit. Don't get up.
I've stolen your car by the way. I'll try
to keep it on the right side of the road.

Love,
Preston

He's real! I crashed back into the pillows, gloriously giddy from it all. Still holding the piece of paper and the rose in my hand, I heard him walk in.

He sat next to my knees balancing a box of doughnuts and two cups. "Sorry, not a lot of options. Unless I missed the main drag. —Do you often sleep this late?" He teased with a smug look.

I glanced at my clock. Quarter after nine. "Hardly. I'm up at the crack-ass of dawn every day. I can't believe I slept that long."

He crawled in next to me, placing his long arm along the pillow behind my head and wearing a very seductive grin.

"What?"

"Well, Love, I could swear you weren't sleeping the *entire* night." He pulled his shirt over exposing his shoulder and a faint pink curve on his skin.

I reached to touch it. "What happened?"

"You *bit* me! —But considering *why,* —I take it as a compliment." He rolled off the bed and hopped to his feet, full of energy. "Cup of sugar in your coffee? The way you take your tea?"

I sat up keeping the sheet tucked under my arms and took one of the cups in my hands. "You're one of those annoying *morning* people aren't you?"

"More likely than not I suppose." He bit his bottom lip as he sauntered around the foot of the bed. "Are you aware that you sort of...babble away in your sleep?"

I squared my shoulders. "I do not."

He raised one brow, "I'll take that as a *No*. Well Love, you do in fact. More importantly, you are... *informative* at it. If you catch my drift." Both eyebrows rose as he took a drink from his cup. His face curled in on itself as he scowled at the drink in his hand. "I think I'll give up tea altogether while I'm here."

I laughed but got right back to the point at hand. "What did I say? Or do I even want to know?"

He flipped open the box and grabbed a doughnut, a chortle under his breath before he answered. "Let's just say, ole Trent may begin to wonder just who the hell Preston is. Especially when your chest begins to heave and those sexy little moans come out of your throat." He began to laugh hysterically as he covered his cup so he wouldn't spill it.

I snatched the pillow from behind me and flung it at him. One smooth glide toward the window, he dodged it laughing.

He pressed a finger to his lips to force a serious tone. "All joking aside, he's going to hear you plain as day."

Trent never told me I talked in my sleep. He took any and every opportunity to rag on me about things like that. When was the last time we even slept in the same bed anyway? He's a general contractor, traveling from this project to the next, week in and week out; at times he's gone a month before we see him again and when he is home, he almost always falls asleep in his office downstairs.

I shrugged my shoulders. "Problem solved. He doesn't sleep in here."

His disbelief couldn't have been any more apparent than if I'd told him I'd previously been a mule in a past life. "You were *serious* about that?"

"Preston, I bought this bedroom suit over seven months ago. You and I are the only ones to sleep in this bed *together*."

He sighed and ran his hand through his hair. "I can't even express how much better that makes me feel." He made a sick face and added, "Pardon me for saying this but he's a real wanker for letting your relationship get so off the mark. Remind me to thank him someday."

"I'll be sure to tell him next time we speak." I said somewhat lost in the thoughts that bounced around in my head.

He cleared his throat a little. "Sorry, I shouldn't say things like that."

I picked nervously on the edge of the green and beige cup. "I bet you think I'm some crazy woman who doesn't know *what* she wants."

He held my chin in his hand and dipped his head to look me in the eye. "Crazy ... yes. But in the best way. That is what you said about people from Louisiana. Didn't you?" He laughed a little and pinched playfully at my toes. "And to think I thought I'd be all alone on my birthday." He stood and picked up his cup again.

I sputtered and choked on my coffee with the reminder of our age difference. Too easy to forget until something reminded me of it.

"Seriously?" I'd been avoiding the subject too long. "Okay, hit me with it. How old are you?" I closed my eyes and braced myself.

"Twenty-one! I can buy beer now!" The juvenile ring in his voice stung my brain like a swarm of angry bees. My mouth and eyes flew open in shock. Then I saw the sadistic grin spread across his face. I launched another pillow, which he very deftly dodged again.

"That is not even remotely funny!"

He looked at me with a sideways glance and a smirk across his lips. "I *knew* that was bothering you! Exactly how old do you *think* I am?"

I looked directly at his face and tried to make a serious guess. "Twenty-four."

"Cradle robber! You think I'm twenty-four?" He rolled his eyes and ran his fingers through his hair again. I loved to watch him do that. "I'm twenty-nine, Love."

Oh, thank you *God*! Eight years isn't so horrible. He made a face letting me know it was my turn.

I sighed and stared down at the tiny hole on the white plastic lid. "Thirty-seven as of March 17th."

"St. Patrick's Day?" He said with a snigger. "See, I told you. You're my lucky girl."

"It's fitting. My great-grandmother Delia was Irish."

"Must be where those beautiful green eyes come from." He sat at the foot of the bed and peeled the sheet back revealing my bare leg up to my thigh then traced his finger down the curve of my calf. "So where does this lovely tan skin come into play? That's definitely not Irish."

"That's my Cherokee blood showing. From Daddy's side."

He smiled. "Nice to know the roots that captivate me so."

Although the house was empty aside from us, my nerves were plucking a wayward tune that my heart could not keep time with. The tiny monster of guilt tried to peek and climb over the edge of my mind; my former state of reason and responsibility. But the beast was fairly small and easily shooed aside.

I swung my feet over the edge of the bed and wrapped the sheet around me, trying to think of what we could do to spend the day together someplace else. I got up and headed to the bathroom.

I heard him expel a great sigh and I turned to peer over my shoulder. "What?"

He shook his head and smiled. "You look like a bride with that long white sheet trailing behind you. And the contrast between that and your skin…" He shivered playfully and growled.

I turned to face him, thinking of how long it'd been since I was a bride. "Well, we can't have that now, can we?"

I let the sheet fall to the floor to see if he even liked what he saw. Because a big part of me wondered why he was interested. Was I just an easy target? But the look in his eyes as they trailed down the length of my body told me, I'd better get in the shower before we wound up in bed again. I walked backward three steps into the bathroom and closed the door with a smile in my heart.

After my shower, I dressed in jeans and a comfortable red tee, my favorite ensemble, but today my preferences had a practical purpose. Preston walked in my room when I was putting my tennis shoes on.

"So, what's the plan for today?" He asked.

"Well, I've been known to listen from time to time. You said you like to walk. –Does walking include hiking?" I stood up and straightened my shirt.

"You like to hike?" He leaned against the door frame and looked down at my pants. "In dungarees? It's hot as bollocks out."

I looked up at him, my hands on my hips. "Do I *want* to know what a bollock is?"

He laughed and crinkled his nose. "Literally? Probably not."

"Well, I don't know what the woods are like in London, but here, occasionally you run into green briars, sticker bushes. Call them what you want, they hurt like hell. So, you up for it?"

"Sounds like a perfect day to me."

We went downstairs to the foyer; normally I kept my keys on the little table there. I walked away remembering I'd left them on the dining table yesterday but he reached out and took hold of my hand, pulled my keys from his pocket and dangled them in front of me. He half smiled, his face, soft and warm but his eyes —open books of expression —they gave him away.

"What's wrong?" I asked.

"It's just...I finally find you and now..." He shook his head and harrumphed miserably. "I don't want to leave your side let alone cross an ocean. And I don't know when I'll be able to come back."

A painful fracture shot through my heart and my eyes burned at the realization. "You're not coming back, are you?" It sounded too much like an accusation.

He pulled me close and hugged me. "Of course I will. It's just the idea of coming back and finding a different you." He sighed deeply. "I'm afraid you'll regret being with me. Eventually."

I pulled away a little to see his face and reached to cup my hand around his neck. "That won't happen. And I understand Preston. If your father needs you, you should go."

I studied his face and realized there was more to it than that. His mouth opened and shut as if he wanted to tell me something. The same pain I'd seen in his eyes yesterday was back. I decided not to pry. He cradled my face in his warm hands and kissed me, giving me the courage to say what I wanted but my heart raced just the same.

"I love you." I whispered then shut my eyes tight wishing I could rewind the last five seconds. "I'm sorry," I bit my lip as I began to flounder at my own mistake.

Dammit! Stupid! Stupid! Stupid!

He buried my head against his chest, his rapid heartbeat the same as mine. "Adena, I told you last night I felt the same. —Didn't I?" He paused and I felt his head shake. "Perhaps I didn't say it as clearly as I should have." He lowered his head and kissed my cheek. "I love you and I *don't* want to share you with anyone." He breathed the declaration against my cheek.

Did he just say he loved me? He isn't sprinting for the door?

A loud knock and the door swung open before I could even think to reach for it. Preston's arms held me tight as the fear of Trent walking through that door seized us. In half a second, I realized he'd grabbed me protectively. He didn't jump away to look as though we weren't together. I looked up and saw that the man would've stood in front of an oncoming train for me.

Oh yeah, he'd already done that once.

"Dena, you home!" The voice boomed into the house. Then he saw us. "Oh, sorry Hon. Didn't realize you were right there."

I let out a sigh that told Preston there was no need to panic and he relaxed.

Owen was the only person who barged in like that. His curly blonde hair blowing wildly out of place from the breeze until he shut the door behind him. Always dressed as if he just got off a fishing boat, a dark complexion and weathered skin from years of too much sun. Deck shoes and a Guy Harvey t-shirt, a typical Floridian. If Crocodile Dundee and Jimmy Buffet could have a kid, he'd look like Owen.

He rapidly assessed the situation between Preston and me, worriedly observing the extra moisture in my eyes.

"Everything's fine." I tried to assure him before he gave his concerns a voice. His loaded glance told me he'd be waiting to hear all the juicy details.

"Owen Stanley. Nice to meet you." He looked at Preston from head to toe and shot me a quick dart of his eyes that clearly said, *Where the hell did he come from?* Owen had never, ever...*ever* been accused of being subtle.

Preston shook his hand as I introduced them properly.

Owen's laugh is so ridiculous; it's contagious to anyone within earshot. We met three years ago walking around the neighborhood. He owned the ugliest dog I'd ever seen and the five pound mutt ran up to me one day, avoiding capture by hiding between my feet. His name ... Spaz. Missing several teeth, his tongue hangs out in a pathetic lack of control, even when his mouth is shut. And every time he saw me he'd get loose and run straight at me. After many attempts to get the dog away from me, Owen and I had become friends. We walk together several times a week, and he pops in to say *Hi* and eat on a regular basis. Owen and the dog. Sometimes, they even come together.

Preston had leaned very casually against the wall with his arms folded across his chest. His smirk and the set of his brow both saying, *What are you going to do now?*

Owen cast Preston a knowing grin before strolling into the kitchen to raid my bottled water. He walked back through the dining room and helped himself to a chair obviously in no hurry to leave so Preston and I took a seat.

Owen rolled his head on his shoulders as if the effort of asking the obvious was a waste of good air. "Oh, come on. How long has *this* been going on?" But he was looking to Preston for an answer.

Preston looked taken off guard but politely said, "I feel inclined to let

Adena answer that." He leaned back in his chair, threw me a brutally sexy grin and waited for my response.

After hearing Preston's accent clearly, Owen turned to me and banged his fist on the table. "Where did you find a gorgeous fucking Brit in the middle of High Springs?"

"Watch your mouth!" I said and smacked his arm again.

He looked at Preston. "Don't mind me. Getting her all riled up is my favorite pastime. She turns the prettiest colors." He turned and pinched my cheek.

I swatted his hand away from my face. "Remember Sunday when *you* stood *me* up?"

He nodded but stopped me. "You can write a story but God knows you can't tell one. Boring, no offense." He looked at Preston again. "You tell me what happened. A man's version, please."

Preston gave me a questioning look, maybe for permission to tell him the truth or not.

"Go ahead. He'll torture me later to find out anyway." I gave in, sulking in silence over Owen's insult.

Preston took a deep breath, flashed me a wicked smile and I swear he sounded like one of those speedy disclaimers at the end of a used car commercial. "Well, she ran into my hotel drenched from her head to her toes. As luck would have it, she didn't tell me to sod off straight away. Lucky bastard that I am, she had a few drinks with me, and we chatted away for quite a while. She came upstairs, we drank some more and she passed out in my lap. Then a tornado came and ripped my suite apart while we made out in the tub. Yesterday, we came back here, danced in the rain and then made love *all* of last night. She slept half the morning away and here we are talking to you." He raised his eyebrows and looked at me. "I think that wraps it up nicely."

He squeezed my leg under the table to let me know he was joking for Owen's benefit although I was a little dumbstruck, that he so *openly* provided so very much frikkin detail in such a bare to the bones story.

Man's version! Kiss my country ass.

Not a word from Owen's gaping mouth. I counted to seven in my head before he slowly turned his head to gawk at me in disbelief. "I stand corrected. You're not boring at all. *You* are a *slut!*" He started guffawing like a jackass, swatting at Preston for a juvenile high five. "Now that's a man's story! Straight to the point!"

"Are you two finished?" I looked at both of them, Owen holding his stomach and Preston laughing. Meanwhile, even my bones were irritated. "I don't think that's exactly how it happened."

"Name one thing I said that wasn't one hundred percent true." Preston defended himself.

It was unsettling that I had to think for a minute. "Okay, we were *not* making out in the tub. You kissed me when it was over. So there." I folded my arms defiantly but without much satisfaction. It didn't really sound so much better.

Preston got up and stood behind my chair, hovering next to my ear and nestled his face in my hair. "Sorry, Love. I only gave him the Cliffs Notes version. Everyone knows you have to read the whole book to get all the good bits." He pressed his lips to my temple and I felt his long fingers slip beneath my hair to tickle my neck.

Preston had to squeeze past Owen's chair on the way to the kitchen. Owen whipped his head around to check out his butt with his mouth hanging open.

I frogged his arm and whispered, "Stop ogling!"

"What?!" Owen whispered about as discreetly as a four-year-old and rubbed the lump in his arm. "I was just looking. Don't be so fucking stingy, Dena!"

"Anyone ever tell you you've got a filthy mouth?"

"Just because *you* teach a bunch of rug-rats doesn't mean *I* have to watch my mouth. I'm a little older than a third grader."

"That's funny, you don't act like it. Ever hear of respect for a lady?"

"When I meet one I'll watch my mouth." He chugged his water and raised one hand to block another expected blow from my fist.

Preston laughed from the kitchen and called over his shoulder. "Care for a drink, Love?"

"Yes, please."

Owen fell back in his chair feigning a fainting spell, only kidding around of course, then rolled his eyes and pretended to barf before Preston took his seat next to me.

"So Dena, speaking of the whole book, you gonna take the time to write all this down? I mean, come on! Who finds love during a tornado? That's priceless."

I felt Preston staring a hole in the side of my face as Owen kept blathering away. I slowly peeked at him through a tiny gap in the curtain of dark curls to find a knowing grin lighting his face. At least he wasn't mad that I didn't just come out and tell him.

He started to play with the fine hairs at the nape of my neck causing goose bumps to erupt down the length of my arms. I heard him barely snicker when he saw what he was doing to me. I'd almost forgotten Owen's question until he kicked me under the table.

"Well? Don't tell me the thought never crossed your mind."

"Did you still want my help editing?" I asked through my teeth, giving him reason to mull over opening his big mouth. It took discreetly stomping on his toes under the table to get the goober to wake up and realize I wanted him to shut up.

He then caught on to the possibility of me leaving him high and dry and finally chose to change the subject.

"Preston," Owen began, "Now that I think of it, I get a feeling I've seen you somewhere before. You're name is ringing a bell too. You live in Gainesville?" His eyebrows scrunched together as if he were trying to force a memory of Preston to the surface.

Preston shook his head and took a drink of his soda. "London."

I thought I detected a sudden wave of tension from Preston. I couldn't be sure and I didn't know why.

"Been there. Loved it." Owen responded then saw my face filled with envy. He'd been present during several conversations between Beth and me about wanting to go to England.

He smiled sardonically at me. "My cousin lives in Redbridge and I went to his wedding. It was the summer we met so don't start in on me, Hag. I doubt that walking ass-crack you're married to would've been very happy if I'd asked you to go."

My only response to that was a bitter roll of my eyes.

Owen looked at Preston again. "You ever been there?"

Preston chuckled. "I live in Havering-atte-Bower. Just east of Redbridge. There's a pub there I like to go to. The Red Lantern?"

Owen laughed in recognition and then that turned into an entire conversation about all kinds of things. I didn't know much about London, other than the popular landmarks, so I kept quiet while they jabbered away. Preston held my hand as he listened to Owen speak of some music store he'd found in some place called Camden Market and how extensive their vinyl collection was.

I must have imagined Preston's tension from before, as now he didn't seem to have a care in the world.

I was lost in a million thoughts when Owen stood up and said he was going to finish his walk without me.

"Where's your partner in crime today?" I asked as I walked him to the door, noticing Spaz was again missing in action.

Owen pulled a tiny harness and leash from his pocket to show the evidence of his four-legged escape artist.

He sighed. "I should've named him Houdini. He'll show up here or my house. Always does."

Preston wrapped his arms around my waist as I said good-bye to Owen. He turned with a wave and headed down the walk.

It hadn't even crossed my mind what it would be like to introduce Preston to anyone. I'm glad it was Owen, the one friend I could trust given the current situation. The last thing I wanted was to hide my feelings and I had no idea how I would be able to slip back into the same old routine once my family returned. But it wouldn't be the same routine. Not at all. I'd be helping my kids move into an apartment in only a few weeks. Not to mention hiding a secret so big just the thought made my stomach roll.

Should I simply fess up to Trent and admit that I'd fallen in love with someone else? Or just pretend that nothing had changed and see what happened later? The latter made the most sense. If one were stupid enough to allow this to happen in the first place, my guess was, to keep it under wraps for longer than *two* days. That last one smacked of cowardice and I didn't care for the taste one bit.

Preston bowed his head into my hair and began to hum a tune that I didn't recognize. After several seconds of his wordless serenade, we started to sway, almost dancing. Until he stopped and stood still as a statue for a good count of ten. He shuffled us closer to the wall. I laughed at our silly, four-footed walk all the while with his lips pressed to my neck.

"What are you doing?" I asked just as he managed to get us positioned in front of a large framed collage on the foyer wall.

"Who is *that?*" He stood straighter and turned me around to face him. "I saw it this morning and forgot to ask you?"

I noted the very curious look on his face. Something between uncertainty and shock. I looked back at the frame and skimmed over the ten random photos my father had framed years ago.

"Um, my family. Some of them anyway." I touched the smallest in black and white. "That's GG, my great-grandmother, Delia. The Irish one I told you about." The one who's been talking to me. And to Preston at least twice. Sheer mental preservation kept my mind from wandering too far down that train of thought again.

He shook his head a little and touched a specific picture. "No. *That* one."

I looked at the old Polaroid of me, Daddy and oddly enough, that little boy who'd popped in my head the night before last just before the tornado. We were by the pool at that hotel in Texas and Scooter was sitting at my feet, barely recognizable beneath layers of sunscreen and a big white swath of zinc oxide on his nose.

"That was back in '87 I believe. We were on vacation. Why?"

He lowered his head and scrutinized the image, then started to laugh. A bit insanely actually. He ran his hands down his face slowly and pressed in on his eyes until it looked like it might hurt.

"Preston?" I reached to pull his hands away before he blinded himself. "What?"

He kept laughing, barely able to get the words out. "For the sake of my sanity, tell me that photo wasn't taken in Texas."

Shocked that he'd guess anything about it, I was silent as I stared at him and then the picture not understanding. He finally stepped back as if he were presenting himself. It took a minute for that to sink in.

I giggled at his assumption, "No, no. That can't be *you*. That kid's name was Scooter Banks."

He laughed harder, holding his stomach as if I'd just confirmed rather than disproved what he was thinking. He tapped his knuckle against the glass of the frame. "My *uncle's* last name is Banks. And they were the only people who *ever* called me Scooter. That's your father Roger there in the background, if my memory serves me correctly. I dreamed of being a cowboy for at least the next five years because of him."

I stared at the image and nearly gulped. I shuttered and felt a little sick. "This is *so* wrong."

"That's *us,* Adena! This is unbelievable! Wait," He lifted my chin quickly to look at me. "What do you mean this is *so* wrong?"

I stabbed at the picture. "I was fifteen and you were seven! That's gross!" I pulled away and leaned against the foyer table fighting off another quiver. Stuff like that just doesn't happen.

He came at me grinning, his thumbs hooked in the back pockets of his jeans. "Adena, honestly, we're both adults now. Eight years is hardly enough to make you a cougar. We are, in fact, part of the same generation."

I folded my arms across my chest. "It's just..." I shuddered to my toes and couldn't speak.

He came closer and kissed my cheek. "Do I look seven to you?"

I sighed and rolled my eyes. "No."

He lifted me to sit on the little table, pushed my legs apart with his thigh and pressed himself against me. "Did it feel *gross,* as you so eloquently put it, when we made love last night?" He kissed my neck and ran his thumb over my collar bone.

"No." I whispered.

His lips found mine for a heartbeat. "I think it's astonishing our paths crossed again. Sort of like," he kissed me again, "destiny or something. —I think I was declaring my love for you before there was a knock at the door." His voice, deep and sultry and that alone made me weak.

"Oh..." I found it hard to speak with him so close and any trace of our age difference disappeared along with the outlandish possibility that we'd met as children.

He pulled his hands slowly up my ribs and raked his thumbs along the side of my breasts giving my heart a new reason to pound. With his face half an inch from mine, every warm breath rushed over me. So close that when he spoke, his lips brushed against mine. Between every few words, he'd stop briefly to kiss me.

"I think I said I love you and... I don't want to share you with anyone. Yes... that's exactly what I said."

He was driving me crazy. I drew a deep breath, preparing to dive in the waters so to speak and not come up anytime soon. I drove my lips hard into his. It must have sent him over the edge. Nothing less than a guttural growl came from somewhere inside him as he grabbed me up with my legs wrapped around his waist.

"Just stop me when anything about you and I feels *wrong.*" His heady whisper danced across my ear just before he crushed my lips beneath his again.

My mind quickly sank into the abyss of whatever it was that we had. All I felt was Preston against me. His roaming hands, his pressing lips. We were on the couch and I couldn't even remember how we got there nor of exactly when our clothes had come off. And nothing...felt wrong.

He moaned loudly and it accelerated my desire to hear his satisfaction so evident. My need to have him this way was something I couldn't understand. An unquenchable thirst, an insatiable hunger, as if

I'd waited a hundred years for him to find me. Time and space ceased to exist. Only he and I resided in some magical dimension in which only he could take me.

My mind danced along a strange timeline in the middle of our magic. Images I couldn't comprehend flitted past my mind's eye. A strobe of pictures from my past and some I had no clue what they were. A tidal wave of unequivocal pleasure and the images faded. We lay there for a long time just studying each other's faces, neither of us able to fight back the urge to smile.

Another knock on the door sent us scurrying into our clothes. Another rapid knock but I could tell who it was this time. Preston was busy freaking out and cursing under his breath.

I straightened the blue pillows on the couch to put things back in order then checked my appearance in the foyer mirror before I opened the door only to find that I looked just as hectic as I felt. I pulled the door open and an eight-year-old boy I'd tutored was smiling up at me, revealing his missing front teeth.

"Hey, Blake. What are you up to?"

He ran in flailing a paper as hard as he could. "Mrs. Whittington! Look here!"

I scanned over the paper he was so anxious to show me. School let out three weeks ago and he'd gotten his report card in the mail and had come to show it off.

"Oh, I'm so proud of you. I knew you could do it." I reached down and gave him a quick hug.

He smiled so wide it warmed my heart. "Granny still wants you to tutor me though. She said it helps my reading. And I didn't get an A. But a B is good. Right?"

"Absolutely, Blake. I believe there's a treat in the freezer if you want one." He ran into the kitchen and I saw Preston leaning against the wall grinning.

Blake looked up at him. "Hey, Mr. Whittington. You want one too?"

I pursed my lips and Preston chuckled deeply. "Sure. Good marks are absolutely cause for celebration. Excellent job."

Blake handed him a frozen fudge bar and craned his neck up to see him, took a bite then studied Preston for a few seconds. "You sound funny." He swallowed and took another bite.

Preston seemed to be on the edge of cracking up. "Do I?"

The little boy nodded. "Well, I gotta go. Granny's last ten hairs will fall out if she finds out I crossed the street. Nice to meet you, sir."

Preston shook his hand and told him goodbye. Blake hugged me again getting gooey fudge on my shirt. I didn't mind. I'm used to it.

Preston busted a gut as soon as the door shut. "Mr. Whittington? I take it he's never been here before."

I shook my head. "Three days a week for two months straight."

He finished his fudge bar and tossed the stick in the garbage. He pushed himself off the wall with his foot and walked slowly toward me. "So, you're a reading tutor."

I nodded. "But not for money."

He took another step. "And a teacher,"

I nodded again as he got closer. "I told you that at the hotel."

"*And* ... a writer."

I thought about how gratifying it'd be to kick Owen in his teeth. "Owen has a big mouth."

His expression became perplexed. "Is it a secret?"

I walked around him, got myself a fudge bar in hopes of avoiding the conversation, and refused to comment.

"I take it Owen's a writer as well?"

I un-wrapped the ice cream and stuck it in my mouth nodding my head to answer his question. He folded his arms and narrowed his eyes at me. "Well?"

"Oh fine! Yes. Happy now?"

He leaned over the counter propping himself on his hands. "Might I ask *why* exactly you're upset with me right now?"

I stared at the ceiling for a second. "I'm not upset with you. I just don't like to talk about it."

He nodded as if he understood something. "Haven't been published?"

I shook my head. "I write under the name A.K. Whit. Most of my readers think I'm a man. My full name is Adena Keely Whitmore then after marrying Trent I became a Whittington. I don't let people around here know, especially at the school. If the principal got a gander at *my* work, he'd fire me."

I shrugged my shoulders a little and propped my heels across the lower bar of the stool. "I don't know, after twelve years of teaching there, I guess it's become a habit to keep it to myself. That and I don't care much for the spotlight." I reached down to a small bookshelf next to my desk and tossed a paperback on the counter. "Teachers live under a microscope these days and the stuff I write would raise an eyebrow or two around here. It's a small town."

His eyes grew wide. "You are unbelievable! Anyone on this planet would gladly brag to be published and you keep it a secret." He scanned a few pages in the middle of the book, his eyes bulging. "You write stories of —*horror?*"

I raised my eyebrows and licked the chocolate from my lips. "And just what is that you aren't ready to tell me yet?"

He nodded and dropped it.

We went over some quick plans for lunch to escape the house before any other unexpected visitors dropped by. Preston went into the living room to wait while I went upstairs to change my fudge pop-stained shirt before we left.

As I was going upstairs, I took a glance back at him, lounging on the couch with his eyes closed. He was sound asleep. *Typical man.'*

But he was anything but typical.

4

WHILE IN MY BATHROOM, I tried to make sense of that crazy trip down memory lane. Right in the middle of making love to that wonderful man no less. The strangest thing was it's not like I was distracted and thinking of other things. No, it was as if our intimacy triggered them somehow. I closed my eyes, leaned against the closed door, and tried to recall them. That cliff I wanted to jump off of in my dreams was part of it. That green valley, the promised whisper in the wind. The images that bothered me most were those I knew were impossible. Like seeing Preston with Beth on his shoulders when she was a little girl. Preston sitting next to my mother, laughing and swaying on our back porch swing by Lake St. John in Louisiana. He and my father chatting in the driveway back home. But that was impossible.

Preston met me at the foot of the stairs and of all things, Spaz ran up barking like the little lunatic that he is and jumped into my arms.

"Where the hell did he come from?" I asked craning my neck to avoid Spaz's Kiss of Death breath.

Preston looked blown away, nervous as a jackrabbit and confused to boot. "Well, now, —I don't rightly know. Would that happen to be Owen's dog? Because, I was asleep on the sofa and I heard the front door click as it shut. Then that strange little creature started licking me." He wiped his face again in disgust. "Right on the mouth. I think he actually made it to my teeth."

"Oh. Well, Owen probably found him and he just stuck him in here while he finished his walk. He does it all the time."

"Well, can we please leave this house now? God knows who'll come by next. I don't want to push our luck any further."

I had to agree. Having him there was the most insane thing I'd ever done.

We hit the drive thru at a burger joint for a quick lunch then headed north on I-75. Preston looked at the passing country side as we'd reached a section with nothing but cow pastures and billboard signs passing by intermittently. A quiet and peaceful ride and the day was perfect for a hike.

I heard the rumble of a muscled engine beside my window and a blaring horn. I glanced to my left and saw an old yellow Ford Fairlane keeping pace with my car. I tried to ignore the teenagers smiling faces. This sort of thing had happened before.

Preston laughed and gently tapped my knee with the back of his hand. "I believe you're being challenged." His shoulders shook with his amusement.

The gangly driver in the next car revved his engine and the passenger looked familiar. He seemed to be trying to hide his red hair and his face under a baseball cap as he slowly melted lower into his seat.

The driver leaned over to yell through the open windows. "Come on lady! No traffic today; let's see what that old horse can do!"

I smiled tightly and shook my head slowing to a crawl to let him pass. But the brat pumped his brakes to stay at my side, then the yellow car lurched with the loud rattle of glass packs as another invitation. When I refused, he cast me a nasty glare, flipped me the bird and then the little Neanderthal leaned over the passenger and *spit* on my car.

Son of a Bitch!! I gassed it, pumped the clutch hard and fast and my Shelby barked into third, flying past the car in a blur. I hit sixty, quickly checked my mirrors for traffic and cops then slammed the gear shift into forth. The Fairlane still far enough behind, I yanked the wheel to the left, spun my car around and downshifted in a cloud of smoke and screeching tires. I grabbed my Coke from the cup holder and headed straight for the Fairlane in the wrong direction. At the precise second I passed the jerk's headlights, I slammed my drink into his windshield and hit the brakes.

"You're gonna wipe you're stinking spit off my car, ya little shit! Now pull over!" I looked at the passenger again and this time I recognized him. "Scott Ingles? Is that you?" He slid further into his seat and suddenly I knew exactly who the driver was. His rotten brother. I'd taught them both. I pulled over and to my surprise his brother Wayne pulled directly behind me.

He got out laughing and leaned on my door. I pried his hands loose and stared at him.

"Sorry, Ms. Whittington. I didn't realize that was you. If I did, well, I would've known better."

"You should know better anyway, Wayne! I've got a good mind to call your Dad."

A U-Haul passed us sending a gust of dusty wind through my window. Wayne took a step back and looked at the side of my car then pulled the tail of his sleeveless flannel to wipe off his wet insult.

"Thanks! Now you get Scott home and stop acting like a moron. Ya know you could take the time to be a *good* influence on your little brother."

He laughed again and with a dash of false respect he answered, "Yes, Ma'am."

I watched Wayne walk to his car in my side mirror and sat there to get my nerves in check. Then I looked to my right and saw Preston pale as a sheet.

He ran both hands down his face. "There is no possible way, *you* teach grade school!" He started laughing and shook his hands to let go of his tension. "You have," he held his hand up and pinched his finger and thumb together. "just a wee issue with your temper I gather."

I shrugged, put the car in first and eased off the road shoulder. Daddy always said I was part Indian and part bulldog. When I'm not on the warpath, I'm sitting on my ass growling about something.

We drove into the quaint little town of White Springs. Several old Bed and Breakfasts built in the late 1800s lined the streets keeping aged company with the sprawling Live Oak trees that cast giant shadows over most everything. Long branches met in the middle over the streets in some places. Sunlight fell down in dappled patterns along the ground, Spanish moss hung down like ghosts, barely swaying in the breeze. A huge white washed General Store sat on the corner, the sign painted across the top said *Adams Country Store est.1865* in barely visible black paint. It stood there as a beautiful reminder of a time long past, just waiting for its rotting timbers to give way someday.

We admired the charm of the houses, porches that stretched all the way around, rocking chairs in front and porch swings hanging from the ceilings. The town looked as though time forgot it was there —just like a thousand other small towns in the south.

And we were virtually guaranteed no familiar visitors here.

We took a left into the Stephen Foster State Park and as we drove past the historic carillon tower, we heard the melody of *Beautiful Dreamer* ringing out from the giant bells. We parked by the Suwannee River at the canoe launch where the nature trail begins. The sound of our feet scuffling through leaf litter and twigs scared a Great Blue Heron wading in the water nearby. We watched as it landed gracefully on the pale sandy banks across the tea-colored river.

We walked and talked making our way through the clusters of palmettos and soaring pine trees for about an hour to the sounds of birds and bickering squirrels until the trail broadened at a river bend. Then we headed to the banks of a big white sand bar that jutted out into the black water.

We took our shoes off and sat them on a small fallen tree. I hung back and watched as Preston scooted down to the water's edge to put his feet in.

"Care to join me?" He said over his shoulder.

I dug my toes into the cold white sand. "Nope."

"Scared of the dirty water? I have to say I'm surprised."

"That's got *nothing* to do with it." I rested my chin on my knees watching him.

"Then why not?" He looked a little offended that I wasn't glued to his side.

"Alligators." I said calmly.

His feet came out of the water so fast he almost rolled over backward. I fell over on my side I laughed so hard. He crawled over closer leering at me but smiling.

"You might have mentioned that *before* you watched me put my feet in." He gave me a wry smile, tugged at my hair as a payback then lunged at me like a wrestler pinning me on my back.

He laughed and laced his fingers through mine, pulled my hands through the sand above my head, and very tenderly, let his lips find mine time and time again. He rolled to his back and offered his arm as a pillow and we stared up at the early evening's purple sky. An Osprey cried out and swooped down, his talons piercing the surface of the lazy river to snatch a fish, completely oblivious to our presence.

I felt the beat of Preston's heart, his warmth, the rise and fall of his chest. Heard his deep breaths. Knowing how much I'd miss him. My heart was sinking with the sun, afraid that it wouldn't come back until he returned and I had no idea when that would be.

I watched a shapeless cloud drift overhead as I contemplated right vs. wrong and the truth of what I wanted whether it was wrong or not. And I'd lived long enough to know that when life offers you something so extraordinary, you reach out and grab it with both hands and be thankful. Everything has a way of working itself out in time the way it should. That was my final reckoning, my justification for what I wanted. And I wanted Preston.

We stared for the longest, lost in each other. So close, so wrapped in all those new emotions.

The sun touched the treetops. Crickets began playing their violins, joining the evening orchestra.

By the time we got back to the canoe launch, it was getting close to dark. We got in the car again and as we crossed the little bridge that stretched over the Suwannee River right at the Hamilton county line, Preston wanted to stop to get a picture. The sky had turned a deep fiery orange, the river reflected the beautiful sunset, and the black silhouettes of the trees that grew along its banks looked hundreds of years old. Their thick twisted branches trying to hide their treasure, like sentient guardians of the last virgin river in the world.

When Preston was done, he turned away from the bridge railing and pointed his phone at me while I sat on the hood of my car. I hated, detested, and even despised having my picture taken. Future generations will look back and think I suffered from Narcolepsy. I always blink at the wrong time. He looked at the image and laughed as we got in the car again holding his phone up to show me my eyes were shut. Of course.

I stared ahead at the glow of distant red taillights in front of us as he drew little swirls on my jeans with his fingers. Our last day had ended too soon. A tear slipped down my cheek and I was thankful for the darkness that he couldn't see how very much I wanted him to stay.

Once we were home again, Preston phoned his sister, Teena, to give her his flight details. Then he began to pack his things. I couldn't bear to watch so I escaped to my shower. If I couldn't even stand to watch him pack, what would I do when I had to watch his plane fly away?

After washing the sand from my hair, and rebuilding the wall around my heart, I pulled on my LSU jersey to sleep in, fought my obsessive-compulsive cleaning disorder and only half way made up the bed. I set my alarm for 6:30 and flipped on the lamp. I phoned Gavin and Beth to locate everyone and to say goodnight. Beth said Trent had gone out to play a little pool with his cousin and Gavin was cooking fried catfish with his friends and Uncle Ray over at their house next-door.

I let out a huff, relieved and satisfied.

The rose Preston had left me this morning looked a little wilted. I pulled my Bible from my nightstand and placed the rose and his good morning letter inside the pages of the book of Matthew; silently praying for forgiveness. I kissed the maroon leather cover and put it back in the drawer.

"That was heartwarming." He said smiling, leaning against the doorframe.

Caught being sappy was not my favorite thing. I slipped beneath the covers and didn't look directly at him. "I didn't know you were there."

"I know." He walked toward the bathroom, with his toothbrush in hand. Being a classic guy, he showered in under ten minutes then came out wearing a pair of blue and green plaid boxers.

I raked my eyes over him. Unavoidable. Reminding me again, of what he could possibly see in me. He ran his fingers through his wet hair to push it away from his face. I don't think he ever fixed it a certain way. It just fell into a sort of chaotic perfection that worked for him.

I must have looked preoccupied as he crawled in next to me.

He tickled my foot with his bare toes. "What's on your mind?"

I pulled my knees to my chest and wrapped my arms around them. "Nothing."

He narrowed his eyes, studying my expression. "Don't ever play poker. You're terrible at hiding your cards. Now what is it?"

"It's just...I don't *get* what you see in me."

"Oh, only everything." He leaned against the headboard and looked at me with sincerity laced with a smidge of confusion.

"Seriously Preston, I'm *older* than you. You could have any younger woman you wanted obviously. Skinny, beautiful, younger women, I'm sure would just fall all over you. Why me?" I regretted it instantly. Looked like it pretty much pissed him off.

"Just so you know, I meant *everything* and all it implies when I said it. And just when the bloody hell did skinny become a compliment? Women are *supposed* to have curves; it's natural. And for the last time, I don't give a damn about your age! It's completely irrelevant to me. "

I let out a deep breath once I realized I had stopped breathing and didn't really know what to say.

"Adena, I can't believe you'd wonder about that." He said in a more even tone. "No one is perfect. Not you, not me. But isn't enough that we're perfect for each other?"

I played with a loose string at the edge of the comforter and spoke so low it was almost to myself. "I think you're perfect."

He tugged at my chin to make me look at him. He sighed a little, his fingers tracing the half hourglass from my ribs to my hip. "You take my breath, Adena. Surely you know that by now. I thought you were the most beautiful girl I'd ever seen all those years ago. And my opinion hasn't changed."

All those years ago. A glimmer of memory made me jump out of bed so excited I almost tripped. I reached to the top shelf of my closet and struggled with an old tattered cardboard box then plopped it on the end of the bed.

I dug through thirty-seven years of keepsakes to see if I still had what had popped into my memory. I pried a Holly Hobby jewelry box, the kind with the tiny ballerina that spins to a clinking metallic music wheel, from beneath a stack of 80's vinyl albums. I peeked inside and laughed at the sight. I shut it tight and held it to my chest giggling. He smiled as he watched me literally bounce with giddiness.

I took a deep breath to prevent sheer spontaneous combustion. "Okay, first, tell me what you remember about when we met the *first* time."

He tilted his head and stared at me. "Well, it was called —Padre something or other."

I nodded. "South Padre Island,"

He scratched absently at his chin as he thought. "We met coming and going to the pool. After playing all day and probably aggravating your poor father to tears, Aunt Gladys wanted to go to dinner and I didn't want to leave. You suggested I could stay until they returned." He leaned back and started to smile. "Your father walked with us to a little concession of some sort and I spent every coin in my pocket to get a trinket from a gumball machine..."

I squealed as that was precisely what I was hoping he'd recall. I flung the lid open, grabbed the purple plastic ring, and tossed it to him. He caught it instinctively and stared at it. "You still have it! Holy sh..." He began to curse but refrained letting the slight die on his tongue. He turned the little purple ring over and over in his hands, a puzzled but playful crush of his brow. "I don't remember it being quite this horrendous."

He took the jewelry box from my hands and filtered through the contents looking at sea shells, another Polaroid his aunt had given me and a page from a coloring book I'd colored with him.

"It's like a time capsule in here. I remember all of this."

An oval frame held a wedding photo of my parents. I picked it up and wiped away the dust.

Preston's eyes bulged. "*Wow*! She's lovely. She looks like..."

"Beth? Yeah, I know. Blonde hair and blue eyes like a new spring sky." But he looked as if he were about to say something else.

"Yes. Like Beth."

Then he went through that same routine as earlier today. And yesterday. Opening his mouth, just on the verge of saying something, then choosing not to. That same struggle over what he wanted to say but wasn't ready to, I guessed. But what could that have to do with my mother? Or Beth for that matter? I pretended not to notice, put the box away and turned off the lamp.

When we got in bed, he pulled the gold comforter tight around us. He turned to his side, stripped my shirt away and tossed it in the corner. "Feel free to sleep in gruesome flannels until I get back."

"How 'bout your blue shirt." I snuggled closer and put my knee between his thighs.

"Not even on Trent's luckiest day will he see you in *that*."

I slid my fingers into his and thought about how perfectly they fit. "Preston, do you believe in Fate?"

"Mmm... Never really gave it much thought until now. But why does Fate have to be so cruel? That or Madam Fate has one twisted sense of humor. —You're married and we live on different continents. Why us? Why would *we* find each other again?"

Neither of us was able to answer that. He ran the fingers of his free hand through my hair. He seemed to enjoy playing with it. We talked, kissed, made love, held each other, and laughed quietly in the dark. Every now and then, he'd pull me even closer and hum this unknown melody from deep in his chest. The same one he was humming right after Owen left this afternoon.

I was still afraid once he was gone he'd lose interest. Not bother to keep in touch. Never find a reason to return. I tried so hard to chase those fears from my mind. The warmth in the way he held me, the sweet things he said, made it too easy to trust him. Like a ping-pong match inside my head, the questions bounced around. Was what we have real or was I allowing myself to be used? Only time would tell. And I knew I was willing to take that risk.

5
PRESTON GRACE

THE ALARM ON MY WATCH beeped twice. I scrambled to pick it up before Adena could hear it then crawled slowly out of bed so as not to disturb her. Luggage in hand, I went downstairs to ring David, a raving lunatic who ran a private shuttle to the airport in Jacksonville. I knew Adena was assuming she would take me to the airport but I didn't want her to. I looked at my watch. 4:27 a.m. It would be at least another half hour before he arrived.

I crept back into Adena's room. The blue glow from her clock radio was just enough to illuminate her face. Her warm brown hair looked black splayed across the stark white pillow she slept on. I wanted to wake her and feel her lips once more. Instead, I crouched next to her bed and watched her. A few moments passed and her eyebrows furrowed with what looked like fear.

"Where'd ya go?" Her sweet southern voice just above a whisper.

I whispered next to her ear. "I'm right here, Love." I kissed her temple and breathed in her delicate floral scent, barely touching her hair. The little crease between her brows became smooth again and she had a faint smile on her lips. I could only stare. How could she ever think she was anything less than an angel?

"Preston," she said it so clearly; I thought certainly she was awake. I started to answer but she whispered before I had the chance. "I love you."

"I love you, Adena." She was still sleeping.

I could feel my heart splintering into pieces. Never had I felt anything so strongly. I couldn't leave without telling her about Kelley. I thought it could wait until later but I couldn't just spring it on her one day. I knew so many details of her life already. And she knew practically nothing about me. I pulled open the drawer just inches from her face as quietly as possible and pulled out a pad of paper with a pen clipped to the side. I started to jot down the words that had haunted me all night. At least, this way, I could think more clearly what to say before I had to go.

I finished my letter and placed it on her bedside table. I took out her Bible and slid it underneath, hope upon hope that she'd get the meaning of it, a promise that every word was true. I wasn't able to completely explain who Kelley was, as it was a longer story than my letter would permit. I'd explain later. I pulled a worn photo from my wallet and placed it on the letter.

Too soon, I saw headlights flash through the window. David was waiting. Time to go.

I was dead wrong. This wasn't easier. I kissed her cheek and she smiled in her slumber. That was the vision I'd take with me. Just as I was in the hallway, I heard her sob once. I turned to go to her and heard her voice again.

"Trent, I'm so s-s-sorry." She sobbed again. *Still* sleeping.

Dear God, what have I done to her?

I should never have allowed this to happen. I forced one foot in front of the other until I got settled in David's van. I closed my eyes as we drove away, a profound aching in my heart. How could I ever be so blatantly selfish?

6

ADENA

THE LONG BOARDWALK ZIGZAGGED its way through the majestic sand dunes. Railroad vines ran chaotic across the sand showing off the purple blooms that clung to them. Tall golden sea oats swayed and rustled in the ocean breeze as if they were whispering something beautiful to me. The sun, high and bright, warmed my skin, the sky a brilliant blue. The boards beneath my feet were bleached by the sun and weathered soft as suede by the salt spray.

I walked barefoot down the steps and across the warm tan sand to the shore. The gentle lapping of the blue-green waters, almost hypnotic with its ancient rhythm. A mixed flock of seagulls and killdeers cried out and landed nearby; half a dozen sand plovers hugged the edge of each little wave gobbling up tiny creatures I couldn't see.

Another salty breeze blew my hair all about tickling my cheek. As I pushed it away, I noticed a man and a little girl walking a good distance away. The child looked so much like Beth, only her platinum hair was straight as corn silk. Beth's had been in ringlets at that age. She looked no older than five, but hard to tell from where I stood. I heard the most glorious laughter from her. But that couldn't be possible. She was so far from me I couldn't make out if they were walking away or toward me. Her squeals of joy at her father seemed to ring out in my head in a strange diminishing echo, slowly fading to nothing. He swung her round and round making her little white dress flutter at her knees.

Something was ... *wrong*. As soon as I heard her laugh, every other sound disappeared. Not as before like the volume on a TV being turned down, but as if a mute button had been pressed. I could *see* the birds, the water, and the wind blowing the tall grass in the dunes. I couldn't *hear* any of it. The empty nothingness pressed in on my ears. I had no idea that absolute silence could be so loud.

I looked back down the beach to the child. She turned and looked directly at me. She smiled and waved, in a peculiar little gesture. Sort of a shy wave, wiggling her pinky while holding her pointer finger down with her thumb. In my mind, it was as if she were only a few feet away from me. She took her father's hand and they walked further into the distance until they were one dot bobbing down the shore.

Everything was quiet still. I turned to look out over the water but it was gone. The blue-green tranquility had simply disappeared. Confusion flooding my mind, I spun around to run away but stopped short at the scene before me. My father, buried up to his neck in a mound of sand as Scooter (seven-year-old Preston) and I decorated him with shells and seaweed. His Aunt and Uncle were laughing a few feet away taking pictures.

Scooter jumped to his feet and stood next to the younger me. "Aunt Gladys! Take one of me and my girl!" The sounds all around seemed to crash into my ears, a great cacophony that hurt my head.

The plump woman stood up to get a little closer and spoke to my father. "Look here Roger, if you're able." She laughed as my father tried to crane his head free from his sandy tomb. She snapped the picture and waited for it to slide from the bottom.

"Alright you two. Let that poor bloke alone so he can have a drink with me." Mr. Banks insisted.

I watched as my father wiggled his way free and just before he sat up, his eyes met mine. Not the fifteen-year-old version of me I saw beside him. *Me*. He smiled and winked as if he had a great secret he couldn't wait to share. He raised his right hand slowly and snapped his fingers.

Immediately, my eyes flew open.

I sat up and rubbed my hands over my face. "Jeez, that was weird!"

I turned to look at Preston in the gray hours of dawn but he wasn't there. I looked around waiting for my eyes to adjust. His luggage wasn't in the corner. I jumped out of bed, snatched a shirt from my closet and ran downstairs. He wasn't anywhere. I swiped my hand over the light switch in the kitchen then reached for my phone on the dining room table to call him. But I screamed and stamped my bare feet in absolute denial that I didn't even have his number.

"I am The Grand High Master of Stupidity!"

My worst fear now dominated every part of my brain. He'd made a clean get away with no strings attached. Tears stung my eyes as I walked slowly up to my room. Nothing made sense. Was I so gullible that I really didn't think this could happen? Fate! Destiny! What a mountain-load of horse shit!

Then that irritating voice inside my brain was coming back in full force with a resounding, *I told you so!* Only my conscience this time.

Tears blurring my vision, I fell hopelessly onto my bed, the pain already more than I could stand. My anger and heartbreak competed to see which would come out on top. And all I could do was cry. I curled into myself and buried my face in the pillow Preston slept on. His scent still lingered and the thought of him being gone forever created a chasm in my heart. A dark emptiness filled me with no light to find my way back to who I used to be. How could I let this happen?

Still clutching his pillow, I finally turned over and numbly stared at a nail hole in the pale green wall. My eyes began to focus on the top of my nightstand as my room grew ever brighter minute by minute by the rising sun. It took a minute for my brain to come around -to remember that I'd put my Bible back in the drawer last night.

I sat up and couldn't believe I didn't see it when I first opened my eyes. I picked up a photo that was sitting on a letter and I could see the side of Preston's face, his hands and his guitar propped on one of his knees as if someone had taken it over his shoulder. A little girl stood just inches in front of him, her little hands placed on either side of his face and her smile was exuberant. The child looked like a tiny angel. She reminded me so much of Beth, only Beth's blonde hair had been curly and hers was —I stopped in mid-thought with a gasp.

My mind abruptly shifted into reverse to the dream I'd waken from almost half an hour before. Impossible. How could *she* be the little girl in my dream? Did that mean the man I presumed to be her father, walking with her; was he Preston? Was this little girl his?

I picked up the letter and began to read.

Adena,

I'm sorry I didn't wake you to say Goodbye. No. Not Goodbye. To say, see you soon. But if I had, I would never have been able to leave. My heart is breaking having to part way so soon. I miss you already as I sit here watching you sleep. You have awakened emotions that I thought would never exist for me. And I know I could only ever feel them for you.

I'll ring you tonight around six o'clock your time. Hope you don't mind me peeking at your cell to steal your number. We still have so much to discuss, but for now, it can wait. The little girl is Kelley Anne Rogers-Grace. She was my goddaughter but my parents adopted her. I'll explain everything. I hope you understand my heart is yours now. It always has been. It just took finding you to know it. Adena, I love you.

Always,
Preston

I read the words at least ten times over. Relief bit by bit began to fill up that terrible crack in my heart. The pain replaced with longing. I looked at my Bible. I sat his letter and the photo on top of it just the way he left it. Then I saw it clearly. The symbolism. It was a promise.

The irritating buzz of my alarm clock resonated throughout my room at precisely 6:00a.m. I reached lifelessly to kill the sound.

For hours, I milled around unable to keep my mind on any one task, literally lost in my own home. I fixed a glass of tea and the only thing I could see was the hilarious face he'd made when he tasted it. I tried to distract myself by watching TV. As soon as I turned it on, the weatherman was still commenting on the tornado that touched down for six minutes right in the center of Gainesville as well as the extensive damage done to a historic building —the image of the balcony side of the hotel was plastered across the screen. I pressed the off button hard as if I could inflict pain on it somehow.

The phone rang and I jumped up to get it, stubbing my toe in the process. It was Trent. He'd only called to get me to email him a file from his computer so he could stay on top of Southeast Construction's latest project, The Sunset Towers Condominiums to break ground in Tampa in less than three weeks.

Talking to Trent was like talking to my brother. That is if I had one. And I felt no guilt for loving Preston. I might as well feel guilty for breathing. I wondered if it all meant I was some horrible heartless monster. But I'd been waiting on Trent one way or the other for the past ten years of our marriage. I'm not sure when I stopped waiting. Maybe it was years ago. Or maybe it was the moment I looked into Preston's eyes. I honestly don't know.

I curled up on the couch with a box of tissues and closed my eyes seeking some measure of escape from my own mind.

Tick … Tick … Tick … Tick … Tick…

I'd never even noticed you could hear that damn clock on the wall. It sounded like it was purposely trying to torment me. An assiduous reminder that I'd have to wait for Preston's call. Wait to see him again. Wait to know with any certainty what the hell was going to happen next. I got up, yanked the batteries out, and smashed it onto the floor. It was ugly anyway.

A loud knock followed by Owen's deep voice rang through the house. Was I even dressed? I looked down. Pajama pants. Good enough.

I yelled back and rubbed my eyes. I'd fallen asleep but for how long I wasn't sure, seeing as how the clock lay in pieces on the floor.

Owen followed my voice into the living room. "I take it Prince Charming is gone." A disgusted sneer on his face.

"Shut up. I just haven't taken a shower yet."

"Is there a drought or some shit I haven't heard about? Its five o'clock. What the hell are you waiting for?"

My heart leapt. I only had an hour to go and I'd hear Preston's voice.

"Hon, seriously. You okay? —You been crying or are you sick?" He glanced around at the pile of tissues on the floor, the couch and the coffee table.

"I've had a bad morning." I pulled my beige throw blanket in my lap and nearly refused to say anything else for fear of sounding childish. I was sure that Owen would think, *They only met a few days ago.* Then I remembered just how understanding he could be underneath his jackass exterior.

"I miss him." I covered my face to stave off another wave of tears. "I don't even know how he got to the airport. He was just gone. But his letter was just so…"

"He left you a *note*?" Disapproval filled his deep brown eyes. "I didn't peg him for the spineless type. I'm usually a better judge of character."

"Owen, stop it! You don't understand and you're kinda starting to piss me off." I pushed myself up and padded across the wood floor in my bare feet.

"Where are you going? Please come back and sit down." But he got up to follow me to my room.

I stood just inside the doorway and pointed at my nightstand. He walked over slowly until his eyes rested on the note and the picture.

"Read it." I bit nervously at my thumbnail watching him. "And tell me what you think."

First, he picked up the picture. His eyes got wide. "He's got a little girl?"

"*No,*" I got frustrated. "Just read the damn letter!" He ignored my impatience and read it for too long.

He's a writer for Pete's sake! What's the delay? Breathe in…breathe out… No more temper tantrums. I like everything in this room. Don't break anything.

He looked back at the little girl holding on to Preston's face and shook his head a little.

"Sorry I jumped the gun downstairs. —He's a good man, Dena. There'd be no point in him telling you this if he wanted to just walk away." He came back to give me a brotherly hug.

The oddity of my dream was lingering heavily, bothering me more than it probably should have. I paced back and forth -eyes closed remembering and relaying the dream to Owen. The little girl's wave, her laugh, the silence.

"And he never showed you that picture? You're sure?"

"Positive." I affirmed.

I didn't know what to consider Kelley other than a part of his family. She was obviously very special to him but why wouldn't he just tell me he had another little sister? He told me about Teena and his parents, Doreen and Nate after all. I did remember him mentioning Kelly's name several times. But the conversation had been generic. He could have been speaking of anyone. He also seemed to quickly change the subject when he mentioned her name.

Owen shrugged his burly shoulders. "Maybe it's just that women's intuition or something. Hell, I don't know. Some things just can't be explained."

"Well, at least you didn't say I was crazy."

He looked at me a little startled by my comment. "Dena, people have weird dreams all the time. I don't think you're crazy." He paused and then his normal smart-ass expression resurfaced. "Now take a walk through this head at night and I'll *show* you crazy."

I couldn't help but smile a little. I glanced at the clock; I still had time to shower before he called. I couldn't wait to hear his voice. I'd never been a more pathetic waste of space.

Owen went to raid my refrigerator. Nothing unusual. I didn't mind though, at least he helped himself and I didn't have to play host when he was around. I hurried downstairs with my hair still wet, t-shirt, old gym shorts, unshaved legs and no bra- Owen wasn't looking so who cares- and my mood was lifting by the minute.

I found Owen sitting at the kitchen counter scarfing down a Dagwood sandwich and a beer. I stood on the other side of the kitchen leaning against the sink and watched him eat like a pig.

"Are you sure you're gay?" I asked.

His eyes popped wide and he stopped chewing with his mouth hanging open. "What the hell is that supposed to mean? I thought you understood me better than that."

"Oh I know, I know. It's just in the movies, gay men are always dressed to a 'T' and have impeccable manners. You are such a hopeless slob! At least when you eat." I could say that to Owen. Brutal honesty was our thing.

"I left my pink shirt at the cleaners and I had my lisp fixed with therapy." He said sarcastically and swallowed a mass of food. "You know damn well I hate being labeled as gay or bisexual, just because I don't limit my options to women. Big fucking deal. You sound like my mother."

I stuck my tongue out at him like a kid. He returned the gesture grossly.

He took another huge bite and tried to speak around half an acre of bread and ham in his mouth. "You seem better. Still look like shit though."

"Hey!"

"Don't dish it if ya can't take it, Hag."

"Alright. You owed me that one. Truce?"

"Truce." He crammed the rest of his sandwich into his mouth.

I sat at the end of the counter, shifted my eyes from the phone to the clock then realized Preston had my cell number and *it* was upstairs. I ran up to get it and tripped over the last step.

"Ugh! Dammit!" Splayed out on the carpet in the hallway. It didn't really hurt it just made me mad.

"Dumbass!" Owen bellowed, followed by his ridiculous laugh.

"Piss off!"

I grabbed my phone and slowed down a little, sure that falling down the stairs would hurt a hell of a lot more than falling up them. I hopped back into the stool next to Owen.

"Glad to see you back to your old self." He said smiling.

"Thanks for coming over."

"Anytime." He got up to put his plate in the sink and then turned around.

I narrowed my eyes at him and pointed at the sink.

"Okay!" He turned around and washed his plate muttering something about me being an 'effin' dish Nazi.

I inhaled deeply and blew it out so I wouldn't sound like a panting lunatic when Preston called, still a little winded from my jaunt up and down the stairs. Or maybe just the anticipation of hearing his voice again. My palms were beginning to sweat.

What the hell is wrong with me?

Six o'clock. I started tapping one finger on the counter and stared at my cell. Owen put his hand over mine to make me stop.

"I *will* choke you if you don't chill." He looked down at my leg and made a face. "You have a bleeding rug burn on your knee."

I looked down. It didn't hurt so I didn't care.

"Preston give you that?" Owen asked then started laughing.

I rolled my eyes and said, "Were you not just here two minutes ago? There's carpet upstairs where I *just* fell you idiot."

He wrinkled his nose and made an ugly face, crossing his eyes, sticking his tongue out and mocking my voice in a nasal wine. '*There's carpet where I blah, blah-blah.*'

An infernal fifteen minutes later, it rang. I had a hard time making my hands work properly.

"Hello?"

"Hello, Love." His voice alone brought back the beautiful flutter in my stomach.

"Oh my God, I miss you already." Okay, that sounded a little desperate. The look on Owen's face seemed to match my thoughts. I didn't care.

"Sooo... you're not furious with me?" Preston asked nervously.

"I was. You're damn lucky I had to wait." I swiveled my chair and put my bare feet on the bottom of Owen's.

"Sorry. The hardest thing I've ever done was walk away from you this morning. A man's man would say he couldn't bear to see you cry. But the straight truth of it is, I wept like a baby all the way home"

I picked up a pen and started doodling on an empty envelope lying on the counter, swallowing my tears internally, fighting against the wave of heartbreak threatening to pull me under again. I held the phone away and breathed out a shaky sigh so he couldn't hear.

I opened my mouth to speak but Owen beat me with an outburst that left me wanting to strangle him. He told on me like a bratty kid regarding my falling *up* the stairs, his insane laugh filling the kitchen. I pressed the phone to my shirt to keep Preston from hearing but to no avail. Preston was laughing just as loud as Owen.

"Thanks. I'm glad you find that funny." My smile was inescapable, so good to hear his voice, to hear him laugh.

"Tell him about that dream you had." Owen said loud enough to wake the dead. In Russia!

I shot a glare at him that said very plainly to *shut up!* "What are you —like 12 years old now? Couldn't you be in another room or something?"

"What dream?" Preston asked.

"It's nothing. You'll think I'm nuts."

"I have news for you, Love. I *already* do. I want to hear all of it. I miss hearing you paint your pictures in my head."

I gave in giving Owen a nasty look and a flip of a finger, a gesture I normally detested but he *so* deserved it. He stood next to me sipping his beer and grinning like a fool as I began to repeat the dream. When I finished, Preston remained quiet. Too quiet.

I gave Owen the evil eye again for bringing it up and kicked him in the shin for good measure. He just smiled, solely to irritate me to death.

Finally, Preston spoke. "You say you couldn't hear anything. In your dream I mean."

"Yes, why?"

"Adena, Kelley is deaf."

"Deaf?" Stunned, I turned and looked at Owen. He threw up both hands humming the theme to *Twilight Zone* and backed into the living room. I grabbed a saltshaker and sent it flying straight into his collarbone. He's lucky it was plastic.

"I'm sorry, Preston. I didn't know."

"You couldn't have. Strange..." He sounded as if he were lost in thought.

"She's beautiful, Preston. She looks a lot like Beth at that age. I love the way she's holding your face. It's adorable."

"She does that when I sing to her. She can feel it. And she likes to watch the words, so to speak. Sorry, I didn't tell you about her earlier."

"It's okay. Did you hear anything more about your Dad?"

"Mmm. His blood pressure is off the charts. He's supposed to be taking something, but refuses to, which explains a lot. Mum keeps yelling at him, in turn making it worse. It's chaos over here."

I could tell he was worried about his father, the sound of his voice was off, strained with stress I supposed. Static started to break up our conversation. "Adena ..." more snowy white noise, "need to ..." more static and broken words that I couldn't make out, then the call dropped.

I flipped my phone shut and laid my face across the cold cobalt blue tiles of the counter. My phone buzzed and it was a text from Preston. - *Ring you tomorrow from land line. I Love You.-*

Owen came back in the kitchen and shook the back of my chair. "See, he called. You alright now?"

I nodded and closed my eyes. I could barely think I was so mentally exhausted. I lay there motionless with my cheek on the tiles. It felt good. My stomach growled angrily.

"Dammit girl! When's the last time you ate?" He didn't wait for an answer and started pulling cold cuts from the fridge.

"Yesterday evening."

He turned slowly and looked at me as if I had personally offended him. "You know it takes a special *kind* of stupid to forget to eat."

He brought me half a sandwich and a soda and stuck around for a few more minutes. Once he was gone, the house was as silent as a crypt. I went to the living room, turned the TV on, needing something to fill the emptiness and ate just enough to get rid of the growl.

7

THURSDAY...
No phone call.
Disappointed.

FRIDAY...
No phone call.
Disappointed and Worried.

SATURDAY...
No phone call.
Worried and Devastated.

SUNDAY...
No phone call.
Worried, Devastated and Pissed!!

8

MONDAY MORNING I ROSE LONG before the sun, giving up on getting any sleep. And giving up that Preston would call at all. I'd tried replying to his text with no luck and the one call I'd gotten only displayed *out of area*.

No shit.

I opened my closet and saw my suitcase crammed in the back. I pulled it out and started packing not consciously aware yet of why. But slowly I knew. I needed to talk to Mama and Daddy and get out of this house where around every corner I'm bombarded with memories of Preston's smile, the way his eyes danced when he laughed. Come hell or high water, I'd get to Lake St. John. I'd go home.

I tossed my suitcase in the trunk, drove two streets over to Owen's house, the street lamps still glowing. I reached under the first brick of a neglected flowerbed for the house key and let myself inside. I followed the bear-like sounds coming from Owen's room. No doubt, the man is single. He had a beautiful one-story red brick home but it's almost bare to the bones. The only proof that he lived there was his desk, buried in his research and manuscripts piled three deep in several stacks and a couch where he crashed briefly between brain storms. I wish I had that level of dedication.

I heard a faint growl that sounded more like the creaking of a door and Spaz poked his head out. Right away, he wagged his curly tail and sprang into my arms complete with a sticky wet lick on my chin.

"Good morning to you too, lil' buddy." I whispered then tucked him under my arm like a tiny football and carried him into Owen's room. He laid spread eagle across his bed and the only thing I could think was, *Thank God he doesn't sleep in the nude.*

I leaned over him about to speak softly when Spaz let out a bark shrill enough to make my ears bleed. Owen's eyes flew open and he grabbed his chest.

"Jesus! You trying to give me a fucking stroke!"

I growled. I glanced to his nightstand and spotted a tiny bottle of hand sanitizer attached to his key ring. I squeezed the green gel onto my finger and smeared it across Owens lips.

He licked them instinctively, spit into the air and started scrubbing his mouth with the sheet.

"What'd ya do that for!"

"Dirty mouth." Spaz was wiggling with excitement and I figured he needed to pee so I took him to the back door across the hall to let him out. It took ten seconds at most and when I got back to Owen's room, he was snoring again.

I jammed my knee into the mattress to shake him. "Owen, I'm going home."

"Good! I can go back to sleep."

"*No.* You're going with me."

He flopped to his side opening one puffy eye. "Oh. *Home.* Louisiana?"

"Yeah, you up for a road trip or is this a bad time?"

He shook his head, closed his eyes and smacked his lips a couple times. "Blah. You, coffee. Me, shower."

I took that as a yes and skipped to the kitchen, brewed the coffee, filled two travel mugs and in less than an hour, we were west bound on I-10. Spaz whined in the back seat for the first thirty miles.

"Care if he sits up front?" Owen asked finally.

"Ugh! I guess. I have a strict no humping policy while I'm driving, Owen."

"Hell, *I'll* behave. I just want him to sit up here so he'll shut up."

I laughed till I cried. Owen could make me laugh no matter what mood I was in and I knew I'd need that for the next couple days.

The twelve long hours didn't seem so bad. We ate junk food and talked about books and the upcoming writer's conference in Anaheim he'd begged me several times to attend, insisting it would relight my creativity.

But as we at last drove over the Mississippi River Bridge and I saw the muddy brown water below, my heart both soared and grew heavy at the same time. The better part of five years had passed since I last saw the sluggish tugboats pushing the long rusty barges along that mighty river. I'd forgotten how green the Kudzu covered bluffs were. How coming through the hills of Natchez, Mississippi and then crossing over the river onto the flat lands of Louisiana always seemed to say, *Welcome home.*

Driving along Highway 84 through the small river towns of Vidalia and Ferriday was always the longest part of the drive for me; the last few minutes following the levee where the houses and yards grow bigger, a mark of the wealthy few who reside on Lake St. John. Out to what most would call sixty miles from nowhere; we rode past the *Duck's Nest*, a restaurant that had been there forever and a day.

With the end of the black top and the pale blue water tower that bears the lakes name in my rear view mirror, I followed the curve around the end of the lake and onto the gravel road where only my family lives on Albright Road. Suddenly, the scenery changed, although still beautiful, these few modest homes among the wild pecan trees, stood long before the wealthy staked claim to the perimeter of the lake.

Owen perked up and stretched just as I parked under a massive sweet gum tree near the gravel driveway.

"I thought you were gonna tell me you grew up in one of those mansions we passed. This is nice though. It's real. Ya know?"

I looked ahead at the simple white two bedroom house I'd grown up in and over to the right where my uncle still lives. "It's home." I slipped the house key from my key ring and handed it to Owen. "I'll be back in a minute. Make yourself at home. I'm going to see the folks."

He smiled a little and nodded. "Take your time then. See ya later."

I waited to make sure he got in okay then backed out of the driveway. My rear was numb from the drive but I needed to see them. A short drive away I parked my car in front of the immaculately kept grounds, walked through the old wrought iron gates and immediately saw them. My feet always felt like cement when I walked through this place, heavy and unwilling to move me forward. I find myself chasing memories, recalling lost youth and trying to relive moments from the past.

Quick flashes of a perfect childhood streamed like a movie through my mind. Mama's pretty blonde hair glowing in the summer sun, sitting on the back porch swing. The smile she always wore no matter what kind of day she'd had. Her and Daddy dancing beneath the cypress trees on the pier.

On my knees, I cried at my mother's feet. I told her everything on my mind, every burden in my heart. But all I saw was the cold granite that bears her name and next to her the matching stone where my father lies. To reach out and hug them one last time would be the greatest wish I could wish, to have my family whole again. GG was blessed with an abundant life; lived till she was ninety-six and she lived it with no regrets.

Mama's life, a candle snuffed out too soon when I was 14, had always been hard to accept. She had simply stood to clear the table after supper, dropped a plate and grabbed her head. And that was it. She was gone. An aneurism, Daddy had explained to me time and time again after I'd wake up screaming for Mama to please just come home. That sort of thing happened more than I care to recall in that first year after she died. It took some time but I finally realized that Daddy had no answers to give and that his own devastation was absolute. He'd lost the love of his life. So I resolved to hide my nightmares.

Time marches on and we did the best we could together. But eight years ago, Daddy's heart gave out on him. Worked himself to death raising cattle and small scale cotton farming. And I hated myself for letting Trent talk me into moving so far away.

I got to my feet, walked behind the standing headstones to kiss them each, and strolled across to GG's stone to give her a kiss as well. With just as much affection, I touched the adjoining stone of Joseph Albright, GG's husband, my great-grandfather. A man I never knew outside of the stories she told me. When I could cry no more, I left and went back home with an unwanted emptiness in my soul.

When I got out of the car, I saw Uncle Ray's yellow front porch light on. He was sitting in his rocker looking down at something, nearly the exact picture I held in my memories of him. Short sleeve blue button up shirt, navy Dickies work slacks and red suspenders. His hair was thinner now. Grayer.

As I've said, time marches on.

I walked the forty or so yards through the weeds between the two houses to see him, ashamed for not visiting more often, my father's only brother.

He looked up and smiled. "I thought I saw that old Pony go by. You go out and see your folks?"

I nodded and walked up the steps to hug him. "Hey, Uncle Ray. What're you up to?"

He took a swig of his Miller and smashed his thumb against the gray painted boards under his feet. "Killin' Ants." Sounding like aints.

I smiled. Uncle Ray was getting on in years and sometimes wasn't in his right mind. His daughter Carolyn looked after him. She's two years older than me.

"How many ya get so far?"

"Not all of 'em. That's for damn sure. How long you here for?"

"Just a couple days, Uncle Ray. Sorry it's been so long. Ya'll wanna come over for supper tomorrow night?"

"I 'magine so. Carolyn'll be right glad to get a break I bet. And she gonna have a fit to see you. Won't be back till mornin' though. —Got a mess a crawfish this mornin. How long's it been since you sucked a head, girl?"

I laughed. Louisiana has to be the only place where that question arises with a straight face.

"It's um ... been a while Uncle Ray."

He squished another ant and rolled it between his bent fingers. "Got a smoke?"

"No I don't and even if I did I wouldn't give you one."

He let out a wheeze and chuckled. "Carolyn won't let me either. Pain in the ass is what she is. God love her though." He rocked far back in his chair and took another swig. "She gets that boy-a-hers to mow around here now. Hunter. Won't let me on my John Deere no more. Says I'll die of heat stroke. I'll die of goddamn boredom 'fore long is what I'll do." Another swig then he smashed another ant. "Who's that feller went inside a while ago. I know it ain't Trent. Boy ain't been around here in a coon's age."

"No sir. Just a friend. You'll meet him tomorrow."

He smiled so wicked his eyes gleamed. "What kinda friend you drag out here to the ass-end of nowhere?"

"Honestly, he's just a friend. But between you, me and the fencepost..." I kneeled down to whisper, "I got one of the other kind too. But that's our secret."

He slapped his knee and assumed I was kidding. And seeing as how Preston hasn't called since the day he left, maybe I was.

Dammit! That's why I came here. To get him out of my head.

"GG find you yet, youngin'? She's been 'round here a good bit lookin' for you."

I blinked twice as I gathered what he said. "GG? Uncle Ray, GG's gone. She died years ago. You remember that, don't you?"

He grunted and tossed his empty can in a five gallon bucket next to the screen door. "Yeah, I reckon I do, youngin'. That don't change the fact that she's lookin' for ya." He mumbled something I couldn't understand but I got the feeling he thought I was being insolent.

"Well, thanks for letting me know, Uncle Ray." He smiled then and I thought about the strange voice I'd heard repeatedly the day of the tornado. "As a matter of fact, I think she did find me a few times."

He smiled with thin lips and swallowed hard, his Adam's apple bobbing beneath the weathered wrinkled skin and if I wasn't mistaken, I saw a tear in the corner of his eye. He and GG weren't related, she was on my mother's side, but she lived right across the street for seventy-some-odd years. She was a mother or grandmother of sorts to all who ever lived on this road. Of course, they were close. Who was I to say he hadn't heard her, too? Maybe GG *was* trying to reach me. There's no way three different people heard her and all three of us were cracked.

I kissed Uncle Ray's cheek and left him there to kill his ants.

I walked around to the backyard, sat at the end of the pier, and watched as the setting sun turned Lake St. John to a sheet of gold. Something about this place revived my soul no matter what troubled me. I tossed a prickly green sweetgum ball in the water, watched a school of brim from below come to investigate, then dart away seeing that it wasn't something to eat.

I walked inside and wrinkled my nose at the musty smell of a house that's been closed up too long. Owen had the windows open but the sweltering heat and humidity called for the window units to run at high for a while.

"How come there's all this food in here. I figured we'd have to go to the grocery store in the morning." Owen said going through the cabinets.

"Gavin was here last week. He likes it out here and he takes care of the place when he comes. I'll go to town in the morning and get some bread and stuff."

Owen turned around and leaned against the old porcelain sink. "You alright? What's this trip really about?"

I shrugged as I sat down at the tiny breakfast table. The old Formica top felt sticky. I'd have to wipe the place down tomorrow despite Gavin's efforts. "Just needed to get away. That's all."

He glanced around the breadbox-sized kitchen and smiled. "I love it here. Man, I could write for months in this place. Maybe go for my first fiction. Life in Louisiana. It's inspiring."

"Well, be prepared. There's a hell of a lot more to Louisiana than flashing your boobs at Mardi Gras."

"That's too bad. My boobs look awesome. Wanna see?"

I rolled my eyes so hard it actually hurt. "Bring your laptop?"

"Yep. There's some beer in here. Want one?"

"Nah. I'm gonna wash all the sheets so we can get some sleep."

"Doesn't look like you need to. They're all neat and folded on each bed. Guess Gavin did it."

I'd have to thank him for that one. I got up and went to make the beds. Owen followed to help and it was weird to have him in my old room. Daddy's unshakable rule: No boys allowed past the bathroom. I opened my closet door to get GG's old quilt from the top shelf. With a window unit in a small bedroom, it turned to an icebox in the middle of the night. Owen fell out laughing and I couldn't imagine why till I saw what he was looking at. On the inside of my closet door was a poster of Jon BonJovi, big hair and all. I laughed as well.

"Shut up! I was in *love*!"

"Yeah, you and every other sixteen year old girl in the eighties."

"True." I tossed the blankets to the bed.

I thought about how Owen sleeps and figured he'd be more comfortable in the bigger bed in my parents' room. I flipped the sheets out and as they settled, I saw someone in the hallway. It startled me and I let out a short scream because the face I saw for an instant, I knew as well as my own. I ran to look down the hallway but it was empty.

"Who the hell was that?" Owen said just as breathless as I.

I spun on my toes to see his face. "Did you just see an old woman standing here?" I searched his eyes and pointed over my shoulder.

"Yeah, why'd she run off like that?"

I swallowed hard, my mouth gone to cotton and my hands started to shake. I wasn't crazy. He saw her too. "She didn't run off. She ... disappeared."

"Say that *one* more time."

I looked up at Owen slowly, every bone in my body vibrating like a tuning fork. "That was GG."

He cast me a sidelong glance then walked through the house, quickly opening doors to the left and right, then I heard both the front and back doors open one at a time. He made his way back to my bedroom door and he was pale as a sheet.

He took a deep breath and squinted one eye at me. "GG. That would be the one I've heard so much about. The one that *died* like, what? —Ten years ago?"

"Fourteen." I corrected. "I think I'll have one of those beers now, Owen."

"You and me both."

I can't even begin to express my disdain for beer. It's not so much a moral issue. I just think it's the most disgusting taste on the planet, nonetheless, Owen and I put away a twelve pack in short order. I wanted to sleep and I wanted to sleep hard and I wanted to *not* think of Preston and I especially didn't want to ponder over whether or not my dead great-grandmother in fact had been wondering the halls of my childhood home.

I did, however, think that I would have a discussion with Gavin as to why this house was stocked with various assortments of alcohol. He's only 19. But, I knew what his argument would be. The legal drinking age in Louisiana is 18-21 depending on the presence of an adult. I don't give a damn. My rules apply in all fifty states.

Late that night as I lay in bed praying for sleep to touch me, I spoke aloud to the house around me. "GG, why would you let me see you then go away? If you're here, I'm listening."

I felt so stupid saying this aloud, not really expecting an answer. But I heard a whisper that sounded like delicate crystal chimes being tossed by the wind in the distance. But it was more than just the wind and this time I could feel her; could even smell the peppermint oil she used to rub on her aged fingers.

I sensed someone watching me and I sat up. "GG? Is that you?" My chin quivered like that of a toddler. I wanted so much for it to be true, to have some link to those lost to me.

The soft tinkling wind sound came again but then morphed into a *Shhh*. The same way she'd shush me when I cried over a skinned elbow as a child. Coolness touched my forehead and I felt as though I was being urged to lie back down. My eyes, wide as golf balls as I strained in the dark to see anything. Any*one*. But there was nothing to see but the slightest indication of lace curtains blowing in front of the small window unit.

The whisper, crisp and clear this time, seemed to come from everywhere and nowhere at once. "Go to sleep, Adena. It's easier for you that way."

She hummed an old Irish lullaby, and it worked like a drug, pushing aside all my worries and all my fears. And sleep finally cradled me and I felt like a little girl safe in my bed.

I saw her round wrinkled face, her silver silken curls, and the smile of her bright green eyes. "Hello, Adena, my precious girl. I'm sorry I startled you, dear. But I needed you to know I was close."

"GG. I've missed you so…"

"Shh, child. You'll wake yourself. Just you listen. Be patient and don't be frightened no matter *what* happens. I'm afraid you will learn of things not meant to know. I learned of some of these things when I was only a girl. Dark things. But as far as I know, that knowledge died with me. Long ago, I left behind all those that I loved in order to take away the darkness someone else cursed upon my family. I bound that wicked woman and she is with me now. Or at least, I'm with her."

"*Bound* her? What woman?"

"Shhh. I can't call her by name. But it's not important now. What *is* important is that you follow your heart no matter where it leads you. You *must*. What I started, you will finish."

I heard a baleful scream and I jumped in my sleep. "GG, what was that? Where are you ... really?"

She touched my lips to quiet me. "Not where you think. We're stuck between, I suppose you could say. Grayland some have called it. We are neither here nor there. And when I bound that vengeful old Harpy, I bound her to me or vice versa, accidently of course, and she's been a little peeved for quite some time."

"Bound? GG you weren't a ... a *witch*, were you?"

She smiled and leaned closer. "You know I was a God fearing woman, nevertheless, there are times when one must fight fire with fire. But the price for dabbling has landed me here. Where ever *here* might be. Perhaps. It could be where she intended for me to be all along. And I'm not alone. There are more of us. How many? I'm not quite certain. But I feel that this place is temporary. Things will be as they should ... come yesterday."

"Come *yesterday*? Don't you mean tomorrow?"

She giggled as if I'd been left out of an inside joke. "You'll understand in time. I may not know exactly how I got here but I do know that what has been wrongly done, can be undone. I love you my precious, Adena. Now sleep. You'll see me no more."

"GG, wait! I love you!" I reached for her but she was fading.

She paused and looked deeply into my eyes, so much like hers. "As I love you. I knew the day you were born that Fate had finally chosen its intended path. A great circle is nearly complete. One side dark, one side light. You are the light, Adena. A hundred years ago, a curse was cast upon those I loved. I did what I could but only when the circle is complete, only when the balance is regained, will the curse be gone forever. But don't you worry. You've inherited more than my eyes and my curls, Adena. You've inherited my memories. Some of them. I hope they serve you well. Just follow your heart, dear. It will not mislead you." And with her blessed Irish smile, she was gone.

"GG?"

Nothing but silence. No more whispers; no more lullabies.

The next day, Owen obeyed his muse, took advantage of fresh inspiration and carried his laptop to the pier under the shade of the grand old cypress trees. He wrote like a man with fire in his fingers and I was tempted to peek over his shoulder, but I knew better. Nothing like an intruder to break your stride.

I laughed at the kitchen window when I noticed a green garden snake slither next to his foot and he nearly dropped his laptop in the murky water, almost fell twice to get away from it then moved his chair back ten feet for safe distance. Talk about breaking his stride. He watched it for five minutes and tried to shoo it away.

I walked outside and rescued the burly forty-two year old man sitting on the pier. I picked up the harmless creature and let it curl around my wrist and laughed.

"Ya crazy woman! Get that thing away from me. I hate snakes." He shivered from head to toe and looked all around in case the serpent had friends hanging about.

"This little guy should be the least of your worries. Water moccasins have been known to fall out of these cypress trees."

"Damn. Them things are poisonous." He said looking overhead at the sprawling branches covered in moss.

He closed his laptop then dragged his chair to the backyard closer to the house. I attempted to get back to prepping for the crawfish boil, but Owen closed his laptop again and looked up at me. "Should we talk about…what happened last night?"

"Nope."

"Didn't think so. You okay?"

"Yep."

"What about Prince Charming? He call yet?"

"Don't wanna talk about that either."

"Got it. Need any help?"

"Write while you can. Looks like you're on a roll. Me and Spaz can hold down the fort." I ruffled his curly hair and stepped up on the porch.

I let the snake crawl onto the white painted banister, not bothered by the little green guy. I'd played with them as a child. A bite from him was somewhere along the lines of getting pinched by a new clothespin.

A breeze blew in from the lake, cooling the perspiration on my neck, a glorious reprieve from the heat. The tinkling of a wind chime tickled my ear and it made me think of GG again.

I looked at the end of the pier and I could almost see her throwing stale biscuits to a drake mallard duck that she'd spoiled year after year. He'd waddle after her, fat as a barrel, quacking for more food. Somehow, this scene in my mind settled me to some degree and gave me the feeling that with her guidance, everything really would be okay.

Evening rolled in the way it always does and the back yard brimmed over with the sounds of old George Straight tunes, lots of laughter and the delectable smell of crawfish boiling. The whirring noise of the propane cooker stopped and Uncle Ray pulled the big stainless steel basket from the steaming pot and spread its contents across the picnic table covered in newspaper.

"Dig in," He flourished his arm across the spread of spice-covered potatoes, corn ears, onions, garlic, sausage and crawfish. "It's ready as its gone git."

Owen looked around as though something was missing. "Paper plates?"

My cousin Carolyn laughed. "Just eat 'em from the table."

She looked a great deal like me only she had the darkest brown eyes, her hair not so wavy. Her skin is a deeper russet than mine due to her less diluted Cherokee blood.

Nothing like Irish Cream to lighten your coffee.

She enjoyed introducing Owen to the bayou style buffet, showing him the easiest way to peel the crawfish. She popped the open end of the head side between her lips and sucked on it. Owen looked fairly appalled, staring at the tail still in her hands.

"What the hell is that yellow gunk on it?" He asked.

"We say it's something like fat. But who cares, its good. Now suck it and don't think about it so much."

It was all I could do to remain standing as I laughed at the look on Owen's face. Uncle Ray was nearly crying as he peeled his tenth bug in the time it took Owen to get the hang of one. But being a good sport, Owen closed his eyes and sucked the head. He let it drop from his mouth to the ground and laughed.

"Nothing but that spicy water came out. And some of that yellow gunk. What's the big deal?"

"Ain't no big deal. What'd you think was gonna come out? Brains?" Carolyn leaned into him giving him a jovial bump with her hip.

Owen popped a tail in his mouth and gave her a loaded grin obviously captivated by her every word and throughout the evening, I saw something grow between them. Call it love or lust or just plain old chemistry, they definitely had something. Watching the two of them laugh, seeing the way Owen stared at her, made me miss Preston.

No matter how I tried to avoid thinking down that path, my mind took me back to the short time we'd spent together. It didn't matter where I was or the company I kept, my heart was somewhere in Havering-Atte-Bower, London —a place I've never seen and likely never will.

Our bellies full and the beer all gone, Carolyn and Owen disappeared to someplace along the banks of the lake or maybe a ride on the levy. Uncle Ray retired to his bed and Carolyn's boy, Hunter, left with some of his friends. A friend of Uncle Ray's pulled away in his bass boat and headed across the lake back to his place.

Alone again, I watched the last few red-orange embers of the campfire dwindle to little more than glowing ashes and it no longer served the purpose of smoking away the mosquitoes. I had the welts to prove it. I cleaned up as much of the mess as I could, disposed of the crawfish carcasses into the lake to prevent an invasion of raccoons in the middle of the night then got the house ready for us to leave in the morning.

I decided to hit my bed early, not much in the mood for conversation and Owen wasn't back yet anyway. Spaz jumped on the twin bed with me. I ran my fingers mindlessly through his errant gray and brown fur wishing my life could be so simple. That a simple petting could make me feel so content. Maybe that was my problem. Preston had acted like he cared. He acknowledged a love for me without really feeling it. A few days of attention and what felt like love after so many years of stagnation between Trent and I and now, after just a few days with Preson, everything inside me felt cold.

I lay there in the dark and tried hard not to think of Preston, or of GG paying me a visit. If that's really what happened. Most of all, I tried not to think of how lonely and broken this house felt. Every fiber in my being told me that life was not supposed to be this way. My mother's laughter should still fill this place. My father should still be here to welcome me home. The kitchen should still smell of chicory coffee, fried chicken and buttermilk biscuits. I shouldn't have lost them both. But life offers no guarantees. Still, I'd always felt that there was something here that was severely incomplete, unfulfilled. Life itself had not been satisfied in this place.

Does everyone in my position feel that way?

Maybe so.

Back in High Springs at 5:08 a.m. -Wednesday morning - my cell rang. I fumbled around on my nightstand and looked at the display. *Out of area.*

Don't get your hopes up.

"Hello," My voice too heavy with sleep to reveal my angst ridden heart.

"Hello, Love."

I could hear the nervous tenor to Preston's tone but my heart sang to hear his voice. But part of me was angry. A big part of me. Still, I forced myself to think with reason.

Don't jump the gun too quickly. Give him a chance to explain.

"Are you...*okay*?"

"Yes," he said quietly.

"And your Dad?"

"Still contrary, but he's fine." Quietly again. I waited. Nothing.

I sat up and pushed my wild hair out of my face. "So then why the hell haven't you called?"

"I'm sorry, Adena."

I waited through a solid minute of silence for an excuse but none came.

"Tell ya what. Don't bother." I flipped my phone shut and threw it on the bed.

I'd recently had an overdose of crazy. GG's stories about curses and light and dark circles and this and that. And *I'm* the light? All I could do was try to reason out what it all meant and right now ... well, head games I can *definitely* live without.

It started ringing again.

I think not!

I threw the covers off and went down stairs. I stood by the coffee pot waiting for the gurgling to stop; all the while hearing the incessant ringing from upstairs.

Sorry for what? If something had happened, he'd have told me right off the bat. In any case, he shouldn't have left me hanging like that. No excuse. I didn't even have to answer. I could already hear it. *Adena, this just isn't going to work.* How did I ever talk myself into believing him? I know how. Cause I'm a simpering idiot sucker for his gorgeous eyes! And that smile of his. And his voice. Stupid, tall … too young … super sweet … Urrrrgh! Come on brain, make up your mind! Hate him or love him. It just pissed me off even more that I couldn't dig up any true derogatory remarks on his behalf. Other than he didn't call me like he said he would. Bingo! That was enough. Conniving liar!

Ringing again! I sat at the counter, finished my coffee, and tried to calm down. I found myself counting. Counting what? I've no idea. Just counting in my head. Sometimes I whispered the numbers between sips of coffee. It seemed to keep me grounded to the kitchen floor. I paced the kitchen. I sat in the barstool. I drank my coffee and I counted.

The phone upstairs finally at rest, I trudged upstairs to count some more only in my shower. I was too wired to go back to sleep.

I counted the steps upstairs; there were seventeen. Thirteen steps to my bedroom door.

And then my phone rang. Again. I threw my head back and screamed to the ceiling as loud as I could, "Dammit!"

My temper, my temper —I snatched the damn thing off the bed. "What!"

"Don't hang up! Adena, I'm sorry. *Please* listen to me."

I plopped down on my bed, teeth on edge and tried to hold my temper. I nearly bit a hole in my tongue just to keep quiet.

"I know you're angry with me. I wish I had an adequate excuse but I don't. I…I just…"

"Oh, spit it out! You just what? Out of sight out of mind? Maybe you forgot all the bullshit you spouted while you were in my bed! So why bother calling now —what is it? A *week* later?" I jumped to my feet again and starting pacing along the wall by my window.

"Adena, no. You know I meant everything I said. I just needed a few days to think. I'm sorry, really I am. All I've *done* is think of you. But mostly what I've done *to* you."

I stopped pacing as though I'd hit a brick wall. "What you've done to me? I've been worried something happened to you or your dad. Now, I feel like you just had a little fling and now you're home and it's done!"

"No! *Please* hear me out. —The morning I left, you said something that's had me in absolute turmoil. You were apologizing to Trent in your sleep. Crying. It's all I can think about. Adena, all of this is my fault. I thought if I didn't hear your voice I could think more clearly. I didn't mean to hurt you. I didn't mean to make you break your promises to him. I didn't mean to fall in love with you. But I can't leave you alone either."

I stood limp at my window looking down on my backyard. Looking down at the very circle of grass where we'd danced. The place we'd made love. The very spot we'd surrendered to whatever was turning our world inside out. I leaned my forehead against the cool window pain and stood there silently crying. There wasn't a cell in my body that wanted to hate him.

"Adena, I do miss you. I do love you. Please talk to me. Tell me I'm not too late."

I swallowed hard, trusting him again. "Don't *ever* do that to me again, Preston."

"I promise, Love."

That wall around my heart, —never had a chance.

I had the house to myself the next few days barring the occasional visit from Owen. I was glad for his visits though. He kept me from losing my mind.

The morning I took Preston to a hotel and drove away was only a hint of what I felt now. As I'd driven away, the nebulous pull got stronger the further I got from him, as if an invisible rubber band bound us. A band that wouldn't break with distance but the strain against the bond was excruciating. Now that band stretched and strained over an entire ocean.

The conflict between my head and my heart over what I was doing — in love with another man – was tearing me in two. But none of it made a dent in the way I felt. Someone once said …*The heart wants what the heart wants. And there is no reasoning with it.* I'd never appreciated how true that is until now. And GG's words rang in my head. *Follow your heart no matter where it leads. And don't be afraid.*

Could she possibly know about Preston? I'd tried very hard not to dwell on the conversation we'd had when I went home to Lake St. John. It was too weird to be real. But too real to ignore. And I didn't understand everything she was trying to tell me.

The very worst had been when Gavin came home one day and in so many words sort of blurted out the question, "Ya still seeing the dude with the guitar?"

Needless to say I nearly fainted. *He* had been the one to let Spaz in the house that last day Preston was there -not Owen as I had previously guessed. Spaz had been on the doorstep when Gavin came by to pick up a few things to take to his new apartment in Gainesville. He'd driven through the night from Louisiana. When he came in, he saw Preston asleep on the couch then came upstairs to find me and discovered a strange piece of luggage in my room. He'd slipped out knowing what he'd stumbled into.

What a nightmare! Puking right there on the kitchen floor was a definite possibility. What my son must have thought of me! But he'd been very understanding and I'll never forget what he told me.

"Do you feel guilty?"

"In the sense that I never wanted to betray your father, of course I do." I'd said.

He shook his head like I didn't get it. "We're not talking about Dad right now. We're talking about you. Maybe guilty was the wrong word. Do you regret getting involved with the guy?"

"No."

"Do you love him?"

"Absolutely. With everything that I am."

"Then that's all I need to know. Dad's been a real prick the last few years," I tried to protest but he held up his hand for me to let him finish. "He has all but moved out of this house and no it's *not* all work. He's like a stranger around here and he's alienated all of us. All I know is that you deserve better than being his live in secretary and bookkeeper. Me and Beth are all grown up now. I *want* you to find some happiness. 'Kay?"

I only nodded. He'd quite effectively rendered me speechless.

He'd hugged me before he left for the apartment that day and no matter how big he'd gotten, I still felt my baby boy in my arms.

I was glad to have a few more days alone. It gave me a little time to try to come to terms with so many things. The thoughts weighing on my mind were never-ending, a pressing heaviness I could barely keep from crushing me. So to obliterate my worries, I spent the days cleaning above and beyond even *my* norm. I cleaned doorknobs and locks meticulously with Q-tips and brass polish. The tiniest imperfections that every house bears seemed to bug me more than usual. A tiny scratch on the foyer wall where Trent hung his keys prompted a trip to the hardware store for some paint so I could get rid of the bothersome blemish. I scrubbed and painted the dark dingy space beneath the kitchen sink, relined the kitchen cabinets and drawers, reorganized the pantry and the linen closet in the hall. I moved the washer, dryer, oven and fridge to clean under, behind and over.

Maybe by fixing every little imperfection, I would somehow erase my bigger problems, or at least push them out of my mind. In any case, after three days of this madness, Owen threatened to take me to mental facility if I didn't stop.

9

HAVING THE SAME DIFFICULTY AS his mother, Preston spent a lion's share of his days trying to convince his father to take better care of himself. Preston's mother, Doreen, had found several pills hidden under the cushion of Nate's chair where he'd secretly been refusing to take them, insisting he didn't like the way they made him feel. This made Preston furious for two reasons; it wasn't good for his father and that Kelley might have found them and mistaken them for candy.

Hearing his frustration when he spoke of Nate was all too familiar. Remembering how my father had been in such denial over his poor health and how he'd refused to slow down and do what his doctor said was by far one of most frustrating times in my life. I could never win those battles; there was always that line of respect I never allowed myself to cross with him. I still beat myself up for not being firmer -for not pitching a fit to make him listen. For all the grand good it would have done. I was his little girl. What did I know?

Understandably, Preston sounded positively weary when we talked, filling his father's shoes in the orchard and the cellars; keeping peace between his parents over medications and doctors visits repeatedly put off -all heaped on top of his own responsibilities kept him busy from dawn till dusk. But he always found the time to call.

Saturday morning I decided to give him a ring to see how things were going. I sat at the dining table and listened but it rang more than normal. I almost hung up, but finally I heard a muffled, *"Hello,"* It wasn't Preston's voice.

"Mr. Nate? Is that you?" I'd only ever heard his voice in the background before but I didn't know who else it could be. He said something else but I couldn't hear him clearly.

"Please ...help ..."

His words were clear enough that time. There was a grunt that followed and there was no doubt it was the sound of unmistakable pain. The phone clattered to the floor and I could hear him groaning; trying to call for his wife, Doreen, but all he could do was gasp and moan. Panic set deep into my blood. I stood up pacing back and forth not knowing what to do.

Oh God...think, think, think. I banged my fist against my forehead. Obviously 9-1-1 wouldn't cut it.

"Oh!" I hung up and dialed the number to the house line. It rang twice and Ms. Doreen answered and despite my best efforts to stay calm, I sort of shouted for her to help Mr. Nate; that something was wrong.

She dropped the phone. I heard water running and hasty footsteps then seconds later, she screamed for Preston. So much commotion followed until I heard Preston's voice of reason trying to calm his mother. A slamming of a door and everything was quiet. I hung up and prayed that Mr. Nate would be all right.

The day dragged; eternal hours spent feeling helpless -wondering and waiting. Just after five o'clock that evening, my cell rang at last while I was checking the mail at the end of the drive. Preston sounded like he'd been hit by a truck as he delivered the news that I'd feared hearing all day. Mr. Nate had suffered a heart attack.

Preston stayed so quiet. The pain in his silence was unbearable. I walked up the crushed marble path, and sat on the front step -trying my best to comfort him, but the inadequacy of mere words from such a distance ripped at my insides. I stared down mindlessly watching a tiny black ant crawl over the stones. That's how I felt. Miniscule and helpless.

Preston's voice wavered as he finally spoke. "I need you here with me. I'd give anything."

He sounded so broken. I deliberated, but not for long. I only knew I couldn't deny him this request. If it *was* a request. The truth is I wanted to be there for him, no matter the consequence.

I told Preston I'd call him back in a few. I hurried to the phone on the kitchen counter and couldn't dial Nan's number fast enough. (Trent's mother) My hands shaking, my heart pounding —so much so, I had to test out my voice to be sure I could still speak as I pressed the last number. A familiar banging on the door followed by Owen's usual boisterous entrance.

"Dena!" He shouted just as Nan's phone rang the second time.

I swiveled my stool around and swatted my hand to make him be quiet. He settled into the seat at the end of the counter and helped himself to my laptop.

"Hello," Nan answered.

"Hey Nan. It's Adena."

She laughed. "Since when does anyone call you *that?*"

Did I really just say that? I felt like Dena had died and Adena had taken over.

Owen tapped the side of his head and crossed his eyes as if to say,

Duh. He must have the hearing of a jungle cat to have heard what she said.

I cracked my neck to relax as Owen typed away on the keys. "Nan, can Beth stay a little while longer. Gavin's gone and with Trent away so much, well, she really doesn't like to stay here by herself." I wound the cord around my finger until it turned purple.

"Of course she can. Where are you going?"

Owen cocked his head to the side and peered over the computer, studying my face, worry creasing his forehead and obviously showing no shame as he listened to my conversation.

My eyes zoned in on Owen's stare; my heart dropped to my feet as I found the courage to truthfully answer Nan.

"London."

Owen lunged across the counter and slammed his hand on the button disconnecting the call.

"What the hell, Owen!" I slammed my fist against the counter and started to dial again. He ran around me and pulled the cord out of the wall.

"Nope, nope, nope. Are you crazy or just stupid! Yeah, I get that you like the guy and all but you are really about to screw up."

I reached for my cell but he snatched it away so fast, I barely saw him move.

"Owen, I have to go! Now give me my damn phone!" I reached for it again but he staggered backward like a toddler with a treasured piece of candy.

"What about Trent? What are you planning to tell him? Hmmm?"

I leaned back in my seat, closed my eyes and ground my teeth loud enough to shatter glass. I didn't have an answer for that and he knew it.

"Yeah, haven't thought that far ahead now have you? Not that I give a shit if you hurt the jerk's feelings. I'm worried about *you*. Ya can't just fly by the seat of your pants here." He walked to the fridge, threw both phones inside, and grabbed two Coronas. "Have a drink with me and just think about what you're doing first, okay."

I lay my head on the counter and heard the phone ringing upstairs.

"Just let it ring Dena and listen to me." He yanked the crisper drawer in the fridge open and grabbed a lime.

"Owen, Preston's father had a heart attack. I need to go."

He opened the drawer next to the stove then paused, "Oh. Sorry to hear that." He raised his eyebrows in thought for a couple seconds, grabbed a knife, and shoved the drawer shut with his hip. "Well, then, I think I can help. I came by to take you out to dinner. I'm leaving Tuesday and I'll be gone for a week and a half."

"Thanks, but I fail to see how dinner is gonna fix my problems. No offense." I said as I watched him quarter the lime directly on my counter. I just barely refrained from having a meltdown over this.

"Sweetheart, *we* are going to Redbridge."

I sat up and folded my arms across my chest. "Redbridge?"

He smashed a green wedge into the mouth of his bottle then mine, took a purposeful swig of his beer and put the other bottle in front of me with a loud clunk. "Yes Dena, Redbridge. Pull your head out of your big ass for two seconds. Don't you remember? My cousin Chancey lives in Redbridge and Preston said Redbridge is right next to Havering-atte-Bower. Don't you listen to anybody? –Anyway, I just invited you to go to London. With *me*."

A marked measure of calm washed over me as I finally grasped what he was getting at. I couldn't speak and the ringing from upstairs stopped. I got up and hugged him. "Thank you, Owen. I swear sometimes I don't know what I'd do without you."

He patted my back and squeezed me. "Awe, I'm just giving you an excuse to go is all. I was sort of hoping you'd want to tag along anyway. I had a ball at the lake, so I owe you one."

I let him go and rubbed my eyes so hard I saw stars. The ringing started again.

"Think I can have my phone back now?"

He pulled them out of the fridge and plugged the kitchen phone back into the wall. I answered and heard Beth yelling.

"Are you insane?!! You *better* be talking about one of those rancid little towns with a cool name right here in the United States. Like Paris, Texas or London, Arkansas. Not *our* London…"

Why, oh, why didn't I see this coming?

My predicament became more problematical by the second. Somewhere in the middle of her ear-assaulting rant, she called me a traitor. I knew she was whining but the word *traitor* stung like a wasp. My thoughts spiraled and I decided hastily. Owen was at my laptop again sitting beside me so I could see as he pointed at different flights and times. I nodded without really looking as I endured Beth's steady stream of irritation drill its way through my eardrum.

"Okay, Okay! You can go, alright?" I took a deep breath and watched

Owen hang his head in his hands. "But sweetie, listen. This trip isn't gonna be like you think. I can't tell you right this second. But ... I will. I love you and I'll call you later."

I hung the phone up slowly and waited for whatever Owen was about to say.

"Congratulations! That's the dumbest thing I've ever seen an intelligent person do. I'll call Guinness first thing in the morning." He held up his hand to stop me from defending myself and went back to the reservations muttering *dumbass* under his breath. I let that one go. It rang too true for me to argue the point.

I handed Owen my credit card for mine and Beth's tickets. After waiting for the hearing in my right ear to return, I had to steady myself. My heart going ninety-to-nothing, my palms sweating and to be completely honest, mildly nauseated. I dialed Preston's number and Owen looked at me.

"You calling *him*?" I nodded. He took the laptop to the living room to give me some privacy. Something so out of character that I stared at his back as he walked forward two steps then back again to grab his beer, then a banana from the fruit bowl on the dining table. I smiled as I watched him balance his load toward the T.V.

Preston answered sounding a little better. To know I'd get to wrap my arms around him in just a matter of days made me deliriously happy.

"Preston," I blew out a deep breath I'd been holding in for too long. "What would you say if I told you I could be there Tuesday?"

"Adena, please. I can't handle getting my hopes up right now."

"Well, unless the plane crashes I really need someone to pick me up from Heathrow."

Five seconds of silence passed before he responded, "Have you gone *mad?*"

I heaved a sigh. That was the third time in ten minutes someone had questioned my sanity. Then we went through a series of, *Are you serious? —Yes, I'm serious.* So on and so forth and we were both very excited until I got to the part where Beth was coming along with me.

"Are you certain you're ready to do that? I mean..." His voice trailed off with a measure of uncertainty.

"You mean do I want to blow the whistle and you and I don't work out? I've thought of that Preston. But I *can't* hide this from her. Gavin knows, what's the difference?"

"Adena it's just ... I feel like you're standing in a pool of petrol and

I'm handing you a lit match. I'd love to meet Beth but if this is too soon, if it's too complicated, I understand. Are you prepared for her reaction? Really?"

"Absolutely not. Doesn't change anything. So, we'll be there Tuesday night." I said resolutely to close the subject. "Is this gonna be alright with your family?" I asked obviously too late. I should've run all this by him first. I wish they made a pill for impetuous behavior.

He laughed a little. "Well of course. However, I did have to convince my mother that you aren't a clairvoyant today."

"Come again."

"She didn't know you were on the cell with Dad. —When I got home, I found my cell on the floor and I noticed the time you rang." He paused and took deep breath. "Thank you for thinking so quickly. I can't believe I'll see you in a little over two days."

"Is there a hotel close by?"

"You're not staying in any bloody hotel. You're staying here with me."

"Preston, I will not impose on your parents like that."

"It's a big house, Adena. Plenty of room. Besides, my house is here too."

"*Your* house?"

"Yes, Love. You didn't honestly think I'm pushing thirty and permanently residing with my parents, did you? I've just been staying here for Mum and Dad."

"Well, I didn't know." Although I had kind of wondered about that.

I knew the farm house had been his great-grandparents' and passed along through the generations. He'd mentioned before that there were four cottages scattered about the property besides the main house, I'd just missed the fact that one of them was his.

I tried to picture it. It sounded…big. And apparently very old. His great-grandfather? To have that much family history in one home was strange to me. Our little stretch of road by the lake and the few homes that lined it held as much history but I'd never met a family so rooted into one house. And I realized that I could fill the Library of Congress with what I still did not know about Preston.

Sunday morning came and went with great news. Mr. Grace's bypass surgery went well and I could literally feel Preston's relief when we spoke. However, Beth and Trent would be home any minute. I felt as though six months had been crammed into two short weeks.

Now my most pressing dilemma. How was I going to tell Beth? Wait until we got on the plane trapped next to each other for eleven hours and casually blurt out, *By the way, I've been having an affair and I'm taking you to my boyfriend's house to meet his family.* Owen was right. My profound stupidity would someday put me in an early grave.

I never liked the idea of getting comfort or courage from a bottle but I poured a glass of wine at one o'clock in the afternoon and went to sit in my sanctuary. I tried to occupy my mind with lesser things. Like what to pack. Hot and humid in High Springs, the mosquitoes were horrible and everything felt sticky. Do you need a jacket in London in the summer? I knew it would be cooler, but hadn't really given it much consideration. Something trivial to concentrate on was better than dwelling on the things I dreaded.

But before I could give the trivial things more thought, I heard the familiar rumble of Trent's diesel engine pulling into the driveway. My heart pounded against my ribs like a caged monkey fighting to be freed from the bars. Nearly hyperventilating, I chugged the remaining wine in my glass, ran upstairs and locked myself in my bathroom like a big coward. I had to get it together before I talked to him.

I breathed in deeply, let it out slowly, and repeated it until the wild monkey in my chest went to sleep. I blew out one last breath and braced myself, squared my shoulders like a prizefighter who was just about to step into the ring for the match of his life. When I went downstairs, Beth and Trent were just coming in the door with a second handful of luggage.

"Hey, you two. How was your trip?" My voice, surprisingly steady.

Trent stretched and yawned, tussled his almost black hair then walked past me without so much as a glance, apparently already angry that I hadn't discussed the trip with him *before* buying the non-refundable tickets.

Beth wrapped me in a hug typical of a kid who missed her mother for two weeks. Or at least one who was taking her to England.

She made a mockingly tired face, her tongue wagging and dropped her bags at her feet. She wrinkled her nose. "Dang! It smells like bleach and paint in here. You get the place to yourself and ... Gah! You're so boring!"

Wasn't the first time I'd heard that.

We lugged her bags upstairs and right away, she started rummaging through the bottom of her closet. Ironically, everything that appeared to be a forgotten heap on the floor was all of her favorite clothes. The clothes on hangers were the things she never touched. I took a seat at the foot of her bed just watching her. My little girl nearly grown. Seventeen years gone by in a flash.

She dug one garment after the next from the cramped space and threw her questions at me just as fast. "What should I bring? Have you packed yet? Are we going anywhere fancy?"

"No, I haven't packed yet; bring something nice just in case. And I thought maybe we could go into Gainesville to do a little shopping for the trip."

If her smile could have gotten any wider, it would have, but it was already ear-to-ear. She spun around and kicked a pile back into her closet as her answer. If you ever need to find a way into the heart of a teenage girl just take her to the mall. Unfortunately, the mall wasn't going to make *this* any easier.

I walked quietly to my room to talk to Trent, but when I looked in, he wasn't there. No big surprise. I went downstairs and down the hall to his office. His stereo was on but I could also hear that he was talking to someone. It only confirmed what I already knew. There was nothing left. No spark, no butterflies, no real love. We did love each other, but it was not the kind a marriage needs.

I had to knock because the door was locked. A minute passed before he stuck his head and one thick shoulder out meeting me with a crabby glare. "What's up?"

"Well, hello for starters." I couldn't help but be annoyed.

"Oh, hey." He leaned further into the hallway and gave me a half-ass hug.

I shrugged him off. "Jesus, Trent, don't bother. You don't have to humor me."

"What the fuck is your problem?"

"Don't you dare talk to me like that." I perched my hands on my hips for the all out war I'd been expecting over the trip. "I was gonna tell you I'm taking Beth to the mall. But I can plainly see you don't give a shit so go ahead and hide in your little cave!" I turned to stalk away.

"Hold up, Dee," His laziest version of my name. Pretty soon he'd just grunt in my general direction. "I'm sorry. Didn't mean to be so nasty."

I stood there looking down at the long blue rug in the hallway. Trent and I had never been that way with each other. Years of indifference yes, but flat out nastiness? No. This was new territory for both of us.

"What is wrong with you, Trent?"

"I don't know. I just got a ton of shit on my mind. My back is killing me and I'm tired."

"So you don't have any questions about the trip?" I looked up at him surprised that he hadn't brought it up yet.

"You should go. Better you than me." He half smiled. "I can't stand to be with Owen for more than five minutes. If you can hang with him for a week, more power to ya."

"We'll be gone for ten days."

"Pack some comfy shoes to keep up with Beth and some Tylenol to put up with Owen." He smiled unevenly, an unfamiliar expression from him. He seemed to be a little annoyed that he had to speak to me. Then I noticed he still had his phone in his hand.

"Humph, I'll let you cram that thing back to your ear. God forbid it not be fused to the side of your head!" My phone rang. Damn fine timing for what I'd just said.

"Hello?"

"Hi, Love. Can you spare a moment?"

"Hey, Preston!" I smiled with true enthusiasm not a foot from Trent's face.

He stood straight as a board, chest puffed out like a rooster, "Who the hell is Preston?"

All of a sudden, I had his full attention.

I stamped my foot and started screaming. "Ya know, it's amazing how the thought of another man pissing on your territory wakes you up! Other than that, you couldn't care less!"

"Adena, *what* are you doing?" Preston's voice was pleading.

"You didn't answer my question, Dee! Who is it?"

"Someone who doesn't ignore me, Trent!"

"Whatever makes you happy!" He slammed the door so hard a few flecks of paint fell from the ceiling.

I stormed out of the house and sat in the car so I could talk in private. If I knew Beth at all, she was changing her clothes before we left. Preston let me rant until I calmed down again. I felt like such an idiot complaining to *him* about the spat with Trent. Insanity at its highest.

I cranked my car, cracked my window and turned the air on to chase away the stifling heat then I saw the front door open. I dropped my cell into my purse just as the car door opened.

Beth sat down next to me and buckled up. "Who was that?"

"Preston." My heart skipped a beat just to mention his name in front of her.

"Sweet name. Who is it?"

"A friend." I said safely for the time being. "We're going to see him while we're in London."

"Oh. Is that Owen's cousin?"

"No. But he knows Owen." I said truthfully.

"Where exactly are we going anyway? London is *freaking* huge! Like where are we staying and stuff?"

I could tell she wasn't looking forward to staying in a house full of Owen's family. She liked him but he really loved to yank her chain.

"Umm...at the cottage." This was something Preston had mentioned and I didn't really have any details to add.

"The cottage? Mom could you possibly be more vague?" Some sudden understanding seemed to come over her. "Oh, good grief! We're not taking some weird camping trip are we? I'm too old for that. I finally get to go to London and you're planning to torture me in the great outdoors! That's what you meant when you said this trip wasn't gonna be like I expected wasn't it?"

A good old fashion teenage tirade was beginning to brew until I told her there wasn't enough room at Chancey's house, (Owen's cousin) so we'd been invited to stay at the Grace's house instead. She needed no further explanation and was just happy to go.

The best place to begin is always the beginning. I made my way turn after turn as if I'd driven the route a hundred times. A permanent map inside my head. Sitting there like an empty ghost, the front of the hotel looked almost as it did the day I ran in from the rain. The glass doors were boarded shut with caution tape that said KEEP OUT. I parked behind it where the balconies *used* to be. It looked as if a giant monster had taken a swipe with his colossal claw at the center of the building from top to bottom.

Being there again made my skin feel too small for my body.

She gasped. "Oh, wow. I saw this on the news."

I watched her examine the broken façade for a few short moments then pulled away in search of the mall.

"Why did you bring me there?" I could hear in her tone that she suspected something was up.

"I'll explain later. I haven't eaten all day. You hungry?" I wasn't ready. It wasn't the right time yet, if there were any such thing.

After getting a couple egg rolls and some stir fry from the Food Court, we found a table and sat down to eat. Unusually quiet, she picked at her fried rice.

She finally spoke, pushing her tray away. "Is everything alright with you and Dad?"

I sighed and gave up on my eggroll after one bite. "No. Not really." I suddenly lost my appetite and my stomach clenched into a knot.

"I heard him yell at you. Sounded like he started it."

"Actually, I did I guess. We didn't mean for you to hear."

"No big deal. I'm just not used to it. —You think things will get better?"

I tried to choose my words carefully. "I don't think so. Your father and I still care about each other. I don't think that'll ever change."

"But..." Her big blue eyes narrowed infinitesimally.

"But we're not in love anymore, Beth. We've changed and I can't even remember when it happened. It's hard to describe."

"I'm seventeen. I think I can grasp the concept." She slumped in her chair, stared at her soda as she trailed the tip of her little finger through the condensation on the plastic cup. "Does Gavin already know something I don't?"

"Why do you ask?"

"We do talk, Mom. He called me late just a few nights ago and was *way* too nice. Before we hung up, he just said, 'Be prepared for things to change.'"

Words failed me. Pandora's Box had been cracked and I was just waiting for all things wicked to rain down on me.

"Are you and Dad getting a divorce?" She finally asked the daunting question that was apparently weighing on her mind.

"We haven't talked about it." It wasn't a yes or a no, but it was still the truth.

"That's not an answer Mother. Tell me what *you* want." She said it low so no one else could overhear but had we been alone she would've shouted the words. And she always reserved the word Mother for when she was angry.

"What do *I* want? Hmm —I can't actually remember the last time someone asked me that, so forgive me if this takes me a minute." I took a long drink of my tea and gathered my thoughts. "Well, for starters, I want a man who will allow me to be there for him and not build so many walls that he's unapproachable. And Beth, please don't hate me for this but I *want* to be in love again. Am I wrong for wanting that kind of happiness?"

She sat up a little straighter and it took her a long moment to answer. "Sorry. Just thought you guys..." She shrugged a little but didn't say anything else.

"Your dad is a good man sweetie. We've just grown apart." A long silence made me nervous. Just getting that far was horrible and if I had any guts at all, I'd just blurt the whole truth out and get it over with, like ripping a band-aid off. I opened my mouth to do just that but she spoke before my brain and my tongue cooperated.

"This is kinda weird." She smiled weakly. "I mean... me and you talking about this. It's like our first adult conversation." She glanced up into my eyes and looked down again. I reached across the table for her hand.

"I always want to be able to talk to you. I know you're practically grown. In some ways you're more mature than a lot of adults I know."

"That's not saying much. You hang out with *Owen*." We both laughed and some of the tension lifted.

"Are we okay, Beth?"

"We'll always be okay. It's just gonna to take some getting used to."

Beth could walk anyone into the ground. The shopping pro that she is, she had no problem picking out several new outfits. I picked out some nice shirts not really into it, wondering how I'd be able to get into phase two of what I needed to tell her. But she fussed at me for being *horrifically lame* and picked out a few things for me.

"Here try these." She tossed a pair of jeans over the dressing room door.

"These aren't Levi's," I said disappointed, holding them up to look at them.

"Would you *please* get over the friggin Levi fetish already? You already own like twenty pair of the exact same pair of pants."

"Because I like them." I argued and pulled them on.

"You'll like those, Mom. Crap, just put the damn pants on!"

She'd never cursed in front of me before and I couldn't help but laugh. But being the mom that I am, "Watch your mouth. —I'll give you permission to cuss me out later."

"You can be beyond weird sometimes." She mumbled over the door.

I'd thought we were done but then she wanted to shoe shop. Preston called me back, worried and under the false impression that we might actually be done by now. Three hours later. He helped me pass the time while Beth was in and out of view keeping a very patient sales clerk busy looking for her size in no less than five different pairs of shoes. She began to comment on how I was ruining her shopping buzz by talking on the phone.

"Who is that anyway?" She asked as she admired the sandals on her feet.

"It's Preston."

"*Again?* What is he? Your boyfriend now?" She laughed as she pulled the shoes off.

I must have frozen for a fraction of a second. She'd been joking obviously but she did a double take at my expression then her smile slowly dropped into a look of shock and even worse, disappointment.

She nodded her head, pursed her lips, and jammed her feet into her own shoes. "Okay, I get it. So, is this the part where you give me permission to cuss you out or should I just take the liberty and do it anyway?"

She stormed off, her blonde curls bouncing down her back. I followed but didn't speak, trying to give her a chance to absorb it first. Nothing but cold dead silence lingered between us as we walked through the scantly lit parking lot. Once in the car, I opened my mouth to explain but she turned the radio up to drown me out. I hated that she was so angry but I let her have her moment. Ready or not, the time had come. I made my way back to the hotel, the place where the irreversible changes in my life were born.

She reached over with a jolt and turned the radio off. "*Why* do you keep bringing me here?"

"I'll tell you but first -go ahead and let me hear everything you have to say. I won't interrupt."

She bit her lip and tears fell down her cheeks. "Does Dad know? Is this why he's so pissy all the time?"

I cringed at her choice of words. "No, that's still a mystery to me." I gripped the steering wheel to remain upright. This was by far one of the worst experiences of my life, my actions causing pain for my children and I hated myself for that.

"Does he have a girlfriend?"

"It would be easy to say it's possible, but I don't have any *real* reason to believe that."

She sat so still for a few minutes then slowly turned, her arms crossed—accusations flying like arrows from her eyes. "*This* is what Gavin was talking about isn't it."

I closed my eyes and nodded.

"Then why did you wait to tell *me*?" The look of betrayal marring her beautiful features was something I never wanted to witness again.

"Gavin came home when Preston was there."

"So this *man*... has been to our house? —Mom, that's like —ten different kinds of wrong!"

I felt like I was going to be sick. I rolled my window down for the moist night air. She sat quiet for a long while. Her tears stopped and she sat up a little straighter, bracing herself.

"Would you please just tell me why we're here?"

I looked through the windshield at the building before us and told her in length, from the time I left the house that Sunday. Meeting him, the never-ending storm, the tornado. His protection of a woman he didn't even know. I explained the best I could, of my awakening, of the feelings that even I didn't understand. (Of course, I edited for her sake.)

Once I finished, she didn't look quite so stung anymore. She peered through the encroaching darkness, scrutinizing the mangled exterior of the building.

"You were *in* there?"

I hadn't expected her reaction, throwing herself across the seat to cling to me, sobs wracking her chest. I realized through the strength of her embrace what she now understood. The mortality of a parent.

Her persistent sobs strangled any words she attempted until finally she stopped trying altogether.

I rubbed her shoulder and smoothed her hair as she cried and tried my best to explain. "Sweetheart, I didn't bring you here to scare you. I just wanted you to understand the reason behind me staying here long enough to even begin to get to know another man. It wasn't on purpose; I wasn't looking for anyone. It just turned out this way. Now it's something I can't undo."

She cried until the tears could no longer flow. Eventually the sobs began to fade away. I held her close until she was ready to talk again.

At last, without letting go of me she whispered, "He tried to protect you. —I could have lost you forever. But by the grace of God, I didn't."

Grace of God indeed. That's the way I saw Preston. A blessing in my life, not some sordid temptation. And that's exactly why I felt the need to tell her; to allow her to meet him.

10

WHEN I WALKED IN THE house, I could see the light on in Trent's office at the end of the hall. The door was ajar so I peeked in. He was sound asleep with a blanket on his sofa which meant he was there for the rest of the night. I closed the door and it clicked too loud.

Dammit!

"Dee? Is that you?"

I opened the door again. "Yeah. Didn't mean to wake you."

"It's okay. Got a minute?" The only place to sit was the couch or his desk chair. I sat next to him on the floor. "I'm sorry I was such a pain before. You didn't deserve that."

Actually, I did and I knew it. He just didn't know why.

"It's alright. I'm sorry, too." I pulled my knees up to my chest and wrapped my arms around them. "Is everything okay? You don't seem yourself lately."

He sighed and sat up wincing from the pain in his back. A cord from a heating pad fell down from under the blanket. "I've been having a hard time working through some... things. Some tough decisions I have to make." He looked away as he finished.

"Well can we talk about it? Maybe I can help."

"Not tonight. Maybe... when you get back." He sounded strange, but at least he was talking.

"Trent, we used to be so close. Whatever's bothering you, you can tell me. You'd be surprised at what I'd understand."

The idea that maybe he *was* seeing someone else crossed my mind. Of course, that would be hard to bring up. Maybe he just wanted out. Maybe he knew, just like I had for too long now, that peaceful complacency is not the same as getting along much less being in love.

He leaned forward and kissed my cheek the way he sometimes did in the morning, usually when we passed at the coffee pot. I honestly couldn't remember the last time we shared a real kiss. I smiled just a bit. The little peck still held *some* affection. I had no doubt whether I was cared for by Trent. I knew I was, as did he by me. Some things are simply unchanging. The sky will always be blue, the sun will always be hot, and water will always be wet. Trent and I would always be friends. We would always be family. We would always care.

My eyes watered but I struggled to keep them from brimming over.

He looked at me and his face finally softened into the Trent I had known for so many years. The kind and understanding softness of my best friend.

He smiled and for the first time in months, the gesture touched his eyes. "You know I'll always love you, Dee."

"And I'll always love you." It was the truth but not the same love I used to have for him. With no more control than any other time lately, the tears flooded over and spilled down my face.

He leaned closer, his eyes on my lips and I froze. In an instant, so many thoughts went to battle in my head. I should let this happen. He's my husband. I owe it to myself and to him to know.

But Preston. I love *him*.

No! I was ready to back away but just as he leaned toward me, he winced again and reached quickly to grope at his back. I wiped my face hastily and stood up; thankful our lips did not meet. The scant flicker of what might have been the last shred of intimacy left me feeling as if I'd nearly cheated on Preston. How backward my life had become.

"Did you take anything for it?" I asked.

"Couldn't find anything." He stretched out again and readjusted the heating pad beneath him.

I went upstairs and found his muscle relaxers in the bathroom, brought him a bottle of water and held the little pill out in my hand.

"How did you hurt it this time?" I asked, genuinely concerned.

"Draggin damn shingles onto Mama's roof."

"That would do it I guess." I pulled a small folding table next to him, picked his phone up off the floor along with the remote to the TV and put them there within easy reach.

"You're too good to me." He smiled up at me and took hold of my hand. His words cut me in half.

I chewed nervously on the inside of my cheek. "You all set?"

"Yeah. I think I can go to sleep."

I turned off his desk lamp. "Night, Trent."

"Thanks for putting up with me." He said as I turned to walk away.

"Same here." I pulled my phone from my pocket and wiggled it at him. "If you need anything, just ring." It made him smile.

I went up to my room to change into my nightgown. While going through my closet, I came across Preston's blue shirt. I held it close and tried to feel him in it. I started to put it back but I noticed there was something in the pocket. I reached in and dug out the little shadow. It was a guitar pick —a faux tortoise shell look to it, brown and mottled. I turned the tiny hello from Preston between my fingers and examined it; guessing that he had to have left it there on purpose. I hadn't noticed it before.

I promised to call him when I got home but it was already three in the morning there. The thought of him being so far away was too bizarre. I picked up the phone wishing Preston and I didn't have to converse so much through speakers. But it was by far better than nothing. He'd texted me four times since Beth and I left the mall. So I called him despite the hour.

"Hello, Love." His voice was heavy.

"Sorry it took so long. Did I wake you?"

"No, I couldn't sleep." But his words were weighted with exhaustion. "The word angry probably doesn't quite carry enough weight, I'd imagine?"

"You have no idea." I explained the whole process we went through.

He blew out a nervous breath that made a distorted crackle through the phone. "I'd wager she bloody well hates me. This is going to be an interesting visit. What should I do?"

"Just be yourself, Preston. It'll just take time."

"Alright, Love. You're flying this B-52. Hope you know how to land it."

"Bombs away." I said. He chuckled sleepily and yawned. "Oh, I almost forgot. I found it."

"Found what, Love?"

"A little brown guitar-pick."

"Aha! I caught you wearing that bloody blue shirt! Where the hell is Trent?"

Suddenly he was wide-awake. He made me laugh. Now I understood why he'd left it there. It was nothing less than a booby trap.

"He's sleeping in his office. I'm not wearing it anyway. I was just…looking at it." I played with the little pick in my hand.

"Good. You've no idea how sick I've been all day thinking of him climbing into bed with you. I didn't know it would be this hard." He exhaled deeply, sounding like a huge release of built up torment. "I can't wait to hold you, Adena."

"Can't wait to be held."

I went to talk with Beth. I explained what happened with Mr. Grace, how Preston wanted me there, and the role Owen played in our trip.

Knowing the whole truth calmed her to some small degree.

I shared the picture of Preston and Kelley he'd left on my nightstand and explained what he was doing and how she *listened*. I could actually see her heart melt as she stared at the gut wrenching image.

"This is his little sister. She's adopted." I started to say she was also his god-daughter but I still didn't know the story behind that so I kept it to myself.

"Seeing that makes it very hard to be mad. And…I guess… I'm not really *mad* at anyone, just the situation. It's just really…strange."

"I understand." I looked at the picture again then looked at Beth for her reaction. "You know she looks a lot like you when you were little."

"Trust me. I noticed. We could be like -sisters to someone who didn't know us. It's weird, huh."

"A little." I admitted, remembering the strange dream I'd had of Kelley. It didn't hold a candle to hearing and seeing GG though.

Beth looked at me again then looked at the floor, but I could tell she actually saw nothing as she spoke. "Things really are about to change, huh?"

I sighed. "Yes, baby. With or without Preston, things between your dad and me —they have to change."

She didn't say anything else and I knew she was ready to be alone with her thoughts so I left her in her bed with a kiss goodnight and another apology for being human. I went back to my room and crawled beneath the sheets so emotionally drained, I fell asleep quickly and deeply.

Hours into my slumber, my eyes popped open and my heart gave a grand lurch at the all too familiar feel of Trent's embrace. Not that I had any reason to fear him. I just wasn't of a mind to be accepting his advances. I knew that without question. Why now, when we haven't touched each other for the better part of a year. But calm washed through me, as he lay there with his arm over my waist, as though trying to offer comfort for some horrible tragedy that I didn't yet know about. He adjusted his legs closer to mine and I realized two things at once. One, he wasn't under the comforter with me, it was too tight behind my legs where his weight pushed it down. Two, he was still wearing his jeans. I heard the unmistakable rustle of denim when he moved his leg.

I heard him whisper in the dark. "I don't think I'll ever be ready."

Ready for what?

He kissed my shoulder and lay there holding me for about an hour. His quiet whispers told me, I wasn't supposed to hear him nor even be aware that he was there.

When had our marriage become this charade? When did we start pretending that simply not being at each other's throats like so many other couples we knew was good enough? When did we settle for this thing less than being in love? I didn't know the answers to any of my own questions. I only knew it had happened too long ago to repair.

I fully expected my heart to respond, a tear to fall, *something* for God's sake. But I had no reaction. I just waited, consciously bidding the air to go in and out of my lungs until at last, with the one little peck on the cheek, my husband rolled out of our bed and returned to his office downstairs.

The most ominous feeling saturated every inch of my being- that in his own way, Trent was trying to tell me good-bye. Neither of us will want to intentionally hurt the other. So it begged the question: Who would do it first?

I had a feeling it would be me. And I dreaded it.

Trent was a good man. A good husband. A good father. A hard worker. A good son to his parents. He was a good friend to me. My whole life, he was a wonderful friend to me.

We rode our bikes along the levee when we were too young to drive. When he got a dirt bike, I was the first to ride along to the store and we shared one of those old Frostee rootbeers. When he got his driver's license and his father let him use the old Ford they'd used on their farm for hauling hay, Trent came to ask Daddy if he could take me to Big John's, a burger joint in Ferriday. I was so excited when Daddy had said yes. We shared a chocolate malt in the cab of that old Ford. And later, when he drove me home, we shared our very first kiss under the carport just before I went inside.

I can remember feeling so in love, so positively high on the way past my parents' watchful eyes then scurrying down the hall to my room where I could woo over my dark-haired angel in private.

We spent our entire youthful existence on each other. Dating, college, starting a family, seeking and building careers. And at some point on that wonderful journey together, one or both of us had taken an exit that took us off of the 'together highway'. Trent spent more and more time at work. It happened gradually. We stopped having time for each other. We laughed less together. We learned less together. We shared less together. Until at some point in time, and I do not recall that moment, that there simply was no more *together*.

This not only affected Trent and me, it affected our children as well. There was always some impending doom waiting someplace else if Trent didn't get on to the next project, be it a condo, a ground breaking ceremony, a hotel, a new city building, or simply a house in some random subdivision a few towns away. Which very simply meant he missed out on a lot for his kids. Sports, recitals, parades and musicals- all those school related events the kids get excited over; those times where good ole' mom and dad pull out the cameras and grin like idiots with pride. Yes, most of those moments, he missed. Hell, —he even missed two planned family vacations.

I don't say these things to vilify the man. No, far from it. Trent is the hardest working man I've ever known apart from my own father. He loves me and he loves his children. I just wish I knew when he stopped enjoying life, when he stopped talking to me, when he stopped wanting to know every single detail of his children's lives. When did he give up everything he used to live for to chase down another dollar? When did the company he built become his first priority- his replacement family?

If I'd known these details years ago, perhaps I would have been able to fix it. Perhaps I wouldn't be in this predicament now. Perhaps I would still be in love with my husband.

Or maybe, just maybe- meeting Preston was inevitable.

My conscious mind tried for an indeterminate length of time, to reason out why Trent had come to bed and then walked away. Even so, my thoughts filled with nothing but Preston before long and consciousness slipped away again. He came so naturally to my dreams to hold me once again and I could see his beautiful pale green eyes smiling down at me. The most exquisite visions of him filled my oblivion, taking me away from the pitfalls of reality. My craving to have him next to me had reached an agonizing degree.

The day he left, I had no idea when I would see him again. My only time frame was, as soon as he could come back, he would. Every night I dreamed of him. Restlessness filled my waking hours. It's difficult to wait for something when you have no clue as to when that monumental moment will finally arrive.

Preston seemed just as excited as I was about Beth and me coming to visit. It gave me a small measure of peace to know, he was waiting, too.

Waiting…

Everything in and beyond our universe revolves around the intangible concept of time. Memories, both good and bad, a mark permanently recorded into our minds of times gone by. Hopes, dreams, prayers of events yet to come. The future. The things we wait for. The present is oddly the hardest measure of time for me to grasp. It's lost immediately moment by moment to history. However, it is the *now* moments that seem to rule how fast or slow time goes by.

In the few blinks, Preston and I spent together, I could think of no time we wasted. There was the basic human factor of having to sleep. But even sleep had been glorious with him and waking in the middle of the night with his arms still around me, would remain burned into my memory for as long as I walk this earth. Now that I knew I'd see him soon, it made me wonder how I thought I'd be able to wait indefinitely.

Owen popped in around two o'clock Monday afternoon and Trent suddenly decided his back felt good enough to go check on a nearby job site. I knew he was lying. I could tell by the way he walked that his back still bothered him. He just didn't care much for Owen and he never made much effort to hide it, which explains why Owen had such horrible names for him. But Trent really was a nice person. Most of the time.

"You packed yet?" Owen asked from the counter in the kitchen.

"Almost. Well, *I* am. But I have to unpack some of Beth's. She looks like she's moving to a deserted island." I busied myself, wiping down the already clean counters.

He chuckled, but then huffed to get my attention. "Would you knock it off? You're gonna scrub the blue color off the damn tiles."

I gave up, tossed the yellow sponge in the sink and dried my hands. "Thanks again for asking me to go."

"Don't mention it. I know you literally put up with me, Dena."

"Oh, you know I love you." I propped my elbows on the counter and gave him an honest smile.

"You're just saying that 'cause I'm making it easier for you to see Sugar Britches." He sang the last two words. I lost it! He really knew how to make me laugh.

I couldn't wait to tell Preston *that* one. It's really gonna make him squirm.

Owen pressed his hands together staring at the tips of his fingers, an atypical serious expression on his face. "Dena, are you sure you're not setting yourself up for heartbreak? You do realize you barely know him."

I'd been waiting for one of them to say it. If I had to guess, it would have been one of the kids to brandish this particular razor's edge of how there was no way Preston and I could love each other in such a short space of time. I couldn't explain it in any case. I shrugged my shoulders in response to his concerns.

He opened my laptop and looked at me. "Can I use this? I want to send Chancey an email real quick."

That would be his cousin in Redbridge that we were supposed to be visiting.

"Sure. Hey, are you gonna hang out here for a while? If I don't help Beth, Preston's gonna think she's there to stay. I'll just be a minute."

"I ain't goin anywhere. I'm hungry."

I rolled my eyes. "Help yourself."

I went to help Beth sort out the difference between needing to bring something and all twenty of her *what if we go here* scenarios. After twenty minutes, I finally got her down to two suitcases.

"Oh! Put this in there before you zip it." She tossed a bottle of Red Door at me and the top came loose in my hands. I looked down at my shirt and saw the amber liquid spreading, immediately followed by an all out assault on my sense of smell.

Upon my reentering the kitchen, Owen slammed my laptop. After raising two teenagers, I know the look of *I wasn't doing anything wrong* when I see it.

"Everything okay?" I asked warily.

"Yep," He got up and helped himself to a glass of tea, took a long drink and cocked his head to the side. "I was just wondering —just purely out of curiosity. What does Preston do for a living?"

"His family owns a pear orchard. They make this unbelievable brandy. And, his uncle raises Thoroughbreds. He talks about the stables a lot, but I'm not exactly sure if he actually works with the horses. He's over there a good bit with his uncle when he calls, so..." I shrugged a little, "I guess he at least helps."

He sucked air through his teeth, a truly nerve plucking sound then turned to put the tea pitcher back in the fridge. Without closing the lid. This annoyed me to no end but I kept my mouth shut. I noted the angst in his mannerisms from my peripheral vision as he leaned into the counter watching as I unloaded the dishwasher.

"So what does *he* do? Pull his weight with the family business? That's it?"

I stacked one of the plates onto the counter a little too aggressively at his tone. "I guess, Owen. Isn't that enough?"

He held up one hand, advising me to hold my temper. "So you don't really *know*. Do you?" He rolled his head *and* his eyes -looking a tad too much like a person possessed. "Oh, my God, Dena! That is so cliché."

Huh? "*What* is?"

"It's the mystery. He's the suave debonair man of mystery with his precious little foreign accent. –He's James Bond. He's Sean Connery!"

He begins to laugh, guffaw actually.

"Oh good grief! *What*?" I asked.

"I don't know," He pauses to breathe for a second, "Mr. Bean." Now he's all but rolling on the floor, laughing and snorting like a pig. Fitting I thought.

I stared at him for a second before slamming the dishwasher shut. A handful of silverware in my hand, I yanked the corner drawer open and tossed them in, not bothering to sort them into their designated slots, most of my anger due to what he was implying. The really crappy part of that? What he implied was true. I *didn't* know. Was Preston really just a man of mystery? Someone intriguing to hold my attention?

Of course not! Mr. Bean indeed. Owen's an idiot! Why do I even listen to him?

"Jesus, girl. I swear you trust people too much."

Enough was enough. "Christ sakes Owen, why do you care what he does all of a sudden? The conversation hasn't presented itself. Okay!"

He gawked at me, craning his neck like a half-strangled chicken. "Hasn't *presented* itself? What the hell do you two talk about every day? It's a one word response in most cases. It can't be that hard. Plumber, doctor, lawyer, writer, police officer —well technically I guess police officer would be considered two words. But then again... so is Serial Killer."

"Oh, *good* one. Hardy Har! I don't care. Nothing would change who *he* is. I swear —people spend all their energy treating each other like a job interview. What's so wrong with getting to know a person on the inside? His favorite color is blue. He loves the smell of leather. His favorite book is *The Old Man and the Sea*. His shoe size is 12. He loves the outdoors. He adores his little sister and everything she does. –And he's abnormally *happy* in the morning which happens to be the one and only thing that annoys me about him but I can so totally live with that! Anything else you need to know, Sherlock?"

He shrugged a little, giving up the third degree.

"Ya know, I'm surprised to hear this from you of all people, Owen. You and your, *I can love anyone regardless of their wrappings* thing."

He walked a little closer and put his hand on my shoulder. "No, I *do* get that part. But I also know he left you hanging for a week and I didn't like it. You looked like a damn marionette whose strings had been cut. I'm just pointing out that you *don't* know him and just... be careful. That's all." He leaned forward, sniffed me cautiously then leaned away covering his nose with the neck of his shirt. "Peter, Paul and Mary! You *stink!*"

"Sorry, way too much of Beth's perfume is all over me. —Listen Owen, I appreciate your concern. Really. But I know what I'm doing. Okay?"

"Alright kiddo. You know I'm here. One way or the other."

Preston gave me David's number, the man who picked him up to take him to the airport. All we had to do is be ready to leave at 5:30 in the morning. The house was clean, we'd finished packing, and I had little left to do. I sorted the silverware I'd tossed into the drawer as I would truly lose sleep over their disarray then started supper early to pass the time. With preparation, consumption and clean up, I managed to survive three more hours.

I went outside to tend to my flowerbeds just before dark and I was almost done weeding when my back pocket started to play *London Bound*, my new ring tone for Preston.

"Hello Love, you all ready to go?"

"Yes. But my clock seems to be broken. The hands are moving way too slow." In truth, they weren't moving at all since I threw it on the floor around two weeks ago. I walked through the patio door and down to the hallway bathroom to wash the dirt from under my nails.

"Adena...I ehm..." The apprehension in his voice made me nervous.

"What's wrong?" I dried my hands and went upstairs so Beth couldn't hear.

"Nothing really. I just never got around to telling you what I do for a living. You know a bit about what I do with my family, but not so much about me."

"*So*," Annoyed again. Not at him but at the reminder of Owen raising such a stink over me not knowing. And why Owen even bothered to ask about it in the first place was beyond me.

"Well, I just think it's...unusual that you never asked."

"You never *asked* me either. Would it matter to you if I were a waitress or a store clerk? Because I've done that too."

"Touché, I wouldn't care at all. Okay, here goes. I'm a male stripper at a night spot called Sugar Britches."

"You- are -not!"

"What makes you so certain?" He chuckled. And I could just see that grin of his.

"Sugar Britches. Owen called you that earlier today."

"I know. He called me that when we spoke. That chap can be downright unnerving at times."

"When you spoke? When did you talk to Owen?"

"Mmm...he said you were helping Beth sort her clothes. He answered your cell. He didn't tell you?"

"*No.* He seemed to have forgotten that." I ground my teeth. Now I knew what all his questions were about. I had a feeling Owen had a *Come to Jesus* meeting with Preston. Not literally, just drilling him over his intentions.

"So the only thing that gave me away was the name of the club?"

I laughed a little. "Yep. I've imagined you doing a strip tease or two since you've been away." I tried to sound sultry but to me it just sounded stupid.

"I'll strip for you Love, but you know very well, I never tease. You know I'm not that patient once my clothes are off." He pulled sultry off perfectly and gave me the quivers from head to toe.

"So, now that you've brought it up, what's the big mystery?"

"I write songs." He said it cautiously as if I would take it as some great offense or something. I looked up at the ceiling as if it might magically tell me what was wrong with him.

"Preston, have you hit your head today? Why the hell, would *that* be hard to tell me?"

"So, you're alright with that?"

My body actually convulsed with the sheer idiocy of our conversation. "Uh, yeah. Why wouldn't I be?"

He chuckled again and I heard him tuning his guitar. "No reason."

Then he strummed and plucked and picked out the most beautiful sounds from his acoustic, the first time I'd ever heard him play. If I wasn't mistaken, it was the tune he had hummed to me. I lay back on my bed, closed my eyes, and let his music fill me. I could see his music drifting behind the darkness of my lids —could actually *see* the musical notes –stretching and dancing upward and deeper into in the night sky then wrap themselves like ribbons around the moon.

After two or three minutes, the strumming slowed and faded but he said nothing.

"Wow! *That* was beautiful. Was that yours?" I asked opening my eyes slowly as if coming out of a trance, smiling as if I'd just had my arms around him.

"No, Love. That was yours." He made me cry. "Didn't mean to make you cry, Love." His whisper so full of love, I could nearly feel his breath on my ear. "Can you possibly feel my love across that vast ocean that separates us? I'm sending it to you now as much as I can. —I feel you inside of me every day. I dream of making love to you. —I wake missing you. —My heart aches to be near you. I miss so much running my fingers through your hair. —When I close my eyes, I can see us dancing in the rain. Close your eyes, Adena. Can you see it as well?"

I whispered, "Yes. I can see it."

"Then dance with me, Darling."

He sang the song we danced to that day in my backyard –*Raining on Sunday*. Eyes closed, I listened and we relived the memory together, swaying against each other in our minds.

He stopped singing. "I can hardly wait to hold you again. I've never felt so utterly tangled into anyone. And thank you for coming to be with me. You have to be the bravest person I know to do what you're doing all for the sake of love."

"Love is everything, Preston. Your love anyway."

"Then I shall give you everything." He whispered.

Tangled. It was the perfect word to describe it.

Beth came into my room. I quickly hid my face in my pillow and gripped my phone to my chest, clinging to the moment we'd just had. She stood silent although I was aware of her standing at the foot of my bed.

"You really love him don't you?"

The sound of her voice seemed to echo the confirmation that I was indeed painfully in love with another man. I held my tears in front of her but continued to hide my face, not wanting her to see me in such a state. The soft padding of her steps brought her to my side and she kissed my hair. With almost no sound, she retreated, my door clicked shut and I cried myself to sleep.

"Mom. Wake up." I heard Beth's voice in my ear and I felt a gentle shake of my shoulder.

I bolted upright thinking I was running late and managed to head-butt Beth, culminating in a loud crack as our skulls bounced off each other.

"Ow!" She grabbed the side of her head. "Re-*lax* already before somebody dies. Like *me* for example. It's only four o'clock."

I breathed a sigh of relief and rubbed my forehead. "Thanks, Sweetie. Sorry about the concussion."

"Whatever, Your royal Weirdness." She grumbled as she walked away.

Her sarcasm was usually a form of entertainment to me; she could be so absolutely comical. But this morning, I felt like I was in an elevator on the fortieth floor and descending too quickly. I'd see Preston today.

Of course, today of all days, my hair refused to cooperate. Not that I'd ever had much luck with my random wayward curls. I did the best I could with what nature so long ago cursed upon me by gathering it all up in a big barrette. It would have to do. My hands were shaking so badly I decided to wait and finish my eyeliner later for fear of taking an eye out. Beth had lain out one of the new outfits she picked for me (i.e. had a fit until I bought the clothes) along with a dressy pair of brown leather boots that were hers. I didn't have it in me to hear her fuss so I put it all on and went downstairs.

"Bagels are ready." She called from the kitchen.

"Is your dad awake?"

"Truck's gone." She gestured toward the red light on the coffee pot. There was about a cup left in the carafe.

"Nice of him to say goodbye." As I said it, Beth pushed a piece of paper closer to me that was sitting right in front of us on the counter.

Sorry, I didn't get a chance to say good-bye. Had to go to Tampa unexpected. Be safe and have fun.
Love ya'll.
T.W.

"Well, that was short and sweet."

"So what's new?" Her words dripping with disdain.

"Beth, don't be like that. You know he works his butt off." Defending him had become an unbreakable habit. Although, I did not miss the fact that he signed the note *T.W.* Trent Whittington is known far and wide as T.W. among various contractors, home goods stores, architects, every sort of subcontractor, etc. etc. –Not one person from back home, his family or mine, nor any of our friends much less myself has *ever* referred to him as T.W.

"Whatever." She followed with her usual eye roll that she picked up from me when she was two. I silently concurred and went to pour myself the last of the coffee.

Thanks T.W. I thought with an edge of bitterness as I took the first careful sip of hot coffee. Trent was in fact making this whole situation a bit easier for me to stomach.

Beth stood there looking at me and smiled. "You sure you want to add a dose of caffeine to those jitters you've already got?"

I really wanted to finish the cup of brew in my hands but I knew she was right. After pouring it down the sink, I turned the pot off, sat at the counter and proceeded to pick at a stubborn piece of grout rising too far from the tiles. I checked the clock on the stove. We still had half an hour.

She nibbled at her bagel a little then flipped one of her own stubborn curls from her eyes. "Mind if I ask what made you crack last night? I haven't seen you that upset since Grandpa Roger...well, you know."

I explained how Preston had wanted to *dance* with me. I didn't tell her everything he said. It was too private, too intimate. But it was enough to give her a glimpse of how wonderful he was.

Of course she rolled her eyes. "That is the corniest," she stopped and sighed a little "—but by far the sweetest thing I've ever heard." She giggled then and it surprised me. "It's kinda hard to stay mad when Dad makes it so friggin evident why you'd even consider getting involved with someone else." She picked up the short note he left us, balled it up, and tossed it into the garbage. "Who leaves a crappy note when their wife and daughter are going out of the country? —*Love ya'll, T.W.*" She mocked. "Gimme a break! What the hell am I? His stinkin' secretary?"

So she'd noticed it too. It gave me an uneasy feeling that she was somewhat okay with the situation simply because she was upset with her dad. It made me feel like I'd pulled the pin on a grenade and it hadn't exploded yet. It was too easy to see that despite the very words falling from her lips that she had not quite absorbed what was happening. All I could do was go along with her current mood and take it day by day.

Around half way through the flight, Beth laid one of her hands across mine. "You seem a little calmer now."

I sighed. "Yes. I am. I think."

Owen had to add, "That's because Lover Boy is only a few hours away."

I could have gone the rest of my life without him calling Preston *Lover Boy* in front of Beth. He could be such a clueless moron sometimes. I sighed and laid my head back. My stomach was literally hurting. Probably an ulcer.

Owen flicked Beth on her knee. "So, what do you think about his career? How cool is that?!" She looked at him, then at me; a question seated in her brows.

I raised my head off the headrest. "Oh yeah, I forgot about that. Preston told me ya'll talked. Why didn't you tell me?"

He pulled his shirt up and patted his hairy chest. "So shoot me. I asked the guy a few questions. Big ole' stinky deal."

I tried to find my happy place before I reached to slap him. "Preston's a songwriter. Blues mostly. I don't get why Owen wants to make a case to the Grand Jury over it."

"Hey, that *is* pretty cool." Beth mildly cooed.

"I hope you didn't give him the big brother act, Owen. That would really bother me."

He looked extremely guilty. "I didn't. *But*...I may have, out of curiosity...Googled him."

"You did *what*?"

"Sorry."

"You found him on Google?" Beth laughed and turned eagerly to get the scoop from Owen. "Ok, tell, tell, tell."

"Owen probably dug through every stinking link to find the right Preston Grace. Being the nosy old lady he is." I concluded.

"*Actually*, Miss *I-trust-everyone-who-smiles-at-me*, they are *all* about him. No digging required. —Writes songs my *ass*! You might as well be dating Elvis."

I whipped my head around so fast I almost gave myself whiplash. "What!"

Beth laughed hysterically and several very tired and annoyed looking travelers turned around to give us dirty looks.

"You're exaggerating, Owen. He didn't say anything like that to me." I whispered fervently but hushed.

"Well, not Elvis. He's known all over the world. Preston is just known all over Europe. They really like him over in Italy; lots of links in Italian. Thought that was kinda weird." He spoke casually while flipping through a Sky Mall catalog. "Ooh! A doggie potty. Wonder if I could get Spaz to use that?"

"You're going straight to Hell for lying. I hope you're aware of that."

He leaned over, squishing Beth uncomfortably between us and grinned at me. "I'm sure I will, but it won't be for lying. Can I sound out a list of what *you'll* be going to Hell for? Oh wait, I don't have to. We're on a plane to go see your *boyfriend!*"

If looks could kill, he'd be cold. He just laughed and I knew he was joking around to try to get on my nerves. Succeeding as always.

"Okay, I didn't Google him. He told me he's a songwriter yesterday. Just nervous about telling you is all. Modest I guess. Ya know, not wanting to toot his own horn. Just like you really. Which I still think is *stupid!*"

He got up and bowed to a few people still paying attention to us. "I'm a writer. Name's Owen. Good meeting you fine folks." He sat back down and looked at me. "See, it's that easy. Cause nobody gives a shit."

When the pilot let us know, we'd be landing soon, Beth flew to the window. We could see the glow from the lights on the ground. It was amazing to see the River Thames far below in person, although the ribbon of water was miniature from our perspective and since it was night, we could only imagine where else it wound across the land. Despite the thin hazy layer of clouds, London stretched out beneath us in grand majesty —millions of glittering lights as far as the eye could see piercing the darkness as though it were its very own galaxy.

Other tourists on the plane made their excitement clear when London Bridge, the blue lights of the London Eye and Big Ben came into closer view. Others merely glanced out their windows and smiled warmly at the recognition of home. But my happiness came from something else entirely. Somewhere down there, Preston was waiting for me.

11

MY HEART FLUTTERED AS the plane continued its descent. The cabin pressure changed making my ears pop then the wheels touched down with a series of loud chirps. I pulled out my compact, hastily finished my eye make-up and popped a tic-tac into my mouth.

Beth grimaced and rolled her eyes. "Jesus! You're making me sick!" But then she smiled a little and patted my knee "Sorry, this is just uber weird."

It went against everything in my nature to share this with her, but it was too late to second guess my decisions.

After a twenty minute taxiing to the terminal, another fifteen to get off the plane, a not so long jaunt through passport control and yet a rock solid hour to get our luggage and make it through customs even though we had nothing to declare. After all that, Owen led the way to the arrival hall where Preston and Chancey would be waiting. Thank God, he'd been through it all before.

I scanned the room for Preston but there had to be a person per every square foot of that room and chaos seemed to be the theme of the moment. I also didn't see anyone tall enough to catch my eye. Well, there was one that stood out, but seeing as how he had hot pink dread locks and a stud in his lip, I continued my search.

I hadn't expected those strong arms to wrap around me from behind and lift me off the floor but he did and in that one instant, my anxiety, my worries and my loneliness, evaporated. His delicious masculine scent and his warmth, no longer imagined. My toppled world was set right again. That one second seemed to stretch out into eternity until he put me down.

I spun on my heels to see him. What I saw made me laugh. There Preston stood wearing my LSU jersey and a purple Tigers baseball cap. I hugged him needing to know he was real.

"God, how I've missed you." He whispered discreetly in my hair before quickly letting me go, given our small audience.

Preston shook Owen's hand thanking him for his help then turned and looked down at Beth. "Pleasure to meet you." He smiled brilliantly but his apprehension was undeniable.

"Hey." She smiled only slightly timid and looked him over. Then she frowned.

Uh Oh.

"You meet the guy in Gainesville, home of *The Gators* and yet *you've* got him in purple and gold. —What is *wrong* with you Mother?" She smiled at him then gave me a wink.

That's my girl.

I reached up to touch a half-inch thick beard he'd grown. He was still beautiful, but it looked really different. Not being able to see his hair was strange too. He looked like any other country boy you might run into in any small town in Louisiana. Except his cap was too new and too clean and of course when he spoke.

"Hey, I see Chancey over at Costa Coffee." Owen gave me a quick hug. "Call me sometime this week." Then he looked at Preston and smacked him hard on his ass. "You too, Sugar Britches." He walked away cackling.

Preston shivered and turned bright pink from the neck up and Beth was about to lose it. I lightly gave her an elbow to the ribs. There wasn't a word in any language that covered how I felt.

When we got outside it was breezy, lightly raining and *cold* compared to the sweltering nights in Florida.

It was odd sitting on the left side of his red Range Rover without driving and although I did realize he was *supposed* to be driving on the left side of the clogged streets, instinct took over each time I saw headlights coming toward us. I gasped and grabbed the door handle every time, especially in the roundabouts. Yes, taking a round-a-bout going what I felt to be too fast in what feels like the wrong stinking direction is asking just a bit too much of the bladder. Preston was in stitches watching me.

Beth paid no mind as she was too busy taking in the night view of the gothic architecture of a few buildings, as well as the lights, cars and people. She gasped and took her camera out when Preston pointed out a colossal 17th century church, with its towering steeples and long narrow stained glass windows. She rolled her window down insisting it wasn't too cold to take in the smells as well. She rolled it up after a few seconds, admitting all she smelled was car exhaust and something along the lines of a wet dog. Preston laughed and explained the smell was actually a sausage vendor just outside of a pub we'd passed. Beth vowed not to eat *any* sausage while we were there.

Having maneuvered his way through the busy tangle of streets leading away from Heathrow, and a quick detour to satisfy Beth's eagerness to see at least a peek of the historic city, Preston took us on a route that seemed to loop around the main hub of London. The M25 motorway according to the signage of the thoroughfare we traveled on for about half an hour or so until jumped off at exit 26.

The buildings eventually began to thin; the lights grew farther apart as we approached the rural areas along the outskirts of London. Honey Lane, Ongor Road and on to Oak Hill.

About an hour had passed since we left the airport when we finally pulled off of North Road to the left onto a brick paved drive with two huge wrought iron gates with an elaborate scrolled G in the middle of each. I laughed louder than I'd intended. Preston was pushing a button on his visor when he looked at me a little bewildered.

"What on earth is so funny?"

I got myself down to a moderate chuckle, as the gates were almost open. "Graceland." Beth immediately started to giggle.

He looked confused but only for a second. "Oh, Elvis' gates. And my name's Grace." He snickered. "Dad will positively gloat over that. He's quite fond of Elvis."

We drove further up the brick drive; walls of stone on either side stood every bit of ten feet, nearly covered in green moss and ivy.

Preston had reached for my hand several times while he was driving, and was now practically sitting on his left hand, not wanting to make Beth uncomfortable. This was going to be a lot harder than I thought.

"Crap. My camera's dead." Beth mumbled from behind me.

"Already? What did you do, tape the whole ride here?"

"Record, Mother. Not *tape*. No one in the free world uses tape to record anything anymore." She whispered, "Jesus" but I heard her anyway.

I peeked over the leather headrest to find her unbuckling herself to reach over the back seat, then digging through one of her cases to put her camera away. Preston read my mind quickly and leaned over to sneak a kiss as quietly as possible and still watch where he was going.

His lips were on mine for only a fraction of a second and it wasn't nearly enough. Had my heart beat at all while we were apart? In comparison to the present moment, it didn't seem so. It didn't seem so at all.

As my heart found its proper place once again in my chest, Preston drove on past the parallel stone walls until the drive opened up into a wide courtyard paved with cobblestones lain out front and center of a huge three-story stone farmhouse. A massive chimney dominated the left side and it looked...old. Picturesque, *absolutely* and beautiful but incredibly old. The yellow glow emitting from the windows combined with the light mist in the air and the beautiful landscaping, made it look as though a Thomas Kinkade painting had come to life.

My heart beat double time. Or maybe it was a palpitation. In any case, I thought perhaps something may have been wrong with me. It took a moment for it to settle into a normal rhythm and the episode startled me as nothing quite like it had ever happened before. An extraordinarily strange feeling came over me as I looked at the beautiful old house. As I absorbed it, really. I wanted to touch the stones and feel them. I wanted so badly to go inside. To *run* inside and see — to see... The feeling fell away. It was, as I've already said, extraordinarily strange but it bears repeating. Something in the vein of, Déjà Vu is the closest I can come to describing the sensation.

Thankfully, Preston carried all of our bags to the door, insisting we stay put for a minute since it was raining. This gave me ample time to work my way through this bout of whatever-had-hit-me. He opened the door for Beth first, holding an umbrella for her and walked her to the door. Refusing to be ridiculously spoiled, I let myself out as it was only sprinkling.

Teena, Preston's younger sister, who really looked no older than Beth, flung herself outside, excited to welcome us; not so different from any southern homecoming. She never stopped trilling on about the plans she had for Beth. She's a little shorter than I am, around 5'6" with the same dark auburn brown hair as Preston. It fell loosely around her shoulders, straight, sleek, and all one length. Pretty as could be but her face was much softer and rounder than his.

"Let them in the door, Teena, we're bloody drowning out here." He fussed with the unmistakable edge of sibling annoyance.

"Oh alright, Preston! Aren't we just a delightful bucket of suck this evening." A vehement shrill shot back at her brother, which I was accustomed to from hearing Beth and Gavin's daily bickering.

I was amazed when I walked inside, the walls, the ceiling and floors, all of warm wood. The soft color of amber seemed to saturate the atmosphere. I laughed quietly when I spotted a photo hanging in the entryway; Teena must have been about two making Preston around nine. Even then, his hair seemed to fall carelessly where it wanted. He caught me looking at it and pulled me further down the long foyer until we reached a hallway that went both ways.

We made a left and stepped into a large open den where I could now see the big stone fireplace on the north wall, flanked by two towering and ancient looking black oak bookshelves that met the high ceiling. A matching pair of navy blue wingback chairs sat in front along with a love seat and a small round mahogany table in between them with an old style rotary phone.

The strangest feeling of Déjà Vu settled over me once again. The smells of the house seemed to fuel the feeling but almost as quickly as it came, the feeling passed. I soon simply chalked the odd experiences up to jet lag and lack of good sound sleep.

The house could have been a museum for fine antiques. A grandfather clock that stood at least eight feet tall with its heavy brass pendulum swinging back and forth stood in the center of the wall along the right side of the den. A cherry wood roll top writing desk sat in the corner by the fireplace and several other mismatched although magnificent pieces. However, a comforting harmony flowed with the hominess. I didn't feel as if I'd be walking on eggshells.

Preston tossed his keys on a small ebony table as if it were a five-dollar garage sale item and Teena perched herself on a short ornately carved credenza leaving me laughing inwardly at the thought of a museum curator gladly zapping them both with a stun gun for having treated the collected pieces with such blatant disrespect.

I looked up a simple white staircase and heard his mother making her way down. When I saw her, it nearly took my breath. Her hair, also auburn brown with a bit of silver shining throughout. When her eyes met mine, it was almost like looking into Preston's. The same stunning shade of blue-green. She was more reserved than Teena but every bit as gracious. She seemed genuinely happy to meet us but she looked weary. Her eyes and her very tired smile reminded me she'd spent most of her time at the hospital with her husband, Nate.

I heard Teena hammering Beth with a million questions about what all she'd like to do as Preston showed me to mine and Beth's room up the stairs. We made a left on the second floor, walked down the hallway, and stopped at the last door on the left. He gave the door a shove with his foot —I walked in and sat my purse and travel case on the bed. The door shut with a solid click and he had me in his arms.

He gazed into my eyes, looking at them one at a time. No words, just a gentle press of his lips to mine at first, then another, each a little more intense than the one before. His hands caressed the small of my back as he pulled me tightly against him. I thought my heart might stop for not being able to keep up with the erratic butterflies. His kiss quickened into growing passion, parting my lips and devouring me. His hands cradled my head with his thumbs splayed across each cheek, pulling me further into his kiss. A tiny whimper escaped as I delved into that mind melting moment and clung to the realness of him. Every single cell in my hands seemed to drink in the information I so desperately needed. I felt of his neck, his cheeks, his ears, his hair, his lips … right up until my knees buckled and I actually stumbled. He pulled away just a little and smiled at the heated flush in my cheeks. It was a little discomforting to be thirty-seven and know he had that effect on me. And now he knew it too.

"Whew! I thought that only happened in the movies." I said trying to steady myself and regulate my systems. At one point I could swear my heart wanted to breathe and my lungs were pulsing away.

Then Preston hit me with that seductive laugh of his that seemed to make every nerve in my body spark like hot copper wires. He kissed me once and smiled his most wicked smile, backing me up one step and again until I was leaning against the wall behind me.

"Better?" He whispered in my ear.

I tried to utter something in agreement, but it only came out in a shuttered sigh. I'd forgotten how good he was at this.

His lips brushed against my ear and it felt like a wild brush fire everywhere he touched me. The tip of his nose traced my jaw and his breath was warm against my neck.

"Mmm…what to do; what to do." He whispered then pulled away just a bit to take a deep breath. "If we do that again I won't be able to stop. And I'm nearly certain one if not more of the ladies downstairs is probably watching the clock down there."

I had to agree, though not happily. We settled for a hug that, thanks to Preston's bear-like strength, nearly cut off my oxygen, not that I could breathe anyway.

"Later?" He asked hopefully, eyes wide.

"I'd bet the house on that one."

He laughed and gave me one final peck as he opened the door. I still wasn't entirely steady on my feet but I managed to make it into the hallway.

At the other end of the hall, stood a little blonde haired girl with a white cotton gown clinging to her still wet body from a fresh bath, desperately struggling with a brush.

I gasped at the sight of her. "Kelley!" I knew she'd be there and it wasn't that she'd surprised me. No. She looked uncannily like my daughter. So much like Beth. I'd seen the resemblance before in the photo but there in person, I felt like I was in a time warp watching my little girl ten years ago.

Preston beamed with pride. Kelley hadn't noticed us right away as it seemed a particular knot had distracted her until she finally surrendered the war with it and glanced up. She waved the brush at him and ran to meet us. She looked up at me and smiled, even more beautiful in person and with one finger, she pointed at me and looked up at him with a question seated in her eyes.

"Ms. Adena?" She inquired looking up at him and he nodded once. "Hello." She said and she waved at me.

Goose bumps flushed my arms as I recognized her distinctive little wave with her pinky leading the gesture and realizing that there was no mistaking that it *was* her in my dream that morning that Preston had left.

"Hey," I waved back at her and smiled trying to bury whatever stunned reaction I would have naturally had. I couldn't stop wondering why? How could it be possible?

Preston took the brush from her and dealt with the knot she'd given up on, braided her hair loosely and pulled a ponytail holder off the handle of the brush to hold it together.

She asked him with scrupulous interest, "Where's Beth?"

He signed to her and said, "Downstairs."

She positioned herself between us and took hold of our hands pulling us along. I smiled down at the little angel between us and refused to be bothered by the vision I'd had of her. I was far too happy to just be there and meet her and the rest of Preston's family.

When we reached the bottom of the stairs, Kelley ran to Teena. Beth smiled and signed to her as she passed. Preston's mouth fell open at the sight.

"You didn't tell me she could do that." He whispered.

"When she was younger she belonged to a youth choir in church. They learned to sign the songs. She loved traveling to the nursing homes and she got really attached to this one sweet old lady who was hearing impaired. So she learned as much as she could so they could talk."

Kelley screamed with delight and giggled. She jumped up and down reaching for Beth's hair. Beth squatted down so she could touch it. She looked a little confused at first then Kelley signed back to her.

Preston chuckled. "Kelley likes Beth because they look alike. Blonde hair, blue eyes. She doesn't resemble any of us."

She and Beth were in their own little bubble sitting cross-legged on the floor looking far too much like sisters. The resemblance was flat out eerie but I kept any more comments about it to myself. I was the only person in the room who'd seen Beth as a child. Preston, Teena and Doreen would never notice the way I did.

Preston asked Teena what she had done with Beth's luggage.

"I put it back in the car. I thought she and I could bunk at your place and make plans for the week. It'll be like having a sister instead of *you*." She laughed and hooked her arm into Beth's. "Is that alright with you, Beth?" She poked her lip out and batted her eyelashes.

"Fine by me." Beth threw a glance at me then rolled her eyes. "Well, that is, if it's okay with the warden."

I rolled my eyes in turn and walked over to speak to her. I glanced around hoping to have a private chat with her but Preston appeared to be quietly chewing Teena out.

Beth clasped her fingers together, and began to bounce on her knees. "Oh, come on, Mom. *Please*. I'd rather hang with her and have *some* semblance of a cool vacation." She looked at Preston and quickly averted her eyes. "Honestly, the less I see, the better off I'll be. Gimme a break here."

It didn't make sense to me that she wanted to avoid seeing Preston and I together but at the same time leave us sleeping in the same house be it on separate floors or not. It made me uncomfortable to say the least.

I shook my head, "Beth, Preston already has all this planned. Let's not be a pain our first night here, okay?"

"Fine, whatever. We'll see what *they* say. —I thought we were supposed to stay at some cottage anyway." She folded her arms and waited.

Teena came back leaving Preston rubbing the bridge of his nose with his eyes clenched tight, apparent that she had successfully given him a headache. Kelly ran to Beth again to hold her hand.

"Beth," Teena began. "Preston and Kelly both have a room of their own here, so there's no reason we can't go. Is that alright?" Teena apparently ignored her brother completely.

Beth laughed in my face. "Ha! See you in the morning."

Preston took Kelly's hand and led her to her room. I couldn't miss the nasty glare he cast at Teena, knowing he shared my thoughts. He'd changed his previous plans, opting for Beth and me to stay at his parents and him safely tucked away at his place to avoid any awkwardness. At any rate, I didn't throw a fit for Beth to stay, I simply hugged her goodnight and told her which room was mine if she changed her mind.

Shortly after the girls left, Preston came back down the hall followed by Kelley stealthily tip-toeing in his tracks. He winked at me fully aware that she'd sneaked out of her bed. He jumped at her with a growl and grabbed her up setting her to squealing as he tickled her in mid-air over his head. He held her in front of him with her slipper-clad toes dangling just to his waist.

"Tell Ms. Adena goodnight. It's very late." She had her eyes on his lips as he spoke.

She held her hands straight out without a word and apparently it meant something important. He placed her belly-side-down on top of his head and she held herself stiff as a board. A little airplane flying high as they came closer. He paused in front of me, she waved and the plane ride continued until they disappeared down the long hallway to the right of the den.

Preston came back smiling after a few minutes.

"Safe landing?"

He nodded. "The wardrobe is empty if you'd like to unpack. I'll be up in a bit. I really have to tell you just one more thing. It's just..." He stopped and turned his head at the sound of a door creaking open down the long hallway.

"Poppy! You forgot to sing *Sunshine!*"

Poppy?

I stared across the room at Preston with new understanding and the way he pursed his lips explained even more.

He closed his eyes and wearily, not to mention worriedly, rubbed his forehead. "I'll explain, Adena. I'll be right up."

Wordlessly, I watched as he walked with his head bowed low down to Kelly's room. I stood next to the grandfather clock and leaned against the wall listening. He began to play his guitar and the words to *You Are My Sunshine* came out in a way I'd never heard them. The man could sing, no doubt about it. But why would he wait to tell me this now?

I left him to put her to bed and went upstairs to brush my teeth. The barrette felt embedded into my scalp after leaning against it all day so I took it out and let my hair bound heavily down, thankful for it to be loose again. After unpacking, I put on a pair of gold satin pajamas. I sat on the bed and looked at the room around me. Everything seemed so surreal.

Was I really in London? Was I actually sitting in this very room? The windows done up in Battenberg lace, the bedspread and pillows, in the softest blue and yellow toile with nostalgic scenes of children playing. I pulled the dainty accent pillows from the front of the old iron railed headboard and piled them neatly in the corner.

I did not feel as though I was in the home of strangers. Not at all. I was still a bundle of nerves to be sure. But it was more the *place* than anything. The house seemed to have a pulse of its own and something about it felt so good. Like a warm embrace.

After some consideration, I decided the place felt welcoming and comforting simply because it was. To anyone it would. I'd spent an entire day in a cramped seat on an airplane listening to the oddest of topics flow from Owen's lips. At this point, a hollowed out stump would have been just as lovely in my eyes. Especially if Preston was there.

As I sat on the bed, the diamond on my left hand caught my eye. I tried to pull it off but it wouldn't budge. It finally gave way, taking a good bit of the skin on my knuckle with it. Preston walked in to see me with my finger in my mouth grimacing in pain.

I looked up to find his face shaved smooth again wearing nothing but his jeans. My heart lurched at the sight. "Jeez!" I shook my head staring at him. "You should come with a warning label. You know, like the one on a pack of cigarettes. Surgeon General's Warning: Looking for prolonged periods of time may cause light headedness, fainting, weakness in the knees as well as unexpected heart palpitations. Stare with caution."

He made a silly face and tossed a pillow at me laughing. I shook my hand trying to get rid of the sting of the missing skin.

He took my hand and traced the pale tan line at the base of my finger. "You didn't have to take it off, Adena." He rolled my finger between his looking at it carefully. "You need a bandage. Be right back."

He opened the door and walked out but came back in less than a minute to sit next to me with a band-aid.

"You are worse than my daddy." Amazed at how concerned he was over such a small scrape.

"Fussed over you, did he?" Someone knocked on the door and he told them to come in.

I felt uncomfortable sitting there in my pajamas with him tending to me so close without his shirt. And at this point, I had about a hundred and three questions I wanted to ask him. His mother opened the door. I wasn't sure if that were any better than if it had been Beth.

"I'm sorry, dear. I didn't tell you goodnight." She looked apologetically at me. "Are you all settled in?"

"Yes, Ma'am. Thank you for having us."

"Be sure to feel as if you're home while you're here."

"Thanks, Ms. Doreen."

She smiled, said goodnight then closed the door. I heard the creaking of the stairs as she made her way back down.

I was astounded at her open acceptance of my relationship with her son given the circumstances.

Preston winked at me and shrugged his shoulders. "Now then," He crawled over me and picked up a brown box from the floor on the other side of the bed. "Turns out I didn't have to send it by post. Just picked it up today."

He held a hopeful glean in his eyes, so I held my questions about Kelley and opened his gift. I peeled away several layers of red tissue and when I saw what lay at the bottom, my hand flew to my chest to steady the earthquake of emotion. I lifted the beautifully tanned leather book as if it were fragile as spun glass. In elegant gold script across the front were the words,

Dear Mom and Dad...

I opened the cover and on the front page, he had written:

In loving memory of Roger and Gayle Whitmore
For my Adena,
To keep them near and to tell them all of
your hopes and dreams. Hope you like it.
Always,
Preston

I flipped through the pages trimmed in gold leaf, exquisitely decorated with scrolling vines in the top right corner of every page. I'd never seen a journal like it in my life. I closed it carefully and found it hard to speak.

Holding it to my heart, I looked at his waiting smile. "I absolutely love it. Where did you ever find it?"

"I had it made for you." He rubbed his hand over the smooth gold satin covering my leg.

My heart overflowed with his thoughtfulness. Then I realized I'd spoken of my parents but I never told him they were gone. "How did you know?"

"Their wedding photo from that box you dragged from your closet. Adena, no one looks so longingly at someone without holding a great deal of hurt inside. I just knew." He rubbed my knee. "Not quite fair what life takes from us is it?"

I shook my head slowly and looked down at the journal, tracing the gold letters of, *Mom and Dad.*

He lay on his side propped up on one elbow, quiet but smiling. We studied each other in the calm of being alone. I could only imagine he was thinking the same as I was. We were together again, against the odds that it happened much sooner than either of us expected, despite the unfortunate circumstances that made it so.

A more solemn look stole the happiness from his face as he sucked in a tense lungful of air. "So, you must be wondering by now."

I nodded knowing he was referring to Kelly. He exhaled deeply, letting it all go as if what he was about to say would make him weary with the effort. He pulled a blue and yellow floral print pillow down between us and slowly picked at a tiny lint ball stuck to the fabric. Then with another deep breath, he began to speak.

"My best friend Spencer Rogers was Kelley's father. He was married to a beautiful girl named Elizabeth. We called her Lizzy. We were all at Kelley's christening and I was deeply honored when they asked me to take care of her should anything ever happen to them. —One night, while I was away, my father got a call from the trauma room. They'd been in a terrible accident." He stopped and rubbed his eyes more to keep from crying rather than wiping tears away. I almost told him he didn't have to finish but I could plainly see this was hard enough on him without interrupting. So I stayed quiet and waited.

"I'm sorry to have waited this long. But to explain Kelley, I have to speak of things I'd rather not remember. I just...its quite difficult to speak of..." He inhaled deeply again and let it go. "It was like losing a brother." He swallowed making his Adam's apple bob hard in his throat. He seemed to be calming himself and collecting his words in his mind before speaking them. He started again, "Kelley survived. But only just."

He whispered. "She was so little. Her first birthday had just passed."

He grimaced and I'm sure the pictures he relived in his thoughts were things I'm glad I couldn't see.

He cleared his throat and rubbed at his eyes again. "Anyway, to make a long story shorter, I was unmarried, unsettled and at the time had no idea what to do. Honestly, the thought of raising a little girl scared the hell out of me. My parents took her in, not that I wouldn't have, it's just, I was dead myself in a way. Too distraught to think most days, let alone have a baby depend on me. But then, once she was here, something happened. Kelley, for some strange reason, wanted no one but me. And each night as I rocked her to sleep, I knew there was nothing I wanted more than to hold her and keep her safe. I kept my promise to my friends. She's *my* daughter." He looked up and his eyes were red, tears pooling but not spilling over. "I've raised her. Heaven knows not without help but she's mine."

I brushed his cheek with the backs of my fingers. "You get more amazing every day."

Too many days and nights of wishing I were close enough to touch him had passed. I kissed his throat and his pulse quickened beneath my lips. I traced the source of his pulse along the side of his neck with my lips and ran my fingertips down his bare chest and his stomach.

When I popped the button on his jeans, he asked, "Are you attacking me?"

"I'm trying."

He got up, locked the door, and turned off the light. He pulled a string to turn the light on inside the closet. Once shut, the beam that barely made its way through the cracks of the door cast a dim glow over the room.

"Not quite candlelight but it'll do." He unzipped his pants and tossed them to the floor.

I had the sensation of falling as he crawled in next to me. My heartbeat quickened to be next to his bare skin, to feel his warmth. I could just make out the expression on his face and it was full of desire. As I snuggled closer, I could feel his heart pounding away; it made me smile knowing how much he wanted me too. He growled playfully as he pulled me closer and I shushed him clamping my hand over his mouth and stifled my own laugh.

He rolled over me pressing me into the dense feather mattress. "Love, this house was built well over a hundred years ago. The walls are a foot thick with brick and mortar. You could scream and no one would hear you."

"Mmm... good to know."

"Yes," He kissed me once. "It is isn't it?" His close whispers gave me chills that had nothing to do with the coolness in the room.

Happiness rose inside me like the waters of the Mississippi River after a heavy rain. An ever-increasing flood that I could drown in forever.

He trailed his kisses from my forehead to my nose and then my chin. He slid his tongue across my neck and I felt as if I were floating. His hand slipped smoothly over the satin covering my breast and he cupped it gently in his hand. He maneuvered my top upward letting his mouth cover the hard center of it, sucking and kissing, causing me to arch into his efforts. My breath caught repeatedly in my chest from the pleasure.

I brought his face to mine, melting my lips into his. He immediately let his tongue mingle with mine -urgently reaching for more. He skillfully undressed me from my satin wrappings stopping his kiss only to pull the top over my head. He stopped, catching his breath, but still exploring my body with his hands.

"It feels like years since I last touched you." He kissed me deeply again, a low moan building in his throat. The pounding in his chest told me he couldn't wait any longer and I was glad. My body ached to feel his strength.

"This insane need for you —it frightens me at times." His fierce kiss stopped me from telling him the same.

I pulled him tightly against me to let him know I needed him as much. My wishes needed no voice. There was no hesitation as he filled me. We were a faultless union. He knew me and I knew him as if by some unseen magic. We soared together, climbing higher and higher with every touch, every kiss, every whisper. Our bodies intertwined as he slowly and methodically brought me to yet another realm —back to that beautiful dimension, where we both slipped away to when we made love.

Being with Preston, lost in that devastating desire was like dancing with a lightning bolt. Electrifying in a way, unexpectedly shocking but easy and natural as nothing else could ever be.

12

I AWOKE THE NEXT MORNING to the sun shining brightly through the leaded glass window. With no clock in the room, I didn't know what hour it was. A blissful feeling, not having to care. The wait was over; I was where I wanted to be.

I turned to look at the pillow next to me. I didn't really expect to find him there; it wouldn't do for everyone to know so openly that we'd spent the night together. But what I did find made me smile. A bundle of freshly cut lavender lay on the pillow tied together with a little band of lace. There was a ladybug crawling away. Sure that the little polka-dotted hitchhiker never thought it would wind up next to me this beautiful day, I let it crawl from the pillow onto my finger and carried it to the window. I tugged on a hulking black iron latch at the bottom, the frame released and with a push, it swung outward from the house.

My eyes locked on the view outside. Too dark to notice when we'd arrived last night, I now saw the vivid landscape. The farmhouse stood in the middle of rich green rolling hills, the stone wall that lined the private drive connected to another that stood parallel to the house and a small wooden gate hung low in an archway in the center of the stone wall. From my window, I could see what lay behind it. A spectacular garden.

The Secret Garden, a book GG had read to me many times as a child, came to mind when I looked out over the grounds. I never thought I would behold anything that resembled what I had imagined while reading that book.

Preston grabbed me from behind and it scared the living daylights out of me. I screamed and my heart thumped viciously. He let go the most ridiculous laugh I'd ever heard.

"I thought I was gonna fall out the damn window!" I huffed and tried to catch my breath. "Well, I don't need coffee now. I'm more than wide awake."

"You should be. It's half-past eleven."

"Ew, that's embarrassing. Why did you let me sleep so late?"

"Jet lag, time change. You need time to adjust." He gave me a peck. "Besides, I've only just arrived home. Brought Mum to see Dad and sat with him a bit."

"How is he?"

"Ornery. He told the vicar to sod off and leave this morning. Said he wasn't dead yet and not to come back till he was." He shook his head and grinned just a bit. "I know he's sick of being there. But they'll let him out tomorrow or the next if all goes well." He gave me another kiss on my forehead. "Hungry?"

"Can we eat after I get a shower?"

He nodded with a contented smile. "What are you pointing at?" He gestured to my hand in between us.

I looked down at the finger I'd been holding the little ladybug on, therefore it appeared that I was just pointing at something sideways.

"There was a bug." I looked all over my hand then having found nothing; let my arm fall to my side. "I had a ladybug on my finger."

He looked at me sort of funny, chuckled as he closed the door; leaving me alone to let me get dressed.

The lavender was a wonderful sentiment but the smell was overwhelming. I turned to look at the pillow where he'd left it but to my surprise, it wasn't there.

Maybe he'd noticed how powerfully strong they were and took the little arrangement out again just before he scared the bejeezus out of me. But still, it would have been nice to thank him for the sentiment.

When I went downstairs, I instinctively turned to the right to go to the kitchen. But before I needed to wonder where I was going, I heard Preston call out, "In here, Lo-" He stopped short and coughed an unnatural sound. "In here, Adena."

Why I turned right, I do not know. It felt right I suppose but in any case I continued, following his voice until I found Beth and Teena sitting at a small café style table with only a pair of chairs chatting and laughing with empty plates pushed aside. I realized Preston had almost called me *Love* in front of Beth. He was trying so hard to make this as easy as possible for her.

Preston and Kelley were sitting at the dining room table in the next room waiting for me. The two tables were only a matter of maybe ten feet apart. A huge archway framed with heavy timbers separated the two rooms.

"We're having omelettes." He announced but then looked up suddenly. "Didn't think to ask. Do you like eggs?"

"Yeah, she likes eggs. With *ketchup*." Beth said making a face.

He looked appalled but didn't comment.

"Don't knock it till you've tried it." I sat down feeling a little empty handed, hardly accustomed to having breakfast prepared and waiting for me.

"Knock it, Preston. It's gross." Beth chimed in again.

He got up and returned from the kitchen with an unfamiliar bottle of Sainsbury's tomato ketchup. I poured a little puddle on my plate and started eating.

"That looks ghastly," he grimaced then shook his head, "but Dad and Uncle have never eaten an egg in any form without dowsing it in some form of tomato torture." He smiled at me and added, "But do enjoy, Love."

Beth laughed despite herself.

He picked up a bit of his omelette and dipped it in my plate, tossed a bite into his mouth and immediately frowned like he was swallowing a worm.

"Yes, I'm still certain I don't care for it. I'm siding with you, Beth." He washed it down with some juice. A lot of juice. "*But* if Adena's gumbo was good after what *it* looked like, I can try just about anything."

Teena turned in her chair making her glossy hair swish over her shoulder. "What, may I ask, is gumbo?"

Preston leaned sideways in his chair to get closer to the little breakfast nook where she and Beth were seated -to look at her closely- to goad her on. "It looks like something you'd scoop from a hog trough, you know, like something *you'd* cook; only yours tastes like slop as well."

I guess I could give up on the hopes that Gavin and Beth would ever outgrow their fights.

"Teena, how old are you?" I asked.

"She's twenty-two." Preston answered for her. "She was an accident." Teena got up and pinched him between his neck and his shoulder making him cringe in his seat. "Ow! Sorry, you were a happy mistake!" Her knuckles turned white where she squeezed his flesh and then she smacked him in the back of his head.

"So how did you guys sleep last night?" Beth said with a smirk I recognized. My muscles went into a rigid state that the hottest of baths could not relieve.

Preston looked at me. "How rude of me, I didn't even ask. Did you sleep well? Have enough blankets in your room?"

I nodded. "I slept like the dead. Plenty of blankets, thanks."

Beth rolled her eyes at me as if to say, *Give me a break*. She looked across the kitchen nook and smiled at Preston. "Your house is really cool, Preston. You did the decorating yourself?"

"Thanks. Yes I did." He smeared a little butter on some toast and took a bite off the corner.

Beth crossed her arms and leaned back in her chair, the rattlesnake in her, ready to strike. "You know I think your living room would be awesome in a darker shade though. You know kinda like that color in Mom's room."

Preston walked blindly into her proverbial fangs. "Yes, sort of a mossy green. I like that idea."

A triumphant smile lit her face and her eyes found mine. Immediately Preston closed his eyes and mouthed the word *shit* realizing she'd set him up.

She raised her eyebrows and brought her plate to the sink. When she walked past us, she mumbled, "Please don't treat me like a moron, Mother. I'm old enough to know better."

I stared at her as she turned the corner of the short stretch of wall that separated the kitchen and dining area. I stood up and walked quickly to meet her, cornering her against the dark oak cabinets of the kitchen out of sight.

"Beth, I know this is difficult for you but you *will* show some respect for Preston and his family while you're here." I spoke low in an attempt to keep the others from overhearing.

"*Respect*? Ha!" She whispered loudly and threw a finger in the direction of the dining room. "I don't know if I should ask him to be my new daddy or to go the prom! You could have given me just a little warning. What'd you do, pick him out at the play ground? He barely looks older than the guys *I* go out with."

I crossed my arms and looked at her incredulously. "Is that really what this is about? His age? Beth, he's twenty-nine."

Her face and shoulders relaxed a little. "Oh." She raised her brows a little. "Well, that's not as gross as I thought." A smidge of guilt flicked across her face. "Sorry. Didn't mean to be a brat. It's just..."

I waited but she didn't say anything else.

"I know, sweetie, but please just take the time to get to know him. I'm not asking you to pretend to like him, but can we please make an effort not to make things worse than they already are?"

I wanted to say so much more. I wanted to hold her like I did when she was three and smooth her silky blonde curls and tell her everything would be alright when something upset her. I wanted so badly to just tell her that I'm sorry. I wanted to say that life won't be so screwed up for her when she's older. I wanted to assure her that love is a real thing, something to count on, something concrete.

But I couldn't. Love *is* real. But it's not always so concrete. It can be for a long time. Sometimes for a lifetime. But sometimes it just crumbles and blows away in a stiff enough breeze only to land someplace else. To exist for others. Sometimes it comes back. But sometimes…

Well, sometimes love just has really shitty timing.

Her eyes fell to the pale honey wood floor and she tucked a sun lit wave behind her ear. "Sure. So, is my attitude adjustment over now?"

I moved out of her way and she mumbled low. "This sucks. But at least in sucks in London." She went to sit next to Teena. The two of them picked up their previous conversation and even laughed about something.

Preston's eyes filled with apologies as I sat down. I don't know why, it wasn't his fault. I whispered *sorry* to him and tried to let it all go.

Kelley pushed her plate away and drank the last of her juice. Preston tugged her shirtsleeve to see it better. She stood up and stretched it out showing off her new University of Florida shirt. I looked at Beth to find her already smiling, pleased with herself. I gave her a quick wink to let her know I appreciated her unseen efforts. Kelley gave her best monster growl and held her hands one over the other, arms stretched out in front of her and clamped them shut. I knew all too well the familiar Gator Pride gesture and knew that Beth had obviously given her a little coaching.

"Chomp, Chomp!" Kelly giggled and turned to smile proudly at Beth.

Preston looked at Beth and chuckled less nervous than before. "What did you do to her?"

She shook her finger at him. "Learn it, live it, love it. And *burn* that LSU crap you were wearing last night. Just because my mother is an LSU freak doesn't mean *you* have to dress like a dork."

Joking around with him was probably the closest he'd get to an apology from her. At least for now and I didn't want to push her too far too fast. He reached behind his shoulder and retrieved his purple and gold cap he'd had on last night and tugged it firmly onto his head with a defiant grin.

She got up, pulled a rubber band from her hair as she walked toward him then held her hand out. "Give it." She demanded.

He looked at me with a fair measure of uncertainty but he did as she said. She quickly rolled the bill of the cap just so then tightly fastened it with the rubber band. "If you insist on wearing it, at least shape it right." She tossed it on the table without a word then she and Teena left to take a ride around the property.

"Well then," Preston began, once we'd finished cleaning the dishes. "Now that everyone is fed, care to take a ride? I have to meet up with my cousin Robert so he can show me where the fence is down."

"Sure. Unless Kelley doesn't want to go. I could stay here with her."

Leaning against the stove drying his hands, he reached to tap Kelley on the shoulder. She spun her head around.

"Yes, Poppy?"

"Care for a ride in The Beast?"

Her eyes lit up and she bolted through a mudroom at the rear of the kitchen and through the back door. You'd think we were headed to a carnival.

The day was sunny with a few clouds littering an otherwise beautiful sky, around sixty degrees and everything smelled of fresh mown grass and wet earth.

Kelley waited impatiently, dancing one foot to the next, right next to a slightly beat up light green pickup that looked like it was no less than fifteen years older than me. Preston opened the door for her and she climbed in. I tried to let myself in on the other side but I couldn't get the handle to budge.

"Allow me. Merely one of the many reasons she named it *The Beast*." Preston said. He popped it with the side of his fist and yanked it hard. The reluctant hinge gave up with a screech of rusty metal.

He disappeared inside a small stone storage shed of sorts and reappeared with a pair of post-hole diggers, two posts and a small roll of baling wire. They clattered into the bed of the truck prompting Kelley to turn around to peek through the back glass. He climbed in the driver's seat and tossed a pair of wire snips and a wad of bale ties on the dash and away we went with a roar of the old V-8.

It didn't take long to see why Kelley was so excited to go. As we wound through the curves and up and down the rolling hills, occasionally upon going down, we experienced the temporary weightlessness of being on a small rollercoaster. She squealed and clapped her hands every time it happened.

"I thought you said she was seven." I said to Preston.

He nodded. "She's just small for her age. Lizzy was such a slight little creature. I suppose that's where she gets it from."

"I noticed you don't sign to her all the time. Does she read lips?"

He nodded once but for the most part kept his eyes forward as he drove. "You'll see her at times mouth what others are saying. It's just her way of listening. She has a hearing aid but refuses to wear it." He looked down at her and she'd seen what he said.

She poked her tongue out at him. "I've told you a thousand-hundred-million times, Poppy. It makes scary sounds. I don't *like* it."

He raised his brows at her but said nothing more.

After a few moments, he shook his head and laughed a bit as he looked ahead steering with his wrist. "So, when's prom? Should my tie match Beth's dress for the occasion?"

I closed my eyes as my embarrassment colored my face. He'd heard our brief but heated conversation in the kitchen. We both chuckled a little and resolved to accept whatever she may say or do as the days went by.

We drove through a gate meant purely for keeping livestock in then up to a white house roughly the size of Delaware situated under a cluster of massive shade trees.

Preston blared the horn and shortly a man, I assumed somewhere around Preston's age came limping down the gray painted cement steps with his arm in a cast. His dark brown hair was clean cut but mussed, brown eyes and he had a hell of a shiner; his fair skin, almost tanned. His build was tall and lean and he winced with every step. He stopped at Preston's window, pointed to the corner of the property explaining where the broken fence was and apologized for not being able to fix it himself.

"No worries." Preston told him. "Robert, meet Adena. Adena this is Robert."

"Hey, Robert. Nice to meet you."

His eyes widened as did his smile and I could see clearly how kind his face was. "Glad to make your acquaintance." He looked at Preston again and bumped his shoulder. "*Where* did you find her?"

I realized he was referring to my accent. That was going to get old quick.

"Sunny Florida. Well, it wasn't so sunny at the time." Preston looked at me and laughed at his inside joke. Understatement of the year.

"Feeling any better, mate?" Preston asked and poked quite deliberately at Robert's shoulder as he asked, "Does *that* still hurt?"

Robert managed to land a half decent punch into Preston's chest with his good arm. "Bugger off!" Then he grabbed his shoulder where Preston poked him and rubbed a particular spot. "Cheeky bastard!"

Preston couldn't stop laughing and he released the brake to roll past Robert, leaving him cursing alone in his front yard.

Boys will be boys, I guess.

"What happened to him?" I asked when Preston could breathe again. "Did he get run over or something?"

Preston shook his head. "Nearly. He got caught in a stampede."

That was not what I was expecting. "Seriously?"

Kelley pulled the tail of my shirt. "Poppy's exaggerating. Three horses stomped on him." She held up three of her little fingers very close to my face; emphatically showing me how many. "He looked positively wretched a few weeks ago. His face and his legs were all swollen and he's badly bruised."

"Preston! That's terrible. Why would you poke the poor guy?"

He looked appalled that I would even ask. "Because he did it to me first! I've been waiting three years for a little payback. He nicked my crutches so I couldn't go —well, you know,"

Kelly watched his lips as Preston hesitated and when she decided he wouldn't or couldn't, she turned to me and said, "He couldn't go wee!" She giggled.

"Thank you for that, Kelley. And then everyday he managed to be there when my bandages were changed. He'd wait till the nurse looked away and poke and prod the darkest bruise he could find. I would scream then the nurse would overreact and get Mum all out of sorts then they'd find some reason to give me yet another shot. I positively hate needles therefore Robert found this utterly hysterical! Sadistic little git!"

Like I said, boys will be boys.

Preston pulled past the house and drove to the back corner of the fence. Kelley and I got out and waited for him to unload the posts. When he was done, I helped her onto the tailgate and we sat there together watching him dig a fresh posthole. In no time at all, she looked bored enough for her little face to slide right off her skull. I spotted a small roll of bright yellow nylon string sitting in the truck bed and I tried to get a piece free, though I knew it was useless. The stuff just doesn't break like cotton string.

Preston saw me struggling with it. He walked over pulling a pocketknife from his jeans. "What are you trying to do?"

"You'll see." I held out the amount of string I needed so he could cut it.

I tied the loose ends together, wound the loop around my little finger and thumb on each hand. Kelley looked very curious in wonder of what I was doing. I went through each step very slowly showing her how to make a Cat's Cradle.

She smiled and gasped with the gleeful astonishment that only small children possess. "Poppy, look!"

He peeked over his shoulder and smiled then picked up the fence post and dropped it into the freshly dug hole.

I gave the string to her and placed it over her fingers helping her through the process. We did it three times and she had it on her own.

Once Preston finished mending the fence, we drove to a stately white barn and stable that stood roughly fifty or so yards to the rear of the white house where Robert lives. Kelley went running to catch a rather robust orange cat she called Pumpkin. Completely appropriate, he looked like one.

I glanced up at the sky and found that our sunny morning had morphed into an overcast and breezy afternoon.

Walking through the meticulously kept stables, the scent of leather, oats, horses, fresh sawdust and hay took me back to when I was a girl, although, our tiny stable could not begin to compare to this. But large vs. small, that pristine smell was just the same.

Preston introduced me, so to speak, to thirteen stunning Thoroughbreds, pointing out Helena, Athena, and Pandora -the guilty three who'd had a go at Robert.

It was too easy to see how just one of these beauties could have inflicted the damage done to the poor man. If he got tangled in the hooves of three of these large specimens -well, I'd consider him to be the luckiest fellow with a black eye and a broken arm. He got off easy.

When we made it all the way down to the last stall on the right, there stood a dazzling quarter horse, seemingly dwarfed in comparison with her larger stable mates. She had a long shiny black mane and tail, a small white blaze on her face and her forelock fell, partially covering one beautiful, intelligent brown eye.

"This is Dolly," Preston said, "I believe I told you about her once."

"She's absolutely gorgeous!" I breathed in admiration.

She let out a loud whinny and nodded her head up and down as if appearing in agreement.

"Apparently, she seems to think so too." He opened her gate letting her walk out then he put her bridle on and turned to wink at me.

"What are you fixin' to do?"

"Fixin' to?" He looked baffled and scratched his head. "Translation please?"

"Sorry. It means *about to*. Strictly a southern thing. People in New York would be just as confused as you."

He chuckled a little. "Well, the rest are event horses. Dolly is a pet. I got her at auction last year." He patted her shoulder then smoothed her dark sleek coat just under her neck. "The two of you have something in common. She's an American as well."

"Really? Where from?"

"Cody, Wyoming. Some bloke abandoned her not far from here." He shook his head and swatted a single fly from Dolly's ear. "I can't imagine going through all the trouble of bringing her to another country and then not take proper care of her." He shrugged his shoulders and found my eyes again. "Anyway, aside from that, I have no information on her. I don't even know what her name was." He tapped the small scar above his eyebrow. "And like every other horse in present company, she doesn't like me *on* her."

I reached up to run my finger over the little scar, an excuse to touch his face. "And what exactly did she do to you?"

"She scraped me off on a tree *and* adding insult to injury, she stepped on my head. As if to say, 'stay down you smug bastard.'" He made me laugh. "At any rate, I was going to let you give her a go."

"So she bucks *you* off and you want *me* to ride her? Thanks!"

"Teena has no trouble with her. Honestly, I think it's just me."

I stared a little as he pulled a red and blue plaid horse blanket off the railing next to Dolly's stall then toss it over her back. I straightened it a bit as he turned once again to retrieve a western saddle from a large hook on the wall then hoist it into place. I ran my fingers through her silky mane and raised the flank of the saddle admiring the artisanship. I watched as Dolly slowly pawed at the ground doing a good job at digging a shallow ditch.

She stopped, swished her long glossy tail, shifted her weight and if I didn't know any better, took one step back to purposely step on Preston's foot. He scrunched his eyes tight and the muscles in his neck contracted. He pushed her forward patiently, begging her silently to move. She turned her head and nudged his face with her muzzle, then very politely freed his foot from under her hoof. A soft whinny and it nearly sounded as if she were laughing.

I shook my head and laughed myself. "So —okay. You just said horses don't like you. I don't get it."

He shrugged again. "I don't ride much. I'd rather look at a horse than sit on one. I simply appreciate their presence, to watch them. Not to mention at least half of these ladies have had the pleasure of throwing me at least once."

I swatted the same bothersome fly from Dolly's shoulder. "So, why did you buy her when ya'll have a stable full already?"

"I fell in love with her. Sorry, I didn't tell you I had another love in my life. But as you can see, she doesn't feel the same. However, I did find something else just around a year ago that I know won't throw me." He pulled the reins over her head.

"Like what? A dead goat?"

He grabbed his stomach in mock laughter. "Very funny. A motor bike. Got myself an Indian Chief. Another auction. Dad's got me addicted."

"Really? Daddy had one when I was little."

"Well, I'd gladly show it to you but it's lying in several crates in my garage. I figured it'd be worth restoring it. Sooner rather than later. Damn thing seems to call my name every time I pass it. I've never even seen it in one piece."

Preston led Dolly out of the barn, and as I looked out over the broad green pasture, I saw three pale-blue feed barrels set up in a triangular pattern right in the center of a sand filled paddock.

I looked up at him. "Did you do that?"

"Yes, early this morning. I'd like to see what you can do."

"Preston, you can't just get on some random horse and expect it to run the barrels. They have to be trained."

"I'm *aware* of that, Miss Obvious. You can still give her go if you like. But, if you're afraid..." he smiled and the look on his face was nothing less than a dare.

"I didn't say I wouldn't ride her." I pulled myself up on her back and she side stepped twice then settled back down.

He put his hands on his hips and carefully appraised Dolly's reactions then reached for my hand. "This might not be such a good idea. I'd hate for you to be sharing a room with my father at the hospital."

"Preston, if she throws me it won't be my first time." I bumped her gently with my heels and clicked my tongue in my cheek urging her out toward the gate.

"It's that last time I'm worried about." He called to me.

Just as we got to the gate, she stopped and pawed anxiously at the ground. Perfectly lined up with the barrels when I looked up, but I wasn't about to try it, especially on a horse that I didn't know. It'd been twenty years since I'd done anything like that. I attempted to veer her to the left to go down the line of the fence but she wouldn't budge. I tried the other direction. She yanked her head back and held her ground dead center of the gate.

"Oh come on, Dolly. Let's go." Like a strike of lightening, she bolted.

It would be a vast understatement to say it merely scared me. Until I realized what she was doing. And why should that even remotely surprise me? A quarter horse from Cody, Wyoming of all places, had about a ninety percent chance of being a barrel horse.

She showed no signs of hesitation so I tugged her to the right. She shot off to the first barrel and hugged it so tight we almost laid down. I almost fell off but she was up and lunging hard through the damp dirt and sand before I had time to wrap my head around it. I held on for dear life, crouched low over her shoulders and it was absolutely exhilarating. I laughed as we spiraled effortlessly around the barrel on the left and I wanted to see if it tipped but I couldn't look back. We were flying to the blue barrel in the far center and she had no trouble at all whipping around it then off in a wide-open thunder we sped toward the gate, her head and neck pumping hard to assist her forward propulsion.

As we passed through the gate, I pulled her reins and she pranced sideways like a show pony toward Preston nodding excitedly with the brand new pride of a five year old child telling her father to 'watch me daddy, -did ya see, did ya see?' So reluctantly she came to a halt that her hooves sent small sprays of moist dirt near to where Preston was standing.

"Thought you said you couldn't get her to do that?" He smiled leaning against a tall white pole as it started to drizzle.

My heart thundered in my ears as if I were the one who'd done the running. I smiled and tried to catch my breath. "That was *not* her first time. Apparently, the words *let's go* do it for her." I slid off her side and gave her kiss on her velvety muzzle thanking her for letting me fly with her.

Preston came closer to put his arms around my waist. "I could watch you and her do that every day. The epitome of freedom."

I handed him her reins. "Try it. I wanna see you in action." He smiled wickedly and came at my neck. I caught his chest with my hands. "On Dolly, Preston!"

"What? And let you see firsthand my inevitable humiliation? No thanks." Dolly nudged his arm and began turning restless circles around us.

"See. She wants to go again."

He groaned and turned around to adjust the stirrups to make them longer then grudgingly climbed onto her back. He didn't even get both feet in the stirrups before she reared up and pitched like a bronco. I stumbled back to get out of the way before I got a wild hoof in the eye.

"Preston!" I screamed, so scared he'd get hurt.

He rolled his eyes at me and laughed, completely capable of holding his own. He took control, letting her run wild and open around the pasture. His body moved in rhythm with hers and all I could do was stare. His shoulders crouched just over hers, his hair swept back, his shirt billowing, her silken black mane and tail flying behind her as he let her truly stretch her legs. One glorious creature together they seemed and I'd never seen anything more beautiful or more graceful. I felt as though I'd witnessed the final perfect liquid brushstroke on a Master's canvas. The quiet sunrise after a storm. Peace and uninhibited satisfaction. I was able for the first time in all my life to let go of every single thought outside of that moment while I watched him ride. How long had I watched? Five minutes? An hour? Time slows for such moments; I wasn't aware till the moment had passed.

Dolly came galloping back and Preston tried the barrels from the opposite direction and he didn't do bad. Not bad at all.

The overcast sky turned loose a light sprinkle as I watched Dolly slow to a trot in front of me, her nostrils flaring. Preston swung his leg around and hopped down.

"She's *never* let me ride her like that." He smiled holding her reins and stepped closer to me. I was speechless. He was breathless.

Droplets of water began to collect in our hair. Preston came closer. I couldn't feel the chill from the breeze, not when he towered over me like that. Chill? Breeze? Rain? What rain? I felt nothing at all but his lips on mine and his fingers in my hair, his palms on either side of my face so that he could kiss me just the way he wanted. And there was simply nothing like it in this world. His exhilaration from the ride had indeed evoked some excitement that translated roughly to a situation where all I wanted was to -

"Ay! Romeo!" I heard a man's stern baritone voice call to Preston.

Dammit! I thought.

Preston's lips curved into a tight smile against mine. "Dammit!" He muttered and I laughed at the shared sentiment.

A tall slender man, in his late fifties or so stood beneath the shelter of the stables with Kelley right next to him, her little arms overflowing with Pumpkin the cat. We walked over with Dolly following behind.

"Adena, meet Uncle." Preston introduced us.

The man said hello with an unexpected rib-crushing hug, lifting me till I was a foot off the ground. "Yes, I've heard all about you!"

He let me go and I looked up at the two of them again. "Holy cow, ya'll look just alike!" I couldn't keep the comment to myself.

I looked back and forth at them in awe. They were exactly the same height and they looked so much alike it was uncanny. Except for the eyes. Preston definitely got those blue-green peepers from his mother. They looked at each other with matching expressions and I knew that they must get that reaction from a lot of people.

"I'm much better looking." Uncle said aiming the same damn crooked grin at me that Preston had perfected.

"So can you stand what I'll look like when I'm an old geezer like him?"

His uncle punched Preston in the arm. "I'm not old. Just more experienced." His fuzzy eyebrows jumping suggestively.

"Watch it, you old nutter. She's taken." Preston laughed and kissed me with a deliberate display that I belonged to him.

"Bloody show off." Uncle said to him. "Oh, by the by, have you seen Trojan?"

"Robert said he put him in the east pen this morning."

"Who's Trojan?" I asked.

"Well, all these pretty ladies, aside from Dolly, are his ehm —harem, if you will." Preston explained.

I laughed as that sunk in. "Wait. Let me get this straight. —Ya'll have a stud horse —named *Trojan?*" The two of them looked at each other and chuckled.

"Ironic isn't it? That would be *his* sense of humor." Preston thumbed in his uncle's direction. "And leave it to you to figure it out so quickly."

Uncle hooked his arm into mine. "I can see we're going to get along great, you and I. Stick with me and in no time at all, Preston will feel like a spare prick at a wedding."

I smiled and figured he must be quite the character. Not to mention he seemed to have a certain penchant for Greek mythology which I had always found fascinating. All of his horses were named for a god or goddess. Trojan, although technically not a mythological name, but rather a people, nevertheless -Trojan, the present sire was the son of his equine predecessor, Hercules, and he the son of another named Zeus. All nicknames of course, their real names were Hercules Hussle and Zeus' Last Bolt and such as that.

Preston looked up at the sky. "I don't think this will last long." He took Dolly's saddle off and patted her rump to let her know she was free to play in the rain.

Preston and his uncle, I still didn't know his name, were discussing a trainer that hadn't shown up for three days. I assumed it safe to say, Preston was involved with the operation to some degree. Kelley and I left them there, opting to wait in the dry cab of the truck.

I looked through the rain-dotted windshield out over the green expanse behind the stables simply admiring the rolling lay of the land but my eyes stopped at once when I noticed a man standing just on the edge of the woods. He was tall and from this distance, if I didn't already know where Preston was, I'd swear it was him. I leaned closer and in the time it took me to blink, the man was gone.

Kelley looked up at me and seemed a little nervous. She turned her head and seemed to look at the spot where the man had been standing.

"He does that sometimes. Poof! Just like the wind."

I had no idea how to reply to that. And so, I didn't.

13

KELLEY PLAYED WITH HER STRING quietly between us as we drove back. Preston grinned looking down at her. You'd never know that he wasn't her biological father, despite the lack of any resemblance. He adored her.

He took a left in a fork in the road that took us past the long line of trees behind his parents' house. It wasn't so much a road as it was a path with nothing more than parallel ruts worn deeply beyond the grass, into the clay, dirt and stone. At any rate, the path wound its way through a few trees at first then it looked like we were in a forest for at least a quarter mile stretch.

Preston nudged Kelley so she'd look up. "The rain didn't last. Think we should show Adena the magic?"

She smiled and nodded quickly. I must have been in for a surprise as neither of them would explain what that meant. Preston insisted I close my eyes. He didn't trust me and tossed a raincoat over my head so I couldn't see. When the truck stopped, they were both giggling. He opened my door and guided my blind steps until Kelley insisted it was good enough.

"Now, Poppy, now!"

"Not just yet. Wait for the wind." He stood behind me and pulled the jacket away but warned me first, "Don't open your eyes until I say. Trust me, it's worth it."

I played the good sport and did as he said. Then I heard the sound of the wind approaching in the distance, rustling the tops of trees until it was almost upon us.

"Now?" I asked.

He kissed my cheek and whispered. "Open your eyes, Love."

I opened them and blinked twice to adjust my vision. At first sight, it appeared to be a blizzard blowing around us. We were standing in the middle of a massive pear orchard and I looked up and around at the tall, broad trees blanketed in tiny white blossoms. With the help of the breeze, the tiny white flowers fell and fluttered all around us. The delicate petals tickled the skin on my arms and collected on our clothes like snowflakes falling from the clouds. I turned and stared all around, amazed at the breathtaking event. I could see precise currents of wind as the little flowers spun upwards and away in some places, spiraling this way and that before fluttering to the ground.

"What do you think?" Preston asked.

"Are you kidding? It's unbelievable!" I laughed and saw Kelley twirling under the falling blooms and I took a few turns with her. We giggled and spun together until we were both dizzy.

The gentle winds died down after a while and whatever blooms were left were holding fast to their branches and buds for now, so we walked and talked and sometimes we just stopped and stood quiet absorbing the beauty of the day, a passing cloud overhead, or the blue sky making its grand appearance once again. We listened to Kelley tell silly yet scary stories of *The Witch of Grace Manor*-something Preston said she'd made up about a year ago but after a while she got sidetracked and found Pumpkin the cat licking his paw beside a stump.

We strolled down one of the long shaded rows between the trees toward the truck. Preston held my hand as we watched Kelley run ahead chasing after that incredibly fat cat again as he began to enlighten me.

"A distant relative started this orchard. He'd never had much luck with the pears, as they don't taste very good straight off the tree. Not at all like a William's pear. However, many years later, my great-grandfather found a better use for them and with luck and patience, managed to perfect his very own brandy. And that's still the family business. Well, that and the horses. A fine bloodline and an orchard passed along to his two sons, then on to my father and Uncle. Uncle is Robert's father; they live in the white house we stopped at earlier."

I nodded as I began to connect the dots of who was who.

"What *is* your uncle's name? I can't very well call him Uncle."

"Why not? The man at the petrol station does. As does the ginger haired woman at the butcher shop over in Gidea Park. Well, I think she fancies him but nevertheless, everyone calls him Uncle. He used to scrap a lot when he was younger. Apparently, one tough nut. You know, Uncle, like, *I give up*."

I nodded as we got in the truck again. "Got it. Well then just out of curiosity…"

"Phillip. But he wouldn't even look up if you called him that."

Uncle it is then.

He made a right turn and soon another small thick of woods was behind us. We pulled up to a house made of light and dark gray stone framed in thick black timbers. The high-pitched roof looked like it might be slate. A familiar red Range Rover parked inside an open garage standing separate from the house told me where we were. And it wasn't exactly what I'd consider a cottage. I was expecting something small with a little sign that read *Sleepy, Sneezy or Doc.* It must have gotten the reference only because it wasn't nearly the size of neither his parents' grand farmhouse nor that colossal white house.

When we walked through the front door, it wasn't anything I expected. "I gather it didn't always look this way."

He smiled. "No. The place was a wreck when I bought it. Took me two solid years to get it livable. It was built in the 1850's in all likelihood for a stableman or some other such position." He touched the football sized stones on the outer side of the house. "See, same as Dad's place. There are three more but one has fallen, the other two are inhabited by a few workers and if you believe everything you hear —a couple of ghosts."

"Ghosts?" Suddenly, GG's face popped into my head.

I'd pushed that night in Ferriday by the lake to a dusty little corner in my mind. I'd bolted a door shut on that corner and sealed it tight. I'd wallpapered over it then shoved a large and heavy piece of furniture in front of it to forget. I didn't like thinking of GG as a *ghost.* Then I thought of Kelley's statement about the man I'd seen on the edge of the woods. *Poof,* she'd said. *Just like the wind.*

Goosies covered my arms. That's how Gavin used to say it when he was a little boy.

Preston laughed and waved his hand around to dismiss the ludicrous notion. "Just some ridiculous story started years ago by some superstitious old man who used to live here."

Superstitious. Right.

We walked inside and I savored the masculine flavor of the space. Everything in varying hues of brown. The floor was hardwood, very old but recently refinished. A wheat-colored rug covered most of the living room with a large compass rose design in the center. A sofa of worn brown leather, similar to that of a Bomber's jacket, sat facing the fireplace. His coffee table was an abstractly shaped glass top with a rusty ship's anchor underneath. An array of ancient nautical collectibles, compasses, spyglasses, brass propellers, and barometers as well as several other ornate brass and bronze pieces adorned small alcoves in the walls, bookcases and shelves. Very Hemmingway-ish.

A tattered old world map of the earth's continents and oceans hung matted and framed above the fireplace. On the mantel below, were several framed photos. One of his parents and Teena, one of Preston holding Kelley when she was a toddler and the ever present mottled blue background of school pictures.

The tour continued to Kelley's room, all decked out in periwinkle with white lace on the windows. She weaved between us to make her way to a simple but beautiful yellow dollhouse in the corner, occupied at once in her own little world of make-believe.

A narrow staircase led to a small loft where I saw Beth's suitcases sitting on top of an old steamer trunk at the foot of the bed.

Then he showed me to his room. It was unfussy with little decoration; the theme was mostly dark brown suede accented with copper and gold colors throughout. The window treatments were the oddest I'd ever seen. Strips of thick leather about four inches wide hung vertically with a big brass grommet at the bottom of each. It reminded me of a Roman soldier's attire and gladiators and chariots. Very manly, but it looked great. They filled the room with one of my favorite scents. The other, was standing next to me.

I admired a painting of a sea serpent that hung over his headboard. The kind you'd find printed on the ocean of an ancient map or old world globe.

"Is that what this is?" I asked flourishing my hand around his room. "Uncharted, unknown, possibly dangerous territory?"

He looked directly from me to the serpent and back again. A one-sided grin played across his lips. "I'm impressed. Most people don't know what to make of it."

"Most people? How many *people* have been in your room?" I teased him.

"If you're referring to women, none. Well, none I'm not related to anyway. I don't bring women around here to be on this level with Kelley and me." An unmistakable cold edge to the last of his words.

I felt like I'd just walked into the hardest coldest winter. He had said he needed me in a moment of weakness and I took it as an invitation.

He must have sensed my tension. He wrapped me in his arms looking down into my eyes but I looked away.

"What's wrong, Love?"

"I'm sorry. I kinda pushed myself into your world. I didn't mean..." I turned away feeling like such a fool. How stupid can one person be?

"I wasn't referring to *you*, obviously." He pulled me back and dropped his head low to look me directly in the eyes. "Adena, I asked you to come. And you came through for me in a way I never had a right to expect." He sighed and held me against his chest. "I hope you realize, I never meant to make things so complicated for you."

I savored his words and the warmth of his embrace. "I missed this. This space."

He kissed the crown of my head. "This space here? He tightened his arms around me. "Good. This space has been terribly empty lately. And you fit quite perfectly." He pressed his lips to my hair again and whispered, "I missed you as well."

He half released me, looked me over, that crooked grin of his firmly in place. He pulled open a drawer and threw a green and white striped, long sleeved rugby shirt on the bed for me to change into as we were both fairly damp from the short shower at the stables. I had to roll the sleeves up three times just to get them up to my wrists, but it was dry and smelled faintly of him. He pulled his shirt off and tossed it in a wicker basket. And for the first time I noticed a large crescent scar just below his shoulder blade followed by another about six inches down.

I gasped, so surprised I'd not seen his bare back in the daylight before. "Preston, what on earth happened to you?"

"What?" He realized what I was looking at and reached behind to trace the scar with his thumb. "Oh, that. Happened about three years ago. Trojan especially hates me. Uncle says I hold in too much anxiety and he reacted to it. Who knows?" He turned and looked at me, still smiling. "That would be when Robert tormented me for several weeks. Remember?" He chuckled.

After slipping on a dry t-shirt, he shrugged into a chambray button up as well then stretched out on the bed. He pulled me down on top of him drawing his thighs tightly around my hips. "No way out now. You're my prisoner."

"Prisoners are generally not happy, and they usually try to escape. I, on the other hand, am deliriously happy and I think I like it right here." I pulled the V of his tee and kissed the triangle of dark hair on his chest.

He closed his eyes and shivered. "You make it very hard to resist ripping your clothes free."

"Oh, I barely kissed you."

"You can't see what I see though." He opened his eyes and interlocked his fingers behind my back. "I see you looking at me from underneath your long lashes." He ran his finger just underneath my hair pushing it back behind my ear. "I see those crazy pretty curls clinging to your cheeks and your neck. —And if that weren't enough, from this angle, being that my shirt is much too big for you, I can see that blasted sexy little freckle on your boob."

I sat straight up and clambered to my knees as he lay there chuckling beneath me. I peered down my shirt. "I *do not* have a freckle on my boob!"

"Oh, I beg to differ. It peeks out of every shirt I've ever seen you wear. From my perspective anyways." He sat up against me, pulled the top buttons loose and placed his face directly in my cleavage. He kissed me just to the left and darted his tongue out. I quaked on the inside. "And that's exactly what I want to do every time I see it."

"So, you've been peeking down my shirt this whole time."

"Since the moment I met you." The crooked smile that turned my bones to jelly was back as he lay back down, crossing his arms behind his head. "I told you I was no gentleman. I warned you from the start. So in short, what I see right now, is nothing less than a sexy pin up straight from the pages of a dirty magazine, except no one gets to see but me."

I folded my arms. "I should have worn my boots. The crap is getting pretty deep in here."

Frustration bent his brow and filled his sigh. "Adena, you completely underestimate the power you have over me." He practically yanked me down, rolled over me and began kissing me so feverishly, my entire body began to respond.

As bad as I wanted to keep going, I knew we couldn't. I reluctantly dampened the fire and managed to say, "Um, Kelley might see."

He groaned. "Never had to worry about that before."

When I stood up, I noticed a picture of a dark haired woman in a small silver frame beside his bed. She was asleep with one bare shoulder showing, her long hair spilling across her skin and her pillow. I'd never considered myself a jealous person but I felt an undeniable twinge of green when I saw where he still kept her picture.

He saw what I was looking at and went to pick it up. "Ah, quite sexy isn't it?"

I tried for indifference and asked, "So, who is she?"

I thought his jaw would drop to the floor. "You can't be serious." He shoved the photo in my hands and made me look at it. "Is that not *your* headboard, *your* hair?" He kissed it before sitting it back beside his bed. "I took it the morning I brought you breakfast."

I bit my lip and fought to hide my smile as he continued to tease me for being jealous of myself.

We walked together down the hall and found Kelley fast asleep on her frilly twin bed clinging tightly to a well-loved purple bunny. He closed her door leaving it cracked a little before we went to the living room.

As I settled into the deep cushions of his couch, he picked up one of three guitars sitting in the corner. He ducked his head beneath the black leather strap, looked a little befuddled for only a second then barely laughed as if something amazed him but didn't comment on his thoughts. He took a deep breath and began to pick his six-string slowly, and in no time, I recognized the tune.

"That's *London Bound.*" I clasped my hands together as I watched his fingers so surely manipulate the frets, so effortlessly summon the complex chords. His guitar, like an extension of his own body, merely obeyed his command. And he knew the lyrics word for word, the rhythm dead on queue. However, he stopped playing before the song was finished. I looked up to find a distant look in his eyes.

"You were very close I take it." I moved closer and rested my hand on his knee.

He nodded once and cleared his throat. "Best mates since grade school." He pulled the strap over his head and sat the guitar gently on the floor. "Adena, can you guess why I played that for you?"

I studied his furrowed brow. "I guess cause I told you I liked it. And it's your friend's song. You play it better than the version I have."

He stood up, slipped his hands into his pockets and stared out a small window that looked out on a grouping of fig trees in front of his house. He looked thoughtful and chewed on the side of his lip. "We used to play in the pubs together. At age ten he could play better than I do now." He hung his head and I watched the muscles in his jaw contract as he clenched his teeth. "Adena, the download you have is Spencer *and* me. —Twelve years ago."

He turned his head and held my eyes with his. I just sat there and stared back, twiddling my fingers as I thought about what he'd said.

"So, you're telling me that —I've been listening to *you* all this time?"

He nodded. "Weird enough for you?"

I stood up and walked to his side. "I guess stranger things have happened. But this really seems to upset you. Is there something that I'm not getting?"

"He's Kelly's father, Adena."

"Oh!"

He nodded. "I can't stop thinking about it. You finding that song. The dream you had of Kelley. Don't you think that's a bit..."

"Strange? Yes. I guess so. But that's sort of been the theme to my life lately."

"Meaning?"

I stared out the window to watch the wind toss the branches of a tree I couldn't name. "I went home a few days after you left."

He stood behind me and placed his hands on my hips. "Lake St. John?"

I nodded once, thinking of GG and her cryptic message. Nothing seemed real anymore. Nothing made sense.

"Are you alright?" He asked.

I turned around and looked into his translucent eyes. "Yeah. It's just so different now. It was good seeing my uncle and his family. I've always wanted to move back there. But, now it just seems like I don't fit there anymore. Maybe I've been gone too long. Maybe it's just cause Mama and Daddy aren't there."

"I'm sorry, Love."

Encircling me in his arms, he rested his cheek against the top of my head and let me nestle my face against him. We started to sway and dance slowly to nothing at all. Only the sound of our hearts. A lovers' lullaby that only we could hear. But suddenly he stopped and froze. I looked up at him.

"What's wrong?"

He frowned a little. "I forgot they'd be in and out of here." He turned me around to see Teena and Beth coming down the hall from the rear of the house. They'd come through the back door. He whispered in my ear. "I'm sorry. I didn't mean for Beth to see us so close."

Privacy was going to be an issue. But Beth didn't *look* bothered. They came and joined us in the living room. Beth looked around and I couldn't figure out why.

"What's wrong, sweetie?" I asked her.

"Nothing. Just looking for the stereo. I heard music a few minutes ago when we were in the yard."

"Oh," I smiled at Preston. "That was him."

Beth looked duly impressed. "Really? That was kinda awesome."

Her mood swings were going to give me vertigo for sure. I didn't know what to expect. The girls headed up the narrow stairs to the loft,

173

talking over their plans for going into the city the next day.

Preston looked down at me with wide eyes. "I believe your daughter just paid me a compliment."

She heard him. "Yeah well, don't let it go to your head. I still think you're a dork."

He tossed his head back as though her words literally hit him in his face. "Ah, that's more like it." But he looked down at me and grinned. "She's a riot."

We left Kelley to finish her nap and the girls said they would bring her back to the farmhouse later. When we got in the truck, it was somewhat misty and overcast again.

"Is it always like this here?" I asked as we made our way up the road.

"Often enough. But you saw it this morning. We have a sunny day every now and again. They just come and go. Be glad for the on and off of it because around November it pours buckets." He chuckled a bit looking at me. "By the way, *what* were you dreaming of last night? You kept smiling and said something about someplace being beautiful."

I'd almost forgotten till he brought it up. "It was weird. We were standing under an old arbor, I think. Maybe it was part of a building that was torn down or something. Anyway, the beams were huge –like railroad-ties-huge- and just surrounded by woods and green everywhere. It was all wild and overgrown but it was really, well, beautiful. —That's all there was to it. Or at least all I can remember."

He wore a strange expression as if I'd just said something remarkable. He spun the truck around flinging mud all over and I had to hold on to the door and the dash to stay in the seat.

"What the *hell* are you doing? Good grief, you're just like the guys I grew up with. Gotta play in the mud."

"Sorry."

"Where are we going?" I asked sitting upright again.

"You'll see." His expression and demeanor pulled a complete one-eighty, his brow set in staid thought.

He drove through the forest but turned down a small path I hadn't noticed before, the canopy of the trees blocking most of the light of day. Limbs and vines slapped against the sides of the truck and after bouncing over the large stones embedded in the clay for another minute or so, Preston hit the brakes and slapped the gear arm into park sending us lurching toward the windshield. We hiked into the woods along a footpath so overgrown, I began to worry we'd get lost. But he seemed to know where we were going. Finally, he stopped, the trail practically gone, until he pointed out a block of cement completely disguised under green moss and leaf litter to the right. He held my hand as we stepped onto it and it kept going.

"Is this all cement?" I asked looking down. It felt much firmer than the path.

"Stone." He said dismissively and continued to pull me along behind him.

He led me beneath a long forgotten arbor of mammoth sized beams. Wild vines overtook the structure making it look like something from a medieval fairytale. And I recognized it. I couldn't understand why. First Kelley, seeing GG, now this. It scared me.

"Well?" He looked down at me, his eyes afire with expectation.

I cleared my throat and tried to sound casual. "Well *what*?"

"Is this the place you saw last night in your dream?"

I shook my head profusely, refusing to admit it aloud. He eyed me for a minute not saying anything then walked determinedly to one of the broad vertical beams of the framework. He leaned against the post and looked over at me again.

"I can see it in your eyes and the way you're standing. —This *is* what you saw isn't it?"

I didn't deny it again but I didn't say anything either. He ran his fingers through his hair and turned around looking at everything but me. I just watched him afraid of what he must have been thinking.

I walked slowly over to stand in front of him. "You think I'm some weirdo now don't you."

"No, Adena. Strangely enough I don't. I'm just trying to understand. —Has this type of thing happened to you before? The dreams? The bloody *voices*, now that we're getting to it."

"No, Preston, it *hasn't*." I didn't mean to sound irritated but I was a little irked at the possibility that I was a fruitcake. "I've never talked in my sleep or had visions or heard voices until I met *you*."

"Do you have any idea why she would tell us someone might be trying to kill us?"

"GG? Why? Did you hear her again?"

He shook his head. "Not since that first evening at your place."

I hung my head and swallowed my welling tears. Part of me was beginning to fear the absurdity of it all. Part of me was getting angry as to why GG wouldn't give me more to go on.

"I don't know what she's trying to tell me!" I through my hands up in frustration. "I don't understand anything anymore." I folded my arms trying to fight off the chill that suddenly hung in the air. "But I haven't heard her lately either."

Then the strangest sensation of Déjà Vu settled over me again. The next moment in time tauntingly out of reach but with each passing second as familiar as a real memory. But the feeling passed too quickly just as it had before. There was something maddening about the sensation. In some way, it was like looking trough someone else's eyes. Not my own. But I knew this was a foolish notion and I was afraid if I voiced this to anyone, even Preston, that someone would take me to a place where they would feed me colorful pills several times a day and keep me locked in a very plain and institutional looking room.

Preston stood there looking down at his feet and took both my hands in his. "Adena, I don't understand what's happening, either. But *please* don't let it scare you away. I don't really care if you *see* things in your sleep before you see them in reality. The fact is…" He stopped and pursed his lips. He rubbed his face and shook his head a little. "I think I dreamed of you before we met. It was my first night in Gainesville. Three days before we met. The woman in my dream had no face. But I knew I loved her. I loved her with all of my being. Body, mind, and soul, I loved her. And I saw her *here* in this very place. When I found her, it was as if I'd been searching for her forever. The longing I felt for her was such that it physically *hurt*. I remember waking from the dream with such an overwhelming feeling of loss because she wasn't real. Three nights, the same dream. —It didn't make sense to me at the time. I chalked it up as just some strangeness and thought nothing of it. But now, —I think the woman was you." He wrapped his arms around me. "Adena, I feel connected to you somehow. I only wish I knew why."

Three nights. I'd begun to have the dream of the cliff three nights before running into Preston. Was it because we were in such close proximity to each other? Is that even possible? To subconsciously feel your other half so near that the mind conjures such things? Again, I didn't speak these thoughts, preferring to hide my crazy.

"Well, I don't want to talk about it anymore. It's kinda freaking me out. But I don't care. Nothing is gonna scare me away from you. I just don't want you to think I'm a freak."

He chuckled a little. "Love, I wouldn't *dream* of it."

"Very funny. Enough with the dream talk. Let's go."

"Well, it is quite serene out here. And we *are* alone."

He took off his chambray shirt and spread it out on the ground in the center beneath the arbor for me to sit on, leaving him in his white undershirt. We leaned back on our elbows staring up at the lush green foliage all around us. With the warmth of his body so close, it helped me shake off the strangeness of the dreams.

I couldn't get over our surroundings. The mist hung in the air, adding to the mystical image. It really was a beautiful place. The wind blew across the tops of the trees causing the leaves to whisper to us. We heard the sound of rain gently falling somewhere but we never felt it. We lay there alone for hours on the moss-covered stone in the middle of the most magical place on earth. At least, that's what it felt like to me.

14

JUNE 19TH

FRIDAY MORNING TEENA TOOK BETH into the city for a day of shopping and sightseeing. Preston had already taken his mother to the hospital to sit with Mr. Nate until they released him. I'd finally get to meet him today. We took care of every chore so Doreen wouldn't have to lift a finger. We collapsed in the den when we'd finished, nearly exhausted as the house consisted of three bathrooms, five bedrooms, a den, a study, Mr. Nate's small office, the kitchen and dining room, the mudroom in back of the kitchen as well as the laundry room. And we never even went to the third floor.

We went to the grocery store then finished up at a farmer's market in town to get everything we needed to make roast beef for supper. Later in the kitchen, as I was trying to rinse the veggies, Preston kept standing behind me kissing my neck and playing around with my hair.

"You are *very* distracting. Anyone ever tell you that?" I said sort of scolding him.

"It's your perfume. Can't seem to keep my hands to myself."

"Well, pay attention. I'm fixin' to teach you how to cook this."

He laughed and poked the raw roast with his finger. "Fixin' to."

"About to! Jesus, Get over it. I swear, you say *bloody* so much it conjures up images of brutal massacres. So don't be pickin' on *me*."

"I'm not a good cook. I do eggs okay. Fairly good at cereal." He said while leaning against the butcher block counter, arms crossed, watching me.

I slid a chef's knife from its block on the counter, his eyes carefully watching the tip as I pointed it at him. I tossed it up in a half circle, catching the blade carefully so that the handle faced him. "I trust you at least know how to cut potatoes?"

He pulled a cutting board from under the sink and turned his head to me. "You can be right scary at times. Are you aware of that?"

After cutting up the potatoes, onions, carrots and celery, I had him season and dredge the meat and showed him how I browned it first. When he was done, he put it in a roasting pan and put all the veggies in around it. I covered it and placed it in the oven, while he set the timer.

"Mum won't know what to do coming home to a hot meal that isn't take-out." He stood behind me as I washed my hands and resumed his obsession with my neck and hair. "You seem nervous today. Anything the matter?"

"You think Beth and I should stay at your house tonight and give your dad some peace and quiet?" I pulled open one of four drawers and snagged a red dishtowel to dry my hands before turning to face him. He looked down at me, amused in some way but also looking a bit confused.

"What?" I asked.

He shook his head a little, shoved his hands into the pockets of his jeans and took one step back, smiling in a curious way. "I just noticed something. –You know this kitchen as well as your own."

I took a quick glance around the small space and shrugged. "So, a kitchen's a kitchen."

He disagreed with a slow shake of his head. "No. Your kitchen is huge by comparison. Not one cupboard, not one drawer is similar in any way. And you've not asked me once where anything is. It's like you've been cooking in here for ages. It just sort of struck me as -odd." He smiled and reached for the red dish towel, looped it around my neck to pull me closer. "But nice all the same."

I pondered his point for a second or so and realized he was right. I'd taken care of Trent's mother for two weeks last year after she'd undergone knee surgery. I'm familiar with her place and it'd still taken days to figure out where she kept everything. But then again, this kitchen is small; there are only so many places to put things.

"How are you with chocolate cake? Dad's addicted to the stuff."

I looked to the stove and noted the six hours to pass before the roast would be done. "How are we gonna cook it? The oven's a little busy right now."

His bottom lip jutted out a little as he thought for a short spell, then his eyes popped. He spun and stooped to the cabinet next to the oven. A few seconds of clattering pots and pans as he pushed them to the side, then he dragged a small convectional oven out.

"Will this work?"

I nodded. "Perfect. Now if you'll get the cake plate from the cabinet over the fridge, I'll get the pans ready." Immediately, I slapped my hand over my mouth. How the hell did I know there's an antique crystal cake dish up there? But I could see it plain as day in my mind.

He stood up slowly with the oven in his hands but didn't make a move to set it on the counter. He just stood there staring at me with a strange grin.

"What, Preston? You give me the heebie jeebies when you look at me like that."

He sat the oven on the counter and plugged it in. "You give me the heebie jeebies when you do things like that. That's quite a guess off the top of your head."

"So. That's where I keep mine." I watched as he reached for the cabinet over the fridge.

Please let it be ugly avocado green Tupperstuff from the seventies!

But no, there he stood holding a heavy crystal pedestal in one hand, the ornately diamond cut topper in the other.

Then something suddenly occurred to me and it hit me like a gigantic brick wall all at once. GG said I'd not only inherited her eyes and her curls but also her memories. But that still didn't explain how I would know anything about this house. It didn't make sense and it was making my brain itch! The thought had just popped into my head. I remembered GG's last words to me when she was still alive. I could hear her fervent words struggling to tell me to take her memories and follow her home. Follow the music of my heart and follow her home. But what did any of it have to do with Preston? I didn't understand.

I realized I was biting my lip in my fascination with the past. And Preston was watching me.

I changed the subject to get past his stare. "What about me and Beth staying at your place? You never answered me. I don't want us to be in the way." I tugged open the drawer to the left of the sink and took out the beaters for the mixer.

"You're anything but in the way, Adena. Having you here means everything to me. Mum can't go on enough on how Kelley has taken to you both. It's all she talks about in Dad's room." He laughed a little, an impish grin spreading.

"What?"

He pursed his lips as he opened the pantry to get a box of cake mix. "Well, that's not all she said." He cut his eyes at me and saw the expectant look on my face. His shoulders started to shake and soon he was laughing so hard he couldn't breathe. "She told me to go ahead and go to bed with you and not bother sneaking up the stairs so late."

"Preston!" I snatched the box from him, ripped it open and dumped the contents into a stainless steel bowl. "I thought you said no one could hear us."

"She didn't hear *us*. She heard the stairs creaking. They go right next to her room."

"So, she's not stupid."

"Adena, I'm fairly certain my mother knows her little boy isn't a virgin. It's alright." Looking far too smug for my liking.

My face grew hot and his smile didn't help. He gathered a few eggs from the fridge, picked the cake box up to squint at the directions, then got a bottle of oil from the pantry. He sat it all next to the bowl trying his best to keep from laughing again. And it's a good thing. I fought the urge to smack him with something. Something hard. Fuming, I cracked the eggs, thankful for something safe to break and watched them ooze down the side of the bowl.

He chuckled again and wrapped his arm around my waist. "I'm sorry for teasing but I do think it's funny. But aren't you glad we don't have to pretend to sleep in separate rooms anymore."

"What about Beth?"

"She's hardly been in this house since she's been here. You could be sleeping on the bloody roof for all she knows."

I stabbed the beaters into the mixer and poured the oil, only estimating the right amount. "What about your dad?"

I heard him grind his teeth behind me. "He'll think I'm one lucky bastard when he meets you. Now please stop worrying so much."

"Fine." I flipped the switch on the mixer but nothing happened. I shook it and it whirred to life but only for a second. He held the cord for me at just the right angle.

"I'll have to get her a new one. I forgot it has a short in it."

Standing closely behind me, he held the cord as I mixed the dark brown batter until the mixer quit working again. He'd dropped it on purpose and let his chin come to rest on my shoulder.

"There isn't anything I wouldn't do for you. You know that right?" He whispered softly.

"Yes."

"And would you do anything for me if I asked?"

I met the man two and a half weeks ago, fell in love with him, and here I am in London. Would I do anything for him? Duh!

"Of course I would. Why?"

"Then I want you to pretend you're *my* wife for the next seven days." I turned around and stared up at him. "What? Is it too much?"

"No. I'm just surprised."

The indignant look on his face told me I might have hurt his feelings. "Why does that surprise you?"

"I don't know. It just did."

He cupped my face in hands and leaned closer. "Adena, I'm not talking about just sharing a bed. I just don't want you fretting over what anyone thinks. And I want you to feel comfortable here with me, as if you are home. That's all I'm asking for." He buried his nose in my hair and breathed in deeply. "So what do you say? Will you be my wife for the next week and not someone else's?"

"Only a week?"

He smiled and pressed his lips to my forehead. "Well, you've got matters to deal with first. All in your own time of course."

I cuddled into the cocoon of his arms trying to imagine what it would be like to wake up with him for the rest of my life, too easy to see our future as forever. I knew it wasn't a proposal by any means but just that he'd suggested it made my head swim.

A flash of dread made me take a step back, but the counter blocked my retreat. I side stepped him and started turning in circles in the middle of the kitchen, my hands in my hair as reality began to creep up my spine.

"Adena? What's the matter?"

"Preston, I can't even think fast enough to keep up with us. There is something you need to know. For your sake, not mine." Scared that this overlooked bit of information could be what drew a line between us, my pulse thudded in my ears.

He took me by my shoulders and made me stop moving around as if I were lost in a maze.

"Stop it. There is nothing that would turn me away from you."

"Listen, I know this isn't a bridge *we're* about to cross but —I can't have any more children. I had two miscarriages after Beth. I got fixed so I'd never have to go through it again. And you're young. You may want to be with someone who can have your child someday."

He huffed a little and rolled his eyes. "That's it? That's what turned you inside out? Jesus, you scared the hell out of me." He came closer, eye to eye. "I have Kelley. I don't *have* to have anymore. If I have you, I won't *need* anything else."

I had to force myself to try to make him consider longer. But he started kissing me as if the feel of his lips would persuade me not to think about it. And truthfully, Preston's kisses were exceptionally persuasive. I'd almost forgotten what we were discussing and I had no will to push him away. It was something I had to pull out of thin air, something that didn't exist within me to press my hands against his chest and break the spell.

I managed to do it and took in a deep breath to slow my heart. "Preston, I swear we are stuck in fast forward here. Press pause for a second and *think* about what you're saying."

He took my hands in his and squeezed them and for a few seconds, his face turned a fascinating shade of purple. At least until he let go a frustrated whimper. "Don't you think the obstacles that are *already* in place are enough? Without adding to it? Dammit! You're married and we live on two blasted different continents." His tone more than bothered, but then he forced himself peaceful. "Don't you know what I would do for you? The lengths I'd go through?" He shoved one hand through his hair and looked away. "Of course, you can't. You're the one who flew half way round the world for me at the drop of hat."

I tugged his chin to make him look at me again. "I just thought you should know. A child is a huge thing to give up."

"Fine. Duly noted." He smiled and stroked my cheek. "Now, *please*. No more worries."

I smiled but the thought still troubled me for what it might mean if we ever actually made it that far.

Preston and Uncle had a meeting set up with a horse trainer to replace the one who still hadn't shown since I'd arrived, so I went upstairs to wash away the smell of furniture polish and onions.

Still wet from the shower, I stood looking through the antique wardrobe in my temporary room with nothing but a towel wrapped around me when there was a light knock at the door.

"Um, who is it?" I thought it might be Preston but he hadn't been gone that long. No one said anything and the hairs on my arms stood on end. "Preston?" I called walking closer to the door. No response.

I grabbed the first clothes I could get my hands on and dressed as quickly as I could. I gave the old glass doorknob a twist, cracked the door an inch to peek into the hall. No one was there. I stepped out and turned to the right and almost ran into him, my heart slammed against my ribs.

"Shit, Preston! You almost gave me heart attack!" I blew out a calming breath and looked up at him. But he looked strange. Not himself. It didn't take long to begin to notice things. Things like his clothes. It looked like he'd stepped back in time, his trousers not anything Preston would wear. A tweed jacket with patches on the elbows, his shoes, black boots that I'd never seen him wear.

My eyes followed the towering figure before me until I held his eyes with mine. I took a wary step back as I realized the man standing three feet from me wasn't Preston at all. He was actually a good bit taller, his eyes were brown and he was older. But his stance, his looks —from a distance it'd be too easy to make the mistake. He was the man I saw in the woods behind the stables.

I tried reasoning the situation out. Probably just another relative I hadn't met and he'd let himself in. Yes, that's it. Apparently there was another relative that looked so much like Uncle and Preston. Family looks run deep and frequent in some families.

I cleared my throat and stuck out my hand. "Hey, I'm Adena. Um, Preston's with Uncle right now." I realized it wasn't very smart letting this stranger know I was alone, be it a relative or not. "But they'll be back any second."

I looked down at my empty hand as the man had not accepted my greeting. Letting my hand fall awkwardly to my side, I looked up at him waiting for him to speak. He narrowed his eyes at me a little but not in a shrewd way, more like trying to figure me out. Must be my accent throwing him off.

Then he breathed in and with the intake of air, it sounded like a thousand tinkling bells tumbling in a great wind, slowly morphing into words. "Have you seen her?"

My skin turned to gooseflesh in an instant. I felt like screaming but my throat constricted as the recognition of the sound hit me. The windy sound had been the same when GG spoke to me at the lake.

"Have you seen her?" He asked again and took a step toward me, his British accent much sharper than Preston's. "I've looked for ages and I can't find her. I know she's close. I can hear her."

I took a step back into the bedroom and gulped. "Wh-wh-who are you looking for?"

The man smiled —a smile so familiar I almost wanted to touch him. Preston's smile.

"Oh, sweet Dilly. You should know. My Katherine. Please help me. She weeps for me and I can't find her."

Dilly? This man, this apparition, thought I was someone else. I took another step back, but he stepped forward keeping a perfect three foot distance between us.

"I'm sorry, Sir. My name's Adena. Not Dilly. And I'm afraid I *can't* help you."

His face, so forlorn, seemed to fall into further despair. "Don't be frightened. I mean you no harm. You look a great deal like Dilly, only —darker somehow. Your skin, your hair. However, you sound a great deal like Roger. Do you know him?"

My chin began to quiver and tears instantly pooled in my eyes and spilled quickly down my face. "How do you know my father?"

"I only hear him. Never knew the man until we all found ourselves here. Wherever here is –this wretched gray place."

Wherever here is? Gray? GG had said the same things. A brick tumbled into place in my mind. Whatever magic had brought GG back to speak to me was happening here as well. And somehow, it involved Preston and me. Our meeting again had been no accident. I had no way of knowing but some instinct deep within me confirmed this simple fact.

GG had said; *Don't be afraid, no matter what happens.* Did she know this man would find me? With her voice in my head, I took a step closer and looked deeply into the tall man's brown eyes.

"Sir, who are you?"

He smiled. "Preston, of course."

Okay, not only am I speaking to yet another ghost, I'm speaking to a crazy one.

But the resemblance, too strong to not be some relative of Preston's – maybe Preston had been named after him.

The tell-tale creak of the stairs announced *my* Preston's arrival.

The man winked and tipped an imaginary hat to me. He checked an ancient pocket watch that had no hands then slipped it back into his coat pocket. "I don't think he's prepared to know I'm still about. Wiry lad, he's always been. But I quite admire the man he's become." He pressed his finger to his lips as if to say, *Don't tell him you saw me.*

The strangest thing happened next. His figure turned all gray, the whisper wind of a chuckle and he began to spin. Not on his feet, his feet remained planted firmly on the floor, but rather fragments of him swirled, slowly at first, then faster like time sped up the process of turning his body into a whirlwind, a seven foot tornado with the sound of a spring breeze. The faster it spun, the thinner it became, until there was nothing left. *Poof! Like the wind,* Kelley had said.

GG tells me not to be afraid. Some man named Preston tells me not to tell *my* Preston I've seen him. The other side of death sure seemed to have its hooks in me and trying to do a damn good job at driving me to the loony bin.

I faintly heard Preston whistling a happy tune down the hall. I spun to the dresser to look in the mirror. My hands shaking, I turned my make up bag upside down spilling the contents on the dark wood surface. I rubbed the tears vigorously away and powdered my face at the speed of light. I heard another door open, the whistling continued. I had a little more time. Eyeliner, blush, lipstick, mascara, all in record time. I could've done a better job but at least I'd hidden all evidence of crying.

I grabbed my hair dryer to blow out my hair. Just as soon as the loud racket filled the room, Preston walked in.

I gave him a wave, not sure how steady my voice might be. I flipped my hair over to blow out the back fluffing it with my fingers. A few minutes of the loud hot hair seemed to relax me and give me the time I needed to find just the right amount of composure.

I'm not afraid. I'm not freaked out. Everything is fine. I repeated the mantra in my head. Writing this kind of nonsense was one thing. Living it was entirely another.

Questions began to form in my brain. *Who's Dilly? Who's Katherine?* According to GG, she'd started something, that, for some unknown reason, she believed I could finish. What were the connections? *More importantly, why am I still drying my hair? I'm gonna look like a bush rat with all these damn curls if I don't stop.*

I stood up and checked my hair in the mirror. *Whew! Stopped just in time.*

"So that's how you get it to do that." Preston said, stretching out on the bed.

"To do what? Be dry? It's a hair dryer. Awesome little invention."

"*No,* Miss Sassy Pants. The waves everywhere. Looks like you spend hours on it."

I walked a step closer solely to take in his scent. The earthy smell of the stables still clinging to his clothes, the undertone of his very skin; mixed together the scents were enough to intoxicate me.

He chuckled a little, his eyes following me from top to bottom. "You're wearing the same clothes you had on the day we met."

I looked down at myself. "Really?"

He sat up and touched my sleeves. "Brown v-neck. Longish sleeves pushed up to your elbows. It's pretty." He leaned back on the bed and casually folded his hands behind his head.

I couldn't believe he remembered.

"And I get to see the freckle." He added cheerily.

I turned back to the closet and started to search again. "Hmm. I think I have a turtleneck in here somewhere." I didn't even own one.

"No! I was only joking. No turtlenecks." He pleaded from the foot of the bed. "I'll be good."

"Promise?"

He smiled and crossed his heart.

"Okay. Close your eyes. I have to... readjust a few things."

"Readjust? Like what?"

"My bra is stabbing me in the back if you have to know. Just close your eyes!"

He closed his eyes and lay there complaining that he'd already seen me naked and the whole bit of how we were supposed to be married. As he whined, I raised my shirt to fix the uncomfortable problem with my undergarment-as I had put it on far too fast before and it felt like maybe I'd twisted the strap somehow when hooking it. The situation had to be remedied which I managed quickly enough but before I'd gotten my shirt pulled back down, Preston opened his eyes, dropped his jaw then clamped his teeth shut with a loud click. He pulled my shirt up to peek at the bronze lace he'd gotten just a glimpse of.

I swatted his hands away. "You promised to be good."

"Oh, I'll be *very* good, I promise."

I laughed at his insatiable appetite.

He stood up and kissed me once very gently. "I'm only teasing. Between working around here, Dad, and everyone else coming and going, today's the first day we've been alone, save for a few fleeting moments of privacy."

"Preston, we *have* been sharing a room."

He rolled his eyes. "I know and I'm grateful that the arrangement has worked out this way. I just don't like having to wait till the wee hours of night just to touch you. I refuse to make Beth hate me any more than she already does."

"She doesn't hate you, Preston."

He grimaced a little. "You can't know that. I slipped up and held your hand in front of her yesterday, only to find her giving me the snake eye."

"Oh, don't worry about it. And you know what?"

"What?"

"You can hold my hand whenever and wherever you want."

He smiled. "Well, I don't want to hold your hand right now." He glanced at his watch and frowned a little. "The others are on their way home as we speak. Fancy a kiss instead?"

"Always."

And for the next ten minutes, our lips found all sorts of ways to stay busy.

Kelley came running in the den first, straight at us eyes wide and smiling. I fully expected her open arms to be for Preston but she caught me around my waist in a tight hug. I wrapped her warm little body in my arms, returning her gracious gift. Then she pulled the string I'd tied for her from around her neck and showed me a new trick.

"Beth taught me." She held it up. "See, its London Bridge. Did you know Gran and Teena can do it as well?"

"I'm certain of it. It's a very old game. And it doesn't even need batteries."

She giggled and skipped down the hall.

Beth came in next followed by Teena and Mr. Nate. Preston went to his side offering his assistance.

His father swatted his thick right hand through the air. "Nothing wrong with the legs, Preston. I can bloody well walk on my own. — Now, where is she?" He looked up and found my face. "There she is! Come give an old man a kiss."

He had a cute round face, rosy cheeks, and silvery hair. Stocky and square with a little potbelly. With just the right red attire, and a little more stuffing, he'd make an excellent Santa.

Of course I obliged, and walked over to Nate and gave him a little peck on the cheek. "It's good to finally meet you, Sir."

Ms. Doreen walked in carrying an overnight bag, looking so relieved to have her husband safely back home. Preston took the bag from her and brought it to her room near the staircase.

Mr. Grace took my hand and we walked together to his favorite chair by the fireplace. "How are you feeling?" I asked as he sat down.

"Oh, everything is tickety-boo." He replied brightly although it was an obvious wash over to how weary he really felt. He heaved a careful sigh as he pulled his reading glasses from his shirt pocket and sat them next to him on a small table. His hands shook ever so slightly.

But as for his words, well he may as well have spoken Chinese. I looked up to find Preston coming to stand next to me wearing a smile as the others started to snicker at mine and Beth's puzzled expressions. Even Mr. Nate began to chuckle deeply.

"Tickety-boo is an old saying. It means *never better* or something of the sort." Preston explained.

"Oh. Glad to hear it." The others gathered around us and sat down near Nate to talk.

"I owe you my gratitude young lady for helping me out the other day." His father held my hand as he spoke, his chilled hands thickly calloused and dry as a bone. "I remember everything. The pain was just too much for me to speak…couldn't catch my breath. But I could hear how afraid you were for a stubborn old bloke you didn't even know. And when I couldn't call out, you did it for me." He patted my hand. "Thank you, precious."

"I'm just glad you're better now." I gently squeezed his hand before I sat down next to Preston on the love seat nearby.

Preston laced his fingers into mine and he was wearing an expression I hadn't seen before. Elation I think. He was happy when we were together but his father's failing health was a heavy weight on his mind. I think he'd been trying to hide it from everyone. Now we were together, his Dad was back, and Beth seemed to be taking things in stride. (Some of the time.) He pulled our hands up and flipped them over to kiss the back of my hand.

His father leaned over the arm of his chair and winked right at me. "Preston I simply adore her already. Loads better than that *last* girl you brought home. What was her name?"

Preston's mouth fell open. "Thanks Dad." He seemed a little irritated but smiled for Nate's benefit.

Teena chimed in immediately. "Don't worry Adena, she was all fur coat and no knickers compared to you."

I looked at Preston again for help.

"Ehm, fake and shallow, I suppose. Pretty enough on the outside, nothing of substance inside."

"Got it. —Thanks Teena." Teena, at times, made it very hard to believe that we both spoke English.

"Well, I think Adena is lovely. I never liked that girl. Little vulture." Ms. Doreen surprised me with her tone. Sounded like she harbored a bit of a grudge but I wasn't about to ask why.

189

"Well, I agree undoubtedly, but I honestly don't think Adena cares to be compared to my ex all evening." Preston looked flustered. "Scratch that last, she isn't even my ex. We only went out a few times before she stuck that bleedin' knife in me." He squeezed my hand. "And," he directed at his family, "that blunder was over four years ago. So can we please drop it and move on?"

Four years ago? That's the last time he'd brought a woman to meet his parents? Wow!

I don't know why I'd been so apprehensive about meeting his father. The conversation flowed as easily as water down a hill for almost an hour. Beth regaled her and Teena's time in the city, her blonde curls bouncing with her animated gestures, her blue eyes shining with the excitement of her day, which made me extremely happy.

"Mom, did you know that if a person is born within the sound of St. Mary-le-Bow's bells, *that's* what makes them a cockney Londoner?"

"I had no idea." I didn't even know what a cockney Londoner was - but okay.

"We went back the route where Preston took us on the way here and a bunch of other places! We saw St. Paul's Cathedral, St. Mary-le-Bow, The Tower of London…" A good five more minutes passed before she began to wind down. But not before the clincher. "And tomorrow night, she's taking me to SoHo!" Followed by an ear-bleeding squeal.

Teena bumped Beth's knee to shut her up but Preston spoke up.

"No, you're *not*, Teena. She's only seventeen and I *know* some of your flaky friends. Let's leave it at shopping and sightseeing and perhaps you could take her for *lunch* in SoHo. Not hit every club at night." He ran his hand through his hair and frowned earnestly at his sister. "Really, Teena. I truly wonder at what rattles about in your skull sometimes."

Beth and Teena each slumped in their seats like ten-years-olds told that it was too dark to go outside and play. But it didn't take long for Beth to figure Preston's suggestions were just as good, given she'd always been one to choose shopping over partying.

I whispered a quick but quiet thanks to him and it made him smile.

Mr. Nate slapped his knee then gestured to Beth, chuckling with his eyes closed. "I've been trying to puzzle out who she reminds me of." He got up carefully and walked to the right of the fireplace scratching his week-old whiskers as his eyes searched the bookshelves.

"What do you want, Dad? I'll get it." Preston offered.

He swatted the air again never taking his eyes from the shelf. "I think

I can carry a DVD without falling." He heaved a sigh. "But thanks all the same. –Ah! There it is." He pulled a movie from a stack and sat down again, tossing the slim case to Beth.

She caught it, turned it around to read it and died laughing. "Are you serious?" She held the cover of *Sweet Home Alabama* next to her face. "Mom? What do you think?"

"Pretty close."

"She sounds like her as well." Nate laughed again gesturing to the actress on the cover.

"Poppy, I smell chocolate." Kelly announced, climbing between us.

"That's because Adena made a special treat for us. You'll have to wait till after supper."

I tapped her knee so she'd look at me. "Would you like to help me in the kitchen?"

She nodded eagerly, her darling pink smile tugging at my heartstrings. Once in the kitchen, it took only a second for her eyes to locate the source of the smell. She dragged a chair to the counter and looked at me, then the cake, then at me again. She made me laugh.

"Is it finished?" She inquired very seriously.

I tapped my finger on my chin and stared at the bald brown cake. "I don't know. It seems to be missing something. Don't you think?" Careful to turn my head so she could read my lips.

"Frosting! It's definitely missing the frosting! And it should be really thick like this." She held her little fingers up to show me at least an inch worth.

I let her help me smooth the frosting on, which I'd already prepared and left to cool on the counter. She seemed to want to lick her fingers but always resisted and even dropped the spatula in the sink when we'd finished.

"You can have a taste." I told her, rescuing the spatula before water dripped on it. Her eyes lit up and she looked over her shoulder as if she might get a scolding, but then reached for the chocolate covered trophy in my hands.

I pulled it back just out of reach. "Wait. You're not a diabetic are you?"

Her little blonde brows almost touched each other. "A dia-what-ic?"

I surmised if she didn't know the word, it'd be safe to let her have it. She licked it clean giggling the entire time. It wasn't until she'd finished that she explained.

"Gran never lets me have sugar before supper."

I dropped my jaw as though saving that bit of information had been the biggest scandal since Watergate and it made her red-faced with the giggles. A quick swipe with a damp towel removed all evidence from her lips and the darling chocolate smudge on the tip of her nose.

She smacked her ear like she was swatting at a bothersome bug and yanked a tiny yellow piece from her ear. I hadn't noticed she'd had her hearing aid in.

"I hate this thing and its creepy noises. Gran makes me wear it when we go out. She's afraid I'll step into the street and I won't hear her shouting." She stared at me like an insulted mini diva, head and hip cocked to one side, her hands perched at her waist. "I'm deaf, not daft!"

She tossed the offending aid on the kitchen counter as though ridding herself of a disgusting insect then she grabbed my arm. We went to join the others hand in hand and above all else, her acceptance made me feel I belonged.

The timer on the oven beeped and Ms. Doreen jumped to her feet.

"Sit *down*, Mum." Preston said. "We've got it."

"I won't argue once." She said flopping back into her chair. "Well, I suppose I do need to get you something to drink so you can take your pills." She said to Nate and got up again.

"Not right now, Love. They'll make me sleepy and I really want to enjoy everyone tonight." Mr. Nate grumbled lightly but somehow still managed to sound lighthearted.

Although, Preston and I were halfway to the dining room when we overheard his father's reluctance to cooperate again, it was as though the barometric pressure in the room had dropped to zero. A hurricane was brewing and the tension of the approaching storm was palpable. Preston froze in his tracks and his hands drew into tight balls making the veins in his arms stand out in acute definition. I heard something that sounded almost like a low growl building deep in his chest, maybe in his throat and I could clearly see he was in no state of mind to turn around and respond to his father- so I urged him onward so he wouldn't say anything he couldn't take back.

Once in the kitchen, he leaned against the counter and reached backward to smack the digital timer of the stove. Without a word, I pulled out the roast and put the rolls in, adjusting the temperature before closing it again. I looked up and saw the pain etched in his otherwise tender eyes and I watched his anger and disappointment rise to the boiling point. To say he was merely livid would be a woeful inaccuracy.

He cleared his throat, looked up at the ceiling and said very low, "Please, excuse me."

He turned and walked carefully to the mudroom. He must have stopped for a second but then I heard the door creak open then slam shut as he stormed off into the backyard. I hurried to the kitchen sink and looked for him in the limited boxed in view that I had. It took a few seconds but finally from the left he walked within the glassed in frame. Pacing back and forth in front of the long line of trees fronting a section of deep forest that lie between his cottage and the big farmhouse, Preston slowly puffed away on a cigarette- his eyes so deep and dark with worry as he looked down watching his own feet as he wore a path in the pale green grass.

It was then that I realized that he only smoked when he drank, when he was worried, or in this case angry.

Ms. Doreen came in so quietly that it startled me when she spoke. "Excuse me dear, is everything alright?" I gestured to the window without a word. She looked out the window and watched Preston bend over to pick up a rock and launch it across the back yard into the woods. "I see. I suppose he heard Nathaniel's nonsense?"

I nodded; feeling trapped right in the middle of a private war that I had no business seeing.

"No need to fret. He'll settle down and come back in directly. He does that sometimes. Blow off a little steam to prevent saying something to upset his father. He tries so hard. And Nate." She sighed and I looked at her not yet knowing what to say. "Well, he's like any man I suppose. Thick as a brick and just as smart at times. As much as I love the old fool, I'd really love nothing more than to put my hands around his fat neck and give it a good hard squeeze." She looked outside at her son again and shook her head. "Perhaps, the *both* of them now and then if I thought for a second I could drain just a smidgen of their stubbornness out."

She made herself busy setting the long oak table in the dining room. I joined her getting the silverware and glasses. It didn't take long and I found myself back at the window watching Preston wrestle with his anger. He finally stood still, looked up and saw me. His lips spread into a thin line and he motioned for me to come to him.

As soon as I walked around the corner of the house, he grabbed my hand. I curled my arms around his waist and held him as he leaned against the rear wall of the house. He felt rigid and hard as the cold stones behind him. His mood as gray as the early evening's sky.

He reached up and smoothed away several tendrils of hair blowing across my face from the stiff breeze. His features softened but his brows were still drawn. "I hate that you saw me so beside myself."

I pressed my lips to his throat, as that was all I could reach without him bending. He spread his legs a little to make himself shorter and I stood on my toes to kiss his lips. At first he felt a little unyielding, too distressed to accept my offer. I backed away only a bit.

His eyes narrowed only the slightest and the corner of his mouth turned up faintly, the barest hint of my favorite smile. "Still hurts. Do it again."

That was one invitation I'd never send my regrets to. His lips were more than yielding and he kissed me back. His body relaxed and he pulled me against him tighter. Then with no warning he reached down, picked me up and wrapped my legs around his waist then he turned and pressed me hard against the side of the house, with a kiss so brutal it took my breath. You'd think I'd have felt some discomfort from the stones pressed into my back but I honestly never noticed. I'd never been kissed by an angry man before and all I could think of was ways to possibly piss Preston off in the future. Just a little.

The back door opened with a tattletale creak. He cursed and let me slide down till my feet were firmly on the ground; he kissed me again then stood there before me looking just a smidgen abashed.

"Sorry for that. But all the same, thank you." He whispered and kissed the tip of my nose. "Thank you for being here."

"Oh... sorry dear. Just letting you know we're sitting down to eat. Whenever you're ready." Doreen said from the corner of the house.

When she walked inside, he sighed. "Seems like every time we have a moment like that, we get interrupted. What I wouldn't give to be completely alone with you."

15

WHEN EVERYONE FINISHED EATING, MS. Doreen got up automatically to clear the dishes. Beth gave me a hug saying that she, Teena, and Kelley were going to the cottage. Teena kissed her dad goodnight. At first, I wondered why she wouldn't want to visit with him longer. Then I realized it was a ploy to leave the house quiet so Nate could get some rest.

I helped clean the dishes and put away what food was left over, leaving Preston and his father alone. I could tell Doreen was listening to the conversation in the dining room just around the corner. Their voices getting more tense and edgy. With every word, she came closer to breaking down.

My uncontrollable *fix things* nature began to boil over due to my inability to be around people who didn't get along. I tried to fight it, the urge to open my big mouth. But before I gave it another thought, Ms. Doreen excused herself, walking away with tears gleaming in her eyes, apparently unable to bear the discord between her husband and son one more second.

I walked nervously into the dining room taking the seat nearest to Nate. "How'd you like the roast Preston made?" Redirecting their conversation as if I hadn't overheard any of it.

Preston tilted his chair back and didn't say anything.

"I thought you cooked this evening." Nate said as though he and Preston hadn't had one cross word. I shook my head and thumbed at Preston giving him all the credit. Nate patted his full stomach. "Well, I must say it was delicious."

Preston looked altogether irritated staring down at the table at three small amber containers containing Mr. Nate's medicine—the muscles in his jaw clenched and unclenched like he was trying to bite a ten penny nail in half. He flicked a crumb off the lace tablecloth.

I tried to think of something else to say, but my cell rang. Gavin asked me about college credits, prerequisites for engineering and something about a chemistry placement exam at mach one speed, but I wasn't sure I'd get another opportunity to get Mr. Nate alone.

I covered the mouthpiece and looked at Preston. "You went to college, right?"

He nodded. "**Architectural** Engineering. Why?"

Perfect. Thankfully, Gavin had heard Preston say *Engineering* and jumped at the opportunity to speak to him. I slid the phone down the length of the table. Preston looked shocked and let the legs of his chair bang to the floor.

"Take it in the den please; it's rude to talk on the phone at the table." I smiled and gave him a wink that Nate didn't catch.

He picked it up with half of his grin in place wondering what I was up to. When he vanished around the corner of the stairs and into the den, I gave Nate's hand a gentle nudge. "I thought he'd *never* leave."

He chuckled. "Alright, dear. What have they put you up to?"

"Nothing. This is just you and me getting to know each other. Much easier with just the two of us. Wouldn't you think?"

"Yes, I would. What would you like to talk about?" "Nothing in particular. We can just shoot the breeze if you want."

"Shoot the breeze we shall then." He leaned back in his armed chair at the head of the table.

"You know, Preston and I picked up a bottle of red wine today but we forgot to open it for supper. We could have a glass if you want."

"Grand idea. I've heard red wine is good for the blood."

"So have I. Of course I think grape juice does the same thing, but we won't let that ugly little rumor get out." It made him laugh.

I walked to a beautiful antique china cabinet, carefully took out two crystal goblets and a cork screw. I didn't ask where to find these items and it crossed my mind again as to how it could be that I just knew. Mr. Nate didn't seem to notice the oddity so I sat down and set to work opening the bottle but he put his hand on mine to stop me.

"This is a special occasion. My boy having such a darling at last. Follow me under the stairs for a bit and I'll find us something good and old."

I laughed. I loved the man already. I followed him to the stairwell and watched as he pulled open what I'd never noticed was a door. It had no knob; he just placed his nimble fingers along the edge of a wide piece of tongue-and-groove paneling and pulled it.

Down the narrowest steps I'd ever taken, we curved our way down, the temperature dropping a few degrees as we descended. He reached over his head about half way down and snagged a cord to turn on a light without ever slowing. The stone walls and steps were black with age, or maybe from whatever stone the underbelly of the house had been made of. I began to worry the exertion may be too much too soon for him but I kept my mouth shut, although I kept careful eyes on him.

The stairs ended and with another light cord pulled, I could see the massive cellar. Easily fifty feet by fifty feet filled with rows upon rows of large wooden casks covered in dust and cob webs.

"The famous Grace cellars. Is this where you age the brandy?" I asked.

"Not all of it. We have three more like this on the grounds. You've likely driven right over them at some point and didn't even know it."

I nodded with admiration. "So there has to be another way in here. There's no way you got those big wooden barrels down those stairs."

"You would be correct. You've seen how the land slopes just behind the house?"

I had to think about it but then recalled seeing what looked like a retaining wall on the side of hill past the little storage shed next to Kelley's swing and where Preston keeps that old green truck parked. I nodded. "So there's an entrance on the other side of the shed?"

He smiled and shook his head.

Then sudden understanding hit me. "Oh, I see. That's not just a storage shed is it?"

His eyes danced with his smile. "You catch on quickly."

He mumbled to himself as he made his way to the back wall half covered by a rough hewn wooden wine rack rubbed smooth in places from eons of use. He pulled several bottles out one by one, glancing at the labels quickly then putting them back. "Where is it?" He grumbled to himself then reached two rows higher to pull another out just far enough to see it. "Ah, there it is!"

When he freed the bottle, I heard something scratch the wall, the sound of crisp paper scraping as it fell a few inches.

"I think you lost the label on that one." I reached my hand between the narrow spaces and peered through the gaps to see where it went.

"Oh, leave it. There are probably spiders back there anyways. Wouldn't want you to get bitten."

I shuddered at the thought. "Sorry, Mr. Nate. I have a touch of OCD. I clean during my free time just to keep my head on straight. You have no idea how bad it will bug me to leave it back there."

He laughed and went to get a flashlight from a small work bench then came back to help.

"Preston told me you're a writer. Isn't that a contradiction? I thought people of an artistic nature tended to be..." He chuckled again. "Well, not so worried about tidying, too engrossed in their work to be bothered."

"Mmm, I don't know. Maybe that's why I can't finish my book." I wiggled my fingers trying to grasp at anything that felt like the label.

He shined the light closer and peeked himself. "Wait, I see it. But that's not a label at all." He took a step back and squatted a little. "One row down from where you are, pull the bottle out that sits two to your left. You should be able to reach to the right. It's trapped behind that bottle. If we move that one, it will only fall again and I'd hate for you to lose any sleep over it."

I stepped back, handed him the key bottle, dove my hand in, reached to the right, snagged the bothersome piece of paper between two fingers and pulled it free.

As soon as I had it in front of us, a quarter-sized brown spider scuttled to the corner and dropped by a web to the floor where Mr. Nate ended its life with a crunch beneath his shoe.

"I bloody well despise those things." He shivered and did a funky dance that had me in tears. He took the paper from me and almost balled it up, but seemed to recognize something on it. He stretched the curled paper out on the work bench and shined the light on it. "Another one? These things have turned up in every dismal corner of this house. Half rat-eaten. I wish I knew where the lot of them were once and for all."

"What is it?" I looked over his shoulder and he moved to the side to show me.

"Some sort of blessing I gather. But have a look. It's a lovely poem. I don't know if my grandmother actually wrote it herself or if someone gave it to her. But throughout the years I find them in the oddest of places. It has to be rodents dragging them from somewhere in this house. I just don't know." He handed me the flash light and I began to read.

'Infinite Love'
We pray to the powers
Of the Lord above
That all of this family
Shall share our love.
Unable to resist,
Unwilling to try.
Our love will live on
Long after we die.
All along our family tree
Our sons shall know
What's come to be.
From the roots to the branches
And every new leaf,
Our home and our hearts
We vow to bequeath.
Katherine and Preston Grace
Wedded March 17ᵗʰ, 1908

Right away, a wicked chill tickled my spine. I took note of the names at the bottom.

"Katherine. As in Katherine's Private Stock." I said, referring to the brandy labels.

He nodded. "Yes. My grandmother."

I sat down on an overturned milk crate with the yellowed paper in my hand, the brittle edges cracking and falling from being handled. And I felt as though I held a great piece of the puzzle in my hand. The piece that would answer all of my questions. If only I had the coordinating pieces to fit it with.

"And *Preston* —was your grandfather?"

He nodded again. "Is something wrong, dear?"

I shook my head quick and tight, not wanting to think about the man who so resembled my Preston, who'd paid me a visit in this very house, (*his* house) looking for his lost Katherine. Two mysteries solved. But I still didn't know who Dilly could be.

"Nothing's wrong. Just a little tired. It's been a long day." I stood up, sat the poem on the work bench and tapped the date just below the couples' names. "St. Patrick's day. I was born on their wedding anniversary."

He looked surprised and smiled. "You don't say. Lucky day all around then. How about that!"

Yeah…how 'bout that?

I remembered then something else that GG had said. She knew the day I was born that Fate had chosen its intended path. What did March 17th have to do with all of this? Was it merely a coincidence that I'd been born on Preston and Katherine's wedding anniversary? How could our families possibly be connected? Too many pieces were missing. But one thing I'd done was follow my heart like she'd said. It led me to Havering-atte-Bower and Preston's family. So, now what? What could it all mean?

As I sat there looking at the poem in my hand, I couldn't help but feel a sinister presence come close around me. The air became thicker somehow, more solid like a cloak. I looked around as Mr. Nate tended to something far off to the left of where I was sitting, near the wall where the large oak casks were.

I looked to the right and noted a thick wooden door. It showed the age of the house in its construction and its thick black iron hinges. My heartbeat quickened at the sight of it. Darkness had never bothered me before but for some reason I wanted to turn on the light. I needed more light. It took a minute to realize what I was feeling as I stared at this simple wooden door. I was afraid. I was beyond afraid, I was petrified. I watched it and I waited and my heartbeat scampered along faster and faster. It felt like some sort of panic attack and I closed my eyes. I could see a long tunnel beyond that door and I could make out the dancing flame of a candle. I saw a small boy next to me. But how did I get in there to begin with?

We were trapped alone in this dark miserable place all alone and hungry. It was damp and it smelled of mildew. My arm hurt me so and this small boy huddled next to me as he held the candle in his hands.

The scant light highlighted his light cinnamon-blonde hair giving him a halo effect and he looked up at me and whispered, "Dilly, what if they never find us? What if she never lets us out?"

"Ready to head up, dear?" Mr. Nate's voice spilled around me and I nearly jumped out of my skin. He laughed. "I didn't mean to startle you."

"Mr. Nate, what's behind that door over there?" I gestured to the old thick relic I'd been staring at.

"Just an old tunnel that connects to another cellar. It's closed off though. A portion of the cellar collapsed when I was just a boy."

I nodded and eagerly got up to follow. I didn't want to know why I could see what lay on the other side. But something told me I was just beginning to get to the meat of the mystery that had taken hold of my world.

Nate made it upstairs to the kitchen only a little short of breath. I listened carefully to be sure he didn't over exert himself but by the time we made it to the dining table, he'd already started to breathe easier and so did I.

I wasn't exerted from the climb, but the daydream, for lack of a better word, seemed to drain every ounce of strength that I had. I was glad to be back in the bright cheeriness of the dining room. It helped me to shake off the odd experience. It helped me to pretend I had not seen two children hiding in a dark tunnel that I shouldn't have known was there.

Nate poured us each a glass of wine, thank God, and with half a glass gone, my nerves were nearly in check. He told me stories about Preston when he was a little boy and we had a grand time in his absence. If language can be considered colorful, then his was a rainbow when he really got going about something. He filled me in on a little more family history and told me all about raising pears. I enjoyed talking to him, but it made me miss my father so much.

"I'll have just a smidge more. Don't want to overdo it first night home." He said. I pushed the bottle over to him so he could pour it himself and made a toast to his good health.

"Here, here." He said raising his glass.

Okay... here goes nothing, big mouth. "You know, Mr. Nate... not everyone gets a second chance."

"Yes. I know I'm a lucky old fool." He said quietly looking down in his lap.

"Has Preston told you about my Daddy?"

"You still call him Daddy? How sweet."

"Well, I used to. He passed away eight years ago. —Of a heart attack."

"Oh, dear. I'm sorry for you and your dear mother. It must be horrible for her without him and you as well, I'm sure."

"They are together."

His face seemed suddenly stricken with this information. "Gracious child, do you have *any* family left?"

"I have my kids. They're all I need." I paused taking his hand in mine. "Mr. Nate, my daddy was alone when he died. I lived over six hundred miles away." The truth still cut like a razor but I pushed the pain aside and kept on. "You on the other hand, have your family here. *You* are the very heart of the Grace family. It only takes minutes to see the love and admiration they have for you. —I have a feeling I know what bothers you most. And it's just a guess, correct me if I'm wrong. — You don't like being coddled do you?"

"No -I -don't!" He slammed one hand on the table but held mine gently in the other. "I bloody well hate it! I wish they would all just leave me be!" He took a drink of his wine and tried to settle his temper. "I've managed to keep this place going for years, seen to the orchards since I was a boy. Now, the lot of 'em want me to lie down and take a bloomin' nap like a tike."

The hand that demanded respect after its powerful strike against the solid wood began to tremble ever so slightly. The look on his face and the way he tucked it inside his other hand to disguise the subtle shaking, told me it did not do so out of anger nor of Nate's own accord. His hands placed in his lap now, Preston's father glanced up at me thoughtfully and after several sullen moments had passed, he said, "I don't fancy the way they look at me. –Like I'm old."

"I don't think that's what they're thinking. I honestly believe they are afraid of losing you. That's fear you see. Not pitty. And certainly not condescendence. They *need* you. And most of all, they love you. That's not so bad is it?"

He smiled one sided, a little crooked —a familiar smile I'd come quite accustomed to seeing on Preston's face. "I suppose it *could* be worse."

"And besides, you know, once you start taking your medicine long enough to see how they affect you, your doctor can adjust them better to suit you. They may not make you so tired." I tacked on the end trying to sound nonchalant.

The familiar swat of his hand as he'd done over Preston's worrying. "I know. I've heard it all before." He wore a grimace as he said it. But then he looked at me and smiled. "It feels good to get it off my chest though. I can't tell *them* that. I know they mean well."

I nodded. "Funny how sometimes it's easier to confide in a stranger than family isn't it?"

He leaned forward a little and patted my hand. "I don't think of you as a stranger. I think you'll fit in with this lot like a pea in a pod." He chuckled and closed his eyes for a second. "That is if you can stand us."

Preston walked cautiously into the dining room. "Is it safe to come back in?"

"Perfectly." I said letting his father know I intended to press no further.

Preston sat next to me and looked at his dad. Mr. Nate leaned over and pecked me on the cheek. He stood up and placed his hands on Preston's shoulders, a gesture of caring. A sign that the battle was over. For now at least.

He gave Preston a gentle shake. "Don't you dare let her get away from us."

"Nice chatting with you, Mr. Nate."

He looked up at the ceiling in exasperation. "Dear *please* call me Nate. You make me feel ancient."

I laughed considering the conversation that had just passed. "Fine. I'll gladly relinquish my Southern manners *if* you do me a favor. If not, it's Gramps from now on."

He chuckled again. "What would you have me do?"

"I can't say in front of him, I'll whisper it to you." I got up and gave him my secret message.

He stood there stunned for a moment trying hard to decide if he'd heard me correctly, I'm sure. I almost regretted saying it, thinking I'd gone too far. But he grabbed his round belly and let out a rumble of laughter that hit the roof.

"Actually *that* was a joke. —Here's the real favor." I whispered again in his ear and looked hopefully into his eyes. "Someday." I said out loud.

"Someday indeed, sweetheart." He said followed by a happy little jig that somewhat resembled the cha-cha. "Your wish is granted, so long as I can help it." He patted my shoulder. "Goodnight, Adena."

"Night, Nate." I said cheerfully satisfied and sat down.

He walked over to where Preston had been sitting earlier, shook out his pills and popped them into his mouth. "Night, Son."

Preston looked back and forth between his father and me. "What the hell did you two talk about?"

Nate began to chuckle all over again and looked down at me. "Can I tell him the first part? Oh, please? I can't hold it. It's worth sharing really."

"Go ahead." I intertwined my fingers and rested them in my lap.

He turned to Preston. "She told me to stop being such a big pussy and take it like a man. My meds that is. Ha! —Ha! Ha!" His eyes darted to me. "The other half will remain between us. Goodnight." And he laughed all the way to his room.

Preston's mouth hung open for a good ten seconds and then he too started to laugh. "Seriously, what did you two get up to in here?"

I poured him a little of the sixty-year-old pear brandy and added just a dribble to my glass.

"I told him about Daddy. Throughout our conversation, I took a guess, and hindsight being what it is —I think he feels like he's being treated like a child. Like he's got no dignity left if he allows himself to be cared for instead of being the caregiver. And I know that's not what any of you are doing to him. Trust me, I've been in your shoes. It's just the way he perceives it."

"And so you call him a pussy and he took his meds?" He laughed.

"Well there was the *other* thing."

He propped his elbows on the table and leaned very close. "And are you going to tell me?"

I leaned even closer until it looked as if I might kiss him. "Nope."

We walked upstairs together. He pulled the covers back and before my head hit the pillow his arm was already there pulling me next to his ribs. Neither of us spoke for a long time. I knew he was thinking. He rubbed his hand slowly against the bare skin of my back.

"Preston?"

"Hmm,"

"I'm sorry for butting in. I realize it wasn't my place. I saw your mom upset. I heard you and your dad. I didn't want anything to escalate. But I shouldn't have done that. It's sort of a disease I have. Are you mad?"

"*No.*" He kissed the top of my head. "I'm just amazed he listened, is all. He can be so stubborn." He sighed. "I was about to blow and that wouldn't have gotten us anywhere. —You talk to the man for half an hour and he listened."

"Actually, he did most of the talking."

"Hmph. I suppose I do need to work on that."

"I didn't mean it that way."

"I know you didn't. Stop defending yourself. As far as it not being your place, can the thought. I saw my daughter hug you today as if you were part of our family. She hardly leaves Beth's side and my father...well, it just all clicked into place so easily. As if you've been the missing piece to a puzzle."

"How old is your dad?"

"Sixty-four. Mum is...fifty-six. Why?"

"Just curious." They were about the same age as my parents would have been.

He turned to his side and put his arm over my hip. "Curiosity is going to make my head explode. Please tell me what you said to my father."

I took a deep breath and almost gave in. But I held on to my secret wish. "Someday."

I opened my eyes to the early morning light. Preston was still next to me sleeping soundly, the first time I'd awakened to find him still in bed after sunrise. The sun grew brighter as it got higher and he stretched, slowly opening his eyes. He blinked and rubbed his face then turned to find me smiling at him.

We heard a creak on the stairs.

He looked at me sternly. "Don't start flipping out. The door is locked and just waking up with you is wonderful. No hurry to run off someplace."

He was right. I snuggled beneath the covers closer to him.

"Cold?" He peeked under the quilt and smiled. "No need to answer, I can see for myself." I launched my knee into his thigh narrowly missing his groin. "Careful! You nearly got me in the sweets."

He tried to kiss me but I covered my mouth insisting I needed to brush my teeth first. He leaned over me to claim my lips, gentle and loving.

"There now. That wasn't too revolting was it?" He looked from my eyes to my hair and a toothy grin spread across his face. "You're hair is absolutely feral today."

"That's because you play with it all night in your sleep." We heard creaking from the stairs again.

"I'd wager anything that's my mother trying to see if we're up and about."

Whoever it was, they never came to knock on the door. We both got up to get ready for the day, though we did so reluctantly. By the time I went downstairs, Preston was coming down the hall dressed in a pair of khaki's and a white pullover. Very handsome. He took my hand just as Doreen peered around the corner.

"Breakfast is on." She looked back and forth at him and me. "Didn't think you love birds would ever come down." She smiled far too knowingly and walked away wringing her hands through a dishtowel.

I closed my eyes as every ounce of blood rushed to my cheeks. Preston's laugh filled the house as he dragged me toward the kitchen. I was thankful she busied about for a few minutes before she sat down with her tea, giving my face time to return to its normal shade.

She was so well put together. Her silvering auburn hair pulled back in two combs, pressed navy blue slacks and a white blouse tucked in complete with a tidy little belt and leather slip on shoes. She could be ready for a day at the office or a luncheon with her lady friends at the drop of a hat.

I could take a few pointers from her for sure. Maybe I've reached the age to give up on some of my old ratty Levi's and trade off some of my comfy tees for nicer shirts. I had teacher appropriate clothes of course, but I hated them. The truth is, if I had to pick something to spend eternity in, I would likely go for comfort and while away infinity in a man's old t-shirt, a worn pair of jeans and no shoes at all.

"Care for a cup, Adena?" Doreen asked holding a blue porcelain tea pot riddled with chips around the edges.

I opened my mouth to say no thanks, but Preston interrupted me.

"She prefers her tea cold." He shivered.

I shot a glare at him without a word then looked back at her. "I'd like to try it your way thanks."

"Put about half cup sugar in it. That stuff she drinks could be served over hotcakes."

"Stop teasing her Preston, she can have it however she likes."

"However you take it is fine Ms. Doreen. Don't worry. I'm ignoring him. I may continue to do so for the remainder of the week." I gave him a sideways glance and took the cup from her.

He sat straight in his chair and laced his fingers together on the table, his face very solemn. "I promise to be good." His most devilish smile appeared and he grabbed my face, kissed me right in the mouth, and released me quickly. "But I have been known to lie on occasion." He chuckled and reached for one of the delicious smelling fruit filled pastries his mother had made. I kicked him under the table. "Ow! What was that for?" Then he grabbed the other leg and yelled again. I only kicked him once but then realized his mother had done the same.

"Two against one is hardly fair! Where's Dad?" He asked just before he took a bite.

"He's outside. And no need to throw a Benny, he's only watching Kelley play."

"I'm not going to say anything. I'm going to leave him be and see if he keeps his word."

"What do you mean?" She looked at Preston in a curious way.

I dug my nails into his pants begging him silently not to repeat the tasteless joke I'd made to his father the night before.

"I've no idea. Something between her and Dad." He said casually. "He took his pills right in front of me last night. Don't try to get him to take it anymore. Just leave him be and let him do it."

I hoped she didn't resent me for butting in regardless of the outcome. She raised her eyebrows and shrugged her narrow shoulders as she took a sip from her cup.

"Whatever works." She concluded and smoothed her auburn hair as she spoke. "That saves me the trouble of hitting the daft bastard in the head with a shovel."

A beat of silence then Preston and I started laughing. She had such a delicate softness to her that it was hilarious to hear her say something like that.

"Adena, has Preston shown you the garden yet?"

"No, Ma'am. But I can see some of it from upstairs. It's really something."

She looked at Preston and made a tisk-tisk sound. "The most romantic place on the grounds. I'm ashamed of you."

He shook his head. "Mum, there is no lack of romance between myself and Adena. Trust me on that." He made his eyebrows bounce and slid his chair back at just the right time so that we both kicked at nothing but air. "Ha! You *missed* me. I'll go sit with Dad and let you lovely ladies take a walk." He pecked my cheek and stood up. "I killed a rosebush by mistake nearly ten years ago and she's never forgiven me."

Doreen and I went outside. We went through the stone archway ducking beneath the trailing ivy and when I looked up, I couldn't believe my eyes. The roses, so white and pure, appeared to glow under the sunlight as though they lit up from within. They grew in a thick circle around a breathtaking fountain.

The marble statue was of a nude goddess. Her long wavy hair trailing over her breasts much like the depictions of Eve in her Garden of Eden. The water trickling over her sent little splashes into a huge lotus that served as the basin. I could see by the moss and algae that clung to its pedestal that she had stood there for ages. A flagstone path, lain around it, branched out in a cross, North, South, East, and West to different brightly colored flowerbeds, each of them leading to a black iron settee. Other parts of the garden roamed and climbed as aimlessly and vigorously as it desired. The perfect balance between chaos and order in its design was absolutely flawless. The place dripped with color and fragrances that seemed to change with each subtle change in the breeze.

"This is incredible. You did all this yourself?" I asked walking along side her toward one of her little benches.

"Heaven's, no. I take care of it, yes, and keep it thriving with help. But I didn't create this." She paused and looked at me. "Did Preston tell you how old this house is?"

"He said it was his great grandfather's."

"Yes, but it stood ages before he acquired it. Built in 1832. But this garden and the walls around it, he built for his wife as a wedding gift around 1908 I believe. Her name was Katherine." She pointed back at the fountain as we sat down. "That curvaceous creature is supposed to be her. I don't know how true it is, but that's the story I was told."

I tried to see the features in the marble likeness of a woman I'd never know. Time and weather had stained her too dark to see her very well. Surely, she must have been beautiful.

"He was known as Preston as well. His son was Nathan, then my Nate and down to Preston again. Nathaniel Preston Grace the IV." She smiled. "I'll wager he didn't tell you *that* did he?"

"No, Ma'am."

That bit of information would have been helpful to know when the first Preston came to visit me. I tried to hide a shudder and thankfully she didn't notice.

"If you're up for a good laugh, wait until he's aled up a bit and call him by his first name."

"He doesn't like it I take it."

Doreen giggled. "Despises it. He thinks it's silly to hand down a namesake for so long. Regurgitate, I believe, is the word he uses."

I took a deep breath and soaked in the warmth of the sun. It was a beautiful day. Then the sweet stench hit me. I looked around but I couldn't identify the location of what assailed my sense of smell.

"I smell lavender." I said and looked around again for the source. "I wondered where Preston had gotten that little bundle from the other morning. But it's so strong. I used to like the scent of lavender but this is different. It actually makes my throat hurt to smell it." I laughed only a little and realized I was beginning to get a headache.

Doreen looked terribly concerned all of a sudden. "What little bundle?"

I was taken aback, not certain as to why her demeanor seemed to change.

"Um, a few mornings ago I woke up and Preston had left a little bundle of lavender in my room."

She shook her head emphatically in quick short bursts of denial. "There's no lavender here. No place on the property. I'm highly allergic to it. Preston wouldn't have—" she stopped for a second or so then swallowed. "He wouldn't have brought it into the house, dear." She cleared her throat and swatted her hand as though it were all no big deal. "Perhaps, Kelley found some along the ditches beyond the horse pens and didn't know any better. She likes you."

The wind shifted ever so slightly and the overwhelming fragrance of lavender dissipated- thankfully taking my headache with it.

Doreen sniffed the air and seemed to relax once it was thoroughly gone which told me clearly that she in fact had smelled it as well.

She changed the subject entirely, asking about Louisiana, what it was like there and my extended family, what my father did for a living and all the other common exchanges between two people getting to know each other. The history that somehow defines each of us.

In short order thereafter, we talked of how I came to know Preston. I was a little surprised to learn he hadn't told her of the storm that kept us together throughout an entire night, allowing us the chance to connect so deeply. Then of the terror we'd faced and how he'd tried so valiantly to protect me.

Her eyes were misty when I finished. "Heavens. No wonder." She said fanning tears from her eyes.

"Crazy accidental meeting turned into this irrepressible need to be with him." I admitted shamelessly.

"No, dear. That was no accident. Something like that only happens by the will of a higher power." She pointed reverently to the sky. "Not to mention the odds of running into each other after so many years. Uncanny, wouldn't you say?"

I only nodded in agreement. Uncanny seemed to define everything since we'd met.

She covered my hand with hers and looked at me for a long moment. "You really *do* love him don't you?"

"Endlessly, Ms. Doreen." I hung my head and felt truly ashamed. "I hope you don't think less of me considering I'm —" I bit my lip and tried to form the words I wanted to say.

She patted my back. "Adena, you don't owe anyone any explanation. How do you think I felt being the other woman in Nate's marriage? So, you fell in love. It's an unfortunate technicality, not a punishable crime. There isn't a soul who's ever walked this Earth who could choose who they've fallen in love with."

This surprised me almost as much as speaking to the dead. "Nate was married?"

She nodded and hung her head, her eyes on the stone path under our feet. "It's not something either of us is proud of. She was quite mad living here for some reason. His first wife. She said the house didn't like her. She had nightmares of a crying infant and then seeing a dead child in the arms of a dark haired woman. She'd sworn there had been something sinister in her presence." Doreen stiffened strangely and corrected herself. "Well, that's what she said according to Nate. Perhaps, she'd dreamt it all in her fevers. She really was quite ill. Depression I suppose you'd call it in the beginning only it went on to turn into a rash of mental and physical fits. Her preoccupation with this mysterious, sinister woman had driven her truly mad.

"Nate and I started out as friends. He simply turned to me by chance. He was a young man who didn't know what to do and he was losing his wife. I worked in a café' down the lane from the ward. He simply said hello to me. Teary eyed and beautiful, he was. All that we are today grew from that moment. We never told her. Nate was too afraid of the fragility of her mind, that she wouldn't be able to accept or understand that we'd fallen in love. We never had to. She committed suicide. Nate, of course, blamed himself."

She raised her head; her eyes squinted against the brightness of the sky. It was a moment when you find yourself looking at someone and trying in vain to imagine what it may have been like. We think we can, but of course we all walk our own path and only the individual can accurately recall the wounds along the way and feel the pain those old wounds still inflict upon the mind and the heart.

She took a deep breath and continued, "When Preston returned home, he was so distraught. He hid in his old room for days. He kept playing this one song over and over, until I thought I'd go mad." She looked at the sky as if she were trying to remember. "It was *Whatever Comes Monday*. No, it was *Raining on Sunday*." She shook her head and flipped her hand in front of her. "Something like that. —Sheer guilt was eating him alive. He finally told me of your husband and children. Now, I know what happened between Nate and I justifies nothing. Even so, I told him for the first time. A mother will do anything to ease her child's pain. You understand, I'm sure. And I knew exactly what he was feeling. The fear of breaking up a happy home. Although, Nate's home wasn't so happy, the fear is always there. *If it weren't for me, things could get better.* The thought is always there. But Preston —Well, he hasn't been involved with anyone since that horrid little beast betrayed him so badly, so I knew you must be special."

"The girl ya'll were talking about last night?"

"Yes. He hasn't told you?"

"No, Ma'am. Didn't ask. Looked like a sore spot to me."

She leaned back and rested her hands in her lap seeming more at ease with a less soul-dredging topic. "Her name was Melanie. A truly beautiful young lady with hair like fire —tiny little thing. But, looks can be deceiving. At any rate, they only dated for a few weeks but I didn't really care for her from the start. Turns out I was right to feel that way." She hesitated as if she were thinking. "I should probably let Preston fill you in on the rest. I'll just say she betrayed him and he was hurt. He stopped trusting people after her little stunt. Stopped dating all together so far as I know. At least no one serious enough to introduce to the family."

We heard the latch on the gate clatter shut behind Teena, Beth, Preston and Kelley.

"Ms. Doreen, thanks for making me and Beth feel so welcome. I enjoyed our few minutes alone."

"I enjoyed it as well. Please call me Doreen, I'm begging you."

"Sorry. It's a lifelong habit."

"All my friends call me Doreen." She encouraged as she reached to cup the side of my face in her hand. She smiled then got up and strolled off.

Beth made her way through the garden to sit with me. "It looks like one of those botanical gardens in here, doesn't it?" Teena showed me the other day right before we caught you and dork-boy in the cottage crushing on each other."

"Beth, *please* stop calling him that."

"Just kidding."

Curiosity was now getting the better of me. "Did you bring me lavender the other day? Up to my room?"

She looked at me like I'd lost my mind. "Uh, no. To be honest, that house kinda creeps me out. No offence to anyone, but it is just something about old places that irk me. —I like Preston's house just fine. Maybe cause it doesn't *look* old. At least on the indside." She shrugged a little. "Why?"

I shook it off. "No reason." Maybe it *had* been Kelley. I decided it didn't matter and let it go.

I hadn't had the chance to talk to Beth much alone. She and Teena had been so busy together and when we were together, we were *all* together.

"Are you okay, honey?" I asked.

She looked down at her feet and gave a quiet nod. "Ya know, when we first got here, I was pretty much all set to despise him. —But being around him and everyone else ... well, you can't help but like them." She crossed her ankles and watched Teena and Preston talking with no particular interest. "I wish Gavin could be here to get to know them."

"Are you really okay, Beth? Or are you just putting on a brave front?" I looked at her face for any sign of uncertainty.

"You can't be serious. Teena is a hoot and a half. I'm really gonna miss her when we go home." She hung her head a little and took a deep breath. "As far as Preston goes, well, it's hard to see you with someone other than Dad. But I have to admit, Preston is definitely a likeable guy. It'd take a bonified idiot to miss how sweet he is. I can tell he really cares about you and stuff. Thanks for letting me come."

I wrapped my arms around her. She'd rendered me speechless. When I let her go, she turned to watch Kelley splashing her hand in the fountain. "Oh, I almost forgot why I came out here. Can I go to the mall with Teena? She said it's in Romford- wherever the heck that is."

"It's just a piece down the road. We went to the market there the other day. —Sure. Go have fun."

Preston was talking to Teena when Beth reached them. Beth looked like a little girl next to him. He must have teased her about something because she slugged him. He put his hand across the top of her head and held her at arm's length and she couldn't reach him again, no matter how she tried. Seeing my daughter laughing with him and his family so comfortably, left me more at ease. I had been so afraid she had simply been putting up with being at the Grace's for me. And I prayed she meant what she said.

The others left Preston and I to be alone. We talked and held hands, basking in the sunlit afternoon, so warm but I don't think it had anything to do with the weather.

Because the beast of burden, the final fallout between Trent and I, remained fast asleep. Somewhere in the far reaches of my mind lay an ancient dragon, a ferocious being lying in wait to rip me apart. But for now it was dormant.

16

AROUND THREE-O'CLOCK IN THE afternoon on Monday, Preston and I sat together on a little wooden bench between the stone shed and the back of the house watching Kelley play on her swing.

A week had already passed since I'd arrived and it was all a blur in my mind. My time with him was slipping like water through my fingers and I could hardly think on this detail too long or I'd fall off the edge of reason. I slipped into my pretense once again that I could stay there forever with Preston and make-believe that nothing could touch us.

I cast my sweater aside with the raincoats that seemed to be in our hands every time we went outside, although I never seemed to have one when it actually rained. Warmer and an absolutely perfect sky over head, I suggested we treat his mother to another night off in the kitchen.

"Everyone is going over to Uncle's for a cookout. Everyone but you and I that is." His smile suggested he had something special in mind. "I've kept you all cooped up since you've been here. Time to take you out for a night on the town. Some place nice."

"We don't have to go anywhere." I didn't care what we did. However, a quiet evening with just him did sound inviting. We were rarely alone except late at night.

Preston narrowed his eyes and set his jaw. "We leave at 6:00."

He apparently had it all set up according to the sternness in his brow and his demanding tone —although impossible to take annoyance at the charade when his bluster was accompanied by that smile of his. His own personal reset button and the key to my undoing.

He looked up at the sky. "It's a perfect day to show you something. Care for a walk?"

"Sure."

The three of us got in the old green truck Kelley called *The Beast* and we rode past the orchard as well as Preston's house. We continued on beyond the grass-bare lane along the fringe of the forest for about five minutes then stopped when we could drive no further at the head of a rocky trail. We abandoned the truck and hiked up the crooked path through the ever thinning woods for at least a mile until we stood quite abruptly on an outcropping of bare jagged rocks. He held Kelley's hand and warned her to be careful near the edge. I looked to the right of us and saw the cliff not fifteen feet away. My heart accelerated. I'd seen it before.

"Well, what do you think? Some view, eh?" He smiled and took my hand and showed me the distant views of Essex and Kent, then to the north, the wide-open expanse of beautiful open countryside, to the south, the developed area of Collier Row. All of it lain out in surreal panoramic splendor.

"Havering is one of the highest points around here. On a day like this you can see forever."

My eyes found the cliff edge again. I could nearly feel the cold wet rocks beneath my bare feet and hear that haunting whisper in the wind. It was a picture-perfect recollection of my dream.

It won't hurt when you fall. I'll catch you I promise. I could hear the whisper in the wind tickle the very nerves in my ears as I stood there.

I walked closer to take a cautious peek over the edge. I didn't want to look but I had to. And I did. The valley below, the very same I'd seen too many nights in my sleep before I'd found Preston in Gainesville. I swallowed hard and grasped wildly for my sanity like trying to catch too many falling straws at once.

"Adena?" I heard Preston's feet crunching against the smaller rocks behind me.

I swallowed again and gave my best attempt at acting. I would not tell him about this, ever, or anyone else. It was too much. It was in fact the proverbial straw that broke the camel's back and I firmly decided to see a damn shrink first thing when I got back home to figure out what the hell was wrong with me.

I turned around and smiled. "This is unbelievable. Beautiful doesn't do it justice."

He smiled and looked at his watch. "We should get back. I'm going to help Uncle set up for tonight then I'll meet you at Dad's."

As soon as we drove up to the farmhouse, Kelley ran around back to her swing again. Preston tried to get her to go with him to Uncle's. She shook her head no, apparently still wanting to play. He signed something to her. She signed back and shook her head again. He turned to me briefly, wearing a tight smile. And the signing continued. She knew perfectly well what he was saying when he spoke although I had a feeling I was witnessing a silent argument. Kelly's face scrunched up at Preston and the gestures with her hands were so defiant, her hands smacked together at times as if she were yelling at him. Then with one last protest, she jabbed her finger toward me.

I didn't understand a bit of sign language other than the alphabet but

I understood what she meant. I sat down on the wooden bench. "Preston, I can watch her till you get back."

She'd been watching me and she turned quickly to poke her tongue out at her Poppy with a triumphant, I WIN!

He heaved a sigh. "I give up. You can stay. That just means more chocolate ice-cream for me." He happily strolled away, whistling toward the truck, slowing to glance at me and smile at his own guaranteed win. She took one last swing and jumped out running to get to the truck before he did.

I called Gavin before I went upstairs. He'd been so hard to reach lately and I supposed I'd have to get used to his hectic schedule between his job and his classes that would be starting again all too soon. I wanted to hear his voice and tell him how things were going and to find out how he was doing. Apparently, he and Beth had spoken several times as he seemed to be abreast on all of our comings and goings and of course he was fine. It was good to hear his voice though.

I went upstairs to get ready for our evening out. Preston had said someplace nice. I did pack one dress just in case. I gave myself a quick manicure and pedicure so it would be thoroughly dry before I got dressed. I curled my hair loosely all over to smooth and tame my somewhat wild locks. Beth and Teena found me and sat on the bed chatting while I put on my evening face.

Teena got up to take a closer look at the black dress hanging on the back of the door. She held it up and her mouth dropped. "*Where* are you going?"

I shrugged a bit and blotted my lip stick with a tissue. "He vaguely said someplace nice. That's the only dress I brought."

"When did you even get that, Mom? I've never seen you wear it." Beth said getting up to look at it.

"I bought it on impulse over a year ago and haven't had any place to wear it. Never even tried it on actually."

She turned to look at me as if I were the most dim-witted person in the world. "Um…hello? You. Owen. All that walking. You lost a whole size since last year."

I hadn't even thought of it. "Okay, you two turn around and I'll slip it on." I took my robe off and slid the dress over my head. "Alright, one of you hook me up in the back."

They turned around and smiled at each other.

I looked down at myself trying to judge the fit. "What? Too big? Too little?"

"No! It's outlandishly fantastic!" Teena squealed.

Beth walked up behind me. "Hook you up where? It's supposed to hang like that." She grabbed me by the shoulders and spun me around for Teena to see.

"Holy Mary! My brother is going to have a brain hemorrhage when he sees you in that get up."

I checked myself in the mirror. It fit perfectly. I turned around to peek over my shoulder so I could see the back. "Crap. I can't wear this out. The back is too low. Another inch and you could see my underwear."

"So don't wear any." Teena said giggling behind her hand.

"Very funny." I looked at it again. I had no idea the swag that hung from either side of my shoulders draped down so low. "I'll just see if I can get away with wearing my pant suit; that or talk him into going someplace else."

Beth flicked me on my forehead. "Don't you dare! Besides, I actually know where he's taking you. The dress is perfect. I'm just surprised *you* picked it." She dropped down on the foot of the bed staring at the dress and then to my feet. "Okay. Show me the shoes. They can't be some old lady pumps either. Not with that bombshell."

"How do *you* know where we're going?" I asked as I pulled the three-inch strappy black heels out of the antique wardrobe and slipped my toes in carefully just in case the polish was still soft. I pulled the last strap in place and stood up.

Beth ruefully looked down her nose, "I'm gonna have to take a run through your closet when we get back home."

"See, I'm not half as lame as you think. But you didn't answer my question."

"Adena, you look fabulous. How are you going to wear your hair?" Teena got up and pulled at one of the large ringlets I hadn't styled yet.

"I don't know. Up or down? And why won't ya'll answer me?" I pulled it into a make shift twist to test out the effect and let it fall past my shoulders again.

"Up." They said simultaneously like the inseparable twins they'd become.

"It's a surprise, Mom. Don't ruin it by asking too many questions."

I asked Beth for the time. When she'd informed me, it was 5:45 I almost passed out. I must have talked to Gavin longer than I thought.

Beth stood behind me and curled a few strands I missed. Teena disappeared for a few minutes and came back in a half run with a hair clip that looked like a small black butterfly. It looked more like a piece of jewelry it was so pretty. She held it in front of my face to see if I liked it.

All of a sudden, it was prom night all over again. Sadly, the first one felt like a billion years ago.

Doreen knocked softly and peeked around the door. "Preston just came in with his suit. He's getting dressed now."

Preston in a suit. My knees went weak remembering how gallant he'd looked at the hotel.

Teena set to work on my hair. Beth pulled her perfume out and thankfully, I was able to stop her before she got the cap off to squirt me.

"Don't! I've already got mine on." I grabbed it from her and sat it on the dresser in front of me.

"Mine is better." She insisted.

"Well, Preston just so happens to like *mine*." I looked around at each of them a little embarrassed at having said it. Out loud anyway. "A lot actually." I finished anyway then my cheeks went all hot. Then the three of them giggled like little girls.

"There. Don't worry about the wispy bits that are loose. It's lovely that way." Teena stepped away just after securely clipping the butterfly into the top of the twist she miraculously pulled off with my hair. "Thank you. Wish I could get it to do that." I turned around and faced them. "Okay, tell the truth."

"Classy and elegant Adena, nothing less." Doreen said, kissing her fingers like a French chef.

Beth stood and looked at the front of my dress. She found the tiniest hook and eye and fastened it. "There." She kissed my cheek and said, "Have fun, Mom. It's long overdue." We exchanged a long glance that needed no words. One of unconditional love.

Doreen made me wait wanting to see Preston's face when I came down. I wondered how our simple date had managed to turn into such a spectacle as I waited to hear the girls' footsteps on the hardwood floor below. Halfway down, I saw Preston talking to his cousin Robert with his back to me. Robert smiled and thumped Preston dead center of his forehead to get him to turn around. After nearly flooring Robert with a retaliatory punch in his good arm he turned then stayed rooted to his spot until I was standing in front of him, staring at me with a blank expression.

"Did I make us late?"

Preston looked as if I'd waken him with my question. "Late? No. — Wow! You look incredible." He took my hands and held them out to get a better view.

The robin's egg blue shirt under his black suit, made his eyes turn the same brilliant hue. It was an Olympic effort to look away from them, not that I tried. Snickers sounded all around us. He looked around to find everyone smiling at him.

"I thought you all would be burning various sorts of meat on a grill by now. Why the hell is everyone still here?" He pulled me closer and bent his head low to kiss me lightly on the lips. He'd been avoiding showing much affection in front of Beth, but today felt different somehow. Her one sided smile, usually meant she approved of something or at the very least thought it was sweet and she was wearing that smile now.

He looked up at his family and Beth. "Everyone have a good time. *Maybe*, we'll see you later." He gave them all a nod.

I gave a silent wave to my daughter as I walked ahead of him toward the door, the familiar feel of his hand at the small of my back but only for a second, then spontaneous laughter hit the rafters. I turned quickly to find Preston on his knees staring at my bare back.

"What are you doing? Get up!" I whispered loudly, regretting having let the girls talk me into thinking the slinky black dress was appropriate for anything.

"What am I doing? —I'm trying to get the feeling back in my legs, that's what I'm doing!"

Robert let out a loud hoot then laughed all the way through the kitchen and out the back door, the rest of them following.

Preston stood up and dusted off the knees of his pants.

"Stop goofing around." I told him.

"I wasn't goofing. That dress is lethal!"

I shook my head at his attempt to convince me he'd forgotten how to walk. A buzz sounded near the door.

"Chariot's here." He said then looked at me with a sincerity that made me melt and took hold of my hands. "Fair warning. You are about to be spoiled. And I don't want to hear one protest, one complaint. Agreed?"

I bit my lip and wrinkled my nose. "I'll do my best."

"Not nearly good enough. I want you to promise me you will fully accept anything that —well anything that may happen."

"Fine. I promise. Can we go now?"

Out front in the courtyard was a chauffeur waiting next to charcoal gray limousine. We ducked inside and as the car slowly headed out of the gates, Preston pulled two fluted stems from a small pocket in the car and handed them to me. He popped the cork on a bottle of 1996 Krug Brut. We laughed at the mess he made despite his best efforts. He filled the two glasses, placed the bottle back in the ice bucket with a loud crunch then took his flute in his hand.

"Let's see, what shall we drink to?"

I smoothed my dress over my knees and thought for a moment. "Really rainy days?"

He laughed and bobbed his head once. "Definitely. And unexpected surprises." He finished in a seductive whisper at my throat.

He lingered there so closely; the radiating warmth of his skin and his cologne put me in mild trance until he pulled away and tipped his glass to mine to chink the rims together resulting in that pure beautiful crystal ring.

"So, where are we going?" I said, breaking the silence.

"In due time, Love." He downed his champagne and shook his head then tucked the flute away in a wooden tray attached to the door made especially to hold a stemmed glass.

"What's the hurry?" I giggled watching his every move.

"Nothing. Just need my hands free."

His bent smile in the dim light told me he was up to something. He came closer, placing his cheek against mine. I could hear each breath he took as he skimmed his lips along my jaw. He reached his hands behind and I could detect them moving gently but I couldn't concentrate on what he might be doing. His mouth lingered dangerously close to mine as we drew in each other's breaths. His hands came from behind and he used them to guide my head slowly back. His lips touched mine but only briefly, and then he trailed one kiss then another down the center of my throat, my head spinning at the stirring sensation. As his lips found their way just a little further down I felt something lightly tug around my neck.

"Damn," he whispered. "Ran out of rope." With a final kiss high on my chest, I felt something fall from his lips. "Thought I might get lucky and make it to my favorite freckle." He pulled back looking very pleased with himself.

I groped around my neck to feel a smooth herringbone chain and let my fingers follow it to my chest. I locked down as I felt something hanging in the middle. My eyes flew wide.

"Oh, Preston! *Please* tell me this is a really good fake."

But even with the last rays of daylight, it shimmered, casting fragments of rainbow here and there. The perfectly round one-karat diamond, encircled by a satiny ring of gold, laid flat against my skin.

"Careful, Love. You are dangerously close to breaking your promise."

"That's not fair. I had no idea you'd... I can't... I thought it was just din..."

He stopped my inane babble with a kiss moaning, "Mm-mm," He pulled away. "You promised."

I clenched my eyes shut and bit my lip until I thought it might actually bleed. I looked down at the glimmering stone and back up to him. "I don't know what to say. Thank you. It's beautiful."

"Doesn't quite shine like you do." He tapped the end of my nose. "That wasn't so hard was it?"

"Preston, I just don't want you to think I expect things like this. And I'm not complaining. I'm perfectly happy just being with you. Every precious moment we have together is worth more than a king's ransom to me."

"I feel the same, Adena. But knowing that makes it all the more fun to surprise you." I noticed him looking at the side of my head with a frown.

"What? Is my hair falling down?" I reached up to feel it.

He playfully swatted my hands away. "No, your hair is lovely. —But now you're earrings don't match." He pulled from his pocket a satin box of midnight blue and opened it. The earrings, round and a ½ karat each and just as brilliant as the one around my neck.

I looked at him in disbelief. "Are you out of your rabid ass mind?"

He shrugged. "I've been accused of worse." Then he looked confused. "I think. What does that even mean?" He held up his hand to stop me just in case I might explain. "Never mind. I've no doubt it's another southern thing. Just put them on."

He pulled them free from the tiny box and I gave him my onyx earrings to put in it.

I double-checked to make sure the backs were on snug. "Thank you again. Are you done now?" I reached up and gave him a peck.

He chuckled. "For today, yes."

I'd never appreciated the saying *diamonds are a girl's best friend*. It made every woman sound like a gold digger. I appreciated his gifts; they were beautiful. I just wasn't accustomed to that level of adoration.

I noticed Preston's slightly fallen expression.

"Honey, I'm sorry. I ruined your surprise didn't I? I really do like them."

He shook his head and placed his hand on mine. "No, I was just wondering. Earlier today by the cliff, you looked upset for a bit. Are you alright? I don't mean to pry, but did you and Trent have another row or something?"

My eyes popped a little. "A row?"

He smiled. "An argument."

"Oh. No, I haven't talked to him."

This bit of news surprised him. "He hasn't rang you *once* since you've been here?"

I shook my head.

"In that case, I'm sorry for breaking our pretense of happily ever after. So, then, what was troubling you?"

Apparently, I wasn't able to hide my dismay. I tried again. "Nothing. The view is just incredible up there." This seemed to appease him for now but he gave me a sideways grin that said he wasn't buying it.

When the limo came to a stop, he took my hand, leading the way along the back of a massive stage temporarily set up in a park. Obviously, we were here for a concert. We climbed to the top of a grand stand to a covered section and reserved seating. As I looked around at the people gathering in the stands I noted we were definitely overdressed.

"Who's singing tonight?" I asked as we took our seats.

"Several people. It's a blues festival. An annual charity event for the children's hospital."

He popped a piece of spearmint gum in his mouth and bounced his knee up and down, looking like a man ready to crawl out of his own skin.

I laughed at his odd behavior. "What is *wrong* with you?"

"Me? Oh...nothing. I have a friend who'll be performing tonight. Just wondering where he is."

Preston never let on to be anxious about anything as far as I had seen. I looked out over the park grounds at the thousands of people converging on the open grassy knoll in front of the stage, hundreds upon hundreds pouring into the stands.

"Nice for so many to come out and support a good cause." I said.

"It's always a good turnout. I haven't been here in the last two years. Looks like it's gotten bigger. —Oh, look who it is." He pointed down the bleachers.

To my complete and utter surprise, Beth and the rest of his family were coming up to sit with us.

Damn. There goes our night alone. "I thought they were going to Uncle's."

"Guess they changed their mind." He smiled and looked a little calmer for some reason.

Beth sat next to me grinning like the cat that ate the canary. Why, I couldn't begin to guess. Teena sat next to Beth and his parents settled in behind us.

"Where's Kelley?" I asked Beth.

"At Uncle's. She's decided Pumpkin is fat because he's having kittens and he's likely having them tonight." She laughed. "I checked. Pumpkin is indeed a male." She laughed again.

The lights surrounding the park went black, the stage lights went up and the crowd came alive with a unanimous cheer. A young man with spiky black hair wearing jeans and a black t-shirt came out and welcomed everyone to the show.

London Blues had a bit of a different sound than what you'd hear in Chicago or New Orleans. One of the men sounded a little like Johnny Cash to me. The next group had a definite Led Zeppelin flavor, the next something along the lines of Van Morrison; they even sang a few of his songs and yet another very similar to Tracy Chapman and I *love* her. I'd never heard of any of them but they all put on a great show. The crowd seemed to know who they were and the applause was almost louder than the music.

Preston leaned over and brushed my knee. "Thirsty?"

"Sure. Whatever they have is fine."

"I'll only be a few minutes then." He kneeled in front of me, patted my knee and seemed nervous again. He just looked at me for what seemed like the longest, this worried slant to what is normally the cutest grin in the world. He glanced at Beth and his family then back to me. He kissed my cheek and trotted quickly down the steps.

My eyebrows furrowed until I thought they'd touch each other.

223

I watched him disappear to the rear of the stands where we were sitting then slowly turned to look at Beth. She met my gaze of wonderment and shrugged her shoulders. She looked at my necklace and earrings but didn't comment, only raised her brow and gave me that half smile of hers.

Beth, Teena, and I were talking when the spiky haired emcee of the show appeared on stage again to thank the performers for coming and I thought maybe the concert was over. Quite a few minutes passed and the crowds didn't seem to be dispersing. If anything, there were even more people swelling the crowds than when the benefit started.

The emcee started to speak again. "Our next performer needs no introduction. We all know who he is. So let's welcome back one of our favorite sons of London!"

The crowd went absolutely bat shit. Of course, they save the best for last and Preston was about to miss it. He must have found his friend he'd been expecting to see.

"Found Preston, Mom." Beth elbowed me to get me to look up.

"Where?" I looked down the stands and over the side to the ground. I didn't see him anywhere. Then I looked at her hand to see where she was pointing. My eyes went the direction of the stage to find Preston walking across it carrying his guitar.

What the hell is he doing?

"How is everyone this fine evening?" He asked the crowd as he tried blocking the lights from his eyes. An unexpected roar of screams and applause rolled through the crowd. Then a giant screen behind the stage came to life with a forty-foot live image of Preston on it.

Uh…

"Well, it's been two years since I've been here, but I'm glad to be here tonight. He looked in my direction a gave a little wave but I knew he couldn't actually see me. I don't know if I waved back or not. I doubt it. I couldn't move. And my brain was still at, "*Uh…*"

Preston continued, "Ladies and Gentlemen, I wrote this song for the most beautiful creature and this woman, this angel —well, she means everything to me. Hope you enjoy it."

I stared at him, astonished and watched as he began to strum his guitar.

'Come here angel and… Break my pain.
And the memories of you… Lyin' in the rain.

I didn't miss his sheepish grin as he sang the hidden reference to the first time we'd made love.

And no I… can't go back… To the way things used to be.
Can't go on without you,
Want you by my side,
Gotta have you next to me.
And I'm so tangled … tangled up in you.
So tangled … tangled up in love with you.

The melody stopped my breath. It was the tune he'd hummed to me the day Owen had stopped by. It had been the piece he'd played for me on his guitar over the phone.

And the stars at night
They're jealous to see you smile.
Your soul's so bright,
They'd travel a hundred thousand miles,
Just to see you again,
Just to be with you again,
Just to feel you,
Just to hold you again.
And I'm so tangled … tangled up in you
So tangled … tangled up in love with you.
So come here Angel and… Break my pain….

I couldn't move. Couldn't speak. Couldn't wrap my head around what I'd just seen and heard. And I couldn't take my eyes off him. It took until the end of the song before I realized he had me in tears.

Again! Dangit!

He looked in my direction and blew me a quick kiss, a big smile on his face.

The absolute thunder of the crowd snapped me from my stupor. The collective adoration from the crowd was colossal. It took me a moment to realize his family was laughing at me, Beth included.

I turned to look at her feeling as if I'd just snapped out of a hazy daydream. "What just happened?"

"Mom, Owen was right." In hysterics, she wiped a tear from her eye. "Preston clued me in and *made* me promise not to tell you. He was afraid all this would scare you away." She pointed to the far right of us just two rows down and I saw Owen laughing his ass off, waving at me. His cousin Chancey turned with a smile that told me *everyone* knew but me.

Nate leaned over the back of my seat and squeezed my shoulders.

"Are you alright, sweetheart?"

"Yes, of course. I —I just don't understand why he didn't just tell me. This is…" I couldn't finish that thought. I still didn't know what to make of it.

"Oh, he only wanted you to get to know *him* first. Just a regular person. Are you upset?"

I turned around and looked at his parents smiling faces, still fighting to find the right words. Then they started laughing at me again. Beth and Teena, giggling right beside me and I could hear Preston beginning a different song.

"Oh, all of you just…" I bit my tongue to keep from yelling *shut up*, a horrible habit of mine, and joking or not it'd be beyond rude to say that to his parents. I laughed instead, trying to cover my mild disorientation then pointed my finger at every one of them sitting in the box with me. "Filthy little liars, every one of you. He told me he wrote songs. —I *assumed* other people sang them!" Apparently, they took no offense by my good-humored accusation, as they were still enjoying a good loud bout of chuckles at my expense.

I realized now why everyone was there with us. The family was there to keep me from bolting.

I turned my attention back to the stage and thought about what Nate had said as I watched Preston entertain the masses. He just wanted me to get know him first. I guess I could understand that. And I knew I was glad I wasn't aware of this in the beginning. I thought he was just a regular guy, albeit a loose interpretation of the phrase, given that I thought there was nothing regular about him. I'd rather say extraordinary. But I fell in love with him for who he was not for what he did or because of what everyone else thought of him. We loved each other and that's all there was to it.

Just before his closing song, he laughed as someone brought him an electric guitar. "This next one isn't mine but I'm certain most of you know it. —Seems I've found myself under a spell."

He closed his eyes and began to play with such feeling it showed in his face, the intense passion of a true musician. Then I recognized the song. *Voodoo Child* by Jimmy Hendrix.

You're hilarious Preston.

It was getting fairly late by the time the concert was over; we got in the limo, off to somewhere else. I kept silent, crossed my legs, folded my arms, and waited for him to say something. He stayed warily close to his door.

"You're angry aren't you?" He winced like he was preparing himself for a whack in the head.

I rolled my eyes and sort of stomped my foot on the floorboard. "No, Preston, I'm *not* angry. But why did you think any of this would make a difference to me?"

His eyes resumed their natural shape. "I didn't really. It's just, —I've been burned a few times and it all revolves around my career." He slid closer to me and held my hand, running his fingers softly over the back of it. "Some people are quite content living life under the radar. I wanted you to see that I *am* one of those people. It's just, on occasion, I can't." He kept his eyes on our hands.

I gave it some thought and remembered that Doreen mentioned he'd been hurt. Some loathsome, self-centered woman did something to him to keep him from trusting anymore.

"Adena, please tell me what you're thinking."

I turned a bit more to face him, more open. "Honey, I just want you to know you can trust me. I realize that's at least *some* of the reason you didn't tell me. Part of you thinks you can't."

He looked up from our hands and met my eyes. "I do trust you. But we have more than enough hurdles to jump without you worrying where I am or what I'm doing once you go back home." And then it made more sense to me.

"You think I won't trust *you*? Is that what this is about?" *God help me make this man understand me!* I searched above the frame of the door groping for a light switch and thankfully, I found one. I needed him to see me clearly. "Preston, first of all, I'm not a jealous person. Fans…big deal. I get that. I'm still coming to terms that you *have* fans, but that is so beside the point right now. For Pete's sake, my husband is still in our house with me." His body tensed at the mention of it but I wanted to make him understand. "If anything I'd think you'd not trust what happens *there* when you and I are apart. But don't ever think for one second about that. We haven't touched each other in over a year. Not in that way."

He let go a deep sigh, a wind of release, his free hand running through his hair. My favorite smile back where it belonged.

"So, is that it? No more evasive secrets?" I asked glad to get everything out on the table finally.

"None at all." He leaned over to kiss me, sealing his satisfaction that we trusted each other enough to get over our hurdles.

I sighed so dramatically he stared at me. I batted my lashes and pretended to swoon, the back of my hand on my forehead. "Oh, Preston. Can I have your autograph?"

He elbowed me then the car slowed to a stop. He rolled the window down just an inch.

"Ehm...I hope you're not too camera shy. There are only a few though." He got out first and it looked like lightening from the sidewalk. He pulled my hand gently, probably wondering why I wasn't standing next to him yet.

I yanked him down so I could say in his ear, "That's not just a few Preston! There's gotta be thirty reporters out there with a damn camera!"

"Relax, Adena. Just ignore them. Or simply smile and wave if you like. They only want to know who you are."

Oh *that* helps. Did he not just hear me? I'd rather be invisible.

He leaned in further when I didn't move. "Unless, you have the ability to magically pop us inside, the front door *is* the only way in. Ready?"

I'd had a premonition of his daughter and I'd recently talked to two dead people. I saw two children in a phantom tunnel that under all other reason and reality I should not have seen- not to mention the fact that I had also dreamed of not one but two very distinct locations on a farm in London that until recently I had absolutely no connection to. So why, pray tell, should I *not* be able to magically pop us inside?

I squeezed my eyes in a futile effort to do so but of course nothing at all happened.

I was starting to think more and more about a nice long stay in a rubber room. A white rubber room. Yes, that would be nice. Maybe the nice people who own those rubber rooms would let me bring some crayons with me and I could draw some happy pictures.

Preston offered his arm again. "Love, I do agree that it's no one's business as to who you are, however, we do have reservations."

With the thought of 'no one's damn business' in my thoughts, I gave up, got out and we made our way arm in arm to the doors of the restaurant. It seemed like the short walk took ten minutes. I can tell you that there was one particular little man out there that I wanted whole-heartedly to punch in the face after he crammed a very large camera directly in front of me and flashed away repeatedly until I could no longer see where I was going at all. I bumped into someone in fact, possibly the photographer responsible for blinding me. I hope I stepped on his foot.

Preston only looked up once to wave and say, "Have a good evening."

Someone was holding the door open for us and we stepped into the building. Thank God it was over! I felt queasy and the lingering bright blue spots in my vision from the hundred flashes didn't help at all.

A minute or so passed as Preston briefly laughed and mingled with a man he'd introduced me to but I never saw his face thanks to this very large blue aura that seemed to block out everyone's face. But my vision soon corrected itself and just in time to see an older gentleman approach us with a big smile displacing his jowls.

"You just had to come to my restaurant, didn't you?" The old man chuckled and clapped Preston on the shoulder. "Sorry about that foolishness outside. I'll have to educate a few new hires on the meaning of discretion."

The man leaned backward to glare at a particular young lady standing behind a small podium. She seemed a little star struck to have Preston standing so near.

Weird.

Preston looked down at her and smiled. "No harm done." Then turned his eyes to the man. "Frank, this is Adena. Love, this is Frank Reynolds. He and dad are old friends. I think they caught the same donkey to school."

Frank knuckled him in his chest. "One more old man joke from you and I'll put a nice big prawn in your food. Watch that pretty little head of yours swell up like a melon." He turned and took my hand. "Pleasure to meet you, Adena. Sarah here will show you to your table."

"Thanks. Good meeting you, too." I said. Frank smiled hugely again creating deep ruts in his abundant jowls then stepped away to greet a few more guests.

Sarah, the host, led the way to a shadow-filled corner of the restaurant at a semi-circular booth. "Your waiter will be here shortly. And Er...Mr. Grace, I am sorry. I had no idea all those people would show up. I only told my mother. She's such a fan of yours. She must have screamed it in the streets." She seemed genuinely regretful that she'd leaked his arrival. Solid weirdness.

"Sarah, if you're going to work here, first rule is...*ignore Frank*." Preston reached out to shake her hand and gave her a smile. "And tell your mother hello for me."

She hesitated before she walked away, looking over her shoulder for any sign of Frank. She pulled a pen from her pocket and offered it to him with a shy smile. "Please?"

He chuckled and looked around for something to sign. Not a paper napkin in sight. He asked for her mother's name and pulled out a dry cleaning slip from his suit pocket. He signed it and handed it to her. "Sorry, that's the best I can do for now."

She nearly skipped away beaming.

I couldn't curb the urge to giggle at how she was so enamored by him.

"Oh, shut it! Just being polite. She didn't deserve to get into trouble over it." He scooted closer in the center of the tapestry-covered seat and placed his hand on my thigh.

The waiter came and poured two glasses of wine for us. A wonderful, intimate evening, just he and I hidden away from most of the other patrons. Frank himself served us braised venison and tomatoes with a side of apricot glazed veggies. *And,* of all things, fried pumpkin slices. The only way I'd ever eaten pumpkin was in a pie but all of it was delicious.

The room was too dark, the table linens too long for anyone to notice that Preston was tickling my thigh beneath the table, entertaining himself with my battle to keep a straight face. He'd leaned close to give me a playful nibble as someone approached our table. I gave him a little prod to get his attention as I noticed the woman standing in front of us.

She smiled but with a haughtiness that for some reason made me want to smack her. When he looked up, I saw the instant flash of recognition coinciding perfectly with his hand on my leg curling into a tight fist. His body went rigid from head to toe and he wore a scowl — and the intensity in those blue-green eyes made him look like a man I'd never want to cross. I noted her blazing red hair. Attractive but fairly … well … short. Not that there's anything wrong with being so petite, it just seemed strange to think of the two of them standing next to each other.

He closed his eyes and in a raw voice I'd never heard from him, "Melanie, *please* leave. I do not wish to *see* or *speak* to you."

Melanie. So it really is her. I'd guessed as much but now I had confirmation. I'd have to remember to thank Doreen for the heads up.

"Sweet, Preston. Don't tell me you're still sore at me after all this time."

To hear her say his name pissed me off to no end. I still had no idea what she'd done to him but she was not about to ruin our night. Preston didn't say anything and he looked like he could bite the front bumper off a Buick.

"Come now, aren't you going to introduce me to your... *friend*."

That was All. I. Needed.

"Melanie? Is that *really* you?" I slid quickly out of the booth, hugged her and gave her a peck on the cheek as if reunited with a long lost friend. "I haven't seen you in *ages*."

I glanced at Preston. He looked just as confused as she did; his head cocked to the side like a puppy who'd just heard a high-pitched whistle but the demeanor of a pit-bull on steroids. I gave him a sly smile and his face relaxed. A little.

"I'm sorry. Do I know you?" She asked politely enough, the smugness gone for the moment.

"Oh, I was sure you'd remember me. My name is Adena." I kept my voice low, well mannered and reserved so it remained just between her and I.

"I don't know anyone by that name. I think you've mistaken me for someone else." She opened her mouth to say something else to Preston but I stopped her in her tracks.

"Are you sure? I would think something like that would be extremely hard to forget." My voice sweet and friendly. "You see...*I'm* that crazy bitch in your very worst nightmares. I can't believe I'm finally meeting you in person." I smiled graciously.

She glared back in a fashion that let me know I'd hit a nerve. Target acquired. Shots fired. Bullseye!

"Fine. Have my seconds, I'm *done* with him."

"That doesn't make you special, it just makes you stupid. And Melanie, if you *ever* approach him again, that will leave you treading precariously close to a real live lion's den. Now I hope you have a pleasant evening. It's been real peachy seeing you again." Still quiet but not so friendly.

She didn't seem so inclined to say anything else and she turned to walk away stiff as a yard stick. Well, in her case a ruler.

Preston's eyes were as big as saucers and he wore an enormous grin. I reseated myself, put his hand back on my thigh, picked up my wine glass and took a drink.

"That was the scariest thing I've *ever* seen." He laughed in amazement.

"Maybe I'll give her Trent's number, see if she likes my seconds. Little bitch."

"If we could pave that wicked streak of yours, we wouldn't have to fly to see each other, we could *drive*."

"No, that'd never work. People from America would be driving on the right, you guys headed over there would be on *your* left...I can see it now. One big ass head on collision. Flying is safer."

Preston nearly lay down in the booth laughing himself breathless. Then he sat up slowly as though rising from the dead. "Wait. How did you know it was her?"

"Well, first off, you were about to pop a vein over here. Second, your mom told me about her. Red hair and all. Brazen little leprechaun. — But I don't know what she did to you. What is it with her?"

"As a general rule I don't hate people. Everyone has *some* good in them. Apart from her." He took a deep breath. "I met her at an awards ceremony. She seemed nice at the time and we sort of hit it off. Boy, did she have me fooled. We went out for about a month and everything seemed great. —Until I passed a newsstand one morning to find my face and a bunch of lies. *She* did it. She actually works for one of those low life rags of a newspaper. Gossip and rubbish type. Everything we said or did was for all to see, along with a load of deliberate lies. She even dragged Kelley into the mix."

A complete circle of understanding settled over me. Some of the things he'd been through. It must be like being chased by wolves at times. No wonder he'd kept his guard up.

"I can't believe she had the guts to come over here." I said.

"Neither can I. But I thought you said you weren't a jealous person." He raised his eyebrows and wore a quirky grin.

"That wasn't jealousy. She pissed me off."

He smiled wider. "Are you ready to go home now?"

"Yes, I've been spoiled more than enough."

"Oh, that part hasn't happened yet, Love."

What on earth could top this night? Well,I had a few ideas.

He laced his fingers into mine as we walked toward the front door. As we passed the hostess, he spoke to her again. "Good night, Sarah. Tell Frank thanks for me will you?"

"Yes sir, Mr. Grace. Oh, wait! Don't go out that way. There are twice as many as before. Mr. Reynolds is waiting in his car out back for you. Your limo is a few blocks away."

"Excellent." He paused, thinking of something carefully then looked at me. "Mind if I introduce you to a few people?"

"Like *who*?"

"London."

"Uh-uh. You already did that at the concert." I started to back away but he caught me around my waist.

"Of course, I won't make you. But trust me, with the photos they took earlier, if they don't have a story to go along with it they *will* make up their own. And you can be damned certain some of them will be ruthless."

I knew he was trying to spare me any humiliation, although I did not relish the idea. I gave it some thought and realized I didn't want my face along with the word *hooker* plastered on some rag of a newspaper, either. Melanie would just love that.

I decided I didn't care. "Nope. Ain't happening"

"Are you serious?"

I held up one finger to say *wait* and walked to the front door. I opened it a miniscule crack and peeked outside. *Twice as many? Sarah can't count!*

I walked calmly over and looked up at his waiting smile. "Hell yeah, I'm serious."

"You don't even have to say anything if you don't want to." He put his hand on my shoulder trying to encourage me.

"Preston, I think it's great that they adore you that much. But I will gladly finish this date with Frank if you make me go out there."

"*Why*?" He actually stomped one foot like a spoiled kid.

"I've never enjoyed having a camera pointed at my face. I never thought much of it until we walked in here earlier. It almost made me nauseous. Dizzy even. I'm not going." I held my ground. "You go do your thing and I'll wait here."

He ground his teeth and said he'd be back in a minute.

I stood there waiting and realized Sarah was staring at me. I smiled at her. She smiled back. She almost said something but stopped.

"How long have you worked here?" I opened the conversation for her.

"Almost a month, Miss."

"Call me Adena." I walked over to shake her hand. "Nice to meet you."

"Lovely to meet you as well. Do you mind if I ask where you're from?"

"I grew up in Louisiana. But I live in Florida."

Her mouth fell open for a second. "So you are dating Mr. Grace all the way from there?"

I smiled at the thought myself. "Crazy as it sounds, yes."

"I can't get my boyfriend to get on the bloody tube for ten minutes to my flat and you and he are trudging the skies. That's so romantic."

"Well, Sarah, you are very sweet and pretty as they come. No girl should settle for a guy who isn't worth it."

She smiled broadly and blushed a little. "Ms. Adena, thank you. I can't believe you took the time to be so nice."

She did not *just say that.* "Sarah, I've got a good mind to introduce you to my son. He's an eighteen-year-old college boy. Interested?"

She finally loosened up and laughed just as Preston stepped back in.

He smiled down at me. "Just as I suspected. They all wanted to know who you are."

"And,"

"I told them you were a hooker named Cookie. What the bloody hell do you think I told them? You're my girl!" He bent over to kiss my cheek with a loud smack.

17

ONCE IN THE LIMO AND ON our way, I tugged one of my heels off. "I think I can safely say that I *like* living under the radar. I don't see how you can stand that."

"Well, I've had ten years to get used to it. But it's rarely like that. Being a blues singer doesn't exactly bring with it your typical rock-star status. Not unless your name is B.B. It was just the festival that got them all stirred up."

I pulled the other shoe off and when I looked up, I found him scrutinizing me as if he were trying to decipher Morse Code.

"What?" I asked.

"Well, just when I think I might have you figured out, you surprise me one way or the other."

"Meaning?"

"Let's see, you're fearless on a horse, yet bad weather *freaks* you out. Bold enough to openly put Melanie in her place, which I loved. You *drive* like a stunt man with his balls on fire —yet, a few flashing cameras makes you literally ill."

I shrugged. "Everybody has their strengths and weaknesses, I guess. Although, I haven't found your weakness yet."

He laughed softly. "I'll clue you in on that later."

I reached over my head, pinched the wings of the butterfly together to release the twist, and shook it loose. I laid my head in his lap. When I looked up, he was staring at me. Again!

"It can't be any worse than when I wake up. You've already seen that." I tried to smooth it behind my ear and he caught me by my wrist.

"Don't. You look positively edible. —Anymore dizziness?"

"Preston, that had to be over an hour ago. No, I'm not."

"Good. I'd really like to kiss you if you're up to it." He traced his finger lightly down the side of my neck.

"Well, now *that's* likely to make me dizzy again."

"I don't mind if you don't." He pulled me into his lap with ease.

"Umm, before we get carried away, as we sometimes do. Can he see through that?" I jutted my thumb over my shoulder at the glass divider between the driver and us.

"It's not tinted, Love. Its black. He can't see anything."

He pulled my face to his, his lips moving possessively, pressing in more with each passing moment. I could taste his last drink of wine. He gripped my hip firmly and I'd come to know what that meant. His obvious arousal made the dancing wings flutter again in the pit of my stomach. The tips of his fingers slipped beneath the hem of my dress, then slowly up to my lace panties. He felt of it and moaned against my lips. He started to tug them free and I grabbed his adventurous hand to stop him.

"Patience, Honey. We'll be home soon."

He pouted and went for my neck. "I don't *want* to wait that long. Every moment we have gets interrupted."

His voice sounded rough and he tasted a very sensitive spot below my ear. My will went to nearly nothing to try to resist him. But I was intent on not having sex in the back of a car.

"Please," he breathed into my ear.

He wasn't playing fair at all. As a general rule, I didn't tell him no. I honestly believed we could spend a week in bed and never come up for air. The more I thought about it the better it sounded.

I shifted my body to straddle his hips, a victorious smile dominating his face as he watched me unbutton his shirt. "We're still waiting till we get home. —I've just been wanting to see a little more of you since I came down the stairs today."

I flipped his shirt open to see his gloriously masculine chest. I thought for a second that I might not be able to hold off, either. He grinned and lay down in the seat, keeping me steady in place.

"What are you doing?" I asked watching him maneuver his long body across the seat.

"I can wait. If *you* can." He chuckled and bit his bottom lip as he rolled his hips beneath me, the very evidence of his excitement, more than merely noticeable.

My resolve was fading fast and he knew it. His eyes seared through me and I began to grind slowly against him. He shut his eyes tight in what appeared to be agony. I stopped and his eyes flew open.

"Don't stop!" He pulled me down, pressed his lips demandingly to mine then drove himself firmly against me.

He pulled my dress up and groped me, pulling me down onto him harder. At this rate, I wouldn't have to wait; the erogenous feelings were already coming to the surface. The car came to a stop and I couldn't fathom how he thought we'd have time to even think of finishing what we'd started in the short ride to his home. I smiled down at him a little winded, sat up and straightened my dress.

He laughed throatily and grinned. "Just a little farther and I'd have won."

"Hmph, just a little farther and I'd have been smoking a cigarette *without* you." The car began to move again, having only stopped to wait for the gates to open. "So, do you think everyone's in bed yet?" I tackled the loaded question we were no doubt both wondering.

He checked his watch. "It's almost midnight. Maybe they all went to Uncles after the show." His face contorted and he ground his teeth. "No they didn't! I just know they're all waiting up for us. Bugger!"

"Awe, don't be mad." I combed his hair in the back with my fingers, ridding him of the look that we'd already had a go at each other.

"I'm not angry. Just chomping at the bit so to speak." He pulled out his phone and spoke to his mother.

He smiled, clipped his phone shut and quickly buttoned his shirt as we came to a stop in front of the house. He literally ran to the door dragging me behind him, looking like a child eager to unwrap his presents on Christmas morning.

He stopped and turned to me. "It couldn't have worked out better if I tried. Guess I'm just not that clever." He spoke more to himself than to me. I held my shoes in my hand waiting for him to make a lucid statement. "Well, it depends on you actually. Teena and Beth are prepared to ambush you. They've been invited to a sleepover and they are sure you will say no."

"Then they are right. I've never let Beth go off overnight with people I don't know."

"Then let me assure you that I've known these people my entire life." He stopped to catch his breath. "And they live just down the lane. You could easily walk there."

"Oh, I see. So if they go, you and I get to go to the cottage." I looked down at my feet and rolled my toe over a pebble.

"Well, yes, Adena, but I wouldn't put Beth in harm's way over it." He took my face in his hands and tilted my head up to see my eyes. "I'll admit I'm keyed up over the thought of having you all to myself in my house...just us. But if you're not comfortable letting her go, I understand."

Alone. In his home. Too tempting.

We found Teena, Beth, Doreen and two brunette girls sitting in the kitchen. Beth looked up at me with the pre-begging, hound dog look in her eyes that I'm used to. I held my hand up to stop her. She slumped in her chair with her face in a desolate expression.

"Cheer up sweetie, I didn't say no, *yet*." I looked at Doreen. "What do you think?" Kelley came running in and Preston took her back to her room as she answered me.

"You should have no worries, Adena."

"That's good enough for me." I looked at the chair where Beth was sitting but she slammed into me from the side to give me a hug.

I heard Preston playing his guitar for Kelley.

"Doreen, would it bother him if I peeked in?"

"Of course not. We can all go. It's precious to see them together. She would not go to sleep until he got home."

We hurried to the end of the hall and cracked the door to see. He saw us right away and tried to smile but her little hands held tightly to his cheeks. She stood in front of his guitar as he sat on the bed, playing and singing her bedtime favorite, bound to her with invisible shackles and chains. We all ducked away leaving him to put her to bed. I said goodnight to Beth before she left and then Doreen turned in.

I waited alone in the den reflecting on all the events that had blown in to my world three weeks ago, at the speed in which a person's world could be completely turned upside down. Or right side up for that matter. I laughed quietly as I realized that tonight, as amazing and unbelievable as it had been, actually fell into the category of normal compared to the *other* things I'd seen and heard lately.

The click of his dress shoes echoed down the hall. He stopped at the wall next to the long foyer. "I'll get the Rover and pick you up in a second?" His way of confirming we'd go to his place. I nodded and watched him spin on his heels then disappear around the corner.

I trotted silently up the stairs, grabbed everything I needed for one night and went back down. Beth must have been rifling through my things. I couldn't find half my clothes.

He'd just pulled up when I shut the front door behind me. He held up one finger telling me to wait. He ran around, opened the door, and tossed my bag in the back seat.

When he got in and started down the drive I said, "You know you don't have to open every door for me."

"I dare to think, you of all people, could appreciate and even expect a little courtliness. Yes ma'am, yes sir, please and thank you all the time in your sweet voice. I'll never stop treating you like my queen." He drove with one hand on the wheel as we bumped along the dirt road.

"Yes sir, *Nathaniel*."

He looked as if someone doused him with the contents of a spittoon. His head lulled back in disgust and he shivered. "Who told you?"

"Your mother. And I think Nathaniel is a very noble name. I don't know why you hate it."

"Stop saying it. Makes my teeth hurt to hear it. I vowed years ago that I'd stop this whole Nathaniel Preston business if I ever had a son."

I didn't even have time to begin to worry about me not being able to have any more children. He glanced quickly at me and covered my mouth with his finger.

"Don't you dare read too much into that statement. I've already been through potty training and sippy cups and first words. Kelley *is* as good as mine. I don't need another."

I didn't say anything and lightheartedly bit his finger still covering my lips. Then I held his hand and sucked at his finger ever so lightly.

Preston stared at me and whispered. "Sweet God in Heaven." The Rover bounced unfamiliar to the normal path to his house.

I looked up and screamed. "Tree!"

He swerved just in time to miss it. He looked at me again. "I'm *sorry*. Did you once say *I'm* distracting?"

"Eyes on the road, Mister."

We pulled up to his house, got out and strolled hand in hand to the front door. He stopped and turned to look down at me then raised his hand to trace the gold circle that went around the diamond on my neck. "Care to know why I chose this one? —It's a diamond and a gold ring. The closest I could get since I can't put one on your finger." He picked up my left hand and kissed it. He smiled then turned to go get my bag from the Rover.

I stumbled blankly into the dark house, desperately trying not to weep as I absorbed his words. I pulled the diamond up to my lips and held it there, knowing the true intention of his gift. The door closed. I looked up and saw him smiling, holding my bag.

"You win my heart the most when I catch you. Those sweet things you do when you *think* I'm not looking."

I wrapped my arms around him. No words would do.

He pressed his forehead to mine and kissed my nose. "I love you. Far more than I ever thought possible. Far sooner than I ever dreamed. All I want is to make you happy, to keep you safe and to have you with me."

"Preston,"

"Yes, Love."

I fanned my eyes and took my bag from him. "You're making me cry again."

He laughed softly as I walked away to the bathroom to change out of my dress. I slipped a floor length brown silk gown on and cinched up the velvet laces on the front. I opened the door to find him standing in front of his stereo putting a CD in. I leaned against the doorframe and waited for him to turn around. He lit a candle and burned his finger in the process.

"Bloody son of a..." He stuck his finger in his mouth before finishing his expletive.

I bit my tongue to reign in a giggle. It wasn't often that I got to admire him while he was unaware. He'd already taken his jacket off and draped it over the chair in the corner of his room. He kicked off his patent leather shoes and took off his shirt, dropping it to the floor then pressed a button searching through the songs.

"Adena, are you lost?"

"I'm right here, Honey. How's your finger?"

He spun around, his eyes following the length of the chocolate silk gown to the floor and back up again. He closed the gap between us and ran his fingers over the soft laces on the front. "Care for a little music?"

"Sure. What did you pick? Something of yours?"

"I don't sit around listening to myself sing. That's just weird."

"If I had a voice like yours, I might."

He laughed. "If you had a voice like mine, you'd be a man."

I saw his eyes drift to the nightstand and back to me. "I believe you've a gift waiting."

A crystal vase filled with a myriad of flowers of every color, with one yellow rose skillfully arranged in the center sat next to his alarm clock.

"I thought flowers came first."

"Those *aren't* from me." However, his expression told me he did know who'd left them.

I walked over to find a card placed next to the vase. Preston stood behind me with his hands at my waist, his chin on my shoulder as I opened the card to read next to the candle.

Mom,
I can only hope that someday I'm lucky enough to find a man who loves

me as much as Preston loves you. I can feel your happiness. So here is one last gift for you tonight. My blessing. Spend what time you can together. I'll take your room for the rest of our visit. I insist on this. It's not fair for you to have to steal time with each other only when you can. It's not like he lives across the street. Don't worry; I am fine with this. I love you so much.

Love,

Beth

I swore if I cried one more time, I'd surgically have my eye ducts welded shut. But of course, I did. I turned to look up at him. "Did you know?"

"She spoke to me yesterday. I didn't know she would do it tonight nor of the sleepover. *I* told her no. But I learned she is just as stubborn as you are when she sets her mind on something. And apparently she has." He tilted his head to the other side of his room.

I walked around the bed and looked through a stack of my clothes folded neatly on a small bench. Four outfits. One for each day left and one to go home in.

He came to stand next to me again. "I take it her gift has trumped mine."

"Sorry, but yes. You gave me diamonds. She gave me you. That's way better." I stood on my toes to kiss him and he met me half way.

Just before our lips met he whispered, "I can live with that."

18

HE GUIDED ME BACKWARD sitting me at the foot of his bed. I started to slide back to the pillows but he grabbed my hips and stopped me.

"No, Love. Stay right where you are." He whispered getting down on his knees.

He kissed me bringing my blood to a simmer as he tugged the velvet ribbons loose and slipped the silk away. His mouth parted, lingering so closely to my neck, my breasts and back to my lips as if he wasn't sure which he'd like to try first. He thoroughly tasted all three.

He brought my ankle to his lips and held my eyes with his as he kissed and tasted his way to my knee, up my inner thigh. Gently he pushed me back. He watched as he brought me from boneless to rigid to quaking, moaning against me as if he were feeling the same satisfaction he gave me. He crawled over me and my heart struck a tempo that I was afraid might be beyond its capacity. He stared into my eyes for an eternal minute.

I reached up to kiss him but he pulled away smiling. I begged in a whisper pulling him closer.

"In a hurry?" He kissed me and pulled away again.

"Yes, Preston. A big, big hurry."

"Patience, Love...I'm *fixin* to." An airy chuckle for only a second and then his rapturous kiss engulfed me. His warmth covered me and our emotions flowed like a current from him to me and back again. My legs intertwining with his, he centered himself over me and hesitated.

"Please, Preston. I'm begging you, don't tease me anymore."

"Now?" He growled at my throat.

"Yes, now."

He lunged into me and I almost screamed in pleasure. He hitched one of my legs over his hip and drove into me again. He'd stop for a second to watch my face with each deliberate thrust. I rolled my hips to meet him quicker and he groaned, no longer able to toy with me and his desire over took him. Repeatedly his strength filled me until I thought surely I'd climbed as high as I could. But each time he kept me just shy, delaying the rush and the freefall that comes after.

As he worked his body into mine, sweat dripped from his brow and fell onto my neck. I abandoned any restraint and screamed his name; the earthquake within me, the aftershocks rolling in more powerful one after the other far past what I thought possible. His penetration to its fullest as he groaned to his own peak. He kissed me again, roughly biting at my lips. As his rhythm and heartbeat slowed, his lips became tender and soft, until we were both completely spent; our minds thoroughly shattered.

He lifted his head and smiled down at me. I smiled back out of breath, languid, more sated than I'd ever been. "Go ahead...I'm waiting."

"Waiting for *what* Love?" He panted.

I pushed him onto to his back, cuddled next to him, and pulled his arm around my shoulder.

He laughed. "Oh, that. I was getting there." He pulled the corner of the sheet free and wiped his face dry. "Why is it I'm the only one dripping with sweat?"

"Because you never let me do all the work."

"I didn't hear you complaining." He laughed again. "Unless...*Preston*! *Preston*! Means: *Stop, you're doing it wrong*."

I jabbed him in the ribs. "Don't make fun of me. It was nice not having to hold back the noise for a change."

"*Noise?*" He chuckled softly. "That's like saying breaking the sound barrier, sounds like a bottle rocket."

I forced a pillow down over my face but laughed in spite of myself.

A muffled ring came from the bathroom.

I flung the pillow away. "Crap! Who'd be calling me now?"

My cell stopped ringing before I got to it. Looking at the screen on my way back, my feet caught in his pants lying on the floor and before I knew it, I was flat on the rug with a loud thud. The covers at the edge of the bed shook with Preston's fit of laughter. I couldn't help but crack up over my own inability to do two things at once. He peeked over the side of the bed with a toothy grin.

He offered me his hand. "Step in a hole?" I allowed him to help me to my feet and got back in bed. I looked at the display again.

I showed Preston the text from Owen. "I can't believe I got out of bed for that." I watched his eyes squint and move while he read the message. He was clearly drunk somewhere.

I sighed and stated the obvious concern lurking throughout my mind. "This week has gone by so fast. I can't believe I've only got three days left with you." I tried to swallow the dread of it and curled up next to him again.

"You do not have only three days left with me. You have three days left of this particular visit." Sure to accentuate the difference. He didn't sound all that concerned and I probably started to pout at least just a little. Then he smiled, rolled over me so I could see his face. "Time isn't so much a bother when we're together. —Now when we're apart, when I have the immeasurable fear that I'll never see you again —that is the very center of Hell for me."

I stared back into his translucent eyes. Everything else in my life disappeared, like selective amnesia. The feel of his lips on mine, the taste of him, the touch of his hand on my face, those were the only things that existed. He was right. As long as we were together, there were no worries. At least for now.

Later that night, I dreamt of many things. Strange visions of Preston sitting next to my mother as they laughed and talked on the swing on the back porch that looked over Lake St. John. Then the cliff and the whisper took center stage once again. But the one I remembered perfectly, as though plucked from an actual memory, had been of Daddy and I walking along the banks of the lake back home. I watched as Daddy loosened the rope that tethered our small green johnboat to a large cypress knee. He offered his hand and as I took it, I saw my own hand in front of me. I was a young girl again.

He helped me in and kicked us off the muddy banks. I picked up a boat paddle, plunged it deep into the silt, and shoved us further out into the lake. He yanked the outboard motor to life and I glanced behind us as the motor churned the muddy water until it looked like swirling chocolate milk. He guided us to the north end of the lake to our favorite fishing spot.

My father tossed a makeshift anchor made from a lawnmower rim tied to a vinyl rope into the water. I held my favorite Zebco fishing pole, cheap as they come but never failed me, and offered the line to Daddy to bait the hook. And for the first time in eight long years, I heard my father's deep chuckle and saw the weathered crow's feet crinkle at his eyes.

"Lil Doll, it's about time you learned to do that yourself, don't you think?"

"Daddy, I know how. I just don't like it. It's messy."

"Well, you're fourteen now. There are a lot of things in life that are messy, but if you're gonna enjoy certain things; you have to be willing to clean up the mess." He dug through a Styrofoam bowl and pulled out a long fat night crawler, dangling it in front of my face. "So, all you have to decide now," He gave the worm a wiggle setting it to squirming. "is all the fun worth the mess?"

I reached out and took hold of the sticky, slimy, ill-fated little creature, picked up an old rag off the floor of the boat and rolled him in it. "If I have to hold it, I'm not gettin' worm poop all over me."

He laughed louder than he normally would have, always one for not scaring the fish with too much noise. "Hand it over."

"No, I got it. I just better catch something big if I personally have to kill this poor worm to do it."

He laughed again as he watched me bait my hook. "Atta girl. Should've made you do that years ago."

"I've watched you a thousand times." I cast my line into the water just near a fallen tree.

"Good spot, Doll. One day, you'll have no trouble doin' this on your own."

"Why? You'll always be my favorite fishing buddy."

He chuckled again and with the sound of his raspy laughter, the scenery changed. We were standing on the pier along the lake behind our old house. A massive Sweet Gum tree cast its shade over us. I played with the tasseled end of the rope I'd swung out from, into those muddy waters so many times as a child. I was no longer fourteen.

Daddy held his fists in front of me, to play the *guess which hand it's in'* game. I loved it when he did that. It was usually the beginning to a great surprise, a tiny piece of something much bigger. He'd presented the key to my Mustang for my sixteenth birthday that way.

I looked at each of his tanned fists then up into his hazel eyes, wishing I had an ounce of the wisdom they contained. He smiled down at me as if he had a wonderful secret he was about to share. I looked at his hands again and picked the one on the right.

"Are you sure, Doll? Be careful this time." And without waiting for me to respond, he opened both of them palms up.

I stared down to take in what he wanted to show me. In his right hand lay my wedding rings from Trent. In his left, the diamond pendant from Preston. When I looked up the scenery had changed again.

Daddy, wearing his gray suit, (the one he only dragged out for special occasions) looked strong and handsome as ever. We were standing alone underneath the ancient arbor that Preston had taken me to only a few

245

days ago. Even in my dream, it seemed odd to see him there, but comforting at the same time, still presenting me with the two tokens of love in his hands.

"Daddy, I know what I want more than anything. But —at what cost do I put others through for my own heart?"

"Adena Keely Whitmore. Never put your heart so low on your list of priorities. This is just another one of life's little messes. Everything will be right as rain. Come yesterday. You'll see."

Come yesterday? GG had said the same thing.

"But I'll lose Trent's friendship. And I don't want to hurt him."

"He'll forgive you in time. He'll always be there for you and the kids. He was a good catch."

I looked up to find a slight smirk playing across his mouth. "So am I stupid for throwing him back?"

"Not if you're sure of what's next."

"But how can I possibly know?" I wrapped my arms around his waist and laid my head against his shoulder, feeling the warmth and the love I had missed so much for so long. My tears flowed silently onto his gray jacket.

"I think I have a pretty good vantage point, baby. As for you choosing, well —you could never go wrong with a good fishing buddy. You know, just in case I'm not around some day." He ran his hand lovingly across my back.

"Daddy, I've missed you so much. I love you."

"I've always been close. And I'll help you through this however I can. I love you, Doll."

Just as his embrace became warmer, more real, he chuckled once and the words began to fade. But I heard him clearly. "Tell Scooter I'll be seeing him soon."

The tears became a warm wet spot on my pillow where so many had fallen so quickly. I opened my eyes to find Preston holding on to me, wiping away my sadness. I remembered my dream vividly, could still see the smile on Daddy's face. Almost as if it floated before me, like the smile of the Cheshire cat. I hadn't dreamed of him in years and never as real as that. Every word he said echoed through my thoughts as I looked into Preston's eyes.

"Have a bad dream?" He pushed my hair back out of my eyes.

"No." I took in a calming breath. "Daddy was here...under the arbor."

"Really? Does he disapprove?"

I shook my head but wondered where the dreams kept coming from.

"Good to know. And just so you know, that isn't an arbor. It's the ruins of a really old church." He tugged me closer and held me, his chin on top of my head. "You miss him a great deal don't you?" I nodded. "I'm sorry you're so sad."

I sat up and felt strangely... awake. I wasn't sad. Not at all. On the contrary I felt alert and strong and clear headed. An invisible burden nearly gone. As if, Daddy had come to lighten my load. His approval even now apparently still meant the world to me.

"So, what's on the agenda today?" I asked to change the subject.

"Hmm. No plans. But I do have an idea. Let's see if Dad wants to go fishing. It'll get him out of the house but he'll still be taking it easy. He'd enjoy it. Unless... that's not really your thing. I could take him another day."

I heard my father's faint chuckle somewhere in the depths of my mind as if he'd just delivered the funny punch line to a good joke. *You could never go wrong with a good fishing buddy.*

Good one, Daddy. You're a real riot.

Preston went to get his boat and to pick up his father but he called right after I'd gotten out of the shower to say we'd have to postpone fishing until the next day. His father had an appointment with the specialist that he'd forgotten about. Doreen was on her way to drop Kelley off so she could go with Nate.

I dressed as fast as I could, dragging my brush through my hair hard and fast when I heard someone let them self in the front door. Kelley ran to meet me with another precious hug and Doreen stayed to chat but only for a few minutes. As soon as we were alone, Kelley took hold of my hand pulling me along to her room. She sat down on her white shag rug and I joined her. She reached up to her nightstand and pulled down a picture frame.

"This is Mum Lizzy and Dad Spencer." She placed her pale pink finger on each of their faces as she introduced me to them. "I was in Mum's belly. See there."

I could plainly see Lizzy was due any day and indeed, she was a carbon copy of her beautiful mother. Another brick tumbled into place in my mind. Or perhaps the bricks tumbled down, revealing more of the mystery with each one gone.

Lizzy looked so much like my mother, like Kelley, like Beth. My mind went back to the last night Preston spent in my room and the surprised look on his face when he'd seen my parents wedding picture. Now that I could see the resemblances for myself I knew that he'd seen the remarkable likeness as well.

"Thank you for sharing them with me." I said slowly as she watched my lips. She mouthed each word perfectly just after me.

"You're welcome." She sat the picture back on her nightstand. "I wish I could remember them." She shrugged her shoulders and looked a little sad. "But Poppy tells me stories of them."

"Your Poppy loves you more than anything." Whatever sadness she had quickly turned to absolute happiness.

"And Poppy loves you." She giggled and crawled into my lap sideways.

I smiled down into her pretty face. "That makes us two very lucky girls, doesn't it?"

"Lucky girls." She agreed as she looked down running her finger across the white polish on the tips of my fingernails. I tickled her beneath her chin to get her to look at me.

"You know what?" I asked her.

"What Adena?"

"You've stolen my heart."

She gasped. "What about Poppy?"

"My heart is big enough ..." I waited until she mouthed each word and she nodded for me to finish. "for you and Poppy."

I tickled her ribs and we laughed together until we were breathless. I let her sit up straight again and she peered over my shoulder. "Hi Poppy! Want to play too?"

I spun around with her still in my arms. Preston smiled but his eyes were red.

Kelley stood up, walked behind me, and pulled my hair into a ponytail, flipping it this way and that and tried to braid it. Preston came in and squatted on the floor in front of me.

"We had a nice little chat while you were gone." I told him.

He nodded once. "I stopped in the hallway when I heard her talking about Lizzy and Spence."

"You must have come in right after Doreen left."

He nodded again.

Kelley peeked around the side of my face, kissed my cheek then bounded into Preston's lap knocking him on his rear. She put her feet in my lap and laid back into his chest with a contented smile. He reached over and took my hands in his. She wrapped her little hands around ours. She tilted her head back, lips puckered for him to give her a fatherly peck. He did so and smiled down at her. He looked up at me; his eyes glistening, and laughed in spite of himself. He reached for me, slid his long fingers beneath my hair, his thumb resting at my temple.

"*I'm* the lucky one." He whispered.

Kelley hopped to her feet and went into the living room to dig in her toy box by the sound of it. Preston pulled me to my feet and held me close.

"I used to be good at lying to myself but I can't lie to you. I'll go mad missing you." His breath caught in his chest and he buried his face in my hair. "I feel you in the very depths of my soul. Being with you is like —I don't know how to explain it. Only one word comes to mind but it doesn't make sense."

Before I even knew it, the words that didn't make any sense at all slipped out. "Like a memory."

He pushed me away just enough to see me, his eyes wide. "What?"

"I don't know. It just came out." It's the word I'd been thinking of for a while but I couldn't understand it. And I wished so much that I hadn't said it. The weirdness back again because it didn't have anything to do with our meeting so many years ago. It had to do with what GG had said. I'd inherited her memories. I felt it in my bones but I still couldn't connect the dots.

"It's *exactly* the word I've been thinking. I haven't been able to figure it out. But when I'm with you everything feels so perfect, so right, so familiar. It's not a *memory*, I know that, but it's like something trapped in my mind that I can't find. All I know is that what we're doing isn't wrong. It can't be."

I couldn't speak. His words shook me to my core. He felt it too.

"I'll have to come to you soon. —Or do you need time? Time to figure things out?"

I pulled away further to stare at him. "Preston, there is *nothing* for me to figure out." I backed away and sat down on Kelley's bed.

"Believe it or not, I do realize a lifetime friendship not to mention a marriage of nearly twenty years is a hard thing to just toss to the wind."

I stood up too swiftly. "Preston, when you left I was so lost, so empty. I moped and I cried and I slept and all I could see was your face. *That's* why I went back to the lake. I was running from memories of us!

But guess what? They followed me! —And then later, I felt so exhilarated every time we spoke that you could never know how I felt the rest of the day." I confessed so quickly, I wasn't sure he'd heard me and I wished I could suck every traitorous word back into my stupid mouth. I looked down at my hands clinging to the sides of his flannel shirt not fully aware of when I got close enough to grab it.

He pulled my face up to look at him, his eyes angrily seeking an explanation.

"In nineteen years I've never missed Trent so much, never physically needed him near me. I have no decision left to make. As soon as Trent is home long enough to sit down and talk to him, I *will* tell him I'm in love with you. I swear it."

"I will *not*..." He started to yell something but we heard Kelley coming back toward her room.

He rubbed his face quickly and I spun around pretending to look out the window. He met her at the door and told her we'd be right there to play with her. He came back and gripped my shoulders from behind.

"You've cut my heart open. I don't know if I'll let you go home now. Not if when you get there, you'll fall apart on me. You have to promise me you won't. I swear to you, I'm not worthy of it."

I turned to face him abruptly. "It's not something I did by choice." More harsh than I'd intended. "And you *will not what?*"

He held my shoulders and spoke softly. "Let you lose everything. You tell Trent and then what? I don't know anything about him. What if he hurts you? What if he kicks you out? I don't want to put you in any more jeopardy than I already have."

"Trent would never hit me and I know I've cried every damn day since I met you but I'm not some weak ass little sap who needs a man to take care of her! I'm perfectly capable of taking care of myself!" I shrugged his hands away then turned my back on him. My heated breath fogged the glass of the window just a few inches in front of me.

His arms curled around me. "I know that, Adena. I didn't mean to insinuate that you did. Jesus, you've got to be the strongest person I've ever known. I don't think your tears make you weak. They just show how intensely you love."

I closed my eyes and turned to cling to him. "I'm sorry I yelled at you. The last thing I ever want is for us to start fighting."

"We won't, Love. Now let's go play Candee Land."

19

PRESTON

Thursday Morning June 25...

STANDING OUTSIDE MY FRONT door watching the sun peek over the trees, the all-consuming feeling of dread pulled me under. A riptide of despair threatened to take my last breath and I honestly had no idea what to do next.

In less than twenty-four hours, she'd be gone. My self-deception of the past week and a half, now taking its toll. My biggest fear was that once she got back home with him, they'd work things out. And if they did? —God in Heaven help me if they did —what would I do? The fact is I wanted her. Needed her even. But she cares and does for everyone around her. Would she really have it in her to hurt Trent?

I could give her anything she asked of me. Anything apart from the upcoming dilemma of choosing a new path or remaining on the one she'd held loyally to for half her life. Until I botched everything up for her. I've got to be the biggest prick on the planet. I'd never even considered pursuing a married woman before.

I laughed as I lit a cigarette. Her perfectly polished toe nails hanging over the side of the boat, her tanned skin glowing beneath the afternoon sun yesterday, and she *still* caught more than Dad and I put together. I've never seen a woman so excited over reeling in a fish.

The morning breeze wrapped her floral fragrance around me and from behind I felt her arms curl around my waist. That was all it took for me to lose all train of thought. As I turned to take her in my arms and I looked down, the wind tossed her long waves, scattering a few across her face. She looked like that painting ... Botticelli's *The Birth of Venus*, only with darker hair.

I touched her cheek and stared at her and I knew at that precise moment that the love I saw reflected back at me in her deep green eyes was real.

She watched me toss my cigarette into a bucket by the front steps.

"What are you worried about?" She asked.

"Why do you think that?"

"Process of elimination. You're not drinking. You don't look angry. So that leaves worried. That's the only times you smoke."

Perceptive as always.

"Today is Thursday. I've just been thinking."

She reached her hand to my face and ran her thumb over my cheek. I held her hand against it, closed my eyes and felt her warmth.

"My parents picked up Kelley at daybreak to pay Aunt Gladys a visit. Sorry for not sharing you with them, but I really just want to be alone with you. Is that alright?"

She smiled. "I'll see them next time."

Next time. Easy enough to say but nearly impossible for her. She got away with it this time, thanks to Owen. We'd taken *long distance relationship* to the extreme. If Trent happened to be home when I went back, how would we see each other? Have lunch and make hurried love at my hotel then part ways until the next day? How many heartbreaking goodbyes were either of us able to endure?

She stood on the tips of her toes to kiss me. It's what I'd been waiting for. She beckoned for me with her finger. Perhaps the one I'm so thoroughly wrapped around and I carried her back to my room.

The last thing I ever wanted her to think is that I was only in it for the sex. But now, all I wanted was to sear every detail of her into my mind. As if I could forget how she felt. A sword and scabbard forged to fit no one but each other. Her hand in mine, the way we slept, the way we made love, all of it fit perfectly.

We stayed in the sheets throughout the afternoon, lost in each other for hours on end. I lay there, holding her, still and quiet. She had drifted off to sleep with her head on my chest. All I could see was her long hair spilling over her soft tan shoulder, her breast pressed against my ribs, her elegant fingers splayed across my chest next to her cheek.

The day had gone by far too quickly. I hated to wake her, but it was five o'clock already. I didn't have to; she opened her eyes and looked up at me. I held her closer for as long as I could in the silence of my room. She didn't say much. She didn't have to. As the shadows of evening grew longer, I felt her hot tears roll down my ribs.

Later that night at my parents' house, I sat on the bed watching her neatly fold her clothes. Then with the same orderliness, she began filling her suitcase. At first. Then she cast the last of the pile into her case and slammed it shut. She just stood there silent with her eyes shut. I got up to meet her at the foot of the bed and tried to take her hand but she jerked away.

"Adena? What did I do?"

She sat on the bed and hung her head low, pushing her hair back, hard in mad frustration, inhaled deeply, then let it go. "You didn't do anything, Preston. It's me."

That didn't help at all. She'd never been cold to me before and it felt like a dagger.

"Darling, what do you mean?" I knelt down so I could see her face, her eyes still shut tight.

"I don't even know! —I feel like I'm standing on the edge of a cliff, ready to jump but I'm so scared it's gonna hurt like hell when I land."

I reached to touch her face. "Adena, look at me please." I pleaded. She opened her eyes as I held her face in my hands. "It won't hurt when you fall. I'll catch you, I promise."

She seemed to catch her breath at my words although I couldn't imagine why. Then her face grew desolate at best. Her eyes looked uninhabited and I began to get a glimpse of what she must go through when we were apart. I could relate.

"Preston, I believe you. But how is this gonna work? I mean..." Her hands balled into fists and she banged her knees furiously. "Everything has been so perfect *here*. But now what? How is this gonna work for us? Honestly! How are we gonna keep seeing each other?" Her voice cracked and pitched over every word.

"I *will* come to you. We will find a way to make it work. *Please*, don't give up on me." I prayed with all my heart I could make her hold on. I couldn't lose her.

I pulled myself up to kiss her, desperately trying to bring life back to her eyes. To let my love bring her back from wherever she'd gotten lost. At last, she put her arms round my neck and pulled me closer. When we finally released each other, I searched her eyes. Alive again.

"Adena, all I ask is you trust in what we're feeling. Trust in everything I've said to you. Every touch we've shared, every breath taking moment since we met."

Her chin quivered as she tried to smile.

I lifted her left hand. I wanted her to know the choice was hers and I would give her time. No demands. "Now, where are your rings from Trent?" It felt like jagged glass in my throat to say his name. She pulled them from of her purse and held them out in the palm of her hand. "Put them back on, Love."

She balled them into her fist and refused.

"Surely you must see that you are at a critical junction in your life.

This is *your* decision to make. Make it carefully. If the time comes that I see you've taken them off again, I'll know you've jumped, and I will be ready and waiting when you do." I brushed a wayward curl from her eyes. "But Sweetheart, take your time. No rash decisions like two fools in love. Think of what's best for you. You know I love you. I realize we haven't gone about this the best way, but I want you to understand. I'm yours no matter what. We'll take this step by step. I don't want you to feel as though you have to hit Trent with divorce papers as soon as you get home." I heaved a sigh and stroked her cheek. "Am I making any sense? I've never been in this position before so you'll have to help me a bit here."

She nodded and let go a deep breath as if the weight of the real world had settled upon her shoulders once again. I watched her push the rings back onto her finger and suddenly, the burden of reality filled my heart as well.

We heard muted laughter from the next room. Mum's study. Adena and I went to investigate. We found my mother showing off baby pictures. *Spectacular.* But it was a better way to spend our last night together than crying in the next room. I'd rather hear Adena laugh any day.

She was already smiling as she sat down in the floor with Mum and the girls. I sat down just in time to see my mother point out one of myself —naked holding a toy guitar at age three.

"Mum! Do you mind?"

Beth was in tears and just near to rolling on the floor. However, Adena's short-lived smile faded as she looked at something else. She wasn't just looking at it, she was staring, entranced. Then I could see what it was.

"Can we have a minute?" I said to the others.

Beth was the last to go, looking over her shoulder. The look on her face told me she'd recognized the man in the picture as well. Roger, her grandfather. She looked at me seeking an explanation. I nodded to her as if to say *we'll explain later* and she closed the door.

Adena touched her father's face on the page. "You *did* meet Daddy."

I stared at the image, then at her. I held her and let that bit of information sink in. I remembered it as if it were yesterday. I held her closer rubbing her arms trying to make her trembling stop. I shook my head at the absurdity of it all. I looked at the photo of me standing next to a teenage girl, her father buried in the sand in front of us and wondered exactly how and why this world worked the way it did.

She flipped the page and froze. She put her hands on her hips and cocked her head this way and that. She touched a black and white picture. "Who's that?"

I looked at it carefully. "That's Katherine. My great-grandmother. I don't know who the girl is."

"I think I do." She looked as if she were working out an algebraic equation in her head. "Preston, go get your dad. *Please.* Before my brain falls on the floor."

I couldn't tell if she were angry, shocked, or what. So I went to get my father. How could she even begin to think she knew someone Katherine knew? The photo had to be close to a hundred years old. When Dad walked in, Adena picked the album up and sat it in his hands as though it were fragile as glass.

"Nate, do you have any idea who that is?" She touched the young lady's face and looked expectantly at my father.

Dad pulled his glasses from his shirt pocket and put them on. "Ah, yes. Katherine and Preston adopted her and her younger brother. Their father abandoned the family when the children were small and the mother passed. Preston, you knew the boy. Well, he was an old man to you. Lizzy's grandfather. Adam Mac Dermot. But the girl. *Her* name was Dilly."

Adena nodded her head slowly as she sat in Mum's desk chair, her hands shaking slightly and I saw her gulp. I didn't know if she were swallowing or trying to breathe.

"My great-grandmother's name was Delia Mac Dermot before she married." She sat there so still with her eyes closed and I hadn't absorbed any of it yet. Till her eyes popped at Dad. "Wait! Did you just say her brother was Lizzy's *grandfather?*"

Dad nodded slowly as the two of them stared at each other. Then the puzzle pieces slowly began to shift themselves into place in my head.

"Preston, don't you see? The resemblance between Kelley and Beth? Lizzy and my mother?" She gasped and sat up straight. "Oh my God, that makes Kelley..."

"Your cousin." I finished for her. "Distant —but nonetheless, *related.*" I whipped my head around to look at my father. "You're sure they were adopted? I swear if you say Adena and I—"

"Oh, relax, Preston. They weren't blood relations." Dad heaved a sigh and stared at Adena for a long moment. "Sweetheart, are you alright?"

"Yes. I think so. —I just don't understand. GG was from Ireland. Delia I mean. How did she wind up here? She lived on Lake St. John until Gavin was five years old. She never once spoke of living in England."

"I'm afraid all of that took place before my time. I do know the story though. Dilly's mother was a well-known seamstress and Katherine had sought her out to make her wedding gown. However, when she went to the shop to pick up her dress, it was closed. When she peeked in the window, she saw a girl of around eight or nine trying to give a younger boy a bath from a bowl of water. Poor Dilly had been caring for her brother in the shop for weeks with no family to turn to. Katherine brought them here. Preston made every effort to locate any relatives but he'd found none. So they took them in and raised them.

"She'd been more of a little sister to Katherine as my grandmother was scarcely seventeen when she found the pair. Dilly met and married a pastor at around age eighteen. He was from America so it was only natural that they went back. Adam stayed here and worked the orchards with Preston the rest of his days. He married and lived in one of the cottages. His daughter lived on a farm just a stone's throw from here. She was Lizzy's grandmother.

"As for her being from Ireland, well I knew that as well. But to my knowledge, Dilly's mother had settled the children in the Kilburn area, just a short ride from Brent Reservoir. My grandfather took me there to see the sailboats when I was a boy and he showed me the old building where the children were found. At least, what was left of it. He was always very distressed when he spoke of Dilly which wasn't often at all. You see, she cut all ties with the family once she was gone. Even her brother. No one ever knew why."

I couldn't help but stare at my father, my mouth agape, my brain trying to catch up with what my ears just heard. Unbelievable. Impossible. Yes, impossible. We were assuming that Dilly and Delia were one in the same when in fact we had no proof. Then I had an idea.

"Adena, what was Delia's husband's name, but don't say it out loud, please." I looked at Dad. "Do you know who Dilly married?"

He nodded once.

Adena rolled her eyes at me. "Preston, I recognize the picture. It's almost the same one I have at home."

I held up my hand to politely sway her from saying anything else.

"Please, this is for my own sanity. Nothing more. Now, do you both have the man in question's name in your head?" They both nodded, agitated with me. "Fine then. On the count of three."

They looked at one another like a wild west show counting down to the inevitable draw. And simultaneously they said, "Joseph Albright."

Bugger me!

Things just get more absurd by the second.

Poor Adena looked more confused than ever. She rubbed her brow and sat forward in her chair. "I do remember GG telling me once she was adopted. And she said I was named after the woman who raised her. But now *that* doesn't make sense. Not if her name was Katherine."

Dad raised a brow and rocked back on his heels. "What is your given name?"

"Adena Keely."

"Hmm," He scratched his chin and walked over to Mom's computer, tapped a few keys and waited.

"What are you doing, Dad?"

"I'm only curious. There's more than one way to name a child after someone." He tapped again like a chicken pecking, one slow letter at a time while he spoke, "Your mum likes this site. She and her friend Deb poured over it for days when Deb's daughter was expecting. And through much distress I was asked my useless male opinion on every one. —Mmm, yes. Have a look." He pointed to a popular website for picking out baby names as Adena and I looked over his shoulder. "It's not your first name at all. It's Keely. I imagine she picked that one for several reasons. It's Gaelic for one; from her Irish roots. And have a look at the meaning. Full of *Grace*. And Katherine's first name was Ania. A. K. —You have her initials."

There wasn't much else to say.

***

Friday morning at the airport, Beth wrapped me in a tender hug. "I'm gonna miss you, Preston. I'm glad I got the chance to know you. Kinda makes things a little easier to accept. Ya know?"

She looked like she'd just admitted to kicking a young pup.

"I do. And I'm truly glad you came along, Beth. —You know, just because you sort of like me, despite my being a dork," She smiled and blushed a lovely shade. "Well, that hardly makes you disloyal to your father."

She sighed and nodded quickly. "I know. But thanks for saying it anyway."

"I'll be seeing you soon." I smiled down at her, pleased again, that she'd accepted me as part of her mother's life.

"See ya, Dork." She flashed a smile then walked away with Owen.

Adena pouted like a child. "This sucks."

I took her hand in mine. "Yes, it does. Give me a ring when you land."

But that wasn't all I wanted to say. Only one thought kept recurring — trying to form words that I really wanted to say but shouldn't.

Stay, Adena. Just stay.

She murmured, 'I love you' against my cheek with a last hurried kiss, an audible hitch in her throat.

I kissed her again then held her close, whispering in her ear. "You wanted to know my weakness. It's you."

I watched her walk away again. Quickly. Reluctantly. But eager to be done with our sad so long. Just as she nearly made the right ahead directing her to security, she pulled the strap of her black carry-on tight across her shoulder then swiped broadly at her wet cheeks, one then the other. She sniffed long and hard and deeply as though she could somehow summon the strength she needed purely from the air around her.

The things I'd noticed about her in those last ten seconds —how tall she was for one. Rather, how tall she seemed. Her stature. Her poise. The strength that somehow came from within as well as in the way her shoulders seemed always to be squared —ready for battle in some strange way. She was feminine. Always. And yet, she had a soldier-like quality about her. Roll with the punches? No. Not her. Adena took life's punches straight on and squarely in the teeth. She swallowed them whole and digested them. And there inside, those miseries resided. Hidden away to affect no one she cared for. No one but her and her alone. And only when no one was looking did she break. There were endless things I'd discovered about her, be they real or imagined, long after she'd gone. I saw all of her or so I believed. I saw all of her. I stared and I stood and I stared some more.

I don't know how long I stood there looking at the spot where I last saw her.

20

Three weeks later...July 17th

AFTER A LONG DAY OF waging war on weeds in Mum's colossal garden, and swapping an assortment of curse words as varied as a box of chocolates with the bastard trainer who *used* to work for Uncle, I went home and stood there in my garage ready to tackle my bike as a bit of relief from the eyeball deep tension I seem to find myself adrift in daily.

I'd worked on the old Indian nearly every night since Adena left, finding it more than difficult to sleep without her. When I was ready to put that beautiful flared fender on, I noticed something for the first time. Just above the chrome trim was a bundled mess of touch-up paint. The paint was too red; too bright to be of the original deep burgundy that had long ago lost its metallic luster.

I scratched at it a bit with my thumbnail and wondered out loud, "Who on earth would do that to a bike like this?"

I got some solvent and tried to get it off. I figured it was a wasted attempt, thinking the layered piss-poor paint job was too old to budge. But it came off straight away. Then a faint familiar smell.

"That can't be *nail* polish." I laughed.

So I'd wound up with a girl's motorbike. Leave it to a woman to do something like that. I knew I could fix the scratch properly. However, when I examined what lay beneath the botched paint, I nearly dropped the fender. Couldn't be. I rubbed it harder.

It had to be a coincidence. Simple as that. The odds —too astronomical. Nonetheless, staring back at me were the letters D-E-N-A etched into the original paint. The scribble of a child. I wanted to call Adena and ask if she may have, at some point, defaced her father's old bike in anyway. I convinced myself it was simply too outlandish to be her father's. Could've been an entirely different model. But a nagging curiosity wouldn't allow me to let it go.

The title!

I ran inside and dug through a file-o-folder I kept on the top shelf of my wardrobe. I pulled it out in a flurry of rustling papers as the rest of what I wasn't looking for fell to the floor. Several bits of old papers stapled together that I'd found in one of the boxes with the bike parts along with a cracked leather document holder.

The bike must surely have passed through several owners. The stapled batch turned up nothing but suddenly there it was in plain sight.

The old leather portfolio lay upside down at my feet and in the lower right hand corner were the initials R. W. embossed in the grain.

I bent down, picked it up and flipped it open. My search had suddenly come to a halt. A yellowed piece of paper, an agreement between seller and buyer. The second signature, in a perfectly legible scrawl read, Roger Lee Whitmore.

My legs went to jelly and I surrendered to gravity, sitting at the foot of my bed. I ran my finger over the signature feeling gooseflesh raise the hair on my arms. I could literally feel the indentation the pen had made in the paper where Roger Lee Whitmore, the man himself, had signed over the bike to a man who lived on Orleans Street in Natchez, Mississippi on May 5th, 1979.

There was simply no mistaking that it was his. And somehow, her father's bike had found its way to England. Long after he'd sold it and long before Adena's path and mine crossed again in Gainesville.

Lost in some sort of trancelike obsession, I went to work with much reverence for each piece and finished the project that night around 2 a.m. I was exhausted. Bushed, beat and beyond. At that moment, that was the only truth I knew. Yet I couldn't have kept my eyes closed with a roll of tape.

I poured myself a stiff drink and carried the bottle of Scotch along as well and proceeded to avail myself to the hangover I was no doubt to have by morning. I sat out in the garage staring at that damn bike. And I drank. And I tried to think through the strangeness. I drank some more, stared some more. I thought about cranking it. But I wanted Adena to be here to hear her father's old '48 Indian Chief come to life.

In an eerie way, the machine nearly looked like it was breathing. Long forgotten and neglected but now thankfully brought back. I didn't understand why I had a part to play in its resurrection. But it was one more extraordinary connection to her. Almost disturbing. The coincidences piling up to the point that I knew better than to refer to them as chance any longer. But to dwell on the reasons for too long, would surely lead to nothing but madness.

Adena was persistent in her belief that she'd already made her decision. All I'd been doing was talking her into thinking on it longer. It's no wonder she got so bent with me at times. If anyone tried telling me to be sure how I felt, I'd go ballistic. Yet still, I wait like a fool risking losing her.

A flash of bright light blinded me from the head lamp of the bike and the deafening roar of the motor reverberated throughout my entire body. The handlebars turned, sending the blinding beam askew and I could see although I couldn't believe my eyes. A man was sitting astride the bike, wearing a brown plaid western shirt, cowboy hat, jeans and boots; his hazel eyes staring right through me. His light colored eyes seemed to glow against his russet colored skin and his ink black hair.

I knew this gentleman or at least I had once long ago for merely a week. For the rest of my adolescent years, I'd dreamt of being a cowboy and attempted to emulate his manner of dress and speech and I'd dreamed up all sorts of fantasies chasing down cattle and such with a rope in my hand.

He let go a deep chuckle that seemed to echo through the entire sky. "Damn good to see ya again, Scooter." Then a one sided grin and he tilted his head. "So whatchya waitin' on, son? You're supposed to be together. That's the easy part. Don't wonder so much about why? Just know this. People can't see much beyond what happens in their own lives. But there are wheels turning all around us. Stuff you can't see, stuff you can't even imagine."

"Ehm, Mr. Whitmore, how exactly...?"

"How am I here?" He laughed and rubbed the chrome letters on the gas tank. "Jeanie in a bottle I guess you could say. Man, I loved this thing. Dena was so upset the year I sold it. She was only eight at the time and I watched her do that." He pointed with purpose at the etching on the fender. "She felt bad right after and tried to fix it up with her mama's nail polish." He chuckled, shook his head and looked up at me. "Never had the heart to fuss at her for it.

"But listen up. I don't know how much time I got so I can't take a detour down Memory Lane. —I've been hearing stuff here for a long time that I didn't understand. Can't see anybody, but this place is full of folks. My folks, your folks and they almost never shut up."

"So — why can't I see *my* folks?"

"Shit, *I* don't know, Scooter. One minute I'm alive, the next I'm in no-man's land. Can't see anything here but I hear all these voices. And listen, that little girl of yours hears them, too. It's why she don't like wearing that hearing aid. It scares her."

A blood veil blurred my vision and my neck suddenly felt like it was on fire. "My daughter can *hear* you!"

"Calm down, Scooter. We're all real careful around her, now that we know. Nobody here wants to upset her. They're just stuck like me." He

261

looked over his shoulder at something I couldn't see then turned to face me again and his southern drawl hit double-time. "You gotta get off your ass and do something. I don't get why, but somehow you and my girl are the key to this whole mess. I heard something one day about the attic. Something about the windows. I think there might be something up there that might shed some light on all this."

"Whose attic? What... *windows?*"

"Scooter, I hear fragments of what all these people say. It's like a bad AM radio here. Mostly it's just noise but it's enough to make a man wanna take a damn hammer to his own head. Now, I know it ain't much to go on. But I feel it in my gut. The windows Scooter, not at your place; your Pop's. Oh, and something about a poem? I don't know what the hell that could mean but I know that's what I heard."

He looked over his shoulder again and although I could never have imagined a man the likes of Roger Whitmore being terrified; that's exactly how he looked now. "Outta time. She can't know there's a way through. If I can get out, I'm scared she can, too. The whole damn universe is off kilter 'cause of something she did a long time ago. Ya know? Like ripples in a pond. They just keep going and going. I can't piece it all together here. It's chaos times a million in this place. But maybe you can. You take care of my girl, Scooter."

He revved the motor and in an instant I jerked upright scared out of my wits, stumbling backward over the chair until I fell ass over shoulders into the dirt.

I lay there staring at the bottom side of the gutters on the garage and realized the sun had risen. I looked at the bike sitting there quiet and untouched. I'd fallen asleep with a bit too much to drink. But the hair on the back of my neck was standing on end. I stood up and popped the dust free from my pants.

"Bugger! What the bloody hell was all that about?" I thought better of what I'd just said. "Never mind, Mr. Whitmore, for God's sake, *please* don't answer me."

I had to get a firm grasp of my wits. I took two long strides to the bike and reached to feel the muffler but stopped before I touched it. Did I really want to know if it was warm?

Not on your bloody life!

My parents would arrive any minute to take Kelley on holiday before she went back to school and I still had to pack her things. I sat at the breakfast table while she ate her favorite cereal. She must have noticed I was a bit unnerved.

"Anything the matter, Poppy?"

I looked down into her sweet face and thought hard. I didn't want to frighten her but an overwhelming urgency to know the truth made me ask.

"Kelley, the noises in your hearing aid —what do they sound like?"

She seemed to shrink a bit in her chair and I knew what that meant. She pushed her bowl away and shrugged her little shoulders. "Scary sounds sometimes. I've told you that."

My hand curled into itself and I fought with every ounce to hold my temper. "Kelley, do you hear — *people*?"

Her tiny chin began to quiver and tears pooled in her sky blue eyes. She nodded slowly.

"Why didn't you tell me this, Kelley!"

She jumped in her seat —*away* from me and I reached instantly to grab her. "Sweetheart, I'm sorry. I'm so very sorry." I kissed her head and held her close. She pointed to her ear to show me she was wearing her hearing aid.

She looked up at me and wiped a tear from her cheek. "But it's not so bad any more. The nice man made it stop."

"The nice man? Do you know who he is?"

She nodded with so much sadness in her young eyes. "Adena's Dad. She's just like me, Poppy. Her father was there as well."

I blinked twice. "As well?"

She nodded. "At first, the nice man found Mum Lizzy for me. Then Dad Spencer. Mum sang for me once. They said they miss me. They said they loved me. But I told them that you take excellent care of me. Mum said she knew that and to tell you thanks. They both send their love, Poppy. They miss you as well."

I broke down like a child and my daughter, sitting in my lap, comforted *me*. "It's all right, Poppy. I don't hear them anymore and I'm not frightened anymore. The nice man said you'd figure it all out and make things right again. And Mum and Dad are happy now. They aren't stuck like the rest. They only stayed to look after us for a bit." Her pale little brows bent in consternation for a moment. "Poppy, I think that's why they could leave that place. They were together when they passed. They didn't have to find each other. They left when they were ready to go. All the rest are lost. The others, they call for each other and they cry a lot. It's a very sad place, Poppy. I think they're all just afraid.

That's what frightened me so. The sadness."

I dried my face on my sleeve and gently took her chin in my hand. "Kelley, you have to tell me everything. From now on, no matter how unbelievable it may seem, if anything happens to you, if you hear so much as a whisper, you tell me. Do you understand? I can't take proper care of you unless I know everything."

She nodded. "I will." She clasped her hands to my cheeks the way she does when I sing to her. "I love you, Poppy."

I hugged her tightly. "I love you, Kelley. Now let's go to Gran's house. I've got work to do."

Pulling up to Dad's place, I put the truck in park and helped Kelley out. "You go inside, Sweetheart. Tell your granddad I'll be in shortly." She nodded and let herself in through the front door.

I leaned against the front of the truck craning my neck to see every window of the house. My hands in my pockets, I strolled slowly, looking from one floor to the next down the length of the house until I circled the perimeter twice.

I must be losing my mind. What can the windows possibly have to do with anything? I couldn't understand the logic. Is it something I would see through a particular window? I didn't know where to begin. Sitting on the little bench next to Kelley's swing staring at the back of the house, a beam of sunlight reflected off of one of the attic windows blinding me for a moment. I looked up; shielding my eyes from the sun and suddenly the answer stared back at me.

I bolted into the house passing Dad on the stairs.

"Good morning to you too, son. Where's the fire?"

"Morning, Dad." I jogged up faster, my heart racing as my mind fit another puzzle piece into place. "How many attic windows on the back of the house, Dad?"

I heard him following so I slowed down, allowing him to catch up.

"Four. Why?"

"How many in the attic?"

"Well, there are four of course. Have you been drinking? What are you doing?"

I stopped and turned to him. "Four? Really? You're so certain aren't you?" I laughed. Incredulous that none of us ever noticed.

I opened the door in the second floor hallway that led to the attic and lunged up the stairs taking them three at a time. I had to heave my shoulder against the door at the top as it always seemed to be stuck. It flew open under my weight.

Dad gave a final huff as he trudged up the last steps and stopped to hold on to the door frame.

I watched him carefully. "All right?"

He swatted his hand at me as he always does. "I'm fine! I'm wondering the same about you."

"Not quite fine. Look." I pointed to the attic windows and walked over to touch them each. "*Three* windows Dad. Four on the outside. Where the hell is the last window?"

Dad stood there scratching his head. "I can't believe I've lived here my entire life and never noticed." He weaved his way through the waist high clutter to look out the farthest on the right, same as me.

I walked past at least ten old steamer trunks, paintings, furniture, the entire floor filled with rubbish from everyone that had ever resided in the house. I made it to the far wall on the right and heaved on a heavy hutch to move it out of the way.

"Careful, Preston. Do you have any idea what that thing is probably worth?"

I shoved it out of the way and watched it topple over. "It's worth shit, Dad! It's got twenty coats of horrendous green paint and a broken leg and it's been that way for decades."

My father shrugged in agreement and helped me move the rest of the piled pieces.

He stopped to wipe the sweat from his brow. "Why exactly are we moving all this, Preston?"

"So I can really piss you and Mum off. Stand back."

I pushed with both hands at different sections of the wall checking for studs. Thankfully, there weren't many. It wasn't a weight bearing wall at all, merely a divider or something of the sort. I stepped back and kicked as hard as I could, watching the wall bow in the middle. With some effort, I knew it would give way. But I'd never be able to kick it down. I looked all about the attic for something, anything, to pry it apart.

"Poppy," Kelley called from the door.

I kept searching. There had to be something I could use. "In a minute, Kelley. I'm a little busy."

I heard her feet just behind me then she tugged my shirt. "Poppy!"

I turned to find her struggling with a pry bar and a heavy sledge hammer. "The nice man said you might need these. I got them from the shed."

I smiled and took them from her. "The nice man, you say?"

She nodded and wiped the rust from the tools on her brand new pink pants.

"Tell him thanks, okay?"

She smiled and headed carefully back down the stairs.

My father looked at me. "The nice man? What man?"

"Dad, I don't even know where to begin. Just stand clear."

I tried to get the pry bar beneath the panel but it was far thicker than I thought. I dropped the bar to the floor and grabbed the sledge hammer and wailed away with all my strength. I was surprised at the density and strength of the old wood; it was like hammering through solid plastic for a while, but finally, bit by bit, the wall gave up before I did. Having managed to beat out a hole big enough to climb through, I stuck my head in and looked inside. The space ran the width of the attic but the distance from me to the outer wall of the house, merely six feet.

I crawled through and looked around. "I don't get it. It's only more junk! Why was it boarded up this way?" I took two steps away from the window and immediately regretted it. In two seconds flat I'd found a shortcut to the second floor through the rotting boards. Thankfully, I caught myself before going completely through. Dad started to come through to help.

"NO! Stay where you are, Dad. I'm fine."

He tried to smother his laughter. "I suppose you now know why it's been shut off."

I stopped struggling to stare at him. "Thank you for that brilliant observation."

21

I MANAGED TO EXTRICATE MYSELF from the floor and looked around. In the middle of the floor, a closed hatch with a bit of rope tied round a thick black iron handle. I walked cautiously, testing each creaking board before putting my weight down. I tugged the rope and it took all my strength to get the heavy hatch up and back.

I stared down into the darkness. "Dad?"

"Yes?"

"It's another stair case. And it stinks."

"I'll get a lamp. Hold right there."

The smell, so revolting, I had to cover my nose. What could possibly smell like that? It's a wonder the odor hadn't permeated the walls. I heard Dad come back.

"Catch." He tossed a small camping lamp to me. "Preston, do be careful. I'm too old to drag your long narrow ass out of there."

I pressed the button on the lamp and made my way down; the steps so narrow my elbows scraped the walls. It didn't take long to see the source of the smell. Dead rat. I held the lamp up and stumbled when the putrid place filled with the dim circles of white light. Strange symbols scratched into the wood of the walls, like something out of a horror movie. And there were papers all over the stairwell, tacked to walls, littering the steps from top to bottom, literally everywhere. I held the lamp closer to read one.

That *Infinite Love* poem again. But this one had the same strange symbols from the walls framing the outer edges of the paper. I plucked one from the stairs at my feet. The same. Over and over they were all the same. I hurried down the steps to get away from the rotting rat corpse, swatting cob webs out of the way, eager to see where it led and breathe uncontaminated air.

At the bottom, there didn't appear to be a door. I pushed the wall in front of me and it shuttered. I could see light around the cracks. I dropped the lamp low so I could see. The wall lay in a crude wooden track. I slid it to the right and stepped out. My mother screamed when she saw me walk out of the wall.

"Sorry, Mum." I slid the wall back in place and saw Dad coming down the hall.

"What on Earth!" Mum tried to open it again but I stopped her. "Dead rat in there. It's disgusting. I'll clean it up but don't go in there.

It's not safe."

Dad made his way to my side and stopped to stare at the wall. "I guessed this was the only place it could lead." He said still amazed. "Preston, what's going on here?"

I waited till Mum walked far enough out of earshot before opening the wall again. We stood on the first two steps as I showed him the walls. I explained all I could, all I knew so far which didn't amount to much and told him to go ahead with their holiday to get Mum, Kelley and Teena away for a while.

He shook his head and stood there staring at the symbols. "I never believed it was true."

I pulled a double take. "Never believed *what* was true? Dad, do you actually know something about this?"

He ruffled his silver hair and stepped forward. "Follow me."

We went back up to the main part of the attic. He nodded for no apparent reason and appeared to be debating on whether to tell me something important or not. A battle over the right thing to say. He'd worn a *similar* look when I'd asked if St. Nick was real. And when I'd asked how babies were made. The *same* look when he had to tell me Spencer was dead.

He rubbed the day old scruff on his chin and looked down at his feet, not helping my state of mind, but I waited. He started rummaging through all that stuff stored up there.

"Preston, I'll ask you this once. If you don't understand what I'm saying, I'll never speak of it again. —When you met Adena, did you ever have the feeling that maybe you knew her already? As if you knew you should love her because it was familiar to you. Like recalling a memory only there's nothing to remember because you know you never met her. Of course, you two have discovered you actually *did* meet when you were children, but this is different. Something deeper, something profound that lurks just out of reach."

I had to find a place to sit down. I thought my head was going spin straight off my shoulders. What he was saying was spot on what I'd been feeling the whole time. And more than that, Adena used the same word to describe it. A memory.

My father came to stand in front of my make shift chair of filthy crates. "I don't pretend to understand it. I just accepted it. But only just. I almost lost your mother by ignoring it. Don't make my mistake and try to figure this out. I don't know why it's happened to every man in our family."

I looked up surprised. "Every man? Who else?"

"Uncle. He never figured it out either. It's why he never remarried after his wife died. My father remarried but it was never as it was with my mother."

Dad set to work pulling things out of one of those old steamer trunks. He pulled out a tiny drawstring purse of dark green velvet and tugged it open. "Here. Have a look."

I held my hand out as he shook two gold rings from the little bag. I dropped them instantaneously. An electric shock that stung all the way up my arm, the same I felt when Adena first touched me only then it didn't hurt.

My father laughed insanely. He picked them up and held them out to me again.

"Dodgy old prankster!" I shook my hand half expecting to see burns on my palm.

"No joke. Only happens once. Have a look at the inscription."

"I don't want to!"

"Aw, fancy a spot of tea to calm your nerves? —Don't be such a pansy. I'm holding them now aren't I?"

I gave him a not so friendly look which only resulted in his laughter. I carefully picked the rings up, completely boggled as to what just happened. Just as he said, nothing. I turned one around to see inside the band.

"Infinite."

"Put them together." He urged me.

I stacked them together and read it again. *Infinite Love.* Gooseflesh erupted down my arms. That damned poem again.

"You'll find connections to Adena everywhere you look Preston. They all seem to be different for each of us, but they are always there. Have you noticed that Adena's birthday falls on Katherine and Preston's wedding anniversary?"

"No, I hadn't."

I handed the baffling set of rings back to him. Then he handed me a stack of yellowed letters. I opened one and began to read.

Dearest Katherine,
I hope this letter finds you, Dilly, and Adam well. I'll be home soon and I'm bringing more bulbs for your garden. So sorry I had to leave so soon after our

wedding. I miss you terribly. At times, all I can see is you standing there in the clearing at the old church site. Remember Darling, the day we met? Just know I'm thinking of you every moment and I love you. I've always loved you; it just took finding you to know it. Take care my Love.

Always,

Preston

I'd written the same words to Adena. Nearly... *'my heart is yours now; it just took my finding you to know it.'* He even signed the letter the same. Then I wondered if he'd been referring to the ruins on this property. *The old church site.* This triggered my remembering the dream I'd had of the faceless woman which I thought to be Adena when I was in Gainesville. Adena herself had dreamed of the old Church site while she was here. What was it about that place that had such a hold on people?

I had a difficult time grasping at...whatever it was. I never believed things of this nature existed. I always thought people who rambled on about such as being a bit odd or maybe seeking attention. I could not entertain this train of inane thought another second and I cast the letters back into the trunk.

"This isn't helping, Dad!" I stood up and kicked a box out of my path as I stormed the length of the attic; my mind raging ever on inside my skull. "Don't you see? It's just making it worse!"

"What exactly are you afraid of, Preston? Losing your free will?" His voice rumbled deep as if he were scolding me for being insolent.

But yes, that's exactly what it felt like. As if meeting Adena again were inescapable. As if I had no choice in the matter. Call it shear stubbornness, but the notion didn't sit very well. I walked slowly back and sat down again. Not understanding anything at all any longer, I felt as though I were drowning and couldn't breathe.

My father's anger grew; I could hear it in his heavy breaths, see it in his face and his drawn fists.

"What else would you have happen, Preston? You deny this and believe you me, you'll live to regret it the rest of your life! Just ask her to marry you and all the nonsense will stop. It did for me anyway."

I strangled on my own gasp. *"Marry* her? Dad..." So tongue-tied, I found it hard to speak. "She's already married! I can't propose to her. Damnit! We just met for Christ's sake! And even if she weren't...Jesus, Dad! So I ask her and then what, you think she'll just drop everything and move to London? I can't leave this place. I have too many responsibilities here." I closed the lid of Katherine's trunk before he could show me any more. I didn't much care for the direction all his *connections* were headed. I thought about what he'd said a few minutes before. I sat down again and took a few breaths. smoothed my hair and tried to calm down.

"Dad —It does feel like all of this will take my free will away. And Adena's as well. That's not how it's supposed to be."

He took a cleansing breath solely to hold his patience and not wail on me with both fists flying. "Destiny, free will, Fate, God's will, who bloody cares!! Stop and think boy. Do you *love* her?"

I ran my hands through my hair again. "I have a feeling love has very little to do with this. And whatever peculiarity going on has followed this family through the generations. The only reason I know as much as I do is through some blasted *quirk* in Kelly's hearing aid!" My anger grew exponentially again at the memory of my little girl's tears this morning as she told me at last what had frightened her so many times.

I glanced around at all the steamer trunks and wardrobes as a thought came to mind. "You said you never believed it was true. What exactly did you mean?"

He lifted the lid to the smallest trunk and gestured inside. "See for yourself. I thought it was the imagination of a young girl. But apparently it's all true. I almost cleaned this old place out years ago, but when you sort through the chaos you start to see the real history of this house. Of this family and all the hearts that have beat beneath these rafters." He touched my shoulder and gave it an encouraging squeeze. "This little traveling trunk was Dilly's. She started writing at around age eight, before she'd even lost her mother. It's quite the tale. I'll give you some time. —You'll see."

Dad left me alone as I sat on the dust covered floor for hours spilling over five journals, hand written by the woman Adena had known as GG Delia. And the words I read explained a great deal.

The first was that of a small child just as Dad had said. She talked a fair amount of how much she missed her mother. Of the time when her mother had fallen sick. How as time went by she was forgetting more and more about her birth father. She wrote all she could remember about each of them so that she wouldn't forget everything and so her little brother Adam would know them in some small way. She wrote a great deal about the farm and the land, obviously when everything here was brand new to her. In the second journal, one entry revealed a marvelous day when Preston had taken her and Adam to The Great Stadium in White City to see the summer Olympics.

Wow.

The third was a small green journal. It had personal entries about people close to her. Some entries were soaked in her sadness but more than anything it seemed to be a log of how her relationship with Preston and Katherine had grown. She loved them. And there was no mistaking they loved the children as well.

Another just a bit larger, covered in black leather, fastened with a broken strap that had a clasp that once locked was the one that shed the most light.

Another woman I didn't even know existed once lived in this house. Katherine's older sister, Constance. Which would make her my great-great aunt if one were keeping track. According to Dilly's stories, Constance was a shrewd harpy, the word used several times throughout her writings and it was quite plain that Dilly did not care for her.

Constance had been jealous of Katherine when she and Preston (the first one) were married and Dilly suspected Constance had had her eye on him for her own.

A spinster of her own choosing, she'd lived in what is now the study upstairs due to her own parents' travels to India. Dilly's room had been the one Adena and I shared the first half of her visit. So odd to place these people in the house I grew up in. I'd just never given it any thought.

Dilly made it clear she suspected a great deal of darkness from Constance. There were beatings and unspeakable cruelty at the hand of this horrific woman. All cleverly hidden from the eyes of Katherine and Preston. But there was something deeper. Something darker and Dilly felt it. With the birth of a baby girl, Emmeline Grace, Preston and Katherine's first child of their own, Dilly confirmed the woman was capable of evil. Katherine gave birth to the child, in her bedroom; Constance had helped her deliver it. Dilly had been present but Constance asked her to get some clean linen from the wash line. The baby had been crying and appeared to be perfectly healthy when she walked from the room. When Dilly came back, not five minutes later, the infant lay dead and Katherine was in a deep sleep.

When Preston came in from the orchards, Constance did everything she could to make sure Dilly never got the chance to tell Preston what she'd seen. She'd locked poor Dilly and her little brother Adam in the cellar and told Preston they were sleeping in their rooms, too upset by the tragic news to even eat their supper.

That night, Constance at last let the children out of the cellar and sent them straight to bed with a beating that assured Dilly's silence. When Constance turned to strike Adam, Dilly took his beating as well to prove she would remain quiet although Constance had admitted nothing and Dilly had accused nothing; they both knew what Dilly suspected.

Dilly was so afraid and she had no idea how to tell Preston what she supposed Constance had done. She sneaked out of her room and listened in the stairwell to see if Preston was alone. She'd heard him talking to his sleeping wife, heard his bellowing cries muffled in the confines of their bedroom so distraught with grief.

The aforementioned is a summary by myself as I'd read through fifteen or so entries so far. But the following are Dilly's own words:

I flinched as I heard the front door open then slam shut heavily. Constance had come to tell Papa his prize horse was in danger of falling over the cliff at the lookout, that his hoof was wedged into the rocks. I ran to the stairwell to listen closer and I heard Papa tell Constance to stay and keep an eye on Katherine and Adam and me. She promised, the snake that she is and I prayed with everything I had that she would leave us be - alone upstairs. I couldn't take another wailing from her. But she waited still by the foyer for only a moment before leaving as well. I checked on Mum Katherine. Papa had fetched Dr. Bainbridge down the lane to see to her and he mixed her strong powders to keep her asleep. Adam was sleeping as well so I followed behind Constance the entire way without her taking notice of me. It was a dreadful long walk from the house all the way up the lane, hurrying in my night dress to keep up with her much longer legs.

At last I was able to witness firsthand the woman's wickedness. Breathless, I hid in the bushes and watched Constance make her way to the outcropping at the end of the trail near the cliff.

I watched Papa. He must have heard her footsteps on the rocks because he turned and he cursed her soundly for leading him out in the dark night for no reason. There was no horse up there nor any sign of one ever being there. Then, bold as Satan himself, Constance disrobed in the moonlight, dropping her long expensive dress to the rocks and dirt below. She spread her arms inviting Preston to come to her, but he rebuffed her with disgust etching his face despite her ample beauty. But he could see past her perfect face and her bare breasts - he could see how truly hideous she was, as could I.

Having felt the sharp blade of rejection, she began to spew the most foul and unholy curses upon him and Mum Katherine and their children to come. She stooped to retrieve a dagger hidden in her gown and went for his throat.

I screamed and ran out to help him but she swung the blade wildly, slicing the side of Papa's neck and on the back swing of her own arm, I myself caught a gouge in my shoulder. When Papa realized I'd been injured he was infuriated to such a degree that he wrestled the naked harpy to the ground and bound her hands with his. I staggered backward from the burning pain and I saw the blood pouring from my shoulder; my white night dress now stained with an ever blooming crimson rose. The sight weakened me and I lost my footing.

I didn't know how close I was to the precipice and in a flash Papa let Constance go and lunged to save me from a death fall. But as he saved my very life he went over himself and I screamed to the heavens for God to save him. He'd loved me as his own when I had no one! He couldn't die! I turned in a panic and saw that witch running at me still naked and her face was filled with so much malice that I knew she meant to murder me.

"Papa!" I screamed and stared over the edge searching and I knew I was trapped. I had no place to run.

Out of the black of night I heard Papa call to me, "Jump Dilly! It won't hurt when you fall! I'll catch you, I promise!"

Without a second to spare, I took a leap of faith over the edge scarcely escaping the grasping fingers of the wicked woman behind me. Constance went over with her lunge for me, ripping out a handful of my hair by the roots, my head snapped back, my neck made a popping sound and I screamed all at once. Papa nearly lost me but he held on tight and pulled me closer. Constance tumbled half way down and managed to grab hold of a protruding root on the side of the cliff.

Papa held on so tightly and he pulled us both up the boulder he'd clung to. Safely on higher ground, he hid my face and covered my ears. But I heard that woman's screams echo in the night. "It's too late! I'll have you in death, Preston! I'll have you all in death!" She laughed and the root broke free sending her to her own demise.

Dilly's last entry was years later, about the time she'd gone to the United States.

No two people have loved one another more than my parents. Nor as they have loved myself and my dear brother. I leave now and take with me the darkness of our past. Constance will hurt no one else I love with her Infinite

Love. I've lain a path to set things right. I don't know how long it will take however should my diary ever find its way into the right hands, they will know what they must do to set things right. Follow your instincts; the energy will lead the way. The poem is a curse. The rings are the key. This, I'm afraid is all I can give you. I do not wish for this wretched knowledge to tempt nor to stain another soul.

Dad came back just as my stomach started to growl. I looked at my watch and stood up to stretch the kinks from my muscles. Nearly noon.

"Well, what do you think?" He asked.

I closed the black journal and stretched again until my elbows popped. "Under normal circumstances, I'd have assumed the same as you. Big imagination from a child. But knowing what I know and after seeing that stairwell...I have to say, I can't simply dismiss it. I think the wall up here was simply added just to keep people away from the weakened floor and perhaps out of sight, out of mind and the floors were simply never repaired. But Constance found the entrance in the main hall which gave her a way to keep that blasted poem hidden in this house."

Dad trudged the length of the room and pulled something out of yet another trunk. I was only mildly paying attention as he came back to shove a small ornate silver box into my hands.

"I'd give you the other set but I don't imagine you'd take much pleasure in the possibility of literally shocking your bride. Those were my parents. Think on it, Preston. Don't worry so much on how long you've known Adena or where you'll live. Let *her* decide. I happen to know she's made up her mind."

I sighed and tried not to get frustrated again. "Dad you had *one* conversation with her that I wasn't privy to. How would you know what she's thinking?"

He smiled and plucked his shirt proudly. "I'm a man of my word and I promised I wouldn't say." He chucked me on the chin. "I've been in your shoes, son. But don't let this part bother you so much. Least of all the time you've known her. Time is only important if you twitter it away over silly traditions and society's expectations. I knew your mother for two months when I decided she was the one for me despite my circumstances at the time. It was difficult, yes, given Edith's illness, but I've never regretted loving your mother, Preston. Not once. Not ever."

I pulled a tiny catch on the little silver box with my thumbnail and the top released. Inside, a complete set, not just an engagement ring.

And suddenly nothing else mattered. No more why or how. Only that I knew I couldn't live without her.

"Dad, are you sure? I can get our own. She may want to pick one out."

Then I thought of her. I took them in my hands, contemplating. She'd love the idea that they were special and that Dad thought so much of her, he'd be willing to let us have them. And they were undeniably beautiful, the kind of elegance you simply don't find any longer. Much like Adena.

"On second thought, I think she'd love these. Thanks Dad. This means... a lot." I glanced around and for the first time in twenty-nine years, realized that all of what I'd considered rubbish from the past was my history. "And, thanks for showing me all this. Sorry, I got so upset earlier."

He clasped his hand on my shoulder. Then he stumbled and grabbed his chest. His face contorted and I jumped to my feet to grab him.

"Dad!"

He started laughing and pointed a stubby finger at me. "Got ya!"

"You're a ruthless old bastard," I wrapped my arms around him and held him tight. "But I love you." He hugged me back quickly and tried to step away. I'd outgrown him years ago and he couldn't get free.

"Turn me loose, Preston. I swear you're the strangest Brit in England. Always hugging people. No wonder you love her. Adena must have hugged me twenty times while she was here."

"So she can hug you and I can't." I let him go and laughed at his ruddy cheeks.

He straightened his shirt all flustered. "When you're as pretty as she is, I'll let you hug me that much. I wouldn't hold my breath though."

I looked at the rings again. Then to the journal still in my hand. I opened it to Dilly's last entry again. *Follow your instincts.* Okay. Got it. Easy enough. *The energy will lead the way. The rings are the key.*

Energy...electricity...yep, got it. Something Adena's father said began to echo in my thoughts. *Jeanie in a bottle.* He'd loved his bike. An attachment maybe? It gave me a hunch about the rings. Preston and Katherine would have a very strong attachment to their wedding bands. And Dilly said they were the key. I wasn't sure exactly where I was going with my hunch but I knew I was getting closer. I could feel it.

I turned around and pulled the green velvet bag from Katherine's trunk, tossed the little bag in my hands and gave the silver box back to

Dad.

"Changed my mind, Dad. I think I'll take the risk of shocking Adena after all. Just a hunch."

Dad laughed and watched me head down the stairs. "Where are you off to?"

"I've got a meeting with the devil. The bitch just doesn't know it yet."

My parents left with Kelley and Teena and I went back to my house with one of the poems from the stairwell in my hand; I dialed a number I thought I'd never dial again.

"Hello?" Her voice alone made the bile rise in my throat.

"Melanie. It's Preston. Can you meet me at Frank's place? Say in, — half an hour?"

Dead silence for a five count but then she agreed a little too happily for my taste.

I hopped in the Rover and set off to Frank's, eager to get there early in case she got the wrong idea. When I got there, Frank eyed me at the door as though I'd lost my mind, pointing in the direction of the dining area.

"What are you playing at, Preston? Meeting up with that woman. You know she's bad news."

"It's not what you think, Frank. I've got this well in hand."

I walked through till I saw her sitting at the table where she'd approached me and Adena. There was no end to the ways that woman could piss me off. I looked her over, dressed to the nines, her red stilettos peeking from under the table. A bottle of white wine sat on the table with one glass empty, the other in her hand.

"To what do I owe the pleasure of your company, Preston? Your little hillbilly run back home?"

"Utter one more word about her and I'll feed your lips to the next mongrel I see in the streets. Now, get up."

"No. I think I'll stay right here if you don't mind." She tipped her glass to her lips. I don't know why she bothered with the wine. She stayed drunk on her own blasted ego.

I grabbed the bottle and the extra glass and sat at the next table. She gave in and followed me, her curiosity too wild as to why I'd asked her to come.

"What do you want from me, Preston? An apology?"

I laughed. "After four years, I didn't think that word was in your vocabulary."

She slid into the booth next to me. "You must understand my purpose. You were the boom back then and the boss asked me to go to that awards show to see if I could —accidentally bump into you. The truth is, I really was quite fond of you. But a girl has to make a living."

"Your *purpose*? Melanie, Kelley may stumble across that article on the internet someday. She's lost enough in her young life without doubting where she really comes from. What? The lies about me weren't enough? You had to make up some outlandish rubbish about me being her biological father? A love child with my best mate's *wife*? It sickens me to know you could stoop so low.

"I told you I was there when Kelley was born, watched her be born because her mother didn't want to be alone just in case Spencer didn't make it in time. You twisted a perfectly innocent relationship into something ugly and untrue. Why? Who deserves that? —What? Because I stumbled blindly into a drop of fame, that makes it fine and dandy to rip me apart? To tear my world down, to make people I don't even know completely despise me and call me trash?"

She tucked her straight red hair behind her ear, looking far too much like a decent human being. "Preston, *no* one hated you. Yes, I admit a few people said some nasty things. But it didn't stick. The story died almost as soon as the ink dried. You exude class and high standards and I think people simply knew it wasn't true. And yes, I know that I deserve to have you hate me for it anyways, but truly dear, I *am* sorry. I know it means nothing now, but I did quit *The Rag*. I don't want to be a villain but now I have a reputation for it. Now, I can't get a respectable paper to hire me."

"Are you out of work now?"

I hadn't known she possessed a humble bone in her body, but she hung her head and spoke low, "I've been trying to do some freelance stuff. Haven't had much luck."

I pulled out my wallet, fingered through a few bills and tossed six hundred quid in front of her. "You told me all about your college days. I need some research done. I do recall you being excellent at that. Now, can I trust you this time?"

"Preston, I'll research anything you want. But I'd feel dreadful taking your money."

"I know. So keep it. Keep your mouth shut and get this for me by tonight."

Her eyes grew wide and her mouth popped. "Tonight? That's a bit soon, isn't it?"

"If you can have it ready sooner, you'll get a hundred more for every slanderous word in that article. Assuming you're good at math, I believe you understand how important this is."

"What if I can't find what you're after?"

"I trust you. And if not, then so be it."

The word 'trust' hit a nerve and she recoiled slightly. She knew she didn't deserve my trust although this was the first actual glimpse of any real remorse from her. Then again, I likely never gave her the opportunity.

She sighed then slipped back into the stone cold bitch I'd grown to hate. "I'll call you in few hours then." She took another drink of her wine. "Cripes, I never knew you could be so mean."

"Don't cross me again, Mel. You owe me." I left a large envelope on the table containing what I wanted researched and one of the poems from Dad's house then left without another word.

After leaving Frank's, I went back to Dad's place and called Adena to talk for a bit. Hearing the honey drip of her voice calmed my nerves. Although, she didn't sound so great. Said she'd been feeling tired but explained she'd been helping Beth and Gavin pack and move for college. The only mental stability she could draw from the pair of them moving out was the undeniable fact that they were moving all of ½ an hour away.

I didn't tell her anything about Dilly's journals. I almost did. But a nagging feeling told me to keep it to myself for now.

I tackled the stairwell, hauling out every desecrated piece of wood and all those damned poems to the yard and burned them all along with the rat carcass. I watched the licking flames in the growing darkness begin to consume the lot of it and I was glad to have the remnants of that Constance out of the house once and for all.

I popped the top of a bottle of ale and raised it to the sky. "Here's to you, Dilly. Thank you. Don't really know what I'm doing, but here goes nothing."

A few minutes passed and I heard the front gates beeping as they opened. I turned around expecting to see Robert or Uncle but instead, a white Mercedes pulled into the courtyard, the headlights blinding me. The taste of metal filled my mouth.

How the bloody fuck did *she* get in?

I watched her legs swing out and I didn't hold my laughter a bit when she attempted walking with some dignity across the cobblestones of the courtyard. The spikes on her feet dipping into the cracks between the stones made her look like a swaggering drunk. She finally stopped and tugged them free, knocking her down to only four foot, ten inches tall.

I nodded, trying for polite. "Mel. That was quicker than I thought."

"Bullshit. That's why you called me. What are you burning? Cripes, that stinks." She fanned her nose, tucked her flaming hair behind one ear then handed me the same envelope I'd given her at Frank's.

I opened it and found several printed sheets from the internet as well as page after page of feverishly hand written notes from her. Two small books that looked ancient and something photocopied.

"Is this self explanatory or will I need you?"

"Depends on what you know about that stuff. Preston, I must say, I never expected that kind of curiosity from you. What's all this about?"

I didn't answer but I invited her inside so we could go over her research. We sat side by side at the breakfast table, as unsettling as this was for me, but it was necessary to properly see what madness she had unearthed. She fanned it out page after page then folded her arms one into the other and stared at me.

"So, what is all this?" I asked.

She glared back in true Mel fashion. "I haven't the foggiest, Preston. I can't explain even a tenth of what you want to know unless I know what it is you're looking for. Why are you after *any* information on a lost pagan tribe that existed roughly a thousand years ago?"

I despised her but this is why I needed her. She's bloody brilliant. I took a deep breath and told her what I knew. Every odd experience, every dream of Adena's, every voice I'd heard. I told her of Dilly's journals in the attic, the hidden stairwell and the carvings on the walls.

She didn't comment; she only eyed me for a long moment then turned her attention to the pile on the table. She became the intelligent woman I'd met four years ago, the serious academic her parents had always hoped for and she dug in her heels and focused between the smallest book, the symbols and two particular sheets of interest that were photocopied.

After an hour and a half of going over various sordid religions, witchcraft and God knows what else, not to mention her laptop opened to at least thirteen different tabs of open library sources, as well as a private database that required a series of passwords and the blood of a virgin to access, we at last found the correct location in the smallest book to compare only some of the symbols I'd found on the poems.

Just as she had indicated when she first sat down, the symbols belonged to a pagan tribe whose actual name or religion had been lost to a dead language. Some of the scantly documented research insisted that they predated the Roman Empire, while another group of people, far smarter than I, insisted not quite so long ago and even pegged a location somewhere in North Scotland. The closest to their era and territory would have been the Picts. There was very little information to go on other than somehow a handful of tablets filled with spells masterfully disguised as blessings had survived eons of superstition and persecution. Passed over as nothing more than legend, many scholars believed them to be riddles of sorts to hide their rituals from Christian Crusaders which would have placed the tribe in any number of places across Europe around 700 to 900 years ago.

At last. We were finally getting somewhere. The two other books Mel had found only had one small chapter devoted to what I needed to know. There had been enough evidence to prove that these people existed but none so far had discovered any further instruction on how to use the spells, again lending to the legend and myth theory. For the most part it was a guessing game as to their true culture and much relied on ancient Gaelic fables for guidance.

So, how the hell had Constance, a young British woman born and raised in Havering of all places come to figure it out?

Dilly had said the poem is a curse. And something about that poem had always given me the creeps. It sounded nice enough, a blessing Dad had guessed. But the more I read it, the easier it was to see. Not exactly, but if one reads between the lines, so to speak, the curse becomes somewhat clearer. *...All of this family shall share our love...unable to resist...unwilling to try...our love will live on long after we die. All along our family tree, our sons shall know what's come to be. From the roots to the branches and every new leaf...our love and our home we vow to bequeath.*

I did not believe that this family, nor I, had in fact inherited my great-grandparents love. Life simply does not work that way. However, whatever curse lie hidden in the words that Constance had conjured so many years ago would somehow affect the Grace's for generations. That part was obvious to me. The name of the poem was the very inscription on Preston and Katherine's wedding rings. Was this Constance's way of secretly damning them? I was guessing wildly, of course but it was one of many theories dancing about in my mind.

In the end it didn't matter, how or why she'd done whatever she'd done. Right now, it boiled down to Adena and myself. The curse had affected every son in the family and the women they loved, but they were missing something vital to bring any resolution. Adena and Kelley. *Dilly's* descendents. Something I couldn't identify -be it in my heart or my mind- told me to listen to Dilly's advice. In a way, I felt her with me, silently guiding me.

Melanie was pointing this and that out to me; some I understood, some sounded like pure rubbish, some was simply because Mel liked to hear herself speak. But strangely enough, she stopped for a bit and studied the strange symbols surrounding the poem on one of the tattered sheets. Her brows crammed into one another like two puzzle pieces that didn't quite fit giving her an unattractive expression as she continued to scrutinize something in the corner of the pages.

"Preston, if these two symbols here are correctly translated, they usually accompany each other and it means roughly 'through blood'. That means something would be inherited generation after generation. In this case, it was intended to be something bad, like this curse for example. Whatever it is supposed to do, which I don't understand. Only the person casting the spell or what have you would know that. But it would take one blood line for this curse to carry down to you. Therefore, if you and your lady friend are experiencing any strange happenings of the same sort, then you would, in fact, have to be related by blood."

"We're not related. My father assured me of that."

She leaned back and sighed. "In that case, I think we're barking up the wrong tree entirely. I'm 99% positive that you would have to share blood for this to happen. But hey, I've been looking into it for all of one day sooo —what the bloody hell do I know." I got up and offered her a glass of ale which she declined with a frown. "Preston," she began again, "What ever happened to this Constance person? Where is she buried for instance?"

I shrugged indifferently. "I've no idea."

I lied. Why? It didn't feel right to say. But it gave me an idea and in short order I'd managed to wrap things up with Mel, pay her for her time and very productive effort and let's face it, to keep her mouth shut.

I went upstairs for Dilly's journals, flipped through to the night that Constance died and there it was: the blood link Mel insisted had to be there. No, Adena and I weren't related but I have a feeling that there was one precise instant that changed all of Constance's intentions. The night she died. Before she'd gone over the cliff, she had tried to kill Preston. She caught him in the neck and immediately after, quite unintentionally stabbed Dilly with the same bloody knife. Preston Grace's blood had been transferred to Dilly's. Or perhaps, it was something far more symbolic and less literal. Dilly had fearlessly gone out to help Preston and as well, he'd risked his own life to save hers that night. Either way, I think either event was a pivotal point and something Constance could not predict.

I sighed. Perhaps. What the hell do I know?

I went home to pack. I had enough mumbo jumbo in my head to hopefully know what to do when the time came. I still didn't know what all this information would do to help, but at least I knew the source of the madness.

I burned the contents of the envelope, ancient books and all. The bloody library or museum that carried such a disease could sue me. But in all likelihood they'd come from Mel's parents house. That's why I'd asked her in the first place. Her father, although he never completed his doctorate, had, for nearly thirty years, worked closely with and aspired to be a philologist, which is in short, a person who specializes in the study of ancient texts. A fascinating field. One that I knew Mel, especially, would love to sink her teeth into.

At this point, I didn't particularly care if she told anyone. No one in their right mind would believe her.

Saturday July 18th…

I HELD THE LITTLE GREEN VELVET bag in my hand with my great-grandparents' rings inside, about to be crushed beyond measure or be the happiest man on earth. No more time for anything in between. I'd never been so nervous for so long on the never-ending flight to see her. I must have looked like a damn fool smiling by myself waiting for my luggage. And waiting. Bastard airline lost my bags. To hell with it. I had the rings and my carry on so I headed to customs with what I had.

I was about to ring Adena when my phone vibrated. It was her and my heart started to sing to know I was so close to putting my arms round her again. I spoke to her early this morning, which was last night at her house — but I hadn't told her I was coming.

When I answered and heard Beth's cries on the other end, my world came crashing down in flames.

Please God, No! Don't take her from me.

22

Adena

Saturday July 18th...

I CAME HOME TO FIND Trent in his recliner watching TV. The kids were gone. We were at last... alone.

"Trent?" I called as I put my keys and my purse on the counter then walked into the living room.

"Yeah, Dee?" He replied dully never taking his eyes off the baseball game.

"We need to talk."

His chest rose and fell with an audible and deep sigh. "About *what*? Shit, I just want to sit here and relax!"

I ignored his attitude —too determined to get everything off my chest. "Before I went to London you said you had some things we needed to discuss. We never did and now —I *have* to tell you something."

He slammed the footrest of his recliner down. "Can't it wait?" He stood up and lumbered down the hallway to his office and slammed the door, shutting me out once again.

I felt sick and not for the first time. For at least the past two weeks, I hadn't felt quite up to par and whatever was wrong seemed to be getting worse by the minute. I went to the kitchen and took an antacid. I sat at the counter and hung my head in my hands, sure that I was developing an ulcer. Or maybe it was some kind of virus.

As for Trent, aside from standing in front of him and screaming at the top of my lungs, I had no idea how I was going to get through to him. I went upstairs to gather a few things for 'show and tell'. I looked at my wedding rings on my left ring finger for the last time. The first and only time I'd taken them off had been in London and the act had taken the skin on my knuckle with it. Now, they didn't seem to fit at all. Maybe I'd lost a few pounds since I got back home. I slipped them off and lay them on Trent's nightstand.

A charade of marriage, no more.

Would Preston ever come?

I couldn't help myself from wondering. I knew he was busy what with the list as long as his own arm he always seemed to have to tend to. Taking on his father's responsibilities along with keeping up with his own as well as stepping up to assist Uncle from time to time left very little time for his music, his manager, his friends, or anything else for that matter. He made time for Kelley. He made time for talking to me. But I knew very well he was spreading himself too thin and when I realized this — I felt like an ass for wanting him to come. Preston simply couldn't handle one more needy thing in his life.

And I refused to be *that* woman. The whiner. The nag. I never had been and I wouldn't become one. I loved him. I missed him. He'd come when he could. I knew this and I reminded myself almost hourly around the clock to get by.

Three weeks had passed and at times I felt the fingers of fear probe and stroke my mind and at times, strangle my heart. I was afraid that the strangeness woven throughout our time together had been what held Preston at bay. Who could blame the man? But I missed him so much. He still called everyday and that gave me the hope that somehow we could hold on long enough to be together again.

We'd spoken just last night and Preston sounded positively exuberant for the first time since I left. Nate must still be doing well and recovering nicely. I thanked God for that however there was still no word on any upcoming visit.

But whether Preston came or not, my time with Trent was over. And today was the day.

I held my hands to my aching stomach, fighting off the oncoming urge to wretch and I wished I had something strong enough to knock out the pain and to ease the nausea. But I couldn't put this off another second. I took Preston's blue shirt from the closet, gathered the letters he'd written me and the picture of him and Kelley. I walked determinedly down the stairs and for a second, felt lightheaded. Probably just my nerves.

I lay the shirt across the dining room table, placed the guitar pick strategically on top of the pocket, along with the picture and the letters. I tossed a pack of Dunhill's Preston had left in my gazebo on top of the display.

I sat there for an hour just waiting for Trent to come out of his office, feeling worse by the second. And at last, I heard his door open. I watched him put ice in his glass and pull a pitcher from the fridge.

"I'm in love with another man, Trent." The words so lifeless they didn't sound true.

He stood frozen for a fraction of a second — he poured his tea, took a long slow drink then turned to stare at me, his dark brown eyes full of dismay. "What did you just say?"

"You heard me. I've been trying to tell you. But it's not something I wanted to say over the phone."

He walked over calmly enough and stared at each article on the table then at me, his face and neck turning bright red despite his already dark leathery skin. "So start explaining!" He grabbed the cigarettes and threw them at me. "For starters you can tell me who all this shit belongs to!"

"Preston!" I screamed and slammed my hands on the table. The release to say it and get it over with, like the Hoover dam breaking.

His eyebrows went from angry to questioning as he sat down. "Why do I know that name?"

"Our little screaming match in the hallway just before we left for London. I told you his name."

Why do I suddenly feel dizzy?

I rested my forehead in my hands and concentrated on the light blue and green paisley pattern of the cloth napkins on the table to keep the room from spinning.

"Do the kids know?" He glared at me, the anger in his voice building again.

"Yes," I wasn't trying to be curt with him. But the pain I'd been feeling for days, getting exponentially more painful, made me sick and my head started to swim even more.

"You owe me more than this! I'm your husband, dammit!"

He shot up from of his chair and it skidded back so violently it knocked over one of the bar stools at the counter. As it fell, it caught the cord of the phone and pulled it off clattering to the tile.

I couldn't respond to Trent's outburst. The pain in my abdomen grew brutal. A wave of heavy nausea hit me at once. I stood up and made my way carefully to the kitchen holding on to a chair at first, then to the counter just to hold myself upright. My energy draining as quickly as water through a sieve.

"Dee?"

I faintly heard him right behind me as I tried to make it to the sink for some cold water on my face.

"Dena, talk to me. You look like hell."

As I turned the faucet on, it felt as though a white-hot blade had slashed through my insides. Blinding pain in my abdomen made my vision go to nothing but a flurry of shapeless black and white. Falling, but I don't remember ever hitting the floor.

Somehow, I'd fallen further. Off the earth, altogether. I saw the swish of a long black braid. The flash of a malicious grin. The laughter of the Devil himself. Only ... only ... it was the laughter of a woman. The sound of chaos rolled in waves upon my ears in a sickening rhythm that could only be melodic to a sadistic ear. Just beneath the dirge that filled my mind was the brief cry of an infant. Then its tiny echo faded. And then – there was nothing.

Nothing at all.

23

BETH WHITTINGTON

GAVIN AND I WENT SHOPPING for a few things we'd need for college and for our new place in Gainesville. His crappy old truck overheated twice on the way home and in the suffocating July heat, I couldn't wait to get inside. I was surprised to see Dad's truck at the house during the day. Gavin made it inside before me, leaving the front door wide open. That's when I heard Dad yelling my mother's name.

Gavin ran to the kitchen with me on his heels. Mom's body lay splayed across the kitchen floor, Dad kneeling over her trying to turn her over. Her skin so pale, she looked paper white.

My heart lurched into my throat and right there, I swear it stopped beating.

Gavin and I turned to see the disarray in the dining room. A man's blue dress shirt and — Oh No! Preston and Kelley's picture.

Gavin spun on his sneakers and glared at Dad. "What did you do to her!" He might as well have brandished a pistol, aimed at dad's heart and pulled the trigger all while staring our father in the eyes. My poor dad. The look on his face –it was the purest pain I'd ever seen.

"I would *never* hurt her. Dammit! I didn't do this!" He sobbed and held my mother with the cordless phone gripped in his hand.

"Is she breathing?" Gavin asked, trying to be calmer.

"Yes. But something is hurting her." I'd never seen Dad so devastated.

I asked if he called 9-1-1 which of course he had. I looked at the mess in the dining room. If we assumed it was a fight by seeing it, other people who didn't know us would too. The last thing we needed was Dad winding up in jail. I righted the stool and pushed it back under the counter then picked up the phone and some junk mail that had scattered.

I kneeled down next to my lifeless mother on the floor. My chest started to heave and tears flew down my face. Dad wrapped his arm around me. Gavin went outside to flag down the ambulance.

"Dad. I know you didn't hurt her."

He squeezed my shoulder. "I need you both to know, I'd die for her."

"We know. Gavin was just scared, that's all."

Mom moaned.

"Dee!" Dad lifted her and she threw up everywhere.

I got up, got some towels, and grabbed Dad a clean shirt from the laundry. I did my best to clean her up. She was still out. Her face looked the palest shade of green; a sheen of sweat glistened on her forehead.

Gavin flung the door open. "They're coming!"

Dad and I stopped and listened to the sirens wailing down our street. He patted his back pocket searching for his wallet then reached up and grabbed his keys off the counter. "You and Gavin take my truck and follow us to the hospital."

Two EMTs came in and took Mom's vital signs. As they lifted her to the gurney, her cell fell to the floor. I grabbed it and ran outside. The sirens blared again as the ambulance sped away. Gavin cranked the truck and threw it in reverse. But Dad's diesel wasn't made for instant speed; it was powerful. It was infuriating.

I looked down at Mom's phone, just fidgeting with it. The screen blinked on showing a picture of Preston and her on the banks of the Suwannee River up in White Springs. Figures she'd take him there. She loves that place. It reminds her of Louisiana.

Gavin glanced at it. "Call him. He should know she's sick."

I hesitated. If I learned anything in London, it was that Preston would get on a plane to get here as quick as he could and it still wouldn't be fast enough. I didn't know what I should do. Then I put myself in Preston's shoes. I'd want to know.

I dialed, pressed 'send' and waited.

"Hello, Love!" His voice was so happy and I knew he thought it was her. I sobbed again before I could speak. "Adena? What's the matter, Sweetheart?"

"It's Beth. Mom's unconscious. She's in an ambulance."

The tiniest pause followed. His breath finally found him again and his voice had changed. It was the sound of panic. "What hospital, Beth?"

I told him and he shouted Regional Medical to someone and said to forget the hotel. The call dropped and all I heard was one of those pre-recorded messages. He'd lost his signal. The phone fell to my lap as I realized what I'd done.

"Oh my God, Gavin. He's here. Preston's here and he's on his way. What are we going to do with him and Dad in the same place?"

Gavin kept his eyes on the road, chewing feverishly on the inside of his right cheek. "Don't know, Sis. —But it had to happen sooner or later." He checked his mirrors —rearview and sides then switched lanes to get in the HOV lane.

Our lack of speed was no longer a problem. Dad's diesel was all warmed up and we were hauling ass. The day was nearly spent so people could easily see the hazard lights on Dad's truck and most got out of the way. Much to my relief, a cop edged his way in front of us to escort us the rest of the way. This was good. Gavin is astonishingly and annoyingly level headed for a nineteen-year-old guy but the way he was driving was starting to unnerve me. The cop allowed him to speed but he acted as a pace car so to speak. Not to mention there's nothing like a cruiser with sirens at full wail and the *red and blues* spinning to part traffic like the Red Sea.

Gavin wasn't saying *anything*. Just staring ahead and I knew he was thinking a hundred miles an hour. I couldn't stand it.

"What?"

He glanced at me for a split second then refocused on the road. "*What*- What?"

"Oh Geez, Gav! What do you think about all this? What are we gonna do!"

He looked at me as earnestly as he could and still pay attention to the road and the cop ahead. "We're not gonna do a damn thing, Beth. This is *their* business. We don't have to choose a parent here. We're not little kids having to decide where we live and who gets us at Christmas." He stole another peek at me then stared ahead. A distance found its way into his eyes and I couldn't tell what he saw beyond what was physically there. "You got to know this guy a little bit, right?"

I shrugged, "Yeah. I mean, as much as a person can in a week. He's good to her. He'd give her the world if she asked."

Gavin nodded. "Dad would too. But he never gave her his time. And that's all Mom ever asked for. She begged for it until...well, until she just stopped begging." Gavin triggered his blinker and carefully switched lanes again. We were getting close to the hospital. He looked at me for a second as safety allowed. "Is that what? Just my thoughts?"

I nodded. "I guess. But...Preston can't stay here. Mom will leave."

"*So*. Time to grow up. We go see *her*. She comes to see us."

"What about Dad? I mean...what if,"

"What if *what*? Dad suddenly shits fairy dust and learns to fly?" Gavin whips off the interstate and heads east on Newberry Road. "Listen, I'm not entirely sure I'm even rooting for Dad at this point.

There's only so long you can ignore somebody before you pay the ultimate price. Ya know? I mean, if Mom's happy and healthy, I got no preference. I'll go to the damned Serengeti to see her if that's where she wants to go. She can marry a witch doctor and dance around with a bone in her nose. So long as that's what *she* wants." He reached for my hand and squeezed it. "But first things first here, Sis. Just pray she's okay. None of this other shit really matters right now."

Of course it doesn't. Cause without her…nothing matters. Not to me.

The double doors of the waiting room swung open and Preston's anxious eyes swept the room. When he saw me, I thought he might break into a full run but his legs were so long he was next to me in seconds, completely oblivious to my dad pacing twenty feet away. Then again, I didn't know if he knew what Dad looked like.

He hugged me tight and reached to shake Gavin's hand asking right away how Mom was.

"All we know is that she's in shock and her blood count is low. We haven't heard anything else yet." I told him. I glanced at Dad and back to Preston. "Be warned. Dad already knows about you and he's right over there." I nodded to avoid pointing him out. "Big guy. Black hair. Mad as hell."

Preston's eyes were puffy and bloodshot but he zoned in on my father. He didn't seem overly concerned at his presence. On the contrary he simply leaned back in the hard plastic seat and covered his face with both hands. Dad took notice and made his way like a Brahma bull through the maze of chairs to stand right in front of him.

"Dad, don't." Gavin cautioned under his breath hoping to avoid a scene in public.

Dad didn't say anything. He just stared down at Preston. Preston slowly pulled his hands down from his face and glared back at Dad. I felt awkward sitting next to him instead of standing next to my father, but it didn't really feel wrong, either.

"You got a hell of a lotta nerve showing up here, pal." Dad threatened.

Preston stood up slowly, a head taller than Dad and forced the words through his teeth. "Trent, just so we're perfectly clear, I'm *not* leaving."

Gavin stood up and in a hushed rush of direct warning, "Unless you both sit down and shut up, they're going to kick you *both* out. Now knock it off!"

A solid tense minute passed before Dad and Preston sat down opposite each other. Gavin didn't sit until they were settled.

Dad looked Preston up and down. He chuckled maliciously with a shake of his head. "You're just a kid."

Preston ignored him. Thankfully. I watched him clenching the muscles in his jaw. It looked painful and I was just waiting for one of his teeth to crack.

Gavin asked Dad if he wanted to go get some coffee. Dad replied by walking away without a word. I knew Gavin simply wanted to separate them to keep the peace and he jogged along to catch up.

Preston sat forward and rested his head in his hands. A tear splattered across the toe of his black shoe. Then another hit the floor. I plucked a tissue from the box next to me and put one beneath his face so he could see it. He sniffed and took it immediately wiping his nose. He rubbed his thumbs over his eyes to squeegee away the remaining tears.

"Thank you for calling me, Beth. I know you didn't have to." He sat up straight again not entirely composed.

I showed him the picture on Mom's phone. "Sure I did. She wants you here."

He took it from me and looked at it then handed it back. The pain in his eyes told me it must have been a special day.

A short stocky doctor with receding brown hair came out in blue scrubs. "Who's waiting for Mrs. Adena Whittington?"

Preston and I jumped to our feet.

"We are." He said anxiously. "What's wrong with her?"

The doctor looked up at him. "Are you her husband?" The question looked like it wounded Preston.

I grabbed his hand and held it. "He's family." I insisted and I felt Preston's fingers tighten appreciatively around mine. "What happened to my mother?"

"It's an ectopic pregnancy. The embryo can only grow up to six or eight weeks before this happens. Her fallopian tubes ruptured and she was bleeding internally. Pretty bad. She's in surgery now."

"Pregnant?" I couldn't believe it. Preston's mouth hung open and his hand felt dead in mine.

The doctor nodded and patted my shoulder. "Don't worry. She'll recover just fine. I'll send someone out when her surgery is over and let you know how she is." He nodded once the way doctors do then walked away.

Preston practically fell into the closest chair behind him, his hands covering his face as he shook his head back and forth. "*I* did this to her."

"Don't be ridiculous, Preston. It's not something that can happen on purpose." I tried to reason with him, hating that he felt that way and totally hating that I was the one talking him into believing that it was perfectly okay that he'd had sex with my mother. Gross. But okay, whatever, I was mature enough to deal.

I looked behind me for Dad and Gavin. I never even heard their footsteps. The look on my father's face told me he'd heard enough. He turned and went for the elevators. Gavin, once again, ran after him.

"I need a smoke." Preston said. He looked lost.

I went to the nurse's station and asked for directions to the closest smoking area. She rambled through a rapid series of directions in the mundane voice of someone who'd repeated it a hundred times a day. They weren't short directions and ultimately directed people across the street to a bench.

But Preston didn't get up. He just sat there with his head in his hands. "I won't leave her. I can't ever leave her again. I have to be here when she wakes. I can't leave her."

I sat down next to him and felt like my heart just started beating.

My mom is alright. She's going to be fine.

24

PRESTON

GAVIN CAME IN ALONE AND took a seat on the other side of me. The waiting, driving me mad. I held the green velvet bag in my right hand still hidden in my suit pocket. All I wanted was to see Adena; to know she was all right. The next half-hour felt like days as the three of us sat there in silence.

"Here comes Dad." Beth whispered close.

He came to stand in front of us not really looking at anyone, just stared at the speckled white tile floor for the longest. That was the moment, I really saw him. He didn't look angry any longer. Just beaten. A distraught shell of a man standing there in his work clothes. A white pullover with his company logo stitched into it. Dungarees and boots that showed the wear and tear his job had inflicted on him physically as well. He'd sacrificed his relationship for his career and I didn't hold that against him. It happens too often. The lack of balance in one's life can be detrimental.

I couldn't imagine what he must be feeling. I loved his wife and his children sat on either side of me. He took a seat across from us. When he was looking away, I nudged Beth and tilted my head in his direction in hopes that she'd get the hint. She got up, sat next to him then curled her fingers into his. He squeezed her hand in his and cleared his throat then rubbed at one of his eyes.

At last, a different doctor than before came out. He looked back and forth between Trent and myself. "Who's the spouse of Adena Whittington?"

I looked at Trent expecting him to get up. Or to speak up and have me removed from the premises entirely. However, he did something that nearly knocked the wind out of me.

He cleared his throat and said, "He is." Then gave a half-hearted gesture in my direction.

I tried to look him in the eye trying my best to convey my thanks but he wouldn't look up. My heart leapt just the same. I'd see her at last. I followed the doctor through a maze of hallways until we found the recovery room.

The doctor jotted something down in her chart. "You can sit with her until we put her in a room. Then the others can see her."

I thanked him as he walked away. I looked her over, so aberrantly pale. Tubes and tape still hung from her arms. Big purple bruises covered the back of her hand where she'd been repeatedly assaulted by a needle. To see her so frail broke my heart. She opened her eyes for a second but I knew she didn't see anything. I lifted her right hand and held it gently.

I whispered in her ear. "Let me see those green eyes, Love." It took her a few seconds but she did.

Confused at first, she looked at me. She blinked and studied my face. Then clarity seemed to punch a hole through the fog of drugs. "I missed you." She tried to whisper.

I pressed my lips to her forehead. She looked like she might go to sleep again. But then her eyes opened wide.

"Where is everybody? What happened?" Her voice, rough and hoarse, her brows knitted together. She'd waken up enough to worry.

"They're all in the waiting room."

She closed her eyes again but looked more confused than ever.

I brushed that ever present stray curl from her face. "It's a long story, Love. One that can wait. How are you feeling?"

"Hit by a train."

"Thirsty?"

She nodded. I pulled the white and blue blankets tighter around her, flagged down a nurse, and asked if she could have a drink.

"Only a sip. Too much and she might get sick." She came back with a cup of ice water.

I lifted her head slowly and she tried to hold the straw but her hands were shaking as if she were freezing. She managed to take a sip and swallowed hard. I pulled the cup away.

"Sorry, Love. That's all for now." She nodded her head to let me know she understood and licked her lips.

"I can't believe you're here." Her head rolled to the side, tears streaming freely across the bridge of her nose.

"I'm such a fool for waiting so long. I'm sorry, Love. So sorry." I kissed her hand over and over, the tips of her fingers, her wrist.

She moved trying to sit up a bit. I hoped it didn't hurt to try. She winced and lay back down, pulling her left hand from under the blankets to push her hair back, then rubbed at her eyes. Her wedding rings were gone. She looked at me and smiled, the grogginess fading.

"Adena, are you awake? Really awake?"

"Yes. Unless, I'm vividly dreaming. Wouldn't be the first time." Her voice much stronger, eyes wider.

I pulled the green bag from my pocket but stopped before pulling it out. Something in my head, telling me, *Not yet.*

Mentally, I shouted at whatever nonsensical other worldly rubbish made me stop.

I'm following my instincts here. I never want to let her go again!

An aged woman's voice, a whisper of wind in my ear said, *So ask her already. Just wait for the rings. It's not the right time yet.*

Fair enough. Now get out of my head Ms. Dilly. I can do this part on my own.

Staring into her eyes, I got down on one knee. "Adena, —will you marry me? Be my wife, please. And no, not just for this visit. Forever."

She cried quietly but smiled. "Of course, I will."

I felt dreadfully empty handed. "I…have a ring. Only…it's not quite ready yet."

She giggled softly and rolled her eyes. "I don't care. Get off your knees. It's too hard to see you down there."

"You *are* feeling better. You're getting bossy already."

I kissed her letting my lips linger over hers for only a moment then looked longingly into her beautiful eyes.

She laughed but almost to herself. "It's someday now."

"Someday?"

"The favor I asked of Nate. Remember?"

"Ah, yes. *Please*, tell me." I smiled, waiting anxiously to know what she'd said to my father to make him take such an unexpected turn in taking his health seriously.

"I just asked him to stick around so I could call him Dad someday."

I looked down at this amazing woman and wondered if she would ever cease to amaze and surprise me.

Just over an hour later, they moved her into her own room. She was sleeping and I didn't bother her. I pulled a chair right next to her bed, held her hand and lay my head down to rest next to her, tired but not about to leave her side. A little while later, I heard the crinkle of plastic as someone sat in the other chair. I raised my head to find Gavin smiling awkwardly at me.

"'S'up?" He managed. Trying for polite but a bit uncertain as to what to say to the low-life bastard that knocks up one's mother.

I replied with a staggeringly weak, "Er, everything, I s'pose."

I looked at Adena to find her awake again, her hand still in mine. Beth, Trent, and Owen all walked in at once.

Surprised to see Owen at all, but at same time, glad to have an ally. "Hello, Owen. When did you get here?"

"Just now. I called Dena and Beth answered." He made his way to Adena's side and gave her a kiss on the cheek. "Ya doin' okay?"

"I'll be fine. Thanks for coming."

He looked at the clear bag that dripped into her IV and asked, "What's for dinner?" He made her laugh and that made everyone in the room smile.

Her nurse came in to check her vitals and logged it into her chart. "Any pain? I can get you something."

"Will it knock me out again? I don't want to go straight to sleep."

"Adena, are you hurting?" I asked her sternly. She sounded like my father.

"A little."

Thankfully, the nurse left straight away to get her meds.

Getting closer to the end of visiting hours, and knowing I'd pushed Trent about as far as any man could be pushed, I decided to give her some time with her family. A promise to be wed someday would have to suffice.

Owen followed me into the sterile white corridor. Shortly after, Beth and Gavin came out. Trent and Adena were having a heart to heart and I was glad for that. Owen and I talked for a few minutes more before he left. Gavin and Beth said their goodnights to me and went to sit in the waiting room.

An hour had nearly passed by the time Trent came out and stopped to look at me for a guarded moment. "Thanks for giving me a minute."

"Same here." I watched him take two careful steps then stop to hang his head. His massive shoulders seem to hang. "Can you take care of her?"

"I can. Not that she *needs* anyone to do so. But I get your meaning."

He glanced at me briefly. "Hey, I ain't no saint so don't look at me like you owe me anything. I love her like crazy, always will. But my head's been turned too so I got no real right to be mad. We shoulda split a few years back. You just gave us a reason to move on."

I nodded and swallowed hard. "Thanks."

His cheek twitched. "Don't be nice to me. I'd love nothing more than to kick your skinny ass." His work boots clumped several feet down the hallway.

"Trent," He stopped but didn't turn, offering only a slight of his head to listen. "You should know how much your friendship means to her. She still considers you her best friend."

He turned then and took ten quick steps, reminding me a great deal of a rhino charging. Honestly, I was mildly alarmed and quickly I'd decided that if I was about to get my duly deserved ass kicking, I was at least close to the trauma room. Not that I can't hold my own in a brawl but the man was large. Not fat. Not tall. He was LARGE. He stopped two feet in front of me, raised his thick finger fairly close to my nose and growled quite literally, "Me and that girl go back to Slush Puppies and mud pies boy. I fucked up and lost her. *You* do it and you gotta answer to me." He lowered his hand and took a breath big enough to put out a campfire twenty feet away. Dowsing a raw temper no doubt. I squared my shoulders, held my tongue and only nodded while my very own balls shrank from keeping quiet. "So you keep my big ass in the back of your mind and that whole best friend status, 'kay. Cause I'll happily beat you till you don't know your own damn name."

"Fair enough, Trent. I'd expect no less." Blame it on testosterone but I had to somehow regain a shred of dignity. "I thank you for your graciousness in the waiting room. For allowing her happiness to prevail over some antiquated need to know you have a woman at home. But since we're laying it all on the table, there's something I need to say. You nearly come off as though you're gifting me something. Adena's a gift, that much is certain but she's not yours to relinquish be it grudgingly or with grace. She chose me. I bloody well love her more than life ten times over and I'm certain at some point we'll have our ups and downs just as anyone. But don't be there only for the downs on the hopes you may once again gain her hand. Be there as a friend alongside your children and continue to be part of her life. Be a man about the lot of it or else you're welcome to sod off now you pumped up prick of a redneck."

He stared at me for a few seconds and began to laugh a heavy, congested laugh until his face turned red. He pointed at me again then held his arms on either side as though he had a barrel under each arm. "Huge nads you skinny prick. HUGE." He nodded once, tossed his hand up in farewell.

I only stood there, trying to absorb the day's events, and quite honestly, reveling in the fact that that mountain of a man had not broken several bones in my body.

I sort of jolted awake upon the realization that I would have to leave soon, as well. One glance down the corridor and into the waiting room to verify I would or wouldn't get to be alone with her — Trent and the children were making their way slowly toward the elevators so I pushed the wide wooden door to her room open, peeked in and saw her meet me with her smile. I walked in and took a seat next to her bed. I would stay until the nurses kicked me out.

"Everything alright, Love?"

She nodded. "We had a good talk. Said a lot of things we should have said a long time ago. We're okay."

"You get your pain meds yet?"

She nodded again.

The nurse came back with a pitcher of water and left it with two cellophane wrapped cups on the bedside table. She looked at me. "If you're staying the night, there's an extra blanket in the closet. I'll be back later to check on her."

Elated that I wouldn't have to leave, Adena and I stared at each other for the longest with no words exchanged. Then I thought I should ask her. "Adena, do you know what happened?" She closed her eyes and nodded a little. I rubbed my hand over her leg. "I'm so sorry to have put you through this."

"Do *not* blame yourself." She reached for me, trying to sit up for a kiss.

I pressed my lips to hers and pushed her back into her pillow, far easier than telling her to lie down. She ran her fingers through my hair and caressed the back of my neck. It made me want to kiss her deeper but I pulled away slowly. She giggled. So good to see her smile.

"The butterflies are back."

"What?" It sounded like the meds talking but I didn't think enough time had passed.

"You always give me butterflies when you kiss me." She smiled wider. "Do I give you butterflies?"

"All the time. Care to know what else you do to me?"

She wrinkled her nose and flashed my favorite smile. "What?"

I placed her hand over my heart. "Can you feel it?" She nodded.

I stared into her eyes holding her hand tightly to my heart. I kissed her with the longing I'd felt since she left me in London and tasted the sweetness that could only be her. I placed my other hand on the side of her face and felt a wet trail of tears. I backed away afraid I'd hurt her somehow, but when I looked, I found only happiness.

"See. Like a stampede of wild horses." The velocity of my heart, like a thousand thundering hooves.

"Are you really mine?" She looked afraid as though she may wake from a dream and it would all be over.

"I've always been yours, Love. And I'll be yours until the day I die. Perhaps even longer."

She looked drowsy again, her meds taking her away from me bit by bit until her eyes closed.

"Butterflies and horses." She whispered with a sleepy smile. "Would have made a beautiful nursery." My heart broke again as I watched her. Her smile faded and tears fell from underneath her closed lids. "I'm sorry I couldn't...couldn't have our baby."

She fell asleep mourning the loss of a life we'd created. One that never had a hope of surviving. The last untarnished piece of my soul shattered at the thought of never seeing Adena hold a child of our own. I laid my head next to her waist and cried quietly into the blankets, clinging to her legs, wanting to hold her closer.

25

Adena

AFTER A WEEK OF MOVING Beth and Gavin to Gainesville, the time had come to say good-bye. Standing under the baking sun at the Stratford Court Apartments, Beth gave me a hug.

"You're handling this like a big girl, Mom. I'm proud of you."

I laughed and kissed her cheek. "You promise to come see me, right? Every break you get." I looked at Gavin as well to confirm.

He kissed my cheek and chuckled. "Yep. We'll be in Havershon before you can miss us."

"It's *Havering*, Gavin."

He exaggerated a nod and pulled the waistband of his boxers out. "Wanna write it on my underwear for old time's sake?"

Preston cracked up and put his arm around me. And painfully, I handed the keys to my Shelby to Gavin, his smile a bit too big. I snatched them back and pointed at him. "This is temporary! And if you two get so much as a scratch on my car before it gets to London..."

Beth held her hand up and closed her eyes. "We know already!" She grabbed the keys. "It has to be perfect for your funeral."

This caught me by surprise. "Um, my *funeral?*"

She and Gavin shared a playful glance. "Yes. Didn't you know? We're planning to bury you in that thing. Anyway, we can walk to class from here."

Preston pulled a brochure from his pocket and handed it to Gavin. "It should arrive in two weeks. If not, ring that number ask where the bloody hell it is." He chuckled and avoided my stare.

Gavin gasped, jumped twice and hooted loud enough to send two birds fleeing from a small bush near the curb, then for the first time, clamped a true bear hug around Preston till his eyes bulged.

"Oh, man! Thanks!"

"It's not just from me. Hopefully, this is the first of many peaceable agreements between your father and I."

Beth snatched the brochure from Gavin's hands and gaped. "You guys got him a friggin Chevy Avalanche! What the hell!"

"A cherry *red* Chevy Avalanche! Ha ha!" Gavin added to rub the salt in.

Preston pulled her to his side laughing quietly. "I'll miss having you around. And you know, Teena really misses you. Consider college in London next year and I'll give you my Rover. Well, that is... *if* you could bear to let go of your precious *Gators*."

Beth screamed the way only a teenage girl is capable. "Preston you're the best!" She pulled away craning her neck up to see him and pointed her finger. "You tell Dad I said that and I'll deny it till I'm dead."

A final round of hugs then we watched my children walk through the door to their apartment. It hurt to watch them go, but I knew Gavin would look after Beth. They squabble at times like two roosters in the same pen but when it comes down to it, they love each other.

After several sighs and a good minute after the kids had closed their front door, Preston gave me a squeeze. "We should go if we're going make our flight. Ready?"

I nodded with a considerable lump in my throat.

At the airport we waited in line, our tickets in hand, and I couldn't remember being more sad or more happy at the same time. I'd turned the first page of a new chapter in my life and although I couldn't wait to start the rest of my life with Preston, my feet felt less than firm in my convictions. I wanted to go, it just hurt to put so much distance between me and my children.

Preston bounced on his toes and pulled something from his pocket. "I can't wait any longer. It has to be now." He chuckled and took my hand in his.

He seemed to be listening to thin air for a second then smiled wider. He looked down at me. "Now to do this the right way." Lowering himself to one knee, he gazed up with those celestial eyes of his and placed a beautiful gold ring around the tip of my ring finger. "Adena Keely Whitmore, will you do me the honor of being my bride?"

A full circle of onlookers had converged around us, all with baited breath as if their lives would equally be affected by my answer. They didn't know I'd already told him yes.

I shook my head and smiled down. "Yes, you know I will."

He hopped to his feet and kissed me to the scattered round of applause of strangers and picked me up to give me a twirl. And my heart sang to be free. Free to love him for as long as my heart kept beating.

The crowd dispersed with giggled whispers and kind eyes that wished us well. I saw the little velvet bag in Preston's hand and reached for it. It had a slight weight to it so I peeked inside and fished out a matching band for him. I smiled and took his hand in mine. Reading my thoughts, he looked surprised.

"Isn't it tradition to wait for the wedding for this one?"

"Tradition? Phooey! I need a divorce and we need a wedding license. Paper work to make it legal. You and I are all that counts. Now get over here and kiss me."

"Well, in that case...I do."

I sighed so deeply I thought my lungs might burst. "So do I." And I slipped the gold band onto his left ring finger.

My finger began to tingle, a buzz of energy starting at the base of my finger then spreading quickly throughout my body, like the pins and needles of a foot deprived of blood for too long.

A pulsating current flowed through every vein and every nerve until it felt like –like – well, I had absolutely nothing to compare it to. It didn't resemble normal on any level and oddly I didn't feel like myself at all.

I took in a great lungful of air as though I hadn't taken in the sweetness of breath in years. I looked up through new eyes searching for the face I'd longed to see for the past 42 years since death had claimed me.

"Preston?"

He touched my cheek, and the physical warmth at last matched the flames that still burned strong in my heart. I had so long searched for the love of my life - lost in the endless darkness. And finally the light is before me, the other half of my very soul. My reason for being. I searched his precious face and found his brown eyes full of wonder and love and the sun shone down upon us both. He reached for me. He touched my face and my heart danced among the angels to feel his strong hands so tender on my face once again. Hands filled with real warmth and hope and love and strength. My Preston! My husband! I fell into his arms and clung to him, weeping with joy.

"My Katherine. I've waited so long for this moment. We've lingered here far too long. Kiss me darling and let us go where we will truly have eternity together."

He was saying something else to the woman that had come to the surface of my mind and pushed me to some other backseat realm; this man I'd met only once in the upstairs room of the Grace farmhouse. The first Preston Grace. Katherine's Preston. But I was slipping away as he spoke to his Katherine —as they rejoiced in their reunion and I felt all of their love; all of their hope and the release of their despair. I could feel the cease of the longing they'd known only to feel it grow exponentially again as they embraced and yet could not hold on to each other tight enough. I felt the flicker of fear, licking like the flames of Hell as they each wondered if their reunion would last; if it was real.

I knew it was him as I knew it was her. The love that they felt was divine and longing and yes even painful and there was an undeniable, unbound passion that would never die between these two hearts. Their spirits had come so fully to this world, connected once again through the rings they'd once exchanged before God to love one another every day of their lives. And apparently beyond.

There was no room in my body –in my mind —for both Katherine and I; no room in my heart to feel her love as well as mine. So where was I to go but to where she had been. I felt myself slipping further and further away. I could no longer see her Preston or mine. But I heard my name. Over and over, I heard my name. It was a chorus of calling, searching and I heard my Preston calling for me. I heard my father calling for me. I could see nothing. It was like a bank of fog around me though I was not even aware of my own body. An awareness settled upon me that I no longer had a physical body. I was gone in some strange way. I had ceased to exist and yet my mind raced and therefore I knew that certainly I must exist. But where was I?

Preston called for me again and I called to him in turn. Desperately, I called to him over and over. I called to my father. But the level of chaos in this place, the din of voices simply absorbed any sound I could muster. My cries to anyone were no more than a tiny drop of water in all of the oceans that covered the earth.

This place —so gray, so dark, so full of despair, it was a place that Pain called home and claimed a throne to rule all that were trapped within its boundless territory. I felt the place was infinite in some ways and yet stuffy and close in others. I felt no ground, no sky, no walls, no borders of any kind but there was a closeness all the same. Yes, we were confined by something. But I could not tell what.

How could any *place* with no physical boundaries hold a multitude of bodiless souls trapped like prisoners? I did not know, but I was certain that that was the case. There was no source of light in this place where ever we were. I called out to Preston again. I called out to my father. I began to weep and beg for someone, anyone to help me find my way back. It did no good to search for there was absolutely nothing to see. It was like trying to see through milky gray water. Panic set in. How long would this last?

After a period of panic and searching in vain through the endless gray fog of this place, after what seemed an endless and fruitless search for Preston and my father, the only two voices I had clearly heard once I had descended to wherever we were, my mind settled to some degree. For there was one tiny call of authority that had gathered my attention and my wits with such force that I snapped to attention. It was the voice of GG. Only two words. *BE STILL.*

I don't know how long I had tried to locate the source of the many voices although it seemed like a very long time indeed; I also felt that no time at all had passed. It was as though time simply had no relevance in this place. With this thought in my head, I stopped calling out. Which, the best way for me to explain since I did not actually use my mouth to call out, was to not cast my thoughts, if that makes any sense at all. Imagine, being in a stadium and hearing every thought, every wish, every memory of every single person there. That was the bedlam that filled the fog.

As I became quiet, as I became still, eventually so did the others. I realized then that the constant babble were simply the others searching and pleading; trying to find their own way out, trying to locate those they'd lost. I closed my eyes in my mind and stopped trying to *see*. I used my mind's eye, or perhaps this was a far baser existence; a far baser sight, so to speak. Perhaps this was the consciousness of my soul. I don't know but it worked. I could see the faces, although not clearly, in this vast empty space however I could not reach them. I could not see them all; only enough to see that I was not alone. I saw my father and as soon as I did, he saw me.

His lips did not move but I felt him smile. He really could see me but he seemed so far away.

Don't be afraid, baby. He thought sort of *at* me for lack of a better explanation.

Peace filled me. No matter how desolate and frightening it all seemed, there was still love in this place.

I love you, Daddy. I thought back at him then I stilled my mind, my thoughts, my despair. I calmed what was left of me.

I noticed after some time of concentration that the predominant sound was that of a crying infant that seemed to falter in a strange and fearful way. Like something horrible had gone wrong. Or the poor child had been strangled until its little cry had died. It was not a cry of the present moment. It was an echo that seemed to define this stratum of purgatory.

Something was happening. I felt a lightening of something within me and a rush of adrenaline surging through every part of me. I heard the echo of a horrendous scream and it was as if it came from all around, inside my head and out. It was a rumble like thunder and it was *pissed*.

I felt like I'd been shot through the mouth of a live volcano, I felt life in my fingers and toes and suddenly I felt gravity take hold of my body and I felt my weight once again. I could smell one of those five pound cinnamon rolls from the bakery down the corridor.

And with the press of his lips, I felt so much passion, so much love and longing, my heart could hardly stand the pain and the joy and the release all at once. And the memories...the memories that filled my head in flashes of silver light...they were not *mine*. They were Katherine Grace's and suddenly I knew a great deal more yet understood a great deal less about everything in this universe.

The closest I could illustrate their experience is to say that now, I must know what it feels like to be a prisoner of war in an unknown country. Kept in a dark unknown place filled with turmoil and a loneliness that bares no comparison. Possessing only a glimmer of fading hope that those who love you will someday find you, but that wish for freedom has been so long coming that not even hope has the will to last. And for Katherine and Preston, the wait in the shadowy place beyond the grave that was neither Heaven nor Hell, had gone on for over four decades for her and just over two for him. Despair touched me in my inner most existence, my very soul and yet it was but for a few fleeting seconds that I felt it through Katherine's fresh memory of the place and my brief yet terrifying displacement there. I shudder to consider what that would feel like for very long first hand.

At last something broke free, a rush of wind that shouldn't be inside a terminal at an airport and my Preston released me. Each of us stood there staring at each other, his expression as blank as mine. His eyes were the tranquil shade of the ocean again.

"Do you remember what just happened?" I whispered.

He blinked three times. "Yes, do you?"

I leaned closer so no one else could hear. "Yes. But it was like I was in the back seat of a car watching someone else drive. Then all of a sudden I was —well, gone to that —well, you saw it didn't you?"

He nodded and ran his hand through his hair. He shuddered once. "Yes. Yes, exactly."

The line moved at last and we picked up our carry-ons to move forward. Preston started to fidget, keeping extra space between us and I had a feeling I knew why. My heart lay empty and broken with no feeling. Some nebulous force had brought us together for purposes unknown to me, and now that purpose had been served, yet I couldn't find the courage to tell him. What if he didn't feel that way? What if he still loves me?

Panic welled inside me as Preston moved forward two more steps to hand our tickets to the lady at the counter. But just as she reached for them, he dropped his head and pulled them back.

Cupping his hand under my elbow, he led me to the wall of glass that looked out over the tarmac.

So troubled over the right thing to say, he pinched the bridge of his nose, tears in his eyes and looked down at me. "What happened?"

My chin quivered at the overwhelming feeling of loss. I remembered all the feelings we shared. But I couldn't feel them now. Like someone died and no matter how badly you want that person back, they were just gone. "I don't know, Preston."

He shook his head, the anger in his eyes evident. "I want it back. Oh, God! I want it back so badly, Adena. I swear I do but...it's just..."

I squeezed his hand and wiped a tear from my cheek. "Gone. I know."

He rubbed his eyes with the heels of his palms, the veins in his neck standing out with his tension. "My life has been one vast parade of things that once belonged to someone else. My name, my home, my daughter, the orchard. Now a hand-me-down love that's just been ripped away. I can't stand it."

I pulled his hands down to see his eyes, red and pooling with tears.

The last call for his flight came. He touched my cheek and sighed.

I looked into those blue-green eyes for the last time. Speechless. Dumbfounded. Lost.

He hugged me. "I'm so sorry."

"Me, too."

I watched Preston's plane lift toward a pale gray sky taking with it the last remnants of loss. Our invisible rubber band, at last, was severed. So much I didn't understand. But remembering how Preston's great-grandfather had come to me, asking for help finding his wife, I knew the purpose of my pain. And gladness filled me that they'd at long last found each other. They'd been released from that prison and I had to believe that the others had been as well. This gave me the resolve to move ahead with my own life. The strength to begin again on my own. I exchanged my ticket and caught the next flight to Baton Rouge.

After a short flight and four hours in a rental car too small for a circus mouse, I pulled into Daddy's drive way and tried to call Owen for the hundredth time with no luck. I lay awake that night reflecting on the twists and turns of Fate until my head pounded. At 4:03 am, I fell asleep with no dreams, no visions, no voices, and no lullabies.

After a very late breakfast, I dragged Daddy's old johnboat through the cypress knees at the edge of the lake and pushed it into the murky water. If I caught enough fish, I'd get Uncle Ray to come over for supper again.

A flutter in my chest halted all efforts with the small boat. I stood up to catch my breath, the palpitations coming one after the other with such ferocity, I wondered if I was having a heart attack. I sat on the front of the boat, my feet in the mud and breathed in and out to steady the rhythm of my heart. The fluttering stopped then with no warning I felt as though a Harley had been kick started in my chest. A strong steady beat, filling me with a warmth that surged from the top of my head to the tips of my toes. A hundred degrees in the shade but the warmth had nothing to do with the oppressive summer heat in Louisiana.

The blue-green twinkle of Preston's smiling eyes flashed in my mind and it stunned me. I shook my head and grabbed the rope tied to the boat, climbed the side of the pier and dragged the small craft through the water. I tethered the rope to the last piling loosely as my brain seemed to reboot like an outdated computer, filling my head with important files. Pictures, music, kisses, touches, smells, memories! Preston's smile danced through my every thought and my heart beat stronger. Then that delicious pain filled the very depths of my chest and I realized…It came back!

I threw my face to the glorious blue sky and screamed, "I STILL LOVE HIM!"

I jumped in the water —shoes, sundress and all, like a kid —so excited over the irrefutable feeling with a loud splash. As soon as my head cleared the water's surface, I heard heavy footsteps coming down the pier but I couldn't see over it. I swam to the algae covered ladder and hurried up the slime covered treads expecting to see Hunter or Carolyn or maybe Uncle Ray. One last pull as I hoisted myself up onto the edge but what I saw nearly sent me backward into the water again.

"Preston!" I lunged at him not caring about the brown lake water pouring off my white summer dress and skin. "Oh, my God! How'd you know I was here?"

He let me ruin his baby blue shirt and lifted me off my feet with a single spin. "Where else would you be, Love? I certainly hope that was me you were talking about a moment ago. If not, I'm going to be in a world of pain. It's back, Adena. It's all back and I love you. I don't fully understand but I certainly don't care."

I looked down at my watch. "Took you twenty-four hours to figure all that out?"

His always gentle eyes smiled down at me. "No, Love. It just took that long to get here." He scooped me into his arms. "Now I'm going to kiss you and everything is going change. Come yesterday."

I cocked my head to the side. GG and Daddy had said that. "Where the hell did *you* hear *that*?"

He tossed his head back and laughed. "Dilly has been in my brain all day preparing me for this very moment."

"GG? What are you talking about, Preston? I thought all this mess was over with. Your grandparents found each other and they left for the beautiful beyond. You and I both felt that. Whatever was wrong is over now. We can be together now…and…"

He pressed his finger to my lips to silence me. "Are you going to let me kiss you or not?"

"Sorry. Please continue." I smiled and met his lips, wrapping my arms around his neck, reveling in the smell of his skin, the feel of his strong arms holding me and most important, the greatest love I've ever known.

Thunder rolled and I tried to look but he held me tight, kissing me as though to distract me from what I might see. The sky had been perfect, not a cloud in the sky but the wind suddenly pitched making Preston's stance falter.

His kiss slowed, then he pressed his lips to my eyelids, my forehead then my mouth once more. "Don't be frightened, Adena. No matter what happens."

I looked up at the glowering sky, the dark purple clouds boiling over our heads. "What's happening, Preston? Put me down. We have to go inside!"

He let me down gingerly but held me by my shoulders. "What's happening is… we're getting our wish. Any wish." He cast a calm but wary glance to the sky then held my eyes with his. "This isn't like before. It's not a tornado, darling. I've already seen this happen once today."

My brain felt like someone turned it upside down and shook it. "A wish?"

He nodded slowly. "A prayer to be answered. Call it what you like. It's ours." He stretched his neck as though he was releasing nervous tension, closed his eyes for a second then looked at me thoughtfully. "Now, all you have to do is say it."

I took one step back but he kept his hands on my shoulders. "*I'm* not saying anything. Every event is like ripples in that lake when you throw a rock in it and the consequences are endless. One wish could wipe away someone we love. My kids could disappear. Someone could die!" I crossed my arms defiantly. "Everything that happens, happens for a reason and I ain't messing with it."

He laughed as the wind picked up. "I knew you were the cleverest woman I'd ever met!" He picked me up and hugged me again, swinging me back and forth like a rag doll before standing me on my feet.

The wind began to howl ever so softly, concentrating in slow circles around us, kicking up dirt and small twigs as it moved faster. The sky over head, brilliant as it had been earlier but only in the center of a wide...*funnel*.

"Preston, we really have to move." I started to run to the back door of the house but he caught me.

"No Love, we have to stay right here. It won't be long. You'll see."

The wall of wind swirling around us seemed to change the seasons. Backward, from summer, to spring then winter to fall as though time rewound around us. I stood frozen to the boards beneath my feet physically unable to move or to speak. No fear touched me although I saw the equivalent of many years fly by in reverse. I watched the grass shrink into the ground over and over; flowers go backward from full blooms to buds then disappear. Rusty autumn leaves floated up and attached themselves to the trees, turned green again then dwindled away, as though the trees sucked them into the branches. This process repeated so many times, I lost count of the years. All the while, Preston and I remained unchanged.

From the winds stepped two figures that at first, I had no idea what or who they may be. But as they came closer out of the wall of debris kicked up in the air, I could see that one of the figures was GG. Standing just behind her was a strikingly beautiful woman with dark blonde hair, creamy skin and brown eyes. She didn't say anything, she only smiled. GG approached us and she smiled as well.

"You deserve to know what I know although it isn't much. Do you remember the day I passed, I told you that you'd inherited my memories?"

I only nodded, too bewildered to speak.

"Only to guide you and to serve you were my only intentions. It wasn't a perfect plan but I was only fifteen at the time." She smiled ruefully. "I didn't have a clue what I was doing but I tried. I couldn't risk telling you straight out what to do, else Constance would hear me and know. She tried to kill you both that day in Gainesville. Yes, that horrific storm was her. With you both in the same vicinity, she knew her curse could possibly be in trouble. She couldn't let you fall in love. It would ruin everything for her. But when Preston kissed you, both of your hearts were changed forever and the storm stopped. Constance lashed out many times merely because her anger was so easily projected but she did not know how to perfect her intent."

She came closer and touched my cheek then rested her hand on Preston's shoulder. "Constance did in fact drive Nate's first wife insane and while the poor woman was not delusional, it *was* an easy defeat; her mind was far too delicate. She'd tried to do the same to Preston's mother but Doreen was too strong. The lavender bundle you found in your bed was from Constance; the winds in the garden filled with the sweet stench was her as well. It's a poison to the mind. She tried many times to get to you, Adena. But you, also, were too strong." Her expression was one of pride and she smiled but then her lips faded to a grim thin line. "Do either of you know where you had gone to when Katherine and her Preston were reunited? That gray place void of time and hope and light?"

I looked at my Preston and we both shrugged, shaking our heads slightly.

"Constance had taken an oath to serve the ancient curse. I'm certain she had no real idea what that meant. Her very soul would be the vessel —— the chalice if you will — for all those who died beneath the shadow of the curse. You were trapped within her soul. That is where we have all been, although, that was never her intent. You see, she only wanted my father with her. Although, she had her limitations and certainly not every bad thing that happened in our lives was due to her, she is to blame for many horrible events." GG turned and held out her hand, gesturing to the silent woman behind her. "Do you know who this is?"

I shook my head but offered a smile to the woman.

Unexpectedly, Preston said, "I do. Hello, Emmaline. It's an incredible honor to meet you."

The woman smiled at Preston and came closer. "Thank you, Preston. Thank you both. Without you, I would have remained but a pair of broken hearts and a forgotten gravestone." She leaned forward and laid a feather light kiss upon his cheek and she reached to touch my hair. Then she stepped back into the wall of wind and disappeared.

GG hugged me and she also kissed Preston's cheek. "Preston and Katherine were married in the church of St. John in the center of Havering-atte-Bower. I was there. Do you think it's a coincidence that I settled on the banks of Lake St. John?" She smiled again. "It was my only connection to home. I left my family with the hope that if I could put enough distance between the blood bond between Papa and I, that Constance's power would be divided and therefore weakened. I did not understand enough to know what to expect after death had taken me and I did not know at the time that my leaving behind my precious brother and the family I loved would be in vain. But it's all over now, thanks to you both." She looked over her shoulder at Daddy's little white house then over the lake one last time. "The Universe does not care to be meddled with. Time does not care to be altered. God will not be questioned. And even if He did indulge us with such fantasies, we likely would not comprehend His answer.

"Our destinies are lain out in a grand plan not of our making. We have Free Will to get us to our destinations however we wish to get there but it is indeed a very fine line between the two paths and they are always intertwined. When something or someone infects the natural rhythm of life such as Constance and the magic she'd found, the universe will evolve and adapt and it will no doubt try to purge the erroneous element. We may never know to what extent the damage has been. We may never know what now has changed. Remember to always be thankful and always be careful what you wish for. There is always someone listening.

"I know you have many questions still, but I have to go." She hugged me fiercely, kissed my forehead and then she stepped back and smiled.

As the funnel around us continued to spin, I watched GG shrink in increments and her face grew tighter and her hair grew longer; the silver sprang to life in fresh curls and glowed with an innocent blush of platinum. I watched time dissolve her age completely and she giggled all the while. In a matter of seconds, she was just a little girl wearing a precocious smile and a white summer gown; all of life's storms behind her and the sun shone brightly upon her youth.

From the wall of wind came a man that I recognized. It was Preston the first. He took the little girl he'd known as Dilly straight into his arms, gave her a toss in the air then caught her. They hugged one another and laughed. Dilly held something up in her hand and offered it to him.

"Look, Papa. I found it for you."

He took the object and turned it in his hands. It was a golden pocket watch ticking away as it should. He smiled and thanked her.

It took a moment for me to realize that they could no longer see or hear us. They stepped into the wall of wind just as the young and beautiful Emmeline had done; taking their places in another time; another life or perhaps to their places in Heaven. I truly cannot begin to guess.

I looked at Preston and asked, "Who is Emmaline?"

His eyes were saddened as he spoke, "Constance murdered her when she was only minutes old. She was Katherine and Preston's first born. Dilly wrote about her. She was there the day it happened. Your grandmother went through Hell for the sake of her family. For the sake of mine."

I wanted to touch him but the earth trembled viscously beneath us as the wind shifted, blowing clockwise rather than counter and everything went in fast forward nearly knocking us off our feet. Preston held me tight as once again the seasons changed before our eyes. Leaves burst forth in bright new green then bled into darker shades then falling quickly and melting into the soil. The land turned gray and cold and dreary as the winters zipped past repeatedly and it was so strange to watch the rich colors of summer and fall leech away to almost nothing.

Something changed inside me, I couldn't put my finger on it but I felt markedly different. And I lost count of the seasons as time sped by in a flurry of colors. Then slowly, the winds dissipated, the sky cleared and I could move although I didn't.

My eyes slowly followed the length of Preston's face from his chin to his nose, to his eyes. "What. Was. That."

He chuckled nervously. "Give it a moment and you'll remember all of it, Love."

I stamped my foot so hard the pier beneath us wobbled. "Preston, I've had just about all I can take of the other side of this world! I swear if I hear anymore *'come yesterday'* crap I'm gonna scream!"

The screen door creaked open and out stepped … Daddy! My heart clenched so tightly it hurt and I wanted to run to him, hold him and cry. But I was too shocked to move. He couldn't be real. My legs lost all their strength and Preston was literally holding me upright.

Daddy dropped a spatula in the dirt and suddenly I smelled meat grilling. He mumbled a curse word under his breath then walked back inside letting the screen door slam behind him.

I turned very slowly and stared up at Preston as he smiled hugely at me. I was speechless as bit by bit memories trickled through the passages in my mind. New ones, old ones, but at the same time I knew how things had been. My brain again seemed to be rebooting to some other reality. However, both lives felt like a dream and all it did was confound me more. Like oil and water, the memories just wouldn't mix to make one sequence of images of the past that made any chronological sense; they swirled endlessly together and a headache only a bottle of Vodka the night before could induce was quickly taking shape.

I shook my head and I could feel the creeping fear petrify my face. "This isn't real; is it?"

Preston pulled me closer. "He *is* real, sweetheart. It's all real. And according to today's date, it *is* yesterday. The day we said goodbye." He showed me his watch and pointed to the tiny magnified window.

Today should be August 1st, not July 31st. I knew that as sure I knew my own name.

I looked at him again not understanding anything he was saying. "Does that mean you'll leave tomorrow?"

He laughed as if I'd missed something very important. "No, Adena. Things have changed. I don't understand it completely but —." He bit his lip and chuckled again. "Don't flip completely out okay. Some very important changes will become very clear to you in no time."

I grabbed my back and leaned backward to stretch it. "Well, let's go inside. I can't wait to see Daddy! And my back hurts like someone kicked me in it."

He reached for my hands, kissed them then very deliberately placed them on my belly. I didn't understand why until he got on his knees, placed his hands on either side of my protruding stomach and kissed it.

My heart fluttered and tears spilled down my face. "Preston!" I gasped for air and held my very swollen stomach. "I'm pregnant!"

He got to his feet still holding his hands to my belly. "Eight and a half months to be exact."

I shook my head. "But how? We haven't known each other that long. And, I can't have anymore…"

He held his hand up to stop me. "Give it time, Love. All your new memories will come. I'm *still* getting them and I had a few hours on you. Dilly has a strange new way of getting around. Try having this happen to you when you're roughly 30,000 feet over the Atlantic." He smiled then and added, "It's quite the experience. None I'd care to repeat anytime soon, but nonetheless, interesting."

"Where are the kids?" I asked while my heart sat nearly still.

"They're fine. They'll be here soon."

Relief melted every single cell in my body.

"Am I divorced?"

He nodded as we started to walk to the back porch. "You and Trent divorced three years ago. You and I were married last year. Ringing any bells yet?"

So much for being sure of my own name.

I searched through my mind and yes … I remembered. Such an odd sensation to recall two lives at once. But the old life's memories started to fade just a little as the new memories slowly wedged themselves into my new reality. But with both lives still adrift, in my mind, it was difficult to decide which was which as I struggled with my thoughts.

Preston opened the back door for me and we almost ran into Daddy.

"Oops!" He backed up one step to give my enormous belly room to get by.

I reached to hug my father and he grabbed me up like a little girl. "Hey, Doll." He planted a kiss on my cheek then let me go. "I'll be in in a sec. Doc says I can indulge once a month. I'll be damned if I'm gonna burn my *one* steak."

I heard Kelley's laughter coming from the living room. I stopped in the kitchen to look up at Preston. "Lizzy and Spencer are still gone?"

He nodded. The truth was bittersweet. I knew he'd give anything to have Spencer and Lizzy back; for his friends to remain a family to Kelley. But to imagine Preston and Kelley separated to any degree was enough to break anyone's heart. It would have stopped Preston's heart altogether.

Kelley came running around the corner being chased by a little gray kitten. Still didn't know where it came from but I guessed I'd remember soon enough.

There was a young man in his mid twenties or thereabouts lying on the couch in the living room, a dark complexion, and dark wavy hair.

I whispered to Preston. "Who is *that*?"

He leaned close to my ear and whispered back, "Your little brother, Joseph."

I gasped so hard I nearly choked. "My brother! I don't have a brother!"

The young man rolled his head to look at me revealing a scruffy square jaw and bright green eyes exactly like mine; he tugged a pillow from under his hip and through it at me then snorted, "Jeez, don't be so dramatic, sis. What'd I do to be disowned *today*? Leave the lid up again?" He half snort-chuckled again and redirected his attention to the TV. "Don't worry. You're too fat to fall in."

Okay, maybe I do have a brother. "Jerk."

"Fat ass."

"HEY! Joseph, you watch that mouth in this house!" I whipped my head around in response to a woman's stern reprimand coming from the south end of the house. "Preston, are you in there?" The voice called from the short hallway. "I'm in dire need of a tall man."

"Be right there." Preston called back to her.

He reached quickly to steady my already shaking hands. "I'll go with you, Love."

We walked around the corner and at the end of the hallway between the two bedrooms, stood my mother trying to pull a set of fresh sheets from the linen closet.

"Mama?" I took the five short steps to get to her and wrapped my arms around her. Never in a million years did I ever dream I'd see her smiling eyes again.

"Well, baby —you act like it's been forever since you've been home." She kissed my hair, her smile so bright, even the sun would be envious.

"Feels that way, Mama."

A lump grew large and heavy in my throat and I fought to swallow it down and remind myself that she was here in this life. There was no reason to freak out and bawl. My lungs burned with the cries that so badly needed to escape but I held them fast inside.

My eyes roamed over my mother, taking in every detail I'd missed. Her now graying blonde hair swept up in a clip, her khaki slacks pressed neat and crisp. And sky blue eyes, oh how they shined.

She rubbed my belly and looked up at Preston. "Crazy how those little babies can turn a sane woman into train wreck." She laughed and reached up to pinch Preston's cheek. "I'm so happy you kids are spending your summers here now. And Preston, you tell Doreen I want them here for Thanksgiving. We'll make the trip for Christmas again when Gavin goes over." She giggled and clasped her hands together. "Oh, I can't wait! I love it when we all get together." She looked down at a watch I'd never seen her wear. "Beth should be here soon, shouldn't she?"

I opened my mouth to answer but I couldn't find the correct response. Was she here? Was she in London? Gainesville? I was still having some trouble getting it straight.

Preston reached to the top of the linen closet and got her the floral print sheets she'd been after. "Yes'm. She and Teena and Jeremy should be here any moment. But I'm afraid Gavin won't make it until tomorrow."

"Who's Jeremy?" I asked under my breath as Mama disappeared into her bedroom with the sheets.

Preston whispered, "Beth's fiancé"

"WHAT!"

"Calm down, Love. I'm sure he'll grow out of his current idiot phase, and at any rate, they aren't married *yet*."

I didn't get to have the fit that I wanted so badly to have as I suddenly felt a very familiar pain return to my back then slowly tighten like a belt across the underside of my belly.

"Preston,"

"Yes, Love."

"As exciting as this day as been, I think it's about to get a lot more exciting."

He tossed his head back and laughed. "How much more exciting can it get?"

I grabbed his hand to steady myself as the contraction got stronger. "This is my third baby and if you don't get me outta here its gonna get real exciting, real fast, right here in this hallway."

Mama flung herself out of her bedroom door. "Did I just hear you right? Baby, are you in labor?"

I nodded still holding on to Preston's arm waiting for the excruciating pressure in my lower back to pass. He still hadn't said anything. Mama ran past us and dragged Daddy in from the back yard.

"Roger! Get your Jeep! We're fixin' to be grandparents again!"

"Oh, Mama. Preston can drive."

She looked at me then at him. "Honey, I don't think he's doin' so hot right now. He can sit in the back with you till we get to Natchez. Now, come on. And don't you worry, Preston. Even if she has it in the car, we're only twenty minutes from the hospital."

And with that, all six foot-three and a half inches of Preston hit the floor.

"Real smooth, Mama."

Her laughter filled the small space as she told Daddy and Joseph that they had five minutes to get Preston in the Jeep and for Joseph to watch Kelley and to wait for Beth, Teena and The Idiot.

Joseph hugged me on the way out with Kelley strung across his back. "Good luck, Sis." He looked over his shoulder and said, "Hey Kells, ole Deenie and your pop's gonna be busy for a while. Wanna go feed the baby goats?"

We pulled away watching Kelley laughing and screaming 'giddy up' riding high on Joseph's shoulders as he ran toward the small barn next to our house.

He was all new to me, but I supposed having a brother was pretty cool. Within thirty seconds of knowing him, I had wanted to choke him till his eyeballs popped. But I also knew I would lay down my life for him.

By eleven that evening, most of my memories had sorted themselves into place despite the pain of the onslaught of contractions and then the merciful shot of whatever happy juice that the very nice and wonderful anesthesiologist injected into my IV.

I knew that Emmeline had lived a full life and had a family of her own. I knew that Constance had done little harm thanks to Dilly having had the courage to tell her new father that very first night when Constance pushed her down the stairs. Dilly also found and burned that strange and horrible book Constance had hidden under her bed and Preston (the first) had sent the spinster to live in India with her parents, traveling or not.

I remembered flying to London with my great grandmother and my mother to visit the Grace family twice in my youth; my happy years and my not so happy years with Trent. I finally saw the moment when Preston and my mother were sitting on the swing laughing and talking.

That had been a real memory all along. I just hadn't lived it yet.

I wasn't a writer in this new life. My dark horror stories were merely the crumbs of even darker experiences endured by GG as a child by that monster she'd kept a secret. Her memories bled through in my dreams and I'd written them down in my old life simply to get them out of my head.

Preston was still a singer and a musician and as he should be. His voice was too magical to be anything but. I was glad that much remained the same.

I sadly did not have Owen as a friend any longer. I moved from the neighborhood in this new life before we'd had a chance to meet. I will miss him a great deal. Far more than I can express in just a few words.

I remembered Preston decorating the nursery with me at the cottage. On one wall, a mural of horses running wild and free beneath a flock of Monarch butterflies, spiraling upward toward a baby blue sky.

At 11:46, Preston and I held our beautiful son weighing in at seven pounds, two ounces and twenty-two inches long. Aden Matthew Grace.

"He's perfect, Preston."

Aden stretched and yawned, his tiny lips closed into a perfect rosebud, his little pink fingers stretching wide. Preston slipped his pinky into Aden's palm and watched with a smile from ear to ear as the baby curled his fingers around his.

"That he is." My husband kissed me, then our son. "And I couldn't be happier. I love you so much, Adena."

"I love you, Preston."

Surrounded by my family, both old and new, we celebrated this very special day of our new lives. I thanked God for giving us that second chance. And in my mind I saw the gentle smile of GGs beautiful Irish eyes, no longer in a dark place.

Thank you GG. Thank you for everything.

Two days later…

Preston was pushing me and Aden in a wheelchair out of the hospital elevator; we were on our way to the lake where Aden would meet big brother Gavin and great uncle Ray for the first time.

There was an absolute calamity just ahead of us near the nurse's station. A middle-aged man was bellowing for something descent to eat;

his bare buns intermittently flashing everyone as he staggered in his unfastened hospital gown. He was obviously drugged and in no shape to be wandering the halls. His hair was dark blonde and curly; his skin was like leather.

I laughed until I'd inadvertently waken Aden up from a fairly deep nap. I craned my neck around to see Preston's eyes pop in vague recognition.

He made a face, "There's no bloody way that's who I think it is."

A young blonde nurse came running after the distraught man, "Mr. Stanley, you can *not* keep gettin' outta that bed. You gonna rip your stitches open and you can't have solid food yet."

"Owen!" I said loud enough to get his attention.

The man turned instinctively and gazed at me, then at Preston, then stared a bit at Aden. His brown eyes blinked sleepily as the nurse began to gather him and support some of his weight.

"Where'd you come from beautiful?" He said.

I smiled in response then he smiled back and said, "Wasn't talkin' to you. I was talking to him." And he pointed at Preston. But then he laughed and winked directly at me. The nurse was pulling him along, urging him back to his room. "I get to be the god-father!" He bellowed before disappearing.

Preston whispered, "Oh, my God. How did he even get here?"

I guess some people, no matter how wonderfully strange they may seem, are simply meant to be a part of your life.

I can live with that.